The Story That Ties Us

A Second Chance Romance

Nicolette Terry

An imprint of Coffeehouse Classics Publishing

Cover Design by Kristen at Kristen Lee Designs.

kristenleedesign.co.uk

Character Art by Kateryna Kolomiiets

Series Order:

Each book is a connected standalone involving the same group of friends. This is the romance world - everyone gets a happily ever after.

You can read each story by itself, but for the most impact and understanding of the story, read in the following order:

The Story That Ties Us: A Second Chance Romance

The Music That Ties Us: A Rockstar Romance

The Night That Ties Us (Novella)

The Thread That Ties Us: A Billionaire Romance

The Lie That Ties Us: A Dark Romance

The Truth That Ties Us: A Brother's Best Friend Romance

Related:

The Miracle That Ties Us: A Christmas Novella

Extras:

The Story That Ties Us Bonus Epilogue (Coming Soon)

The Bond That Ties Us (Novella)

The Music That Ties Us Bonus Epilogue

The Thread That Ties Us Bonus Epilogue 1

The Thread That Ties Us Bonus Epilogue 2 (Coming Soon)

Italicized books available for free on Bookfunnel

For those who never let me give up on my dreams,
I wouldn't be here without you.
Thank you.

The White Peony.
A symbol of shame and apology.

Playlist

All I Wanted - Paramore
Before You Go - Lewis Capaldi
Dancing With Our Hands Tied - Taylor Swift
Fight Song - Rachel Platten
Gravity - Sara Bareilles
Here You Come Again - Dolly Parton
Let Her Go - Passenger
Middle of the Night - Elley Duhé
Out of Reach (Acoustic) - Shallow Side
Stay (feat. Mikky Ekko) - Rihanna
Tenerife Sea - Ed Sheeran
What a Time (Feat. Niall Horan) - Julia Michaels

Potential Triggers

This book focuses on the PTSD of a military member who served overseas.

There is reference to miscarriage and the trauma that accompanies it.

There is reference to suicide.

Chapter One

JAMIE

My stomach churned as I pulled into my mom's driveway for the first time in five years. My clammy hands white-knuckled the steering wheel as I tried to steady my breath.

I killed the ignition, but my muscles refused to move.

Coming home was a battle I'd avoided for as long as I could.

I'd been back in Fayetteville for eight months, but I hadn't stepped foot in my childhood home since I left. This place had broken me once before, and I wasn't eager to let it happen again.

The October sun baked the inside of my car, yet an icy dread curled around my spine.

Noah had brought me back here—even in death, I owed him that much.

As active-duty Combat Controllers in the Air Force, running into each other on a mission had felt like fate pulling us together. We'd spent the night before talking late into the evening, reminiscing about our childhood and laughing like no time had passed. I couldn't have known then that those fleeting seconds together would be our last.

Images of Noah's last moments surged forward—sharp, unrelenting. The weight of guilt dragged me under, pulling me into the depths of a memory I couldn't escape.

A knock on the window made me jump, and I reached for the knife on my hip.

"Jamie? Are you okay? You look like you've seen a ghost," my mom, Jane MacIntyre, yelled through the closed window.

She had no idea how right she was. My mother had always seen straight through me.

I put on the best fake smile I could because, despite the tragic circumstances, I was still happy to see her. I got out of my car and wrapped her in a hug tight enough to make up for the last five years I spent staying away.

She squeezed me. "I've missed you."

"I just talked to you this morning."

"But I haven't been able to hug you since you left."

"I'm sorry about that, Mom."

"You'll always be my little boy, Jamie. I just wish I could shoulder some of the burdens you carry."

My chest ached with bittersweetness as she looked up at me with all the love in the world. Deepened wrinkles around her eyes showed me how rough these last few years had been on her.

Years I'd left her to fight her battles alone.

She looped her arm through mine, her warmth chasing away the ghosts I hadn't been ready to face. "Come on, let's get inside before we catch a chill."

I let her lead me to the front door of the colonial-style brick house, hesitating as I stepped across the threshold.

The familiar scents hit me, stirring up dormant emotions I wasn't ready to face yet, as the nostalgia washed over me. This house had been my home, my sanctuary, my undoing. While some memories drove me away, others took the edge off my frazzled nerves. So many things, good and bad, had happened between these walls.

"How about something to drink? Your sister said she wanted to stop by for dinner. I'm making your favorite." Mom took a bottle of water from the fridge and handed it to me.

Guilt twisted inside me as I sank onto a barstool. I didn't deserve her kindness. Hell, I didn't deserve to be here.

I sipped my water as she moved around the kitchen preparing dinner. She made small talk, catching me up on all the gossip going on in town. I nodded and hmm'd at all the right moments.

We avoided talking about Noah, as if he wasn't the invisible weight looming over us and the only reason I was in her kitchen now. And for that small gesture of kindness, I was grateful.

I'd mentioned to her I had been with Noah when he'd died. She was the only one I'd told, and I had no desire to relive it.

"Are you happy to be home again?" Mom asked. "I miss having Ruger around the house, you know."

"I hate to say he misses you more than he misses me now."

Ruger was my German Shepherd and the best dog a guy could have. I'd adopted him on a whim, looking for some sort of companion to share my home with. He helped me feel more alive and gave me a reason to get up every day that wasn't work. A dog had to eat and use the bathroom every once in a while. He kept me accountable.

I'd moved back eight months ago, but I hadn't really been here. I'd barely unpacked before I volunteered for a quick deployment—anything to keep moving.

When Noah was killed, my leadership allowed me to

return home for the funeral and stay since my deployment was so close to completion.

I heard the front door open, and my sister's voice called through the house, offering me some relief from talking about myself.

"Jamie!"

I had just enough time to turn and catch her in a bear hug as she threw herself at me, a mass of blonde hair whipping into my face.

"How the hell are you?"

"It's nice to see you too, Ella."

She stepped back, gave me a once-over, then smirked. "You look like absolute shit."

Damn, I'd forgotten how much I missed that sass of hers.

Most siblings didn't get along, but my sister and I had always been close. And when I'd pulled away from my life here, I had pulled away from her, too.

She sat down next to me and stared.

"What?" I finally asked.

"Nothing," she said, cracking her tell-tale grin. "Just can't believe what I'm seeing. The real Jamie MacIntyre is sitting here in front of me."

I rolled my eyes. "Yeah, yeah."

"Alright, children," Mom cut in. "As much as I've missed your banter, it's time to eat."

The scent of the spices and cooked noodles invaded my senses, and my stomach growled for the first time in what felt like ages.

And together, for the first time in five years, we ate the best beef stroganoff I'd ever had.

Sitting around the kitchen table, with a full stomach, surrounded by my family, I could pretend that everything was okay. That I wasn't being held together by pieces of string that had long since frayed.

At least until Ella brought up my second least favorite topic.

"So, have you seen Blakely yet?"

Hearing her name was like a fist to the gut, knocking the breath from my lungs.

Ella looked at me, disdain in her eyes. "You know she's dating Dean Richey now."

The news pierced through me like a blade, sharp and merciless, leaving me reeling.

"What?" Ella scoffed. "You didn't think she'd wait around forever after the way you left, did you?"

"Enough, Ella." Mom's face reddened. "This is far from the time."

"Sorry." Ella shrugged. "Just didn't want you to be blind-sided at the funeral."

Of course. Blake would be at the funeral.

My fists clenched at my sides, nails biting into my palms. Blake was grieving too, and it was my fault.

Noah died saving me. And she was paying for it.

The familiar squeeze of anxiety coiled around my chest and clawed its way up my throat.

My breath came too fast, too shallow. My vision blurred at the edges, the room tilting as pressure clawed at my ribs. I had to ground myself. I had to get out.

"I'll be right back."

I stood and wandered to the living room, shaking my head as I tried to suppress those emotions that tore at me from the inside.

Moving further away from the voices, my feet carried me automatically upstairs to my childhood bedroom.

I opened the door, and my old life came crashing back.

Chapter Two

JAMIE

A hand fell on my shoulder, and my eyes snapped open. Sucking in a sharp breath, my muscles tensed, my body primed to fight off whatever had startled me awake.

But instead of an intruder, I was met with a pair of familiar blue eyes and a worried smile.

Mom.

"How long have I been asleep?" I asked as I sat up, trying to downplay my mini freak-out.

"Only about an hour. I wouldn't have woken you, but Ella is about to leave."

I ran a hand over my face, rubbing the sleep from my eyes. "I'm sorry. I didn't mean to fall asleep. I just wanted to clear my head."

Mom exhaled gently as she leaned back on her hands, studying me in a way only she could. "You will always have a place to rest your head here, Jamie. This will always be a safe place for you."

"Thanks, Mom."

"Now, let's go say our goodbyes. It's about time you headed home, too."

And she was right. It was getting late, and I needed to stop at the store on my way home to pick up some essentials. Plus, tomorrow, I had to go to work.

Adulting. Yippie.

I followed my mom downstairs, where Ella was waiting by the front door.

She pulled me into a hug. "Don't be a stranger. It's like I see you less now that you actually live here."

"Since moving back, I've spent more time overseas. So I feel you there."

Ella scoffed before shaking her head. "Let's grab lunch soon."

"Yeah. Sounds good."

"Promise?" Ella held out her hand, pinky extended—just like we used to do when we were kids.

With a nod, I laced mine with hers, and we locked pinkies.

As Ella walked out the door, I turned toward my mom.

"I'm glad to see you two making plans. You used to be so close."

Wrapping my arms around her, I said, "It's not like we aren't close now, Mom."

"On the contrary. It seems like you aren't close with anyone anymore."

I grunted in response. What could I even say to argue her point? Especially when she was right.

Pressing a kiss to her head, I promised to bring Ruger back over soon before heading to my car.

As I drove through my old neighborhood, a wave of nostalgia struck me.

The houses, the trees, even the people—they hadn't changed in the five years I'd been gone. I hadn't noticed it when I first moved back—my time had been so brief and filled with to-do lists that I never stopped to take it all in.

But now, looking at the familiar streets, it hit me.

Everything had stayed the same... and yet, I was a completely different man.

It was grounding. And strangely unsettling.

While my world had come crashing down, life had moved on without me.

Before I knew it, I was pulling into the grocery store parking lot.

It was inevitable that my Air Force career would bring me to Pope Army Airfield, home to one of the largest Special Tactics Units. My orders bound me to this place for another three years, a sentence I'd been silently cursing since the day it was issued.

Still, a small voice in the back of my mind whispered that maybe—just maybe—it wouldn't be as bad as I feared.

Walking into the store, I grabbed a cart and ran through my mental list.

Since I'd only been in town for about a month before I deployed, my apartment was still bare. The walls were empty, and most of my belongings were still in boxes.

Not that I ever decorated, anyway.

But things like food, toilet paper, and dog food were a must.

I steered my cart through the aisles, grabbing easy meals and necessities without much thought. Eating was just a way to fuel my body, so I didn't pay much attention to what I put in my cart. I had survived on far worse.

But my toilet paper?

That was non-negotiable.

If my deployments had taught me anything, it was to appreciate the little things in life—like wiping your ass with cloud-like softness—whenever possible.

But as I turned into the aisle with men's body wash, a familiar voice reached my ears, and my entire body froze.

A knot formed in my throat, and—ignoring my better judgment—I followed the sound.

I knew I'd run into her eventually. Moving back here meant facing her.

I just didn't think it would be so soon.

Or that I'd be so unprepared.

But I'd promised myself I wouldn't run away anymore, so I kept walking.

I wiped my sweaty palms on my jeans and mentally prepared myself for...

For what? Groveling? Smiling? Small talk?

I wasn't an idiot—most of the time, anyway. I knew I'd made terrible choices. I knew I'd run from things when I should have faced them.

And I knew, beyond a shadow of a doubt, that Blake had borne the worst of my mistakes.

I couldn't erase that damage, but I'd promised Noah I would try.

With a deep, steadying breath—that did absolutely nothing to calm my racing heart—I turned the corner.

And there she was.

Blakely Mason.

Her blonde hair was pulled up into a ponytail that stretched down her back, showing off the sleek curve of her neck. She wore flip-flops, leggings, and an oversized sweater. Even in something so casual, I could still make out her familiar shape, her curves impossible to ignore.

Blake had always been thin, a testament to how she grew up, but that hadn't stopped her from developing curves in all the right places.

A familiar ache stirred deep in my chest—one I hadn't felt in years.

My stomach tightened. My hands shook. My pulse raced.

Was I feeling... butterflies?

The realization hit like a freight train.

But then reality snapped me back to earth.

Because Blake had a boyfriend.

A very real boyfriend who now stood right next to her.

And had his hands all over her.

Okay, maybe not all over her.

But his hand was definitely on her ass.

He leaned against her, his body heavy with grief, and pulled her into him. I recognized that look. He was seeking comfort. Considering he'd just lost his brother—because of me —I couldn't blame him.

But knowing that didn't make it any easier to watch.

The butterflies turned to stone, rotting in my gut.

I clenched my fists and ground my teeth, fighting the urge to stomp over there like a caveman and beat my chest. I'd lost the right to feel anything toward Blake the moment I abandoned her.

Gripping my cart, I turned around before they could see me.

As I walked in the opposite direction, my emotions buzzed like gnats in the summertime.

Guilt. Anger. Jealousy. Pain.

All fought to be at the forefront.

Blakely Mason had owned my heart since we were kids, and I'd foolishly hoped that time had dulled her hold on me.

But seeing her now, I knew the truth.

She still held it effortlessly.

Stopping in front of the frozen pizzas, I closed my eyes and took a deep breath, allowing myself to feel the storm just for a moment.

One... two... three...

Then I locked it all away.

Running had always been my crutch—the only way I knew how to keep moving forward.

And being the selfish bastard I was, I wasn't sure I'd ever find the strength—or the courage—to stop.

Feeling nothing once again, I checked out on autopilot and ran the hell out of there.

In the quiet of my car, I closed my eyes and leaned my head back.

I hadn't been ready to see her.

And I sure as hell hadn't been ready to see her with Dean.

Even thinking about it now threatened to crack the numbness I fought so hard to maintain.

This.

This was why I kept my distance.

But I'd made a promise to Noah.

A promise I wasn't sure I could keep.

Chapter Three

BLAKELY

Something was off.

I couldn't shake the nagging feeling that the universe had decided to throw my life through the wringer once more. Nothing had happened to me yet, but the feeling clung to me—like a premonition, warning of some life-altering obstacle headed my way.

An invisible stone lodged itself in my stomach, an unease I couldn't place. I was feeling anxious for no reason—an unwelcome addition to the despair I was already drowning in over Noah's death.

That feeling had started creeping in yesterday afternoon, but last night—while I was out shopping with Dean—it had sunk its claws in deep. And for a moment, I'd thought I'd seen a ghost from my past.

But that wasn't possible.

He had left this town in the dust, and as far as I knew, he had no plans to return.

Regardless, after last night, that bizarre feeling had remained.

This morning, I'd snoozed my alarm a few too many times, and now I was running behind. I'd planned to stop for coffee on my way to work as a treat for my coworker, Kate, and me for nailing our last stories. As up-and-coming journalists for the *Fayetteville Observer*—her in lifestyle, me in local news—this was huge for our careers.

But now, I wouldn't have time to stop if I couldn't make it out the door in exactly two minutes.

I ran a hand through my blonde, untamable hair as I checked my reflection in the hall mirror. My green eyes and red lips stood out against my pale complexion. Thank God for mascara, or no one would even know my eyelashes existed.

With a final glance in the mirror, I walked out the door, jumped into my car, and headed to Starbucks.

That unsettled feeling clung to me the entire drive, rooting itself deeper into my psyche. No amount of belting *Paramore* at the top of my lungs helped push it aside.

I ordered and grabbed my drinks, keeping an eye over my shoulder.

Honestly.

This was just getting ridiculous. No spirit, phase of the moon, or universal juju was going to throw some big bad boogeyman at me.

But I could barely finish my thought before my jaw dropped and my eyes widened as a familiar figure waltzed into the shop like he owned the place—a living specter pulled right from my past.

For a split second, I questioned reality. Was I seeing things?

I had imagined him there so many times after he'd left. His ghost haunted my weakest, most vulnerable moments.

But this wasn't a phantom.

He was real. Flesh and blood. Standing right in front of me.

Hair the color of wheat lay tousled and windblown upon his head, still styled the same way—short on the sides but longer on top. Long enough that I'd always found my fingers running through it. His face was thinner than I remembered, and the stubble gave him a more rough and rugged look. His eyes were the same though, dark like storm clouds, and they lit up when he saw me.

He didn't look like the young adult that had left Fayetteville, yet somehow, he looked almost exactly the same.

Except for one thing.

The way his dry-fit running clothes hugged an impressive amount of new muscle, a change I couldn't ignore.

I couldn't stop his name from leaving my lips.

The familiar sound greeted me like an old friend.

An old friend who had trampled on my heart and left me when I was at my lowest.

He took a few timid steps toward me, rubbing the back of his neck.

Clearly, this wasn't what either of us had expected on our morning Starbucks run.

"Hey, Blake."

Hearing my name in that deep, familiar voice sent a jolt down my spine, awakening something I'd spent years trying to bury.

"How are you?" he asked, his words barely above a murmur.

My reaction was subconscious, unintentional.

Unwanted.

Heat flooded through me before turning icy cold. The world around me went fuzzy as the air escaped my lungs.

My pulse roared in my ears, drowning out the café noise, making the world tilt just enough to leave me breathless.

How long had it been since he shattered me and walked

away without a second thought? No phone call or letter to see if I survived the wreckage he left behind.

How long?

Too long.

With a resolve I didn't know I had buried within, I hardened my thawing heart and gathered the last threads of my tattered courage.

"No, Jamie. You don't get to do this. Not again."

I brushed past him to the door, keeping my chin held high and my shoulders straight, and—surprisingly—didn't spill a single drop of coffee.

And just like that, I was officially late for work.

I arrived at my office just in time to make it to my meeting.

After stopping at my desk to drop off my coat and purse, I picked up my notebook and gave Kate her coffee with my "gotta go" excuse.

I stopped outside John's office, inhaling deeply in an attempt to shake it off. Work mode. Focus.

But all I could see was steel-gray eyes, watching me like they saw every fractured piece of my soul.

What could have happened during those five years to cause such a shift in him?

What could have stolen his light?

And why did it soothe a part of my heart to know he wasn't living a perfect life without me?

Maybe because I no longer had a soul since I was happy he wasn't happy? That he wasn't blissfully in love with a couple of kids and a house with a white picket fence.

I was so engrossed in my thoughts, I didn't hear my name being called.

"I'm sorry, Mr. Taylor. I was lost in thought."

"No need to apologize, Blake. How many times do I have to tell you—just call me John."

I forced out a laugh. "I know, I just can't break the habit. You've been Mr. Taylor since I was a little girl."

"Thanks for making me feel old, Blake. Come on in."

John and I had an uncomplicated relationship. He respected my work and allowed me to write what I wanted with little censorship. Since he'd also watched me grow up, he often acted like the father figure I never had.

Not that my father was dead, but he didn't know what happened outside of his liquor bottle.

I settled in the chair in front of his desk.

"Blake, I have an assignment for you. But it's not going to be an easy one for you." John slid a manila folder to me. "As you are aware, Noah Richey died last week in combat. I spoke with his family about his obituary, and I'd like to add more than the usual information. I want it to be a tribute to his life in our community and his military career. He has a special place in this town, and he deserves anything we can do for him."

Noah's name was a punch to the gut. Tears burned my eyes, but I forced them back. I wouldn't cry here. Not now.

"It's okay, Blake. I know how close you two were. That's why I wanted you to be the one to write this. No one else can show how much he means to this town better than you."

I closed my eyes as the first tear slid down my cheek. "Thank you," I whispered.

"If you need anything, just ask. And Blake... I truly am sorry for your loss."

I grabbed the folder off the desk and clutched it to my

chest. Standing wordlessly, I walked out of John's office and headed straight for the bathroom.

As soon as the bathroom door clicked shut behind me, the dam broke.

Chapter Four

BLAKELY

I hadn't noticed Kate following me, but as she pulled me into her arms, I began to weep.

Everything I felt was raw and painful. First from seeing Jamie this morning. Then from the painful reminder that I'd lost Noah forever.

Kate shushed me, her voice low and soothing, like I was a newborn baby. "I know how much Noah's death is hurting you. Just let it out. I'm here."

I pulled back and wiped my face, my fingers trembling. "I just can't believe I'll never see that golden smile of his ever again."

"I know."

"He used to sit back and watch as Wes, Jamie, and Erik came up with the craziest ideas. Their idiotic plans were always getting us into trouble, but for some reason, Noah, Liam, Cadence, and I just went along with it."

"I wish I woulda known you guys then. Sounds like my kind of fun."

"There was one time we took Jamie's old truck into the field behind Wes' house and got it stuck doing donuts in the mud. Another time, we went around and threw toilet paper into all the trees in the neighborhood—except ours, of course—so we were totally busted."

Kate grinned as I drifted into the past, my memories painting those days in golden hues. Days spent with laughter, late-night talks, and a family I'd needed to battle the loneliness I'd carried with me.

They'd pieced me back together, filling the cracks in my foundation one by one.

"The boys had turned the treehouse in Noah's backyard into the official clubhouse and wouldn't let me or Cadence in because we were girls. Noah came down and sat with us until the boys decided we would be the only exception to the rule. Noah had always been the sweetest, most generous guy in the world."

"From what you've told me, it sounds like it."

I wiped my nose with the back of my hand. "Even though he didn't come home often, I still miss him."

"I bet. But why do I get the feeling this is more than just the loss of Noah? You found out about his death last week. You've been upset, don't get me wrong, but not this upset."

I chewed my lip, debating how much I was willing to reveal.

Kate and I were close—best friends even—but she didn't know the depth of my relationship with Jamie. She and I had met after the Jamie chapter in my life had closed.

Cadence had been my rock during that time, the one person who never let me fall down that dark hole I'd circled.

But I couldn't bring myself to bother her right now. She was dealing with her own grief from Noah's passing.

"I ran into my ex at Starbucks this morning."

Kate's eyes widened. "The one who broke your heart?"

"The one."

"Ah. Now the breakdown is making sense. What happened?" Kate grabbed a tissue from the sink and handed it to me.

"Nothing. I ran out of there before anything could. But..." Once again, my words failed me.

"Go on."

"It's stirring up old memories, old feelings. Things that I'd prefer to never think about again."

"Like..." Kate looked at me expectantly.

She wasn't going to let this go. But even if I wanted to, I couldn't answer right away. I needed time to gather my thoughts.

"Jamie had always lived like rules were optional. Once, we snuck up onto the top of the hotel in town one summer night. Jamie had surprised me with a rooftop picnic—the stars, chocolate, and that irresistible smirk of his. We'd made love under the stars, and I had given him every piece of me. He always brought out the best in me. Pushed me to find a better life for myself, away from my father."

"It sounds like you really loved him."

"I did. Hopelessly."

"Why didn't you go after him, then? When he decided to break off your engagement, why didn't you fight for your relationship?"

"It's actually really simple. I told you before about losing my baby. Jamie changed after that. He was slowly becoming a shell of himself. But despite knowing he was hurting, I can't forgive him for not being there when I needed him. I should've been able to lean on him, the one person I trusted to wipe my tears and hold me through the worst of it, but he wasn't there. He disappeared like I meant nothing."

I paused, wiping the tissue under my eyes. "I'd always had a pretty cynical view on the world, growing up like I did. But with Jamie, I started to believe that I could live a happily ever after with him by my side. But everything was ripped away from me. I lost everything I ever cared about in one crushing blow. Him. The baby. Myself."

I took a deep breath, grounding myself.

Then he will return to whatever hole he crawled out of and leave this town without looking back once again.

Jamie and I had shared a passion so bright we couldn't contain it. And in the end, he walked away and left me in the ashes.

And I'd be left to pick up the pieces once again.

Chapter Five

JAMIE

I lay awake in bed, unable to find the peace to drift off to sleep.

Everything was wrong.

One minute I was hot, the next I was freezing.

The outside world was too loud, the parking lot lights seeped through my window, making it too bright.

Everything around me was putting me on edge.

And I knew why.

Noah's funeral was tomorrow, and whenever I thought about putting him in the cold, hard ground, that tight lump formed in my throat, setting my heart ablaze and stealing my breath.

I didn't want this.

To *feel* any of this.

To be the one standing here, alive, instead of him.

And I was so damn tired of watching the people I loved get

buried, their lives stolen while I was left carrying the weight of it all.

Ruger rested his head on my leg, sensing the storm raging inside me. I scratched his ears, grounding myself in the one steady presence I had left.

I willed myself to think of anything but this.

So instead of seeing Noah when I shut my eyes, I saw Blake.

The Blake I had run into this morning at Starbucks—angry, resentful, and absolutely breathtaking.

Running into her twice in twelve hours had to be fate's cruel joke.

But it was different this time. Seeing her there without Dean clinging to her was like a breath of fresh air, untainted by the reality that everything had gone wrong between us. When she looked at me, I could see that familiar sparkle in her eyes.

The one that lived just for me.

And the one I never thought I'd see again.

For that brief moment, it was like nothing had changed. Our story had continued on its path. We were more in love than we'd ever been before. Married and surrounded by tiny versions of ourselves that drove us crazy and yet made our world complete.

Living out the future we were supposed to have.

But when her bright green eyes turned cold, while resentment and anger radiated off her in waves, reality came back like a punch in the gut.

I was the one who walked away and left her broken and alone.

I was the reason she was grieving for one of her closest friends.

And I had no one to blame but myself.

Sitting up in bed, I ran my hands down my face. My mental pep talk was clearly not helping me get to sleep.

Looking for another distraction, I got up and went to the kitchen for a glass of water.

Cold water in hand, I walked to the window in my living room and looked out. Everything had settled, and now there wasn't even a gust of wind to disturb the serene surroundings. The orange glow from the streetlights cast shadows in the night. The sky was dark, not a single star to be seen.

There wasn't a single reason why I shouldn't be able to sleep now.

And yet...

I stood in front of the window, frozen and unable to move, for who knew how long. Lost in the endless spiral of self-loathing.

At some point during the early morning, I wandered back into my room. Ruger was right by my side as I slid into bed.

And I fell asleep with his head on my empty, aching chest.

I woke up completely numb.

Hollow. The shell of the person who used to exist in my place.

I knew the day ahead wouldn't be easy. And my default coping mechanism was to box all those emotions away in a steel case with more than enough locks.

But holding on to that numbness would be more challenging today.

Coming face to face with the people I hurt—seeing Noah's family and knowing he should still be here with them—would make it next to impossible.

But I didn't have a choice.

I owed Noah that much.

No one besides my mom knew I was there when Noah died. That I saw the light leave his eyes as he took his last breath. That his blood-soaked body haunted me while I was both awake and asleep.

It—obviously—wasn't information I offered up willingly.

When I'd spoken to the Richeys, I'd only told them we had been at the same location when he died, and I'd helped bring him home. It was all I could say without breaking my own armor and falling apart.

As I stood in front of the full-length mirror in my bedroom, I slid my dress blues coat over my shoulders. The morning light caught the metal of the ribbons on my chest, making them shine.

Each one signified an accomplishment in my military career.

My newest one—a bronze star—represented the success of my last mission with Noah.

It was humorous that such a silly little piece of fabric symbolized such a big event in my life.

Ridiculous, really.

As if sensing the dive in my thoughts, Ruger whined next to me.

"Alright, boy. I hear you. Let's get you some breakfast."

I opened a can of Ruger's dog food and set it down next to his bowl of kibble, refilled his water, and fluffed his favorite cushion on the couch.

Anything I could do to stall time.

Sighing deeply, I patted Ruger on the head as he ate. His soft fur grounded me, even for the briefest moment. I was grateful to have him, even if I didn't think I deserved the company of someone so loyal.

With a final scratch behind his ears, I walked out the door.

Being surrounded by everyone I knew brought me an unexpected warmth and a strange sense of belonging. The old me stirred somewhere deep within, a faint reminder of who I'd once been among these people I'd known my whole life. The ease of being myself caught me entirely off guard.

I stood where the pews began, trying my best to keep my chin high as I greeted people as they walked by.

"Well, I'll be damned. Jamie!" a voice called out behind me.

I turned to see Wesley Parker and his girlfriend, Olivia.

"Wes!" I said as I pulled him into a hug. "It's good to see you."

Wes smiled. "I'm happy you're back. It's been lonely with just me and Erik."

Liv harrumphed as her lips scrunched into a pout. "Apparently, I'm just chopped liver over here."

I glanced at Wes, who rolled his eyes and shrugged.

"Where are the other guys?" I asked.

"I saw Erik pull in after we did, and Liam said he would be here too." Wes wrapped his arm around Liv's waist and pulled her into him. "Come on, I need to find my mom. Jamie, let's catch up soon."

It wasn't long before Erikson walked in with his family, and I waved.

"Jesus, Jamie. How the hell have you been?" He pulled me into a quick hug. "And while I'm genuinely curious about the answer, my mom is being her dramatic self and 'can't handle the negative energy here.' Let's get drinks later."

"Yeah, definitely."

With a nod, Erik walked back over to his family and laced his mother's arm with his.

A smile pulled at the corner of my mouth. Things never really changed, did they?

"How are you holding up, dear?" My mom spoke before placing a hand on my shoulder. Maybe she had figured out my jumpy tendencies occurred when I was caught off guard.

To which she'd be one hundred percent accurate.

"I'm doing the best I can. How about you? Noah was another son to you."

"I'm okay." She paused before glancing at the casket. "It doesn't seem real. Like this is all one big prank, and at any moment, Noah is going to just pop up and tell me both of you are playing a cruel joke on everyone."

I swallowed hard. "I wish that were the case, Mom. But that isn't going to happen."

My mom said nothing as she rubbed my arm just like she did when I was a kid and had been upset. But back then, I'd been mad because my favorite toy broke or it rained and I couldn't go outside to play. This was a completely different circumstance.

With a final squeeze, she said, "I'm going to go find your sister. Come sit when you can."

I nodded and took in the chapel once again. The panic I had become so familiar with began to slowly creep up my spine. As the faces around me began to blur, it was clear I had already reached the maximum threshold of human contact and emotional baggage for the day.

I felt like Ebenezer Scrooge, except all the ghosts I saw were from my past.

The pastor walked to the pulpit and cleared his throat, and I threw a silent thank you to whoever was willing to listen.

"We will start in just a few minutes. Please make your way to your seats."

As the mourners sat, I walked to where the Richeys stood in front of the altar.

I wanted them to know I was there for them, whatever they needed.

"Mr. Richey." My stomach churned as I shook Mr. Richey's hand.

He smiled weakly, and I diverted my eyes from his gaze as the guilt threatened to overtake me.

Mrs. Richey pulled me into her arms, and my skin itched from her touch. When I reached for Dean's hand, his eyes narrowed. Barely controlled anger radiated off his body.

Unable to hold his menacing gaze, I looked down at our hands.

The memory of Dean and Blake together at the store flashed through my mind uncontrollably. My muscles tightened at the thought of him putting his hands on her.

But I forced myself to let go and moved to find my own seat.

I sat in the pew behind the Richeys with my mom and my sister. I'd been so preoccupied by the circus surrounding everyone's arrival, I hadn't realized Blake wasn't here yet.

But then she appeared, seemingly out of nowhere, and slid into the pew in front of me—right next to Dean. He placed his arm around her shoulder and pulled her closer. She rested her head against him, offering the comfort of her warmth and presence in his sorrow.

My fists clenched and my jaw tightened all on their own.

I had expected to feel shame and regret as I stood among our friends and family, but I wasn't expecting the sting of jealousy to hurt just as bad.

The funeral service concluded with no interruptions. They

had asked me to speak, but I politely declined. I didn't have it in me to talk about Noah and his life in front of his family like I was some noble hero.

As the guests made their way out of the church, I approached the casket and rested my hands on the smooth dark wood.

Words would not come as I looked at Noah's resting face.

You could still see the scratches on his skin, but the mortician had done a stand-up job getting him cleaned up and presentable for the funeral.

Bile rose in my throat, and I swallowed, trying to keep it down.

"I'm so sorry." I didn't know what else to say. I couldn't say a little without saying it all. "I am so sorry."

My body felt impossibly heavy, as if the weight of my grief had turned it to stone. I tried like hell to keep my tears from falling. Crying here, now, felt like a betrayal of the memory I was trying so hard to honor. Noah deserved my strength, not my weakness.

I felt someone come and stand beside me.

"I can't believe he's gone." Blake's voice came out hoarse and low, proof of her own grief.

She sniffled, her gaze on Noah, absorbing the last few moments she would ever get to see his face. Tears cascaded down her cheek as she turned to me.

I mirrored her movements, and the sight of her pain caused my heart to contract uncomfortably.

Her tears turned to sobs before she threw herself into my arms.

"Oh, Jamie..." was all I could make out from her mumbles.

Instinct overrode reason as I pulled her in, gripping her like she was the only thing keeping me from falling apart.

Closing my eyes, I embraced her warmth. It felt so good to

hold her again, as if her touch could solve even the most complex problems.

"How could this have happened?" she asked, though her voice was barely audible.

But her words were loud enough, and my body turned rigid.

"Oh God." Blake pulled out of my arms, misunderstanding my apprehension. "I'm so sorry. I didn't mean to..."

Her eyes widened as she stepped back, and I wanted to pull her back against me and never let her go.

"Excuse me," she said quickly before turning around and practically sprinting away, taking all the warmth in my body with her.

I turned and faced Noah again.

"Maybe I'll see you sooner than you think. At this rate, my heart might give out sooner rather than later."

Coming back to Fayetteville, seeing my family, my friends, Blake, was reawakening a version of myself I thought I'd buried the day I walked away.

That version had felt things too deeply, wanted things too much, and carried the kind of hope that only led to heartbreak. I couldn't let him back to the surface—not now, not ever.

I'd promised Noah I would try, that I would make things right, but I just couldn't do it.

Today only proved as much.

If I let that Jamie out, it would destroy me.

After today, Fayetteville would be treated as just another duty station. I'd do my job and live my life like I had been. I'd keep my distance from Blake, my family, my friends, and everyone who remembered the man I used to be.

That Jamie had no place in the new world I carved out for myself, and I wasn't about to let him crawl back into the light.

I managed a weak smile as I looked down at Noah in his casket.

"Love you, man. I wish it were me in there instead of you. You deserved so much more than this." My voice cracked as I swallowed. "Fly high, my friend."

With one last look at the man who had saved me more times than I deserved, I whispered, "See you later," and forced myself to walk away.

Chapter Six

JAMIE

I rode to the graveyard with my mom and sister in the funeral procession, searching for the numbness I'd clung to this morning.

I stood motionless, as rigid as stone, while the pastor spoke of Noah's life.

The cries of Noah's family tore at my soul. My head pounded, but it was nothing compared to the raw anguish etched onto their faces. Their heartbreak settled into my bones, a weight I'd carry forever.

I watched as Noah's casket began its slow descent into the cold ground. His family took turns tossing handfuls of dirt over him, whispering silent prayers. Blake followed, then Wes, who signaled for my turn.

I grabbed a handful of dirt and let it slip through my fingers, landing with a soft thud on the casket. I should've said something, but the words refused to come.

Erik went next, and Liam emerged from the small crowd to do the same.

As Taps played, the Color Guard folded the American flag with practiced precision before handing it to Mrs. Richey. She clutched it to her chest, her face crumpling under the weight of grief.

A gunshot shattered the stillness. Then another.

I flinched as the final rounds of the 21-Gun Salute echoed through the cemetery, the sharp cracks yanking me back to the desert—to the moment I lost Noah.

I could feel my muscles beginning to freeze, the suffocating tightness returning to my chest. I was falling into the dark spiral, consumed by the storm that raged inside me.

The funeral ended, but my feet wouldn't move as everyone else drifted back toward their cars.

The last rays of sunlight Noah would never see again faded as the cemetery workers shoveled dirt over his grave.

The steady scrape of their shovels triggered another memory, pulling me back to my father's funeral.

Years ago, I'd stood frozen, watching as they covered my dad's casket the same way.

But my emotions that day had been different.

I'd been furious at my father for walking away from us. For choosing to end his life, leaving his family to pick up the shattered pieces he'd left behind.

I hadn't understood his demons back then, hadn't grasped the depth of his pain or what could drive a man to that kind of darkness.

But now? Now I understood.

I knew what it felt like to reach that edge—where misery and loneliness weighed so heavily on you that you just wanted it all to stop. To be consumed by hopelessness. To be so broken there wasn't anything left to push you to keep living.

Reaching that edge meant making a choice—claw your way back or surrender to the abyss.

My dad hadn't been able to fight his way out, and his demons had devoured him whole.

Me? I couldn't say I'd won my battles, but I was still here.

For Noah.

He'd saved my lousy life and died in the process. Now, I was just trying to live enough for the both of us.

"Jamie," a voice called out before a hand landed on my shoulder.

That voice yanked me back from the brink, grounding me in the present.

Shaking away the heaviness, I turned to see Liam.

Liam gave me a once-over. "You look like hell. Get any sleep?"

I shook my head. "Not really."

He dropped his hand and glanced at the men shoveling dirt into the hole. "Yeah, me neither."

Wordlessly, we turned from the grave and started toward our cars, letting the silence stretch between us.

No words could make this any better.

Liam finally sighed. "I need a drink."

"When are you flying back to California?"

"In a few days. They can't seem to function without me."

"The perks of being the CEO of your own company."

"That's debatable."

"Private jet then?"

"Definitely a perk."

I forced out a laugh. "I imagine so."

"Let's get together and grab dinner before I go. For old time's sake."

I nodded before realizing my mistake. Hanging out with my

friends wasn't what I'd meant when I'd decided to keep my distance. It was the opposite, in fact.

"Cool. We'll get the guys together. I'll have my people call your people," Liam said with a smirk.

"I don't have people, Liam."

"Semantics."

With a wave, Liam turned toward his rental car, and I crossed to where my mom stood talking beside John and Mary Taylor, her next-door neighbors. I'd always liked the Taylors. They had watched over us all as kids. He and his wife had helped us anytime we'd needed, as well as kept my teenage shenanigans to themselves.

"It's good to see you, Sir," I said as I shook John's hand.

"Good to see you too, son. You've grown into a fine man."

"I'm not sure about that."

"Your mother is so proud of you and what you've accomplished in the service."

I nodded. Comments like those always made me feel like an imposter in my own skin. Even more now, considering the circumstances.

"I hate to ask this now, but I need a favor." John slid his hands into the pockets of his dress pants.

"Sure," I said, eager to get this conversation over with.

All I wanted was to escape to my silent apartment, where I wouldn't have to fake having my shit together. I'd lace up my tennis shoes and hit the pavement with Ruger at my side. Hoping—for just a little while—I could outrun the weight of today.

"We're doing an obituary for the paper on Noah and his time in the service. Mrs. Richey said you two ran into each other before his last mission, and it would mean a lot if we could get some quotes from you for the piece. We have her blessing, and I hope something from you will make this extra special because you two were so close."

Truthfully, I'd rather run barefoot over hot coals or confess my darkest shit to a therapist.

But dammit. How could I tell him no?

"Uh, sure."

"Thank you, Jamie. That means so much. I'll have the reporter contact you. Actually—" He paused, looking over my shoulder. "Blake? Blake, can you come here for a second?"

And again, the rug was yanked out from underneath me for the millionth time today.

There was no way in absolute hell I could work with her.

I was trying to suppress all my emotions, and being around her was like opening the floodgates.

"John, I can't—" I started, but it was too late.

Blake stood beside John, looking just as uncomfortable as I was.

"What can I do for you, Mr. Taylor?"

"Jamie's agreed to speak about Noah for the article. So you can set up a time to meet and interview him."

Her eyes widened, color draining from her face—a reaction I was sure mirrored my own.

But John continued before either of us could protest. "Thank you, Jamie, for doing this. Please let me know if I can help. And I am so sorry for the loss of your good friend. Both of you."

John gave us a sharp nod before taking his wife's arm and walking away, leaving Blake and me staring at each other, speechless.

It only took about three seconds before Blake turned away and ran after John, calling, "Mr. Taylor? Wait."

Shit.

What the hell did I just agree to?

Chapter Seven

BLAKELY

Two days after the funeral, I finally forced myself out of the house and back to work.

I had taken the previous day off under the guise of a mental health day.

When in reality, I hadn't been able to find the motivation to get out of bed—much less get dressed.

So, I didn't.

I'd called in for the first time in—ever—and spent the entire day binge-watching *Grey's Anatomy* with a pint of Ben & Jerry's, an indulgent hamburger from Five Guys, and an assortment of desserts from the bakery in town.

Thank heavens for DoorDash.

Even Dean had given me some space, which was unusual but a welcomed respite. My mind and body were operating on two different wavelengths, and I needed time to get them back on the same page.

It had been so easy to fall into Jamie's arms at the funeral.

So damn easy.

And it had felt *so right.*

He was like *home*—in a way no place ever could be.

He was as familiar as my own heartbeat, and no matter how much I tried to deny it, a part of me would always belong to him.

Forever tethered to his soul.

My body had ached for him, a pull so instinctive I'd given in without hesitation. I'd been completely powerless.

But in my mind, the hurt and betrayal swirled like dark clouds before a storm.

It lingered, a voice of reason screaming that Jamie and I had no future anymore.

Allowing myself to get closer to Jamie was a mistake. One that would only end with me getting hurt again.

And I would not allow myself to be that girl again.

"Blake?"

I jumped when John called my name. I'd been so lost in thought, I hadn't noticed when he approached my desk.

I cleared my throat. "Yes, sir?"

"Can you come into my office for a second?"

"Sure."

As I stood, I caught Kate's lifted eyebrow as I walked by her desk. Was her surprise from me spacing out or from being summoned by our boss?

I lifted a shoulder. I had no idea.

But I followed John anyway.

As I sat in the chair across from him, he chuckled. "Don't look so scared, Blake. You're not in trouble."

I exhaled, forcing my posture to relax. "Sorry. I'm a little out of it."

"Understandably so. But I have some exciting news I

couldn't wait to share. Thought maybe it would help lift your spirits a bit."

"Oh? Well, you have my undivided attention."

"Bob Warren just accepted an offer at another paper."

I gasped. "Bob Warren, *Senior Editor?*"

"The one."

"Positions like that rarely open up."

John's eyes twinkled. "I know. And that means one of our junior editors will be promoted, which will open up their spot." He paused, letting the words sink in. "I'm recommending you for it."

My mouth popped open. "What?"

"The board wants to interview you, and they're using your article on Noah Richey as a trial piece. So put your best work forward." He leaned back in his chair. "Not that you'd do any less."

I forced out a laugh, though my stomach twisted. John had no idea how much I wanted to put off that interview. Indefinitely.

"No, not yet."

"I'm hoping he'll be able to steer your article in the direction you need. Really give it that wholesome feel. Not only were the two best friends, but Jamie was there when he died."

That caught my attention. "What do you mean?"

"It's actually quite sad. Jane was telling me about it before the funeral. With the luck of the draw, Jamie and Noah deployed at the same time and ended up on the same mission. Jamie wouldn't open up much, but... he was *there* when Noah died."

I covered my mouth with my hands, my stomach twisting in knots.

Oh God, poor Jamie.

"You can see it in his eyes," John continued. "That haunted

look when he thinks no one's watching. That boy is carrying more than his fair share of burdens."

"I didn't notice."

And I had tried very hard not to look in his general direction.

"I'm a journalist, Blake. It's what I do. Now, go out there and make me proud."

I stood, still shocked at the new information about Jamie.

"Oh, and Blake?"

I turned back at the doorway. "Yes?"

"The only time Jamie doesn't look like he's carrying the weight of the world on his shoulders... is when he's looking at you."

"What?"

John chuckled. "Don't forget—the MacIntyres are my next-door neighbors. The missus and I watched you two grow up, fall in love. It was hard to miss. Love like that doesn't just *go away*."

"But we broke up."

"Time heals all wounds, Blake. It doesn't mean you won't feel the ache, but as time goes on, it becomes more bearable. One day, you'll realize it's not the wound defining you anymore, but the strength you built while healing."

"...I..."

"You don't need to say anything. Just keep your head up and your eyes open. Things aren't always what they seem."

I gave a final nod before walking back to my desk. Sitting down, I tapped my phone to check my notifications.

Nothing.

I *hated* that a small part of me was disappointed.

Jamie knew I needed to talk to him. He *should* be the one to reach out first.

Sure, I hadn't given him my number at the funeral, but he

should still remember it. I'd deleted Jamie's contact from my phone long ago, yet I knew his number better than my own.

Not seeing his familiar digits on my screen filled me with an unexplainable heaviness.

My phone finally dinged, and my heart *jumped* in my throat. I tried swallowing it back down as Dean's name appeared on my screen.

Hey sweetheart, dinner tonight?

Sure! My place or yours?

How about yours? I'll bring pizza!

Perfect. See you around 6.

I'll be there.

My plans with Dean left a smile on my face, and the courage to do what I needed to do.

Despite finding out the tragedy surrounding Jamie and Noah, the potential promotion was a huge deal. Being Editor was everything I ever wanted.

And if I needed Jamie to get there, so be it.

I opened a new text message, ready to rip the band-aid off.

Hey Jamie, It's Blake. Will you have some time in the next few days to meet up for an interview for the article on Noah? Thanks.

I hit send before I could overanalyze every word.

My phone buzzed again, and I *jumped*.

I swallowed the lump in my throat—until I saw Dean's name.

Xoxo

I blew out a breath, trying to center myself.

Jamie shouldn't be affecting me like this.

Dean's message should've brought me joy. Instead, every ding caused my stomach to flutter as I anticipated a response from Jamie.

It's just because the promotion is a huge deal.

You need him to cooperate.

If I told myself the lie long enough, maybe I'd believe it.

Something was seriously wrong with me.

Chapter Eight

JAMIE

Walking to my car to meet the guys for lunch, my phone vibrated.

Pulling it from my uniform pocket, I stopped dead in the middle of the parking lot.

My heart skipped a beat—like a teenage girl's—as the number I'd memorized long ago flashed across the screen.

Blake.

I hesitated, staring at the message longer than necessary before continuing to my car. Sliding into the driver's seat, I pulled my phone out again.

Do I answer right away? Is that too eager? Should I make her wait, or does it even matter at all?

Play it cool, Jamie.

Play. It. Cool.

Sure

I typed and hit send—then instantly regretted my choice of words. Or, rather, my word.

Groaning, I dropped my forehead to the steering wheel.

What. The. Fuck.

Her response popped up almost immediately.

> Okay, I guess just let me know when you have time.

This time, I tossed my phone into the passenger seat before I could respond with something ridiculous, like 'Okay'.

I wasn't particularly active in the dating world, but even I knew monosyllabic words weren't how you *wooed* a woman.

I threw the car into reverse and backed out, refusing to dwell on the shitstorm I'd just unearthed.

Pulling into the parking lot, it wasn't hard to spot Wes.

Ever since we were kids, he'd dreamed about owning one specific vehicle—a lime green lifted Jeep Wrangler. And seeing it parked in front of me, I knew he'd finally made that dream a reality.

I parked next to him and climbed out.

"Hey there, stranger," Wes greeted, pulling me into a man-hug.

"Nice ride. You finally got it, huh?"

"She was worth the wait." Wes shot an admiring glance at the Jeep before looking back at me. "I almost didn't recognize you in your *granny car*."

I followed his gaze to my car and laughed.

I'd had this thing since my first duty station. A deep purple Buick LeSabre.

"What?" I said defensively. "She's a classic."

Wes choked on a laugh. "I'll say. But I'll drive anytime we go somewhere. Can't risk someone seeing me in that."

"Because your reputation is at stake?"

"Exactly."

I smirked but had to admit, for a twenty-year-old sedan, Betty was still holding her own. The deep purple paint stood out against the black trim, and the aftermarket rims gave it *some* character.

I'd taken her apart and put her back together more times than I could count. She'd been with me through every major moment of my life.

Sure, she wasn't a dream car, but she was mine.

Maybe, though, it wouldn't hurt to start looking for something new.

"Hey, suckers!"

Wes and I turned to see Erik strolling toward us from his white Audi A3.

He beeped his horn as he walked away—like he was *locking in* his contribution to the *Jamie's car is a joke* bandwagon.

At least Liam wouldn't show up in something ridiculous.

He was probably still driving his mom's old, baby blue Prius.

On cue, Liam pulled into the lot—except he definitely wasn't in a Prius.

"You've got to be kidding me," I muttered under my breath.

Liam parked next to me, and I inwardly cringed. He stepped out of a gray Mercedes G-Wagon like it was just another Tuesday.

"Sorry, I'm late. A business meeting ran over."

"No problem, man. I was just out here roasting Jamie's choice of wheels," Wes said.

Liam and Erik both turned, eyeing my purple monstrosity suspiciously.

"It's a classic!" I said, a little too forcefully.

Erik squinted at the car. "Pretty sure my grandma had the same one when I was a kid."

"Aren't guys like you supposed to be all *macho and shit?*" Wes asked. "I imagined you driving a monster truck or something."

"It's just so ugly," Erik added.

"But it's paid off, and the insurance is cheap," I shot back.

Liam nodded approvingly. "Now that I respect. Smart money moves."

"I still couldn't do it," Erik said. "Not in that car."

"Whatever. Let's go eat."

As we made our way inside, Wes turned to Liam. "So, what do you drive in California?"

"I bet it's some fancy sports car. He's always liked fast cars," Erik guessed.

Liam smirked. "I'll never tell."

"Oh, come on, Liam. It can't be worse than Jamie's car," Wes said.

"Gee, thanks," I said as I pulled off my uniform hat and ran my finger along the seam.

Liam's response was interrupted by a young hostess who perked right up at seeing us walk in.

"Wes! Erik! Hey, guys!"

"Hey, Kimmie," Erik said, walking up to her. "Can we get a table?"

"Of course, anything for you, Erik." Kimmie winked as she grabbed the menus. "Are you going to introduce me to your friends?"

"This is Jamie, and this is Liam. We've known them forever."

Kimmie's gaze shifted to Liam, her eyes sweeping over him with the same slow appraisal.

"You must be here for Noah Richey's funeral."

"Yes," was all Liam said.

Kimmie edged closer to Liam, invading his personal space as he instinctively leaned away.

"You look familiar. Have we met before?"

Liam's expression twisted with barely concealed disgust, and I could already hear the sharp remark forming on his tongue.

So I spoke up, trying to extend him an olive branch.

"He grew up here. Maybe that's why. How long have you worked here?"

Kimmie's eyes lit up as she confused my diversion with interest in her. She took a step closer to me, a smile wide on her lips.

All the while, Wes and Erik laughed behind her back.

Assholes. They'd set us up, knowing we'd be treated as new meat.

"I've been working here for almost a year now. I've been able to meet some of the coolest people. Some I've become really, really close with." She winked again before saying, "Follow me, guys."

Kimmie placed the menus down at the table, but before she walked away, she cornered me, pressing her body against mine.

"Let me know if there is anything I can do for you, Jamie. Anything at all... just let me know." She batted her lashes and bit her lip, an obvious attempt at seduction before finally drifting away.

Sliding into the booth beside Liam, I shot Wes and Erik a pointed look.

"What the fuck?"

They laughed, clutching their stomachs as the sound echoed.

"Kimmie is harmless, just a big flirt," Wes said.

"Unless... you think you might be interested." Erik leaned forward on the table. "Then she isn't so harmless anymore."

I lifted a brow. "She barely looks old enough to vote."

"I think I have a pair of shoes older than her," Liam said.

"Oh, trust me. She's legal."

"Damn, Erik. That explains why she knows your name so well," Liam added, picking up his menu.

"Hey. She knows my name, too."

"We all know Liv would have your head on a platter the moment you even looked at another girl," Erik said.

Wes scoffed, picking up his menu. "Whatever."

When our waitress appeared, I was grateful it wasn't an overzealous personality like Kimmie. I could only handle so much of that kind of energy at one time.

It wasn't that I wasn't flattered by the attention.

Because to her, I was just another guy.

And to me, she'd never be Blakely.

Chapter Nine

JAMIE

Even though the guys ordered a beer with lunch, I stuck with water.

I was still in my uniform and had to go back to work after this.

We ordered a little of everything on the menu, and my stomach growled in anticipation of my greasy burger and fries. I hadn't noticed how damn hungry I was until now.

Wes leaned back into the booth, hands behind his head. "Man, still can't believe you're here in Fayetteville. I never thought you'd come back."

"You act like I just moved here. I've been back for months."

"Yeah, months that you spent halfway across the world," Erik said.

"I was here before I left."

"And somehow we managed to continue to miss each other." Erik lifted an eyebrow.

"I'm sorry, I just..." I didn't know what else to say. I'd avoided everyone before the deployment.

"Don't let them make you feel bad because they've never had the balls to leave home," Liam said, crossing his arms.

"Hey. I've left home. I went away to college," Wes protested.

"Duke University is less than two hours away. Sorry to burst your bubble, but that's not leaving home. You were still close enough to come home for Sunday dinners," Liam shot back.

"My mom's pot roast is the best thing on this planet. You'd drive home every weekend if you could've gotten a plate too, asshole."

"You didn't come home every weekend, did you, Erik?" Liam asked.

Erik shook his head. "Naw. I had a life. And friends."

"Okay, listen fucker," Wes turned toward Erik. "Your friends at Duke were my friends at Duke. So don't pretend like you had this grand social life that didn't include me."

Laughter erupted from everyone—except Wesley, since he was the brunt of our joke.

Falling back into our old camaraderie was effortless, and damn, I'd missed it.

But that feeling quickly turned to guilt.

The voice in the back of my mind wouldn't stay quiet, reminding me that I shouldn't be the one here enjoying lunch with my friends.

I wasn't the one who should've survived.

When our food arrived, I shoved those emotions down, locking them away for later. Noah would want me to be here, to live.

As my burger was placed in front of me, the smell alone

was enough to turn me into a rabid dog. Like I'd forgotten what it was like to have a good meal and actually enjoy it.

They'd loaded my cheeseburger with the works, the brioche bun smelling like pure sin. I couldn't wait to take a bite.

I took a huge bite, barely holding back a groan.

"This is delicious!" I said between mouthfuls.

"Uh, Jamie?" Liam's tone caught my attention.

I paused, my burger centimeters from my mouth, and looked up to see everyone at the table watching me.

"What?" I asked defensively.

"No one's gonna steal your food," Wes said as I set the burger down and grabbed a napkin.

"You're acting like you haven't eaten in days," Erik added with a laugh.

"Well," I chuckled nervously, gripping the back of my neck. "This is my first burger since I've been back. So, it's kinda true. And after living off MREs, everything tastes like Michelin-star quality."

I forced a laugh, downplaying my embarrassing display.

"Shit, now I feel like an asshole." Erik tossed his hands up.

"The shoe fits," Wes shrugged.

"At least I've got game. Can't say the same for you."

"I've got game. Lots of game. But I'm in a committed relationship, or I'd show you how awesome I am right now."

"Yeah... I'm gonna call bullshit on that one."

"You can't call bullshit."

"Well, I can. You and I both know the reason you keep Liv around is because you can't find anyone else to put up with your ass."

"Hey! Not true. Liv and I are in love."

"Uh-huh. Yeah. Okay."

I watched the two of them bicker like brothers, enjoying the soap opera as it unfolded in front of me. The two of them had always been close, and it was good to see things never really changed.

At least until their eyes turned toward me.

"What are you laughing at, Mr. Drives-Around-A-Grannie-Car? I bet the ladies aren't jumping at the chance to hop into that abomination with you," Wes pointed at me.

"How do you know I'm not seeing someone right now?"

"Because you are you." Wes took a drink of his beer.

"Actually," I said matter-of-factly. "I have no trouble dating. When I want to date."

Liam finally pitched in. "Keyword being 'when.' You're too caught up on a certain blonde-haired beauty to even look at any other girls."

"I am not. I've had plenty of dates since we broke up."

"I'm going to call bullshit on that one, too." Erik raised his beer in salute.

"How was it seeing Blake at the funeral the other day?" Wes asked.

I popped a fry into my mouth, trying to act like I hadn't even noticed she was there. "Fine."

"You know, for someone who makes a living keeping secrets, your poker face really sucks right now."

I rolled my eyes and let out a frustrated sigh. "What do you want me to say? That it was weird? Fine, it was—really weird. Seeing her and not being what we were. Watching her with Dean, knowing I couldn't just reach out and take her hand like before. Is that what you wanted to hear? Happy now?"

"Not even close."

"Things with us are messy."

"Are you going to try and win her back from Dean?" Erik asked.

I shook my head. "She can't even look at me."

Liam raised an eyebrow. "That's not how it looked at the funeral."

I shrugged again. "I was in the right place at the right time. That meant nothing."

But even as I said it, I knew better. It had been something for me. It had been a fleeting taste of everything I was missing, a cruel reminder of what I'd left behind. Holding her, feeling her warmth, inhaling her familiar scent only deepened the hollow space that once belonged to her. I hated myself for wanting it to mean something to her, for hoping she felt it too.

"Besides," I continued. "She and Dean seem happy."

Wes snorted. "Yeah, I'm not sure about that."

"What do you mean?"

"She just isn't the same. Her smile doesn't reach her eyes like it used to, and she never talks about him. I never see them out together, and it's almost as if she's putting on an act. To show everyone, or herself, that she's moved on from you."

Erik nodded, for once agreeing with Wes on something.

"It didn't seem like that when I ran into them the other night."

"Jealousy suits you, Jamie. Maybe make it your new look." Liam smirked, biting into an onion ring.

"Next time you see her, just pound your chest and call her 'my female.' Real caveman style. Chicks dig that." Wes thumped his chest like an idiot.

"This is why I keep you guys around. Comedic relief." I picked up my glass of water.

"We do what we can," Erik said.

"There probably won't be a next time, anyway. I think I blew my chances at being her friend already."

"Care to elaborate?"

53

I pulled out my phone and slid it to Wes. His eyes scanned the conversation before he started laughing. I felt my face warm as he showed Erik and Liam my message.

As everyone had a grand ol' laugh at my expense, Wes handed my phone back. I explained that she was writing Noah's obituary and needed to interview me.

"We gotta fix this." Wes gestured to my phone.

"No, there is no need to fix anything. It doesn't matter if Blake thinks I don't want to talk to her. Maybe she'll leave me alone if I keep it up."

"Or not." Wes held his hands up in a typical 'you never know' gesture.

"I know what you're thinking, Wes, and I'm sorry, but no. There is no chance of us getting back together, and it will only hurt if we see each other. I'm done hurting those who mean something to me. I won't allow myself to get caught up in nostalgia. I can't get close to her again."

The guys didn't know the scars I carried. I didn't want to be that close to anyone ever again. I wanted to lock my heart in a tower, surround it with a moat, and throw in a fire-breathing dragon for good measure. To protect everyone, and mostly Blake, from the calamity that was myself.

"Okay, okay." Wes finally gave in. "I get it. But even so, for the sake of Noah's article, you have to see her. Talk with her. At least for a bit. She thinks you're pissed at her, and you can't have that. So, make nice with her. For Noah."

Wes had no idea those words cut straight through me, like a blade twisting deep in my chest.

For Noah, I'd do anything.

No matter the cost.

With a deep exhale, I picked up my phone and typed:

> Sorry, I was in a meeting and couldn't text. I can make time whenever you're free. Just let me know, and I will make it work. Thanks.

I hit send and looked up to see Wes and the guys grinning like nuns at church on a Sunday.

"Happy?" I asked.

"Eh, we are getting there. Definitely getting there."

Chapter Ten

Blakely

With the weight of the workday pressing on my shoulders, I wanted nothing more than to go home and fill the tub with water from the depths of hell, drop in a fizzy bath bomb, drown myself in bubbles, and sip a glass of wine.

The heaviness of John's words had shadowed me all day, pressing against my thoughts like a dull, unrelenting headache.

And just when I'd get lost in a task and forget, *bam*—they'd hit me square in the face.

The promotion was everything I'd ever wanted, but the thought of spending enough time with Jamie for him to answer these questions about Noah had me rethinking my five-year professional plan.

The thought of seeing Jamie in any setting unsettled me, and I couldn't even explain why.

Walking through my front door, I exhaled, releasing some

of the tension I'd carried as the familiar scent of lavender calmed me.

Having my house smell good was a personal obsession. I single-handedly kept Bath & Body Works in business with the sheer number of wall plugins and candles I stocked.

"Hey, sweetheart."

I screeched and jumped like a spooked cat. "Dean!"

"Who else?" He pushed himself away from the kitchen counter and walked over, kissing me on the cheek.

"What are you doing here?"

"Dinner? Remember?" He paused, studying me. "You okay?"

"Oh, yeah. That's right." I forced out a laugh, trying to diffuse the awkwardness I'd created by completely forgetting we'd made plans. "Sorry, I've been a bit of a space case today."

"Yeah, you've been like that for a couple of days now." Dean's eyes narrowed. "Any particular reason?"

Heat crept up my neck under his unwavering gaze. I knew exactly what he was hinting at. We hadn't talked about Jamie being back. It was the elephant in the room.

"No, not that I can think of. Just not sleeping well."

Dean's skeptical gaze lingered, but he let it drop—for now.

"Pizza's on the table. I'll grab the wine—go put your things away."

I watched Dean walk back toward the kitchen, his body tense and rigid. I'd have to make it up to him, tell him how much I appreciated him bringing dinner. Reassure him how much he meant to me.

As I walked to hang up my purse, something caught my attention. My usual clutter was gone.

I wasn't exactly messy, but I didn't rush to put things away the second I was done with them. A couple of coffee mugs on the table, books on the couch, and more blankets than one person needed were just part of my normal. It never bothered me.

But maybe Dean didn't feel the same way.

Returning to the kitchen, Dean stood with one hip against the counter, a glass of wine in his hand, wearing the most *un-Dean-like* expression.

Dean was always sweet, easygoing, and calm. I'd never seen him lose his temper. But now, his clenched fist and steely glare made him look like he could take down a brick house with sheer will alone.

"Dean?"

"Huh?" He looked up, his face instantly shifting back to the Dean I knew.

"What's wrong?"

He smiled, but it didn't reach his eyes. "Of course, sweetheart. Let's eat. I'm starving."

He handed me a glass of wine, and I took a sip as I followed him to the table. He'd already taken the time to set everything up for us.

A thick silence settled between us, unnatural and heavy. And for the first time, I wasn't sure how to break it.

Thankfully, Dean finally spoke. "So, I wanted to ask you something."

"Sure." I set down my slice of pizza. Something in the way his body tensed told me to pay attention.

"At Noah's funeral..."

I gulped, feeling a cold sweat break out on the back of my neck.

I wasn't sure if Dean had seen me in Jamie's arms at the funeral, and I didn't want to bring it up if he hadn't.

It meant nothing. And I didn't want to waste our time together discussing it.

But now...

Dean seemed to struggle with his next words, running his thumb along his lip as if unsure how to say them.

"You and Jamie. You reached for him when you should have come to me."

"I know, Dean. I'm sorry. I didn't mean to upset you. I was saying goodbye to Noah, and I don't know what happened. I barely remember making it through the funeral. I wasn't myself."

"Do you know how that looked? My girlfriend, wrapped up in her ex-boyfriend's arms at my brother's funeral."

"I meant nothing by it. I've known Jamie just as long as I've known you. If I had been up there with Wes, I probably would've hugged him too."

"Probably?"

"Dean, please. I'm sorry."

There wasn't anything else I could say. It had been instinct. But it wasn't like Dean to let his emotions get the best of him.

"Now that Jamie's here, are you going to go back to him? I already lost my brother. Am I going to lose my girlfriend, too?"

My eyes widened at his harsh words. Did he really mean that? Did he really think so little of me?

But his eyes filled with regret almost immediately. "Blake... I'm sorry. I didn't mean that."

I reached for his hand, wrapping both mine around his, letting warmth flood my voice. "It's okay. I know you're hurting."

"Still. That's no excuse to lash out at you. It's just that I've loved you since we were kids. I finally get to call you mine, and I have no intention of giving that up. I'll fight for us, fight for you."

"I didn't know that. That you had feelings for me when we were kids."

"I never mentioned it—it was clear you weren't in love with me back then."

I felt the undertone of his statement. That he was referring to Jamie, to how I'd been so hopelessly in love with him as a kid. But I didn't want to bring him up again.

"Well, I'm glad I know now."

"Yeah."

Dean slipped his hand from mine and reached for his pizza. After a few moments, I cleared my throat.

"I actually have some good news I want to share with you."

"Oh, yeah?"

"Mr. Taylor pulled me into his office today to tell me about an editor position opening."

"Blake, are you serious? This is everything you've been working toward!"

A genuine smile crossed my lips. "I know! Mr. Taylor even recommended me to the board. He said they're anxiously waiting to read the article I write about Noah before they make their final decision. Mr. Taylor thinks I'm a shoo-in for the promotion if I do well on it."

"That's amazing! No one else can do my brother justice, so you've got this in the bag. I'm so proud of you, sweetheart."

And just like that, my Dean was back—the man who made everything feel uncomplicated and easy.

We fell back into easy conversations about our goals and dreams, and the weight I'd been carrying felt just a little lighter.

"Well, I still have to write the article, but I'm hopeful."

"You know I'll do anything I can to help."

Dean raised his glass of wine. "How about a toast to you and your upcoming promotion?"

"Thank you." I smiled. Falling back into our groove helped ease some of the weight I'd been carrying.

Dean took a sip of wine, his shoulders losing some of their

tension. His smile grounded me, and for a moment, it was almost like the anger I saw earlier had never happened.

Almost.

"Let's finish our pizza." Dean set his wine glass down. "And maybe I'll let you pick what we watch on Netflix tonight."

"Deal."

Chapter Eleven

BLAKELY

11 YEARS OLD

My dad was drunk again.

Passed out cold in his bed after another bender.

And I was hungry.

There was no food in the cupboards, and we had no money. Dad's phone kept ringing from people wanting their money, and soon, they'd probably shut off our power.

I was only eleven, but it felt like I had to be the adult.

Since my dad spent most of his time outside work at the casino gambling away what little he made, it was up to me to keep the house clean and make sure we had what we needed.

I wrote down when bills were due, and Dad would tell me when to forge another check in his name.

Yesterday, I left a note on the counter asking for money for food, but when I woke up this morning, there was nothing.

I guess eating wasn't a priority for him right now.

My mom had left about a year ago.

She ran off with another man and started a new family. A better one, I guess.

It broke my dad. He wasn't the same anymore. Now, he barely even looked at me, lost in his own world.

Even if my mom knew leaving would wreck him, I don't think she would have stayed.

She'd discarded us like a used napkin. We'd served our purpose in her life, and she didn't need us anymore.

I didn't hate her. I couldn't. She was still my mom. But in my mind, she might as well have died the day she walked out the door.

I never wanted to see her again. I wished I could forget she ever existed.

My stomach growled for what felt like the millionth time today, and I groaned, flopping onto my bed and staring at the stained ceiling.

At least in here, I didn't have to act like an adult.

The only good thing about my mom leaving was that we got to move into my grandma's house. Now, I had a bigger bedroom.

Not that I had much to put in it. Just a bed and a dresser.

But it was mine.

I'd taped up drawings I made with old colored pencils I found, anything to make the room feel like home.

I needed a distraction.

Rolling off my bed, I grabbed my shoes and slid them on.

"I'm going out," I called—not that anyone was listening.

I hopped on my sparkly new bike, the one my grandma had given me.

It was my most prized possession.

It gave me freedom.

Riding fast, wind whipping through my hair, made me feel

like I was flying. Like maybe, just maybe, life wouldn't always be this hard.

It gave me hope.

I'd found a park a few minutes down the road while I was out exploring the other day.

The swings were my favorite. I kicked my legs and soared high into the sky, pretending I could touch the clouds.

I couldn't wait to go back.

I pedaled faster, staying on the sidewalk, making sure to yield to people walking.

My legs burned, my lungs ached, and I laughed, loving every second of it.

Riding my bike was my favorite thing in the whole world. Nothing else even came close.

When I got to the park, some boys were already playing.

They looked about my age, so I went right up to them.

"Hi. Can I play with you?"

One of them caught my attention right away. Dirty blonde hair, gray eyes. Eyes that, even as an 11-year-old girl, pulled me in.

I peeked at him from the corner of my eye as the other boys tripped over themselves.

"But you're a girl," one of them said, like he was confused about why a girl would want to play with boys.

"So?"

"Let her play," the gray-eyed boy said.

The fact that he didn't care I was a girl just made me want to talk to him more.

Or run away from him.

I wasn't sure yet.

"Fine," another boy said. "I'm Wes." He held out his fist.

I grinned and bumped it.

The first boy rolled his eyes. "I'm Erik." He didn't bother with a fist bump. "And this is Liam, Noah, and..."

Now it was his turn.

My heart pounded, and my hands definitely started sweating.

I'd never liked a boy before, but I was pretty sure this was how it went.

"I'm Jamie."

He held out his hand.

I put my hand in his.

His hand was warm, and for the first time in forever, I didn't feel invisible.

"Nice to meet you guys," I said. "I'm Blake."

Chapter Twelve

BLAKELY

T he buzzing from my alarm slowly pulled me from sleep.

I rolled over and picked up my phone, surprised to see it was a call, not my alarm.

My dad was calling? But why?

I stared at the screen for a beat before letting it go to voicemail.

I rarely saw my dad anymore. As far as I knew, he was exactly where he'd always been—casino, home, or work.

As I grew up, my hope that he would change dwindled, and I realized the gravity of his addiction.

The thing about addiction was, if a person didn't want to change, they wouldn't. And he most certainly did not want to change.

That was why I spent so much time at the MacIntyre house as a kid. Not only because I'd nursed a monster crush on Jamie, but because Mrs. MacIntyre knew an emotionally starved kid when she saw one.

She took me under her wing from the very first day she came to pick Jamie up at the park. She invited me over for dinner, and after that, it was like I never left.

Mrs. MacIntyre even let me sleep over in their spare bedroom when I looked especially ragged.

I never had to ask.

She always knew what I needed before I even realized it myself. That was her superpower.

Although, me falling asleep on their couch more than once probably helped clue her in.

Their house had been my sanctuary.

But when Jamie turned his back on me, I couldn't go there anymore. It was too painful, too full of memories.

Losing him hadn't just meant losing the person I loved. It had meant losing the one place I'd always felt safe.

I let my phone go to voicemail. Not surprising—he didn't leave a message.

I wasn't in the mood to go down memory lane with him, and I wasn't about to feel guilty when he inevitably asked me for something and I said no.

I needed to shake this off. Get it together.

Heading to the kitchen, I started up the coffee maker.

A few minutes later, with a steaming cup in hand, I went into the bathroom. I turned on my Bluetooth speaker, cranked up my playlist, and jumped in the shower, letting the music pull me into the lyrics.

The water was scorching hot—just how I liked it.

I tilted my head back, letting the drops roll down my shoulders, back, and chest. Exhaling, I tried to release the tension still clinging to me.

Anything involving Jamie was a touchy subject. And I'd had more than enough of him this past week to last another five years.

Add in the stress from work and Dean's weirdness last night, and I was just about at my limit.

walked into work with a pep in my step and smiled at the receptionist before heading to my desk.

Up ahead, Kate was perched on the corner of hers, talking to someone in a military uniform.

His back was to me, but whoever he was, he must have been a looker if he had Kate's full attention.

She was picky when it came to men. She knew exactly what she wanted and what she deserved.

With her long chestnut hair, deep brown eyes, and curves that turned heads, Kate was a catch—and she knew it.

She flashed her best smile, even threw her head back as she laughed.

The poor guy didn't stand a chance.

Kate was leaning into him, fully engaged, like he was saying the most fascinating things in the world.

Grinning, I walked toward them, silently cheering her on.

Then déjà vu hit me.

Something about the guy seemed familiar.

And the moment his hand went to the back of his neck, I knew.

My heart skidded to a stop.

"Jamie." The name left my lips before I could think better of it.

They both turned toward me, and Jamie's cheeks flushed pink, like a kid caught sneaking cookies before dinner.

"Hey, Blake."

Kate tilted her head. "So, this is the infamous Jamie?"

"Yep." I lifted my chin defiantly.

Jamie's lips curved in amusement. "You talk about me?"

His tone was playful, but the heat in his eyes sent a shiver down my spine.

"Yes, she does," Kate said at the same time I blurted, "No, I don't."

Kate's Cheshire cat grin spread wider as she flicked a knowing glance in my direction.

Not funny, I shot at her with my glare.

The only indication she got the message was the slight lift of her eyebrow.

"So, are you here to see Blake then?" Kate asked, her smirk firmly in place.

She was a professional pot stirrer.

"Actually, I came to see John," Jamie said. "He told me to wait here until he finished speaking with someone."

I frowned.

Of course, John told Jamie to wait by my desk.

He was already trying to push us back together.

"If there's anything you need to tell Mr. Taylor about the article, you can tell me," I said. "I'll pass the word along."

Jamie, who usually carried himself like he owned the world, seemed to shrink slightly, his cheeks turning from pink to bright red.

It was almost comical.

Kate leaned back on her desk, smirk still firmly in place, clearly enjoying the entire exchange.

But something about the way Jamie was acting instantly pissed me off.

"Jamie, you aren't backing out, are you? You can't. Not after you said you would."

Jamie's expression froze, his eyes wide like a deer in headlights.

"You've got to be kidding me. Don't be a coward." My words came out harsher than I intended, but I couldn't stop them.

Even I wasn't sure I wanted to do the interview, but knowing Jamie was trying to back out made me want to shake him.

I clenched my fists at my sides.

"Blake—"

All I could see was red.

"Haven't you wasted enough of my time already?"

I turned on my heel and stormed to my desk, plopping down harder than necessary.

I was angrier than I had any right to be, and I knew it.

I didn't want to spend more time with him than I had to. The rational part of me whispered that I was overreacting, but I didn't care. I let the fire consume me anyway.

How dare he try to back out when I needed him. Again!

When had he gone from someone I could always depend on to someone who never showed up?

My career depended on this article, and as much as it burned to admit, Mr. Taylor had been right. Jamie had the missing pieces, and I couldn't do this without him.

I was so focused on my anger, on the sting of his indifference, that I didn't hear him approach.

"Blake, please."

Caught off guard, I turned in my chair, meeting his gaze head-on.

"No. No more. Just go. That's what you do best, isn't it?"

For the briefest moment, his eyes darkened, pain flickering before fading back to their usual gray.

But I'd caught it—the anguish my words had caused him.

So why did I feel guilty?

He lowered his gaze to his feet, the weight of the moment pressing on him.

When his eyes lifted again, they locked onto mine, steady and unyielding. Lowering himself to a crouch beside my chair, he brought us face to face, his determination clear.

"Let me explain."

But I was past the point of rational thinking, fueled by years of frustration and betrayal.

"I don't think you understand. I'm not interested in your excuses."

"That's not—"

I cut him off again.

"Jamie, I mean it. Just go!"

"Blake!" he snapped, his voice sharp, slicing through the tension like a blade.

I froze, my traitorous mouth twitching into a smile.

It was just like old times—I'd talk until I pushed him too far, and even then, he'd never yell.

Jamie didn't need to. His frustration always burned in his eyes, a flicker of fire beneath his usual calm, and I saw that same storm swirling in them now.

"Will you let me finish, please?"

Slowly, I nodded, my icy exterior cracking.

"Yes, okay, you got me. I was trying to get out of the article. But if you knew what happened in the desert, you would understand why. You wouldn't ask me to do this."

I balked. *What?*

"You can tell me, Jamie. I'll always listen. Help me understand why."

He shook his head quickly. "I can't."

He hesitated, exhaling a deep breath before continuing.

"But maybe I can give you something that will help. Answer some of your questions. Are you free right now? Want to grab something to eat, and we can talk?"

I raised an eyebrow. It was 8:30 AM.

Jamie must have interpreted my look to mean something else because that lovely shade of pink returned to his cheeks.

"Talk about the article, of course. Nothing else. Not a single detail about our personal lives, if that's what you want."

I lifted my chin under the guise of pretending to think about it, even though we both knew what my answer would be.

"Fine. But not now. I'm busy."

Relief flickered across his face.

"Lunch then?"

I flicked my eyes to the calendar on my desk to buy time. I was trying to keep him on the line, not seem too eager.

Just playing the game.

"Pick me up at eleven."

He nodded as he stood. "Okay. I'll see you then."

Then he smiled.

A soft, easy smile that threw me completely off balance.

For a split second, he looked like *my* Jamie—the carefree boy who had yet to face life's hardest battles.

The Jamie I'd loved with everything in me. The one I would have moved heaven and earth for.

Thank God he turned and walked away before the walls I'd built crumbled to the ground.

This was a very, very bad idea.

I couldn't afford to let myself feel anything for him—not even the smallest sliver of friendship.

It would only dredge up the feelings I'd buried long ago.

I wasn't that lost, broken girl anymore—I had Dean now. I'd

built a home and a life I was proud of, one I fought tooth and nail to create.

I couldn't let anything, especially him, pull me off the path to my dreams.

Lunch was definitely a mistake.

But I couldn't stop myself from looking forward to it.

Chapter Thirteen

BLAKELY

The next couple of hours passed in a blur.

I'd been too busy to dwell on my upcoming lunch plans with Jamie, and I was grateful for it.

I needed to be focused and on my A-game when we met.

I'd compiled a list of questions for my article, and once I had the answers, I wouldn't have to think about Jamie MacIntyre again.

But that didn't stop the jitters in my hands or the nervous breaths I kept taking.

A few minutes before eleven, I stood and made my way to the bathroom, intent on freshening up.

I ran a paper towel under my eyes to catch any fallout from my makeup and combed my fingers through my long, blonde hair. My green eyes stood out well against my minimal mascara and eyeliner, but those dormant feelings of self-doubt crept in.

Whatever.

Why should I care if I looked like I just rolled out of bed? I wasn't here to impress him.

Even so, I tried to calm the frizz in my hair and pushed my lashes up, giving them a little extra boost.

As I walked back to my desk, Jamie's familiar dirty-blonde hair and military uniform came into view.

He turned toward me with a smile.

My heart stumbled, racing wildly as it lodged itself in my throat.

What kind of idiot gets butterflies over lunch with the ex who trampled all over her heart?

A masochist. That's who.

"Hi," he said.

"Hi."

"Ready to go?"

"Yeah. Just let me grab my purse."

I moved to step around him, but in the tight space, my chest barely grazed his.

Electricity crackled between us. No matter how much I tried to fight it, I'd always been drawn to him.

And just like always, I knew he felt it too.

I found his eyes, and they met mine with that same hooded expression I knew too well.

His smile was gone, his gaze dark and needy.

It didn't matter how much time had passed—Jamie had never been able to stay away from me, either.

I shook myself free from the fog of him, forcing my mind to clear.

"Ladies first." His voice was laced with something I didn't want to analyze.

I led the way to the doors, craving the fresh air.

It was another warm day for October, the sky a perfect, cloudless blue.

"Which one is yours?" I gestured toward the parking lot.

I tried to imagine what kind of car suited him now, but the realization hit me—I didn't know him anymore.

Hadn't known him for years.

I glanced at his taller-than-average frame. Definitely something big. He'd need the extra room.

A truck, maybe? Or a big SUV?

Jamie pointed to a lifted black Chevy.

I smiled internally as I walked toward it.

Exactly what I pictured. Maybe I do still know him after all.

"Blake."

I looked up, only to see Jamie standing next to a royal-purple Buick, the passenger door open.

"It's this one."

I swore I saw steam come out of his ears as his embarrassment rose.

Covering my mouth to stifle my laugh, I climbed inside.

"It was nice of someone to loan you their car while you're here, even if it is a bit... dated," I teased as he slid into the driver's seat.

He let out a long breath, gripping the steering wheel.

"This is actually my car. I've had it for a while now."

I frowned. "I don't remember you having this car. Something this... unique would've stuck in my mind."

Jamie rubbed the back of his neck, his voice quieter.

"I bought it shortly after we..."

"Got it." I buckled my seatbelt.

"Wait. I just assumed you flew in from the West Coast for Noah's funeral. Are you stationed in Florida again? Did you drive up here?"

Jamie stared straight ahead, silent. That's when it hit me—he was still in uniform.

Why would he be wearing it if he was on leave?

"Jamie?"

He cleared his throat. "I'm stationed here at Pope. I moved right before my last deployment."

"But that was..."

"Yeah. Months ago."

I didn't know what to say.

That threw a major wrench into my plans to avoid him after the interview and wait him out until he left town.

But now?

Now, he wasn't leaving Fayetteville at all.

And just like that, he wasn't a fleeting ghost from my past—he was a permanent one.

Dammit.

"Well..." I fumbled for something to say, unsure where to go with this information. "I think it's time to upgrade your car, Jamie."

"You're not the first person to mention that. The guys said something similar."

"You saw the guys?"

"Yeah, we got together for lunch," he said, pulling out of the parking lot.

A strange sensation crawled over my skin.

Jealousy?

Jealous that Jamie had time for his best friends but never thought to see me? That they no longer included me in our old group?

I grunted some noncommittal noise and looked at my feet, trying like hell to rein in my emotions.

He was slipping past my boundaries—and fast.

Until now, anger and resentment had been my armor.

But now? I wasn't sure what I felt at all.

Anger had gotten me through him leaving, and I still clung

to it. So why the hell was I jealous about Jamie spending time with the guys?

God, I was a mess.

Looking for a distraction from my inner turmoil, my gaze wandered around his car.

And saw... nothing.

There was literally nothing in his car. No work papers, no empty coffee cups, not even a single speck of dirt. It was empty, void of anything personal.

The only thing of him in the car was his scent—sandalwood and lavender.

It was a smell I'd tried to recreate time and time again when he'd been away for training.

A fragrance that had once relaxed and comforted me. That now unsettled me more than it should.

"So, any requests for lunch?" he asked.

"Hmm... I haven't given it much thought, honestly. How about McAlister's?"

"Oooh. It's been too long since I've had their mac and cheese."

"It was always your favorite."

Jamie glanced at me, a slow, knowing grin spreading across his lips.

That devilish look was back in his eyes.

Alarm bells buzzed in my head as my heart flip-flopped like a fish out of water.

Maybe we should've just done this interview over email.

Chapter Fourteen

JAMIE

We arrived at McAlister's Deli with ease, ordered our food, and sat down to eat.

The smell of their mac and cheese wafted into my nose, and my stomach growled in anticipation.

I was beginning to notice a common theme.

Apparently, I hadn't enjoyed eating for far too long.

I eyed my turkey panini, loaded spud, and mac and cheese with delight, ready to take a bite when Blake chuckled.

I looked up to see the laughter in those endless emerald eyes.

"What's so funny?" Once again, I was self-conscious about my eagerness to consume my lunch.

"Nothing. Just noticing how we still eat the same things."

I glanced at her food and had to admit—she was right.

Before, I could've ordered for her in my sleep.

At McAlister's, she always got the Choose Two—half

chicken salad sandwich with a loaded spud, minus the chives, and a cup of baked potato soup. The soup she never finished and always took home for later.

Familiarity settled over me like a warm blanket. Funny how something so small could make me feel close to her again.

"You're right," I said, sliding my irresistible mac and cheese closer to her.

Her cheeks flushed as she narrowed her gaze.

"This is part of our usual dining experience, isn't it? I always order the mac and cheese, and you never do, but once we sit down, you regret your decision and steal bites of mine." I slid my bowl even closer. "This time, I'm offering. No thieving required."

She scoffed, rolling her eyes.

I grinned, thrilled as she fought her smile. "I remember I started ordering the bigger size just for that reason."

"Okay, Mr. Smarty Pants. What if I was secretly eyeing up your mac and cheese? That doesn't mean I want any. Maybe I'm different now and can manage my desires better."

At the mention of 'desire,' the teasing vanished. The air thickened, charged with something I shouldn't want to name.

And, God help me, I wanted to test that control she was flaunting.

"Go ahead, take a bite."

Her eyes narrowed. "No, thank you."

Blake pushed the bowl back in front of me and took a bite of her sandwich, grinning like she'd won the lottery.

"Suit yourself," I said, scooping up the biggest bite of creamy noodles I could fit on my fork.

She shook her head as I groaned dramatically, making the most exaggerated noises I could muster while keeping my pride intact in a restaurant full of people.

"Oh, my God. This is so delicious. How did I forget how good this was? This stuff should be illegal. It's way too good."

"Just eat your food, Jamie. You're making a scene." But her words carried no malice, and the smile didn't leave her lips as she took another bite of her sandwich.

A comfortable silence settled between us as we got used to being near each other again.

She hadn't changed at all. Everything about her was familiar.

The way she held her fork, the way she slurped her soup, the way her teeth bit down on the plastic utensil before she took a bite.

All the little noises and movements that had once been part of my daily life.

And yet, she had changed.

Not physically, but emotionally.

She was guarded, harder than she used to be.

Was that because of me?

Had I done that to her?

From the hostility I felt when we first saw each other, I could only assume the answer was yes.

The years between us blurred at the edges, memories slipping through my fingers every time I reached for them.

What had I said when I left? How did I tell her I was leaving and not coming back?

Was I at least kind?

I cleared my throat, needing to say something. Anything to close the gaping chasm between us.

Blake looked up, eyebrows raised, waiting.

She seemed... unaffected.

The anger and hostility were gone, but so was everything else.

And for some reason, that was worse.

"What's up, Jamie? You okay?"

"Yeah, I was just thinking."

"Don't hurt yourself over there."

"Ooo, ouch."

Blake laughed, and goosebumps rose all over my skin.

"So..." she said. "How have you been these last few years?"

"I've been fine. How about you?"

Blake looked at me hard. "Okay, yeah. The no-bullshit answer, please."

"That is my no-bullshit answer."

"Jamie, cut the crap. Give me a genuine answer. How are you?"

"It's not that I don't want to give you the answer you want. I just don't know how to answer your question."

She exhaled, her green eyes like laser beams. "Fine. I get it."

"I'm not sure you do. Because you seem to think that I don't want to tell you. But you have to know, out of anyone, you'd be the one I confided in."

And I meant it.

She didn't speak right away, mulling over my words. "Can you tell me about Noah? What happened?"

"Is this Blake talking, or Journalist Blakely Mason?"

"Both."

I ran a hand over my face. "I don't know how to answer that question, either."

"It's okay to not be okay, Jamie."

"Is it?"

I looked up, understanding and empathy clear on her features.

"Yeah, it is."

Everything was there, on the tip of my tongue, waiting to be said. To finally tell someone about the shadows that haunted me day in and day out.

But I couldn't.

The words wouldn't come out.

Time to change the subject.

"Well, what about you? How have you been?"

"Jamie..." She knew what I was doing but let it slide. "I'm fine."

I barked out an obnoxiously loud laugh, and Blake pressed her lips together as she tried to stop her grin from spreading.

She'd always been feisty, and I was happy that hadn't changed.

I cleared my throat and used my best 'Blake' imitation. "The no-bullshit answer, if you please."

"Okay, okay." She took a quick drink. "Things have been fine. Seriously." She shrugged. "I'm doing well for myself. I won't lie, it wasn't easy after you left. But I'm a big girl and I can take care of myself. I have a great job. I bought a house. I have everything I need."

Her words cut deep, a blade straight to my chest.

But something she'd said caught my attention, keeping me from drowning in my guilt.

"Everything you need? What about everything you want?"

Her gaze flicked up to mine.

"I have everything I want." Her tone was defensive, and she sat back against the vinyl booth.

"Mmhmm."

Her gaze hardened, challenging me to argue, but I wouldn't.

If I was being one hundred percent honest with myself, I didn't want to upset her any more than I already had. The wounds I'd left were still there, no matter how hard she tried to pretend they weren't.

I didn't want to hurt her anymore.

Not now. Not ever.

"So, you were able to become a journalist. Do you like it?" I asked instead.

Her shoulders visibly relaxed as we navigated back into comfortable territory.

"Yeah, I enjoy it a lot. The job kind of fell into my lap. I had stopped by your mom's one day to grab something I'd left there, and Mr. Taylor was dropping something off for her. We started chatting, and I told him I'd just graduated, and he told me about the position. I was at the right place at the right time, and honestly, I love it. I couldn't have picked a better career for myself."

"You mean your singing career with Cadence is no longer on the table?" I gasped in mock surprise.

Blake laughed. "Oh, come on. I was like... thirteen."

"I'm so disappointed, Blake."

"What about you? Is being in the military all you ever dreamed of?"

I took a sip of my water, deciding how much I wanted to reveal.

How much of myself did I want to expose?

None, really.

I was too afraid to lose someone else.

I couldn't afford to let anyone through my walls and see the real me.

It was selfish of me to keep prying into her life while giving her nothing of mine. I had hurt her, devastated her, broken her.

But my fight-or-flight instinct didn't care that I owed her everything.

It only cared about saving my skin.

"All that and more," I finally responded.

Blake's gaze locked onto mine.

This time, I saw something different in her eyes. Understanding.

"I thought we said no bullshit answers," she whispered.

I shrugged. "It's the truth."

"Jamie..."

"Hey, I'm going to run to the bathroom really quick. Be right back."

I made my escape before she could call me on my bullshit.

In the privacy of the restroom, I placed my hands on the vanity and took a shaky breath.

I never imagined it would be so hard to be near her again.

Honestly, I'd never given it much thought.

Being home. Being near Blake and my family again.

It had never seemed like a possibility.

Pushing my thoughts out of my head, I made my way back to our table.

Blake stood as I approached, a look of apology on her face.

"Sorry, but I have to get back to the office. Kate just called and said Mr. Taylor wants to speak to everyone. She asked me if I could come back. We didn't get much done for the article, though."

"Are you free tomorrow? Maybe we can get together again."

Idiot.

I offered it without realizing I was agreeing to spend even more time with her.

"Yeah, sure. That's fine. It's Saturday, so I don't have much going on."

"We can iron out details later. Let's get you back to work."

"Thanks. And sorry to rush us out."

I grabbed her to-go container off the table and glanced at my empty dishes.

I had strategically left a few bites of mac and cheese in my bowl, knowing if I presented the opportunity, she would eat it.

And she had.
The bowl was clean.
Hiding my victorious smile, I turned and followed her out.
It warmed my heart to know I still truly knew her.
My Blake was still in there.
Fuck me.

Chapter Fifteen

BLAKELY

17 YEARS OLD

I woke slowly, feeling more at peace than I had in years.

I was comfortable and warm, something I wasn't used to.

I didn't want to open my eyes and break whatever spell I was under.

It was my 17th birthday, and I wanted nothing more than to dive back into my blissful slumber. But my consciousness wouldn't let me stay in my happy little bubble any longer.

My senses slowly awakened, first noticing the scent enveloping me.

It was a smell I knew well—clean, earthy, and... Jamie.

I couldn't stop myself from nuzzling deeper into the familiar scent of lavender and cedarwood before realizing my head was on his shoulder, his head resting atop mine.

My muscles froze, an automatic response when you weren't used to another person's touch.

That's what happened when your parents hadn't hugged you for years.

But that wasn't the only reason.

I'd nursed a schoolgirl crush on Jamie MacIntyre for years, too scared to say anything and risk ruining our friendship. He was my best friend, and I couldn't imagine not having him in my life, so I kept that part of me buried deep.

Still, it felt nice to be close to him. Warm. Safe.

I inched closer, my face warming as a blush crept across my cheeks.

He was comforting in ways I never imagined someone like him could be.

I savored the moment, knowing he'd wake soon and put distance between us, maybe even regret it.

When he stirred beside me, I slammed my eyes shut, pretending to be asleep.

I didn't want him to realize I hadn't wanted to break our connection. That my heart yearned for his touch.

He lifted his head, letting out the most adorable sleepy stretching noises—somewhere between a grunt and a groan.

I waited for him to pull away, but he never did.

Each second stretched unbearably as I waited.

I should've pretended to wake up when he did—saved myself from this agony.

But he wasn't pulling away.

Instead, I felt the lightest touch on my cheek, almost like a butterfly landing on my skin.

My eyes fluttered open before I could think better of it.

His striking gray eyes bore into mine, his fingertip tracing the curve of my face.

His gaze held me captive, every muscle in my body locked under its spell.

I couldn't read the expression he wore. A mixture of want, need, and hesitation.

But why would he hesitate?

What was he thinking?

His palm cupped my cheek, and I closed my eyes briefly, the warmth of his skin on mine sending shivers down my spine.

I was falling for him.

Or maybe I already had—and I'd just been too scared to admit it.

What I felt for him now was far beyond the innocent crush I once had. And as his gaze lingered on me, I let myself dream—just for a moment—that maybe he felt the same.

Then, his lips brushed mine—gentle, uncertain, a whisper of a kiss.

And I was too stunned to react.

A deafening roar filled my ears, while his tender touch did nothing to hide the passion simmering beneath the surface.

When I didn't resist, he wrapped his other hand around my waist, pulling me closer until there was no space left between us.

I came alive under his touch, my body arching into his on instinct, craving more, needing everything he had to give.

His fingers threaded through my hair as his tongue grazed my lips.

I opened up to him with all that I had.

Heat bloomed in my chest, spreading through every inch of my body.

I'd burn willingly if it meant having him beside me.

When we finally pulled apart, my heart raced, my breaths quick and uneven.

His chest mirrored mine, rising and falling to the same erratic rhythm.

A crooked smile tugged at his lips, but I saw the red creeping up his neck—proof of how much he was holding back.

"Happy Birthday, Blake."

And I knew without a doubt—I loved him.

I always had.

Ever since that day at the park.

And I always would.

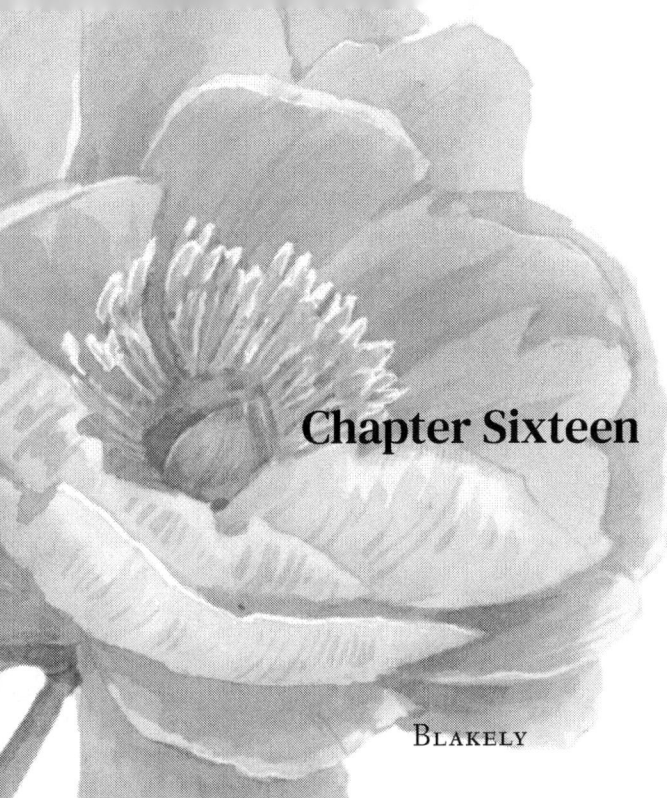

Chapter Sixteen

BLAKELY

I woke disoriented.

My first thoughts jumped to Jamie—our lunch yesterday, our plans for today.

I needed to rebuild my walls, strengthen my resolve against the ease of our banter and the comfort I found in his company.

He'd cracked them so easily.

I picked up my phone and checked the time.

5:36 AM.

I groaned, frustrated with myself for letting Jamie under my skin again, stealing my sleep.

I burrowed deeper into my blanket and shut my eyes tight, determined to fall back asleep.

Sleep refused to come, leaving me staring at my ceiling instead of darkness. When I rechecked my phone, only twenty minutes had passed.

Dammit.

With a huff, I scrolled through my email, checked my social media—anything to pass the time.

But my thoughts turned against me, replaying the haunted look on Jamie's face when I'd asked about Noah.

Like a scene on loop, the sorrow in his eyes was impossible to ignore.

What had happened to him?

And... was he still an early riser?

Biting my lip, I pulled up our messages.

> Hey, are you up?

He replied immediately.

> Unfortunately. What's up?

> Nothing, just couldn't sleep and...

I hesitated, unwilling to admit I'd been thinking about him. Racking my brain for an excuse, I finally typed:

> ... wanted to see if you wanted to meet earlier than 12.

> Sure. Still on for Cracker Barrel?

> Yep, I've been craving their french toast.

> What time are you thinking?

> 45 minutes, okay?

> Yeah, that's fine.

> I can pick you up since you drove last time.

I expected an immediate response, just like before, but nothing came through.

I stared at my phone, watching the screen dim, then shut off.

Maybe he'd gotten distracted?

My phone finally buzzed. Fumbling in my eagerness, I almost dropped it before reading his one-word reply.

Okay.

All that time to text one word?

Address?

Not waiting for his response, I jumped out of bed and into the shower, deciding there was no time for hair washing this morning.

I rushed through my routine, my body wired with anticipation, a thrill humming beneath my skin. I took a shaky breath, trying to steady myself.

This is a terrible idea.

Was I really prepared to go through a Jamie detox all over again?

Then it hit me.

Dean.

Oh my God—Dean.

We had plans for breakfast at 8:30.

Idiot.

How had I forgotten?

But if I was being honest with myself... I wasn't surprised.

Jamie had always scrambled my thoughts, twisting logic into a tangled mess of emotions.

As a teenager, once I realized my feelings for him were well beyond friendship, I could barely form two coherent words around him.

And now? I was caught in that same web.

I shut off the water, stepped out of the shower, and wrapped myself in a towel.

I'd figure something out. I always did.

Still dripping, I pulled on jeans and a button-up blouse, ran my fingers through my hair to create loose waves, and checked the mirror one last time.

Satisfied, I grabbed my purse and headed out the door.

Jamie had sent his address with no extra small talk.

All business. No play.

> On my way

While waiting for my car to idle, I sent a text to Dean.

> Hey, can we push our breakfast a little later? Something for work came up. Maybe around 10?

I'd have to make a conscious effort to not overeat with Jamie. Death by food coma was still a thing.

I placed my phone in the cup holder, knowing Dean was still asleep and wouldn't respond for a while.

But as soon as I pulled my hand away, my phone rang.

Thinking it was Jamie, I picked it up—only to see Dad on the screen.

I froze, making no move to answer.

I wasn't ready to hear what he had to say.

I was still too angry. Too hurt.

The years of irresponsibility, neglect, and drinking had worn me down.

I'd given him chance after chance, listening to his promises to get clean, only to watch him drown in the bottle again.

I can't do this right now.

Setting my phone down, I pulled out of my driveway, shoving thoughts of my dad to the farthest corner of my mind.

Fayetteville's streets stretched empty before me as I drove to Jamie's. The deserted roads, bathed in the eerie glow of streetlights, made it feel as though the entire world had paused, leaving me completely alone.

When I pulled into his apartment complex, I was surprised by his choice of residence.

An apartment?

I'd expected a house. Something with a yard. Jamie had always liked his space, yet here he was, surrounded by neighbors on all sides.

Finding his building, I hesitated—should I knock or text?

Torn between curiosity and caution, I hovered at the edge of a decision.

> I'm here.

> Sorry, I just need a few extra minutes. The door is open if you don't want to wait in your car.

Well. Curiosity killed the cat, and all that.

I got out of my car and walked up to his door, pausing before turning the handle, unsure of what I would see once I crossed the threshold.

To be in his home, his safe place, surrounded by his things, his scent, everything that meant something to him. I wasn't sure I was ready for that closeness again.

But standing outside his door with my hand on the handle was weird, so it was now or never.

I turned the knob, bracing for the overwhelming presence of him. But... nothing.

I looked around, noting he had all the basics—a small table, couch, TV, coffee table.

But just like his car, this apartment was devoid of anything personal.

There was nothing proving it was Jamie who lived here. No photos, no books, no decorations.

The place was completely sterile.

When we were kids, Jamie had filled his room with everything that made him who he was—trophies, photos, posters, and his matchbox car collection. His room had been full of color and life.

The walls of this place were the extreme opposite.

It was strange to think he had changed so much. And I was beginning to realize that I didn't understand the depth of the change.

Jamie hid from life, avoiding attachment to people or things.

This Jamie left the people he cared most about. This Jamie carried scars so deep he wouldn't speak of them.

For so long, I thought I knew his pain, but it was clear that wasn't the case.

"Just a sec, sorry!" His voice came from down the hall.

"Take your time," I said as I peered into the kitchen.

The only thing on the kitchen counter was a coffee pot with remnants of a morning brew. There were no dirty dishes, discarded papers, receipts, or takeout containers.

Everything was so neat and tidy.

How lonely it must be—to have things, but no sense of home.

And that alone splintered the icy dome around my heart.

"Hey."

I jumped, entirely consumed by my thoughts once again. The journalist in me was failing. I hadn't heard him approach.

He smiled sheepishly, rubbing his neck. "Sorry, I didn't mean to scare you."

"It's okay. I spook easy."

"I know."

His words caught me off guard.

Did he still think he knew me?

I doubted it.

I noticed Jamie's casual appearance. He wore jeans and a quarter-zip pullover, but that didn't stop him from looking every bit as handsome.

A soft thud drew my attention from Jamie to the German Shepherd sitting behind him, trained and poised.

"Oh my goodness! Who is this?!" I asked in that high-pitched, annoying voice only reserved for babies and animals as I squatted down to the dog's level.

"This is Ruger."

"Hello, Ruger. I'm Blake." Ruger came forward and smelled my hand. "See, I'm one of the good ones." I reached up and patted his head.

His tail moved, slowly at first and then quickly enough to whack Jamie on the leg. "Aren't you handsome? What a good boy."

Jamie smiled down at his dog. "He really is the best."

For a moment, I couldn't find my voice. It was that rare smile Jamie saved for the people closest to his heart. He used to give me that smile, and seeing it now sent a sharp ache through my chest.

He cleared his throat. "Ready?"

"Mmhmm," I squeaked.

Once outside, I started my car and put my seatbelt on. I fixed my rearview mirror, adjusted the fans blowing the heat out, and picked at something that wasn't there on my steering wheel.

I messed with every little thing I could to keep myself busy while my car warmed up again.

"Nice car," Jamie looked around the interior. "I'm glad to see you in something more reliable than that old Focus."

Suddenly feeling self-conscious, I looked at my vehicle with fresh eyes.

I had splurged on this car after my old beater had broken down. It had been a way to treat myself after everything I had been through.

It was a new Chevy Malibu, LTZ, completely loaded. I hadn't even broken the leather in yet, and you could still smell that new car scent.

"Thanks. I rarely spend the money on new stuff, but this felt right."

"I know," he said again. "This fits you."

My eye caught the faux-leather purse I'd snagged on clearance at Target sitting in my backseat. I only bought something if it was on sale. All of my dress clothes I'd purchased at a resale shop, and everything else was second-hand or clearance.

I wasn't even poor anymore, but if I learned anything from my father, it was that you didn't spend every penny you had.

You never knew when life would come by and leave you out to dry.

But now, with Jamie sitting beside me, I wished I took the time to get my hair done every once in a while, buy some new clothes, and spend a little more time worrying about my appearance.

But in reality, once you hit rock bottom and lost everything you ever held dear, the brand of clothes you wore while crying on the bathroom floor was the last thing on your mind.

"Well, it's definitely a lot nicer than ol' Betty."

"Betty?" I asked.

"The Purple People Eater." He gestured to his car parked next to us.

I barked out a laugh. "That's easy to beat. You ever think about trading her in?"

"Recently I have, just haven't found the car yet," he said as I shifted into reverse.

Music played softly in the background as I drove us to the restaurant. Despite the two of us being awake at this hour, it was still early, and I had never been particularly chatty in the morning.

A fact Jamie was well aware of.

Was that the reason for his silence? Did he really still remember all my quirks?

Once we made it to the restaurant, the hostess sat us quickly. It was just after 7:00 AM on a Saturday, and the place was empty. Ordinary people weren't up and out to breakfast this early.

"I'm starving. I think I'll order one of everything," Jamie said as he picked up his menu.

"You think you can eat all of that?"

"Everything sounds so good! I haven't eaten here since we...." He stopped, his eyes on me.

It didn't take a rocket scientist to figure out what he was going to say.

I haven't eaten here since we were together.

This restaurant had always been our place, and the fact that Jamie hadn't been to any Cracker Barrel with anyone else, with another girl really, sent tingles down my body, warming me.

I wasn't afraid to admit I'd always been a bit jealous throughout our relationship.

Jamie was the football star and popular with the girls at

school. But even though girls threw themselves at him constantly, he never even looked at another girl. He'd only had eyes for me.

I was the one who couldn't contain the green-eyed monster who lurked inside.

I hadn't realized I'd laughed out loud until Jamie asked, "What's so funny?" His tone was defensive.

I scrunched my nose. "Nothing, just thinking about old times."

Jamie rested his elbows on the table, fingers laced. "Oh yeah? Do tell."

I shook my head.

"Come on. You can't tease me."

I laughed. "Oh, fine. It's in the past, anyway." I paused. "I just remembered how jealous I used to get. Whenever we went somewhere, there was always some girl ogling you. I used to get so mad."

"Possessive, huh?"

I raised an eyebrow. "Whatever, like you didn't know."

"What? That you were so obsessed with me? I had no idea."

He flashed me an ear-to-ear grin as I sent him an icy glare over my menu. "Okay, like you never got jealous."

"Only all the time. I would puff my chest out anytime another guy would so much as glance in your direction. I even beat Wes's ass once when we were fifteen because he said he would steal a kiss from you the next time he saw you. Looking back, though, he might have been egging me on. I'm pretty sure they all knew how I felt about you long before I realized it myself." Jamie shook his head, laughing. "But I think all of our friends had a crush on you at some point, except maybe Cadence. Even Noah..."

Jamie frowned, like he hadn't meant to say it—like

mentioning Noah had been an accident. His eyes darkened, gaze dropping to the table. He was slipping into a place I couldn't reach, somewhere deep inside himself, shutting me out.

And I was losing him.

Chapter Seventeen

BLAKELY

As I watched the light leave Jamie's eyes, it felt like he'd taken some of my own light with him.

An ache settled low in my chest, and I had an unwanted desire to make him laugh again.

But that wasn't what I was here to do, and yet... I couldn't seem to help myself from wanting to bring him back into the sun with me.

I cleared my throat. "Well. I'd say there were way more girls into you than guys that were into me. I'll never understand how you were so oblivious to it. Remember Charlotte? She was always trying to get your attention."

Jamie shook his head and pulled himself out of his darkness. His eyes didn't crinkle when he smiled. But it was progress.

"Yeah... sure. All the girls at school were pinning after me." He paused. "As for Charlotte, I haven't seen her in ages."

"She still lives here, and don't act like you didn't know. Charlotte's intentions toward you were about as big as her ass."

Jamie laughed, the sound abrupt and genuine. "Did she have a big ass? I wouldn't know, I preferred looking at *your* ass. I'm certain there was no comparison."

I scoffed as I crossed my arms over my chest.

The familiar spark in his eyes had returned, but it only made me wonder what had triggered the sudden shift in him.

We talked about anything and everything under the sun when we were teenagers. And, as he kept reminding me, he knew me better than I knew myself back then.

Maybe one day, he would feel like he could open up to me again.

Finally, our waitress came to our table to greet us. She was a young girl, probably in college, and was definitely checking out Jamie.

I dropped my gaze as she introduced herself and gave us her spiel. But when I looked back up, I was surprised to find Jamie looking at me with an unwavering gaze.

"I'll just have water," Jamie said, never breaking our eye contact.

My skin prickled and my cheeks warmed under his gaze. Unable to handle it any longer, I looked at our waitress. "Large chocolate milk, please."

She nodded. "Do ya'll know what you'd like to order? Or do you need a few more minutes?"

"I think we're ready," I said.

Jamie nodded to me. "Ladies first."

"I'll have the Mama's French Toast Breakfast."

"How do you want your eggs?"

"Over easy, and I'll have bacon."

"Perfect. And for you, sir?" I could hear a hint of shyness as she addressed Jamie.

The jealous beast inside me stirred, stretching after her long dormancy. I swallowed hard, forcing her back into the cage where she belonged, locking the door tight.

"I'll have the same as her. Thanks."

Jamie gave her a quick smile before turning back to me. She left without a word, and my monster gave a victory shout before retreating.

"Ew. You still drink that. I thought they only gave chocolate milk to the kids."

"You can't drink anything else with breakfast. Chocolate milk or bust. It's like a law or something."

"So, are you going to have me arrested?" Jamie held his hands up toward me, wrists together. "I ordered water."

I shrugged. "Guess I'll have to check with our waitress. She might enjoy getting you into trouble."

"Handcuffs *could* be fun, though."

I laughed as I threw my napkin at him. "Jamie MacIntyre. That's *dirty*."

He caught the napkin mid-air and grinned. "Oh, come on. It's not my fault you've forgotten how to have a little fun."

"Fun? Is that what you call being inappropriate in public?"

"What happened to the Blake I used to know? You weren't always such a prude."

"I am *not* a prude!"

Jamie leaned forward, resting his elbows on the table. "You just called handcuffs dirty. Where is the girl who dared me to skinny-dip in the hotel pool that one summer?"

I gasped. "That was different! It was late, and there wasn't anyone around."

His grin widened. "Still happened. So tell me—where did your wild side go, Blake?"

"She's refined now. *Mature*, even."

Jamie snorted. "Mature. Right. *So* mature you're blushing just talking about handcuffs."

"I'm *not* blushing!" I protested, feeling my cheeks betray me as they warmed further.

"Yeah, keep telling yourself that, and maybe one day you'll convince me," he said with a knowing look. That cocky grin of his made me want to throw another napkin at him.

"Here are your drinks," our waitress said as she set them down and reached for the menus on the table.

As she pulled my menu up, she knocked against my very full glass of chocolate milk.

The milk spread in seconds. I jumped up, liquid soaking both my shirt and pants.

"Oh, my gosh! I'm so sorry," the waitress said, fear lacing her words. "Let me go grab more napkins."

Jamie had jumped up too, tossing our napkins on the table in an attempt to stop the impending waterfall. "Jesus. Are you okay?"

I couldn't do anything but wait for the waitress to come back with more napkins. Laughter bubbled up as I stood there, dripping puddles onto the floor.

"I'm fine. Nothing like a glass of chocolate milk in your lap to wake you up."

Jamie looked at me, bewildered, before cracking a smile of his own. "No kidding."

Our waitress returned with both paper towels, napkins, and a fresh glass of chocolate milk. She did her best to wipe up the mess, but my side of our table was still pretty wet.

"Come sit by me." Jamie scooted over.

Feeling like I didn't have much of a choice, I sat beside him. I'd wanted to keep some distance between us. This felt too intimate.

"Damn, you're soaked."

I looked down at myself and sighed. My baby pink blouse was definitely stained, and my jeans were almost an entire shade darker. The fabric stuck to me uncomfortably. I'd always hated being wet.

So I began to unbutton my blouse, planning to take it off and let it dry a little before we left. I'd worn a silk camisole underneath, so I was decent. I'd be a little chilly, but no more than I already would be in the wet shirt.

As my shirt fell open, I heard Jamie's breath hitch. I tried to ignore the way his body tensed beside mine.

Pulling my shirt down over my shoulders, I exposed my skin to the cool air. The hair on my arms rose as I shivered.

Jamie watched me, his eyes darkening with an intensity that made my breath falter.

I felt a drop of milk travel down my collarbone... and his gaze followed it, as though the tiny bead of liquid held him captive.

Before I could react, his hand moved. He reached out, his finger catching the drip just above the neckline of my thin camisole.

The heat of his touch against my chilled skin sent a jolt through me, starting a fire deep within.

Jamie's eyes widened, snapping up to meet mine, as though he hadn't meant to do it.

There was a flicker of surprise—even hesitation—in his expression, but neither of us moved. We were locked in place, suspended in the charged silence between us, unsure how to break the moment.

Slowly, almost hesitantly, his hand began to move... his fingers following the faint trail the milk had left behind.

Each move was deliberate, his warmth sinking into my skin as my pulse hammered in my chest.

It felt good—too good.

My body reacted, leaning into his touch despite the voice in my head screaming that we were in dangerous territory.

Jamie swallowed hard, his Adam's apple bobbing as his hand stilled against me.

His gaze flicked between his hand, my eyes... and then lingered on my lips.

The weight of his gaze stirred something that I'd locked away long ago.

"Jamie..." I whispered.

Jamie had told me once, when we were together, that he could never get enough of my lips. That they called to him day and night, like an irresistible siren.

He'd said my lips were his weakness, and from the way he stared at them now... I believed him.

He leaned in, slow and deliberate, the heat of him radiating toward me like a flame drawing in a moth.

The familiar glint in his eyes was back—a mix of desire, longing, and something deeper. Something I wasn't sure either of us could name.

But... it was wrong.

So wrong.

Jamie brought his other hand to my cheek, his touch so gentle and soft.

My eyes fluttered shut, a chill racing down my spine, but even as my body leaned into him, I knew I couldn't give him what he wanted.

I wouldn't.

I was approaching a line I wouldn't cross, and I needed to get control of the situation once more.

I wasn't here to rekindle my bond with Jamie.

I was here to do my job.

"Jamie, I..." The heavy air clogged my throat.

"Hmm?"

"I..."

Get ahold of yourself. Snap out of it.

I cleared my throat and tried again. "Jamie. I have a boyfriend."

Jamie cocked his head, a devilish smile curling on his lips, leaving my knees weak.

The heat in his gaze was raw and unrelenting.

I couldn't tear my eyes away, trapped by the wicked gleam that held me captive.

"So?"

I inhaled sharply, my mouth opening in surprise. "You... I..."

My words refused to form, and before I could even think of what to say, his grin deepened—more cunning, more dangerous.

Heaven, help me.

That look in his eyes—it was pure temptation.

And I wasn't sure I had the strength to resist if Satan himself came knocking.

"Your boyfriend," Jamie's voice dropped low, deliberate, the weight of his words sinking into me. "He can't touch what we have. You know it, and I know it."

His gaze burned into mine, unwavering.

"I'm not the same man I used to be. That complacent, easy-going guy? He's gone."

Leaning in, his voice dropped to a growl.

"And I'm not afraid to take what I want anymore."

Chapter Eighteen

BLAKELY

His words sent a jolt straight to my chest, my pulse racing as goosebumps scattered across my skin—and not from the cold.

Suddenly, Jamie's gaze shifted, and his hand fell away from my face. With the connection broken, I felt like I could breathe once again.

"I have two orders of French toast." A man in a button-up dress shirt and dress slacks set our food down on the table in front of us. "I'm so sorry for all the trouble. Ashley is new here and is just getting the hang of things."

I swallowed, hardening my resolve once again, but then I noticed Jamie hadn't removed his hand from my shoulder.

Plastering a smile on my face, I said, "It's okay. Really. I know she didn't do anything on purpose."

"I'm the manager on duty here. Your meals are on the house this morning, and please let me know if there is anything else I can do for you during your visit."

The man's gaze dropped to my bare skin before moving back up to my face. Jamie tensed beside me, making a noise somewhere between a cough and a growl.

"Thank you," I said, cutting my words short.

Taking the hint, he walked away, and beside me, Jamie's tension seemed to shift. His hand dropped from my shoulder, and he let out a low sigh, though his energy still crackled with something unspoken.

But whatever spell had been cast over Jamie was now broken.

"I'm sorry, Blake. I don't know what came over me. I have no right to act like that. To say those things."

"It's okay. Let's just eat."

I was going for nonchalance, but I could still feel the force behind his words and the power behind his gaze.

Jamie peeked at me from the corner of his eye before shaking his head, looking almost defeated.

"I can't sit here with you looking like that."

Scoffing, I said, "Who's being the prude now? You've seen me in much less."

"That might be true." He pulled his sweatshirt over his head, the fabric of his tee clinging to his muscles underneath.

"I'm okay. Seriously. You don't have to do that."

"No. Please. For my sake." He ran a hand through his hair, his jaw clenching as if trying to steady himself. "It's taking everything in me to stay in control, and I can't look at you like that without thinking of throwing you on this table and having you for breakfast instead."

And once again, he'd left me utterly speechless as my internal temperature rose a few degrees.

Without a word, I tugged the sweatshirt over my head, the fabric soft and still carrying the warmth of his body. The faint scent of him clung to it, a mix of cedarwood and lavender that wrapped around me.

This was how it had always been with us.

One pushed while the other pulled, each step a careful balance between tension and ease. Fun, but also deeply passionate. A fire that burned just beneath the surface, waiting for the right moment to ignite.

Somehow, we made it through the rest of our breakfast with no other incidents.

Longing, lingering gazes aside.

I set my fork down and cleared my throat. "So, I guess we should talk about the article. It is the reason we are here, after all."

Jamie's hand stilled for a moment as he went to put his last forkful of French toast into his mouth.

"Okay. What do you want to know?"

"Can you tell me how Noah was at work? Was he well-liked? I only know the Noah of our childhood. I don't know adult Noah that well."

"He was well-liked. He looked out for the other airmen and took his job and the safety of others very seriously."

"And you two were together for that mission? When he died?"

"We were."

"Isn't that unusual? For two of you to be together on a mission? I thought you didn't work alongside other Combat Controllers on a mission."

"It is."

"So, why?"

Jamie exhaled, rubbing his palms over his eyes. When he looked at me again, his face was twisted in a grimace.

"I'm sorry, Blake. Can we talk about something else?"

"Yeah, okay."

Jamie exhaled again, forcing the breath from his lungs like he could force his feelings away.

The manager came back by our table with the bill, which he'd comped, and apologized again with a quick farewell.

Jamie must've unsettled him more than I realized.

"I'm ready to go when you are," I said.

"Did you get everything you needed?"

Did I?

Honestly, I don't think I did. But I couldn't think of something to ask that wouldn't bring back that solemn look on his face.

"If I need anything, I'll just reach out."

Jamie nodded and pulled his wallet out before throwing a $20 bill on the table for the waitress.

"Oh, here. Let me split." I grabbed my purse, but Jamie grabbed my wrist and pulled me toward the exit.

"I don't think so."

I tried to argue, but Jamie wouldn't have it. I followed him into the Country Store before he excused himself.

While waiting for Jamie, I pulled my phone from my purse and saw a message from Dean, sent an hour ago.

> Morning Beautiful. No problem. I'll pick you up at 9:30. Can't wait to see you

I checked the time: 8:42 AM. If I hurried, I could be home and ready to go in 45 minutes. I wouldn't be hungry, but I could pretend.

Fake it till you make it. Or so they say.

"Ready?"

Jamie's voice startled me. I instinctively pressed my phone to my chest—a knee-jerk reaction that only made it look like I was doing something I shouldn't.

Jamie eyed me skeptically. "You good?"

"Fine. Let's go." I turned away from him.

It took a few seconds for him to follow me, and in those brief moments, I realized something.

Somewhere between the teasing, the heated glances, and the moments of vulnerability, the weak fortress I'd constructed was crumbling without me even realizing it.

I'd let my guard down.

Again.

Somehow, I had to get ahold of myself, to put it all back together and protect the fragile thing in my chest.

It no longer belonged to him.

I couldn't afford to let him see the parts of me that still longed for him.

If I pushed him away, did something to make him angry, maybe that would be enough to put space between us again.

While Jamie climbed into my car, I texted Dean back.

> Okay. See you then.

"You sure you're okay?" Jamie asked.

I set my phone down in the cup holder. "Peachy."

"Hmm." He said with a nod. He turned from me and looked out the passenger window.

I squeezed my eyes shut. He'd already been through so much. And I couldn't stomach leaving him alone when I could see how isolated he already was.

Jamie was going through something—something big. And no one knew the details.

If there was even the smallest chance I could help him through it, as his friend, I'd at least try.

At the detriment of myself, it would seem.

My eyes followed Jamie's gaze to the car dealership across the street.

Out front, they had a nice-looking blacked-out Chevy.

"Nice looking truck, isn't it?"

"Yeah, it is."

"Ready to go test drive it?"

Jamie looked back at me. "What? No."

"Oh, come on," I said. "That truck is you, just in truck form. All badass and mysterious. A broody and tough exterior, but I bet the interior is lined with soft and silky leather."

"I'm trying to find the compliment in there somewhere."

I grinned.

Hadn't he just said this morning he'd thought about trading in Betty?

Fueled by spontaneity, I pulled out of the parking spot and drove across the street to the dealership.

"What are you doing?"

"Going to check out that snazzy truck. Maybe I want to take it home."

"Blake. Be serious."

"I am. Maybe I'm ready for the truck life. I am a country girl at heart."

That one pulled the corners of Jamie's lips up, and just like that, the awkwardness I'd created was officially gone.

"We are from North Carolina. And you have never stepped foot on a farm, wore cowboy boots, or touched a farm animal."

"That's actually not true."

"Did you buy yourself a nice pair of boots?"

"No, but I've petted plenty of farm animals at the fair every year."

Jamie rolled his eyes as I parked behind the truck on the lot. I got out, knowing he would be right behind me.

"Wow," I said. "This thing looks fancy. Look at that nav screen. And see, leather interior. Bet it's super soft. I can see it now, me driving it around with the windows down along the dirt road to my farm that I haven't bought yet." I giggled as I watched a smile spread across Jamie's lips.

Was I being over the top? Yes.

Was I enjoying it? Also yes.

Not to mention, Jamie looked like a fox in a henhouse as he circled the truck, inspecting every inch of it.

It wasn't long before we drew the attention of a salesman. I ignored his intro, but Jamie jumped right in, asking all the right questions.

I wandered around the truck, still in earshot, but I wasn't paying too much attention to their conversation.

"Will you join me for a test drive?" Jamie's voice startled me for the hundredth time this morning.

"Yeah, sure."

"Thanks. Figured since this was your idea and all, it was the least you could do."

His excitement was contagious, and this was the first time since he'd been back I'd gotten to see him this way.

The salesman handed the keys to Jamie, giving him yet another rundown of this or that.

And then it hit me.

Shit. I was supposed to be home by 9:30.

"Blakely?" Jamie asked.

The sound of my full name coming from his mouth instantly brought me back to all the times he'd said it before.

I love you, Blakely. So damn much.

You're mine forever, Blakely.

I'll never let you go, Blakely.

Blakely.

Blakely.

Blakely.

My muscles froze, and I was positive I looked like a deer in headlights.

Jamie's brow creased with a worried chuckle. "Seriously. You okay?"

"Can you give me just a second?"

"Yeah, sure, take your time."

I walked to the front of the truck on wobbly legs and pulled my phone out with shaky hands.

It was 9:10 AM, and Dean would be on his way to my house any minute. This time I called him.

He picked up on the second ring.

"Hey, sweetheart, I was just getting ready to walk out the door."

"That's why I'm calling. I'm still working and thought I'd have left by now. I'm sorry, but I won't be home to make our breakfast plans."

Dean didn't respond right away. "Work, you said?"

"Yeah, it's a project Mr. Taylor has me working on."

Technically, that wasn't a lie.

"Well, if it's work, I can't get mad about that. How about we plan for dinner then? Do you think you'll finish by then?"

"Definitely," I said, with no hesitation.

"Okay. Dinner it is. I'll let you get back at it. Love you."

"Thanks. Love you too."

My last words came out as a whisper, but I hung up before Dean could ask any questions.

Guilt twisted my stomach into knots. I clenched my hands, forcing the emotions to the back of my mind. I needed to focus.

I vowed to make the most of this test drive and actually get some work done.

I'd think of something I needed answered for this article. And then after all this, I wouldn't need to see Jamie.

I wouldn't have to feel this way anymore.

But the idea of never seeing Jamie again sent a sharp pang through my chest, one I wasn't ready to admit was there.

I was a walking contradiction—pushing him away while a part of me desperately wanted him to stay.

Moving to the passenger door, where Jamie had it open for me, I lifted my chin.

"Ever the gentleman," I mused.

"I try," he said as he held his hand out to help me get into the lifted truck.

Instead, I reached for the grab bar and pulled myself in, avoiding his touch. I had no idea what I was even doing anymore.

He shook his head with a smile as he shut my door and walked to the driver's side.

I watched as he hoisted himself in. His toned, sleek muscles he'd apparently been working on for the last five years made pulling his large body into the cab look easy.

"Ready?" Jamie asked for the third or fourth time this morning.

"I'm ready."

Jamie backed the truck up and turned toward the exit. The truck drove effortlessly in Jamie's expert hands. He moved us in and out of traffic, and soon I relaxed in the comfortable cabin.

I peeked at Jamie and knew instantly that I should have kept my eyes to myself.

Jamie had never been an 'emotions on his sleeve' kind of guy, but if you paid attention, his eyes always betrayed him.

It had always been my one window into his heart, and right now, I could see absolute exhilaration.

He looked happy and free.

Free from the shadows that seemed to follow him and free to enjoy something good for once.

Gone was that guarded, distant Jamie that had come home.

Somehow, he had morphed into the Jamie I had fallen in love with all those years ago.

He wasn't wrong in saying he wasn't the same person he used to be.

He was so much more now.

He'd turned into a survivor. Someone who kept going in spite of the tragedies that plagued his life. He was still smiling, and that meant he hadn't given up yet.

My heart raced, heat creeping up my neck as my hands grew slick with nerves. I curled them into fists, trying to steady myself.

But I wouldn't. I couldn't. I refused.

So I locked them all away—deadbolt, padlock, and key.

I just hoped they stayed there.

Chapter Nineteen

JAMIE
17 YEARS OLD

J*esus.*

I was so damn nervous.

I had this entire date planned out for Blakely and me, and even after being together for a while now, the idea of us alone together still made me sweat more than a whore in church.

Didn't help that the last few times we were alone, things got pretty damn hot.

I was pretty sure my hands had memorized every curve of her body, my tongue craved the taste of her, and the sound of her moaning my name as she came echoed in my ears.

We'd fooled around plenty, but we hadn't gone all the way.

Blake made it clear the idea of having sex scared her. An unplanned pregnancy, despite any precautionary methods taken, was the root of her fear.

She just didn't want to repeat the mistakes of her parents.

And I respected her for that.

So we took it slow.

Slowish.

I was definitely addicted to every single part of her.

I smoothed out the corner of the blanket I'd laid down on the ground for us.

Technically, we weren't supposed to be up here, but the hotel owners were good friends with my parents. If we got caught, it wouldn't be the worst thing.

Besides, with this view of downtown, the risk was worth it.

We were high enough that the stars were still crystal clear.

The old door creaked open, followed by the soft clicking of shoes—my girl.

It was midsummer, so she'd worn a thin floral dress with spaghetti straps and sandals. Her hair lay down her back in loose waves, and she had no idea how my heart beat faster with each step she took.

She was it for me. No one else even came close.

"You know we're not supposed to be up here, Jamie."

I stood, letting my grin take over my face. She was such a stickler for the rules.

God, I loved this girl.

"It's fine. Trust me."

"That's what you always say, but then..." Her words trailed off as she took in the mini picnic, complete with little tea light candles.

Yeah, I know. Super cheesy. But she deserved the world.

"Jamie... This is... wow. It's so beautiful up here."

I took her hand and pulled her in, my lips finding hers on instinct.

She melted into me, her mouth falling open as I caressed her tongue with my own.

I wanted to devour her.

But I couldn't.

So, I pulled away and laced my fingers with hers.

"Come on, I brought some snacks, and I'm starving."

She laughed. "Of course you are."

We sat down, and I dug into the brown paper bag, pulling out my haul.

"First, plain potato chips—your favorite." I placed it in front of her. "Second, brownies—complimentary of my mom, who didn't know this was why I asked her to make brownies this afternoon."

Blake giggled, her eyes shining in the moonlight. "Thank you, Mrs. MacIntyre, for your unknowing participation."

"Third, Skittles, because again—your favorite. Followed by chocolate-covered strawberries, because this is a fancy romantic date."

"That's all sugar. Not a single healthy thing in sight."

"I brought orange soda. That's healthy. It's basically oranges."

Blake shoved my shoulder playfully.

"That's definitely not the case, and you know it. You're not going to be able to eat like this forever. One day you'll have to stop."

"And until that day comes, there's no stopping me."

"You're going to make yourself sick."

"Maybe if I were eating it alone, but that's what I have you for. Here, say ahhh."

I popped open the bag of chips and held one up for her to take from my fingers.

Which she did, complete with an eye roll and a smile. A smile so breathtaking and radiant it made my insides all mushy.

I want to keep that smile on her face forever.

Placing another chip in front of her mouth, she batted her

eyelashes as she opened her lips and captured the chip and the tips of my fingers.

Licking my fingers clean, she pulled away.

And all the blood in my body ran to one single spot.

I wanted her to do it again.

Picking up a brownie instead, I broke off a small piece from the corner and held it up for her.

Again, she wrapped her tongue around my fingers and I had to fight my own moan from leaving my mouth.

Such a small act, but it was setting my body on fire.

This time, I grabbed one of the strawberries. But instead of turning this into a cute scene from a movie where the couple feeds each other strawberries, I had other plans.

I was already gone, consumed by my desire for her.

Not that it ever took long to get me to that point.

I moved closer to her, and she opened her mouth, but I placed the strawberry on the pulse point of her neck.

She inhaled sharply, the coolness from the chilled dessert sending goosebumps along her skin.

I let it sit against her warm skin, until the chocolate began to melt.

Which was exactly what I wanted.

Fuck chocolate covered strawberries.

I wanted a chocolate covered Blakely.

Pulling it away, I flicked my gaze up to hers, taking in her lust filled green eyes, before licking it clean.

This time I moved the strawberry lower. Blake's breathing picked up and I was becoming lost in haze of hunger.

She was all I could see.

A small breathy moan left her lips as I licked up the chocolate.

But I wanted more.

Placing the strawberry just under her collarbone, I let it sit before squeezing it. I watched the trail of red run down her smooth skin, completely entranced.

Dipping my head quickly, I ran my tongue along it's path, continuing back up before placing a kiss to her neck.

"Jamie... I..." Her gaze bounced around my face, her cheeks flushed and her chest rising and falling to a beat that matched my own racing heart.

"Blakely."

As the sound of her name, she reached her hands into my hair and pulled me against her with a groan.

She tasted of sweetness and everything Blake, and I laid her down on the blanket beneath us, completely oblivious to the fact that we were crushing the chips.

I couldn't stop my hands from running along her body as my tongue fought hers for dominance.

My hand skimmed the hem of her dress, feeling the smoothness of her skin and wanting even more.

But I knew her boundaries. And we needed to douse this fire before it became an inferno.

Breaking our kiss, I rested my forehead against hers.

"We should finish our picnic," I whispered.

"No."

"Our drinks then."

"I don't want that either."

"Then what do you want?"

"You."

"You have me, babe."

She shook her head. "All of you."

I pulled back, looking into her eyes for any hint that she was messing around.

But all I saw in those green depths was resolve.

Determination.

"Blakely..."

"Make me yours, Jamie. In every way."

"Are you sure?"

"I love you, Jamie. Of course I'm sure."

She slammed her lips against mine again and gave me no time to think as she pushed her chest into me, rubbing herself against me.

"I love you, Blakely. So damn much," I said against her lips as I pulled her dress down her body.

I'd tried not to notice earlier that she'd forgotten to wear a bra, but now with her breasts fully exposed, I moved down her body to pull a nipple into my mouth.

She cried out, arching her back as I palmed the other one.

Blake pulled at my tee, impatient as I felt, and tossed it aside. Running her hands down my bare chest, she tugged at my jeans. But before she could push them down my legs, I slid my hand into her underwear.

She gasped, then moaned as I pushed two fingers inside her.

We'd done everything but sex, so I knew just what she liked, but knowing we were going to take this all way sent a wave of nerves throughout my body.

"Jamie, please. Don't make me wait," she said as her body moved under mine, like a puppet on a string.

"I don't want to hurt you."

"You won't. I promise."

I kissed her again, before removing my hand and pulling her underwear down her legs.

She was completely naked, her skin glistening in the glow of the streetlights below.

Stripping off my jeans and boxers, I settled between her legs.

"Are you sure? Is this really what you want?"

Blake rolled her eyes. "How many times do I have to tell you? Just screw me already."

I grabbed my dick—who was happy that it was finally his time to shine, but also slightly afraid he wouldn't be able to last more than thirty seconds.

Because it was his first time too.

When you were in love with the same girl since you were eleven, you didn't really go out and experiment.

Sucking in a deep breath, I locked my gaze with Blake's and pushed inside her.

She gasped at the intrusion before pain etched in her features. My body froze, unable to move and cause her more discomfort. But she shook her head.

"Don't stop."

"You..."

But she moved her hips, taking more of me and ultimately silencing me.

Goddamn.

I wasn't even all the way inside her and I was already ready to tap out.

But there was no way we were going to go without a fight... or... at least feeling Blake unravel on my dick.

What was the point of all this, if not that?

Pushing the rest of the way inside her, I took a deep steadying breath. Trying to not focus on the fact that I could feel every inch of her body.

I leaned back, still concerned it was too much for her.

But besides the furrow in her brow, her mouth hung open and her cheeks were pink.

Her golden hair caught the light and fanned around her like a halo. She was effortlessly beautiful. The kind that didn't need any makeup or fancy clothes. And when she smiled, it lit up her entire face, making her eyes sparkle with a fire that made me feel invincible.

And when she'd look at me, and I mean really look at me, with her wide trusting emerald eyes, I felt like the luckiest guy in the world.

She made me believe I could do anything.

That *we* could do anything.

As long as we were together.

"You're mine forever, Blakely," I groaned as I began to move inside her.

"Yes," she said, pleasure ringing in the sound of her voice.

I could tell by the way she moved, that the worst of her pain was gone and I began to quicken my pace.

I was losing my ability to focus on anything other than the way it felt to be inside her.

This was worth the wait.

But I was ready to hear her scream my name.

My pace turned dominating, and she moaned beneath me.

"God. Jamie. I... I don't what to do."

"Say my name. Say my name as you come apart."

I could feel her body tensing. She was close.

"We can't finish until you scream my name, Blakely."

"Jamie... I... Yes... Jamie!"

She arched beneath me, her muscles spasming as she reached her peak.

Feeling her squeeze my dick pushed me over the edge. And with another thrust, I collapsed on top of her.

I was sweaty, spent, and riding a high like none I'd every felt.

Moving to the side of Blake's body, I asked, "Are you okay? Are you hurt?"

I looked down to see the proof of virginal status between us, but she looked up at me and smiled one of her heart stopping smiles.

"I'm absolutely perfect."

She placed her hand on my collarbone and pushed me down, so I was on my back, and moved into the nook under my arm and rested her head on my shoulder.

"I love you, Jamie."

The stars in the night shinned brighter than I'd ever seen them before. The earlier sounds from the street below were quiet, as if they'd all decided to give us this moment here together. Every touch from Blake felt like a millions pins and needles on my skin.

I'd never be able to figure out how I'd gotten so lucky. How I deserved to have someone like Blakely in my life.

But I knew, I'd never let her go.

Not now. Not ever.

The devil would have to pry her from my cold dead body.

I placed a kiss on top of her head, letting my eyes shut.

"I love you, Blakely."

Chapter Twenty

Blakely

After dropping Jamie off at his apartment, I couldn't shake the melancholy settling deep in my bones.

Jamie didn't seem to notice the shift in me—not that I'd expected him to. He was too preoccupied with the success of the test drive, his excitement practically filling the car. A small, irrational part of me hoped that was the only reason he hadn't asked if I was okay.

The old Jamie would have noticed instantly. He always saw me. The realization stung, and I fought the bitter edge of disappointment that threatened to unravel me.

Back home, I brewed a hot cup of coffee and sank onto the couch, watching as dark clouds rolled in, heavy with the promise of rain.

Fitting, given the storm brewing inside me.

It was strange. Typically, I was full of energy and never sat down. With so much to do, I couldn't remember the last time I stopped and just looked out the window.

But I couldn't make myself move from the couch.

Numb. Completely numb.

My mind flitted between thoughts, like images in a slideshow—past Jamie and present Jamie, and how different the two had become. I found myself reliving moments we'd shared, moments when we gave everything to each other.

I remembered how it all began to change, how he started pulling away during his training. Then his dad. Then the baby. Before I knew it, he came home to our apartment one day and told me he wouldn't be back. That he didn't want me wasting any more of my time on him. I called him over and over, begging him to talk to me, to come back, but my messages went unanswered.

And then there was Dean. Patient, kind, and steady. He helped me find myself again. With him, I never had to wonder where I stood. He was dependable, and at the time, that was exactly what I needed.

But every time I tried to hold onto a memory, it slipped through my fingers—replaced by another. It was like trying to hold onto sand—no matter how tightly I grasped, the harder it became to keep my mind on track.

I took a sip of my coffee, surprised by its coolness.

Hadn't I just poured it?

I glanced at my phone. Almost noon. Had I really been sitting here that long?

Hours wasted.

I wanted to shake the haze, to push through the tangled mess of emotions choking my chest. But I couldn't find the motivation to get up.

Sometime later, still stuck in that detached haze, I jolted awake at the sound of my front door handle jiggling.

I jumped to my feet, thankful I had set my coffee down a while ago.

The handle jiggled again, and I grabbed the baseball bat I kept next to my front door. I gripped it tight, ready for whoever dared to come through.

The door opened, and I prepared to swing.

"Whoa! Blake. Blake, it's just me."

Dean stood with his hands raised, holding a bouquet and a bottle of wine.

Shit.

I'd forgotten...again.

"Sorry," I muttered as I lowered my bat.

Dean shut the door behind him. "These are for you." The awkwardness of me almost clubbing him lingered between us.

He set the gifts down on the entryway table, and I couldn't help but notice how dressed up he was. Black dress slacks, dress shirt, complete with a tie.

Why?

We never talked about going to a fancy restaurant, and even if I hadn't forgotten about our date, I wouldn't have dressed up in black tie.

And that irritated me. More than it should have. But my emotions were already all over the place, and I felt like he was trying way too hard.

Dean looked me up and down. "Oh... You're not ready yet."

Dean looked crushed, and for some reason, that only made my irritation spike.

I should have remembered and canceled. I wasn't in the right headspace for this, and my irritation wasn't fair to him.

I took a deep breath, trying to calm myself down. Dean had done nothing wrong.

"I'm sorry, Dean, I lost track of time. When I got home, I sat down on the couch and must have fallen asleep looking out the window."

Dean eyed me skeptically. He knew me better than that—I

never just stopped to stare out a window. But at least this time, I wasn't lying.

"Work must have exhausted you today."

I blew out a huff. "Yeah."

Something flickered behind Dean's eyes—dark and unsettling. It was gone as fast as it came, but a chill worked its way down my spine.

I must have imagined it.

I'd never seen Dean hurt a fly. In fact, he was all for saving the spiders in the house, which had always creeped me out.

"Listen, Dean. I am really sorry, but—"

Dean sighed, cutting me off. "It's fine, sweetheart. Why don't we order in? I planned this whole thing, but it won't be fun if you're not into it. How about Chinese?"

My body sagged. "Thank you. That would be amazing."

Dean walked to my couch and sat down, loosening the tie around his neck. I followed and sat beside him, resting my head on his shoulder.

"Actually, can we get Chick-fil-A? I'm craving their Spicy Chicken Sandwich."

Dean tensed beside me, his fingers pausing over his phone before resuming their movement—slower this time.

"Yeah, that's fine."

"If you're set on Chinese, let's order that. I can get my sandwich tomorrow."

"No. We can get Chick-fil-A."

His voice came out sharper than necessary, but he didn't argue. He just pulled out his phone, fingers moving swiftly as he placed the order.

I turned on my TV, relaxing back into my couch as I clicked the Netflix button on the remote.

"Any requests?" I asked.

"No."

I clicked on a random *Friends* episode, anything to offer some distraction, and I could literally jump into this show at any point and still know exactly what was going on.

Dean sat beside me, unusually quiet, his thumb moving over the screen while his brows pulled together.

"Dean? Are you okay?"

He stopped scrolling, his fingers freezing as if my words had shocked him.

"Am I okay?"

"Yeah."

He set his phone down, his fingers tapping against the armrest before he finally spoke. "I'm not sure."

I waited, frustration curling in my chest when he didn't offer more. He wanted me to ask.

"And why is that, Dean?"

"Because my girlfriend was running around town with her ex-boyfriend while claiming she was too busy working to keep her plans with me. She canceled and rescheduled, not once, not twice, but three times after completely forgetting about our dinner plans."

Chapter Twenty-One

BLAKELY

My heart raced as heat rushed to my face.

Dean sneered at me, anger radiating off him in waves. He looked like a completely different person. Gone was the gentle, sweet man who had held me through some of my darkest moments.

This Dean was a stranger to me.

"Dean, I—"

"Is that enough reason for me to 'not be okay'?"

"Listen—"

"I'm not sure I want to."

Frustrated, I huffed, "Dean, just listen!"

He took a deep breath. "Why?"

"I was working. Mr. Taylor wanted me to interview Jamie for the article on Noah. Since Jamie was there when he died and they were best friends, Mr. Taylor thought Jamie could add important details to the piece."

Dean's eyes narrowed, but he stayed silent. So I kept going.

"I've been trying to get Jamie to answer some questions, and he was free this morning. I am sorry about canceling on you. I never meant to hurt you. At all. I didn't think it was important enough to worry you by mentioning Jamie."

I placed my hand on Dean's cheek, silently offering him all the love I held in my heart.

"I didn't think it was important because Jamie is my past. You, Dean, are my present and my future. It is you who I love, not him. Not anymore."

I watched some of the tension leave his body at my confession.

A knock at the door interrupted us, and I took it as a blessing in disguise.

It broke the strain between us and gave me a chance to breathe.

A confrontation with Dean wasn't what I'd anticipated tonight, but I could see why he was upset. Hurting him was never my intention.

It was just easier to do what I needed to do without having to explain myself.

Dean thanked the driver and brought the bags of fried goodness to my coffee table. He divvied out the food, and my stomach growled as the smell of fried chicken and waffle fries entered my orbit.

I took a bite of my sandwich and moaned appreciatively.

Dean's gaze flicked to mine, and I grinned sheepishly.

Hunger shone behind his eyes, and not the hunger food could satisfy.

"Enjoying your food?"

My face grew hot. "Yes."

"Hm."

I took a deep breath. "Dean, I'm really sorry. I didn't mean to string you along all day."

Dean exhaled. With each passing minute, he looked more and more like my Dean and less like the stranger he'd been earlier.

"I'm sorry, too. For jumping down your throat. I know how much you cared for Jamie and how much he hurt you. But I love you, Blake, and I don't want to lose you. He gave you up willingly, and I will fight to the death to keep you."

My chest warmed with his admission. His words gave me security, and I felt safe with him. Emotionally safe. That was all I needed.

"I love you, too, Dean."

I leaned my head on his shoulder, and we continued eating in a comfortable silence.

With his last bite, Dean broke the quiet surrounding us. "I miss him, you know. Noah. The way he used to put a smile on my face no matter how I was feeling. He wrote me, and getting his letters was the highlight of my day."

I lifted my head and nodded. "He wrote me too. Not as often as other people, I'm sure. There were more important people to him than me."

"I think you are downplaying how much you meant to him. He always worried about you and how you were holding up after Jamie left." Dean laughed. "I think he had a thing for you, actually."

"No, he didn't. Don't joke about that stuff."

"I'm not." Dean reached over and ran a finger along my jaw. "But I couldn't stop my feelings either, and some part of me wonders if that pushed Noah away."

Dean dropped his hand and looked out the window.

"Noah mentioned Jamie in his letters. He told me they ran into each other a few times. But it seemed as time went on, Noah grew concerned for Jamie. Saying that he became reckless and wasn't concerned with anyone's safety or following the rules."

I frowned, fighting the urge to argue with what Dean was saying. It wasn't my job to defend Jamie, but what he said didn't sound like Jamie at all.

Then again, he'd shown no concern for my well-being these past few years.

"Noah wrote me the night before he died, saying he was going on a mission and Jamie would be there too, and he was worried."

"Worried? About what?"

"Worried about the safety of everyone. Jamie was obviously a loose cannon, and Noah was probably worried they wouldn't survive that mission and Jamie would be the—"

"Don't say it, Dean."

"Why? Why protect him if he is responsible for my brother's death?"

All I could do was shake my head. There was no way Jamie would knowingly put anyone in harm's way. Especially Noah.

"Jamie was always causing trouble when we were kids. He was always getting Noah into trouble, and Noah would just bail him out."

"But Dean, I was with them. We all contributed to the trouble. It wasn't only Jamie with those ideas. Wes, Liam, Erik, Noah, Jamie, Cadence, and I all did those things together."

"Noah rode home in the back of a police car because of him."

"So did everyone else."

"Why are you defending him, Blake?"

"Because, as much as you don't want me to say it, I know Jamie. And I know he would never do anything to put other people at risk. He just wouldn't."

"Maybe the Jamie you knew wouldn't, but he isn't that

person anymore. He knows what happened to my brother and won't tell anyone. Which leads me to believe it's his fault. He's saving his own skin."

Frustration settled over me like a heavy weight on my chest. I pressed my lips into a thin line, realizing this was a dead end.

Neither of us were ready to acknowledge the other's truth.

My goal had been to reassure Dean, not fight for Jamie's honor.

"Let's not talk about this anymore, okay?"

"So now I can't even talk to my own girlfriend about my brother's death?"

"No, that's not what I'm saying. I just feel like this is all speculation. We don't know what happened, so how can anyone try to place blame?"

"Guess we'll have to agree to disagree. But I don't have a problem placing blame where blame is due."

I took a sip of my soda, pressing my lips together. I had nothing to say back.

Dean stood. "Why don't I get out of here? Tonight clearly didn't go as planned. Maybe it's just best to cut my losses."

"No, don't leave. Not like this. Stay."

"Blake..."

"No, really. Stay. Let's watch a movie and cuddle on the couch. I'll make some popcorn and open that bottle of wine you brought." I flashed a baby doll smile. "Please?"

After everything I'd put him through today, I didn't want him to leave like this.

Dean's face softened as I batted my eyes. "Fine... I guess."

I stood to meet him. Rising onto my tiptoes, I pressed my lips to his, his warm breath fanning against my skin as he leaned in.

His arms tightened around my waist, drawing me in, while his other hand traced a slow path up my shoulder before settling at the back of my neck. His fingers pressed gently, sending a shiver racing down my spine.

As the kiss deepened, his tongue brushed against mine, moving with a deliberate, practiced rhythm that made it impossible not to surrender.

I gave in completely, letting him take what he wanted, my thoughts melting away with every second that passed.

When Dean finally pulled back, we were both left breathless, the air between us charged with unspoken tension. His dark brown hair was slightly tousled, his deep eyes flickering with something unreadable.

My gaze drifted over him—his chiseled jawline, the way his muscles filled out his shirt, every inch of him radiating strength and confidence. He was undeniably attractive, and I couldn't stop myself from giving him a quick once-over.

A cocky smirk tugged at his lips as he raised an eyebrow, then took my hand and led me toward the bedroom.

Neither of us were strangers to desire, and I was more than willing to give Dean the comfort he needed—the reassurance that he still had every piece of me.

Standing in my room, he pulled off his button up and dropped his dress pants, before grabbing my waist.

Pushing my hair back from my shoulder, he kissed my neck. I let my body relax in his touch, moving my head to give me better access to my skin.

I let out a little moan as he licked and nipped down my throat to my collarbone.

"Time to take these off," he said pulling the sweatshirt I wore over my head.

Oh. God. *Jamie's* sweatshirt.

I never gave it back to him earlier after...

Jamie's heated look flashed in my mind, and my body

tensed. This was *not* the time or place for my memory to recall those moments from earlier.

Dean didn't seem to notice as he ran his hands down my bare shoulders. I still only had the camisole underneath the sweatshirt.

"Mm. Almost done," he said as he lifted the thin silk material over my head.

I tried to swallow the lump in my throat as Dean continued to kiss my skin and remove the remainder of our clothes.

But Jamie had invaded our intimate space.

And that felt like a betrayal.

Sinking down into the bed, Dean settled between my thighs. I wrapped my hand around the back of his neck and pulled his lips to mine, seeking that same passion and hunger I'd seen in Jamie's eyes earlier.

As Dean thrust inside me, I gasped, fighting to push aside every memory that wasn't of Dean and I.

His touch, his smell, his eyes.

Dean, and only Dean.

But as he moved, the sounds of his pleasure surrounded us, and I was struggling to keep our moment isolated from my storm of emotions.

"God, Blake. You feel so good," he said as he kissed my cheek, my forehead, and then my lips.

I turned my head, trying to forget everything I was thinking and just *feel*.

But the hints of Jamie's scent lingered on my skin and I could smell him. My body tensed as those hints of cedarwood brought me back to a pair of steel gray eyes.

The way he'd looked at me...

It felt like he'd truly wanted to devour me.

Pleasure coursed through me, clouding my judgement and forcing these thoughts away.

Because in those moments, I'd wanted Jamie to make good on his words.

"Yes…" I moaned as Dean panted in my ear.

But I didn't hear him.

And when he growled, "Come for me, Blake."

I did.

My muscles spasmed as my back arched, my release taking over my body.

But it wasn't Dean's voice I'd heard, but the deep timber of Jamie's.

As I came down from the high, Dean stilled, emptying himself inside me. But I was already on way back to detachment. I was no longer living in this moment.

What kind of person did this make me? Thinking about someone else while having sex with your boyfriend?

But it was Dean's words that finally pushed me over the edge and to the point of no return.

The same one's *he'd* said all those years ago.

"You're mine forever, Blakely."

Chapter Twenty-Two

JAMIE

Light streamed through my window, blinding me as I rolled over—again.

It was early Sunday morning, and I was trying to do what normal people did on the weekend—sleep in.

But convincing my body to sleep past its usual four or five hours was like trying to get a vegetarian to eat a juicy burger.

AKA—never gonna happen.

Ruger grunted beside me, clearly irritated that my sleeplessness was disturbing his beauty rest.

I groaned and rolled out of bed.

I knew what my body wanted to do. What it craved.

It was my favorite thing to do when I found no comfort from the back of my eyelids.

Run.

Running distracted me from the pain I felt inside.

The burn in my chest as it fought for oxygen, the heaviness

in my legs as I pushed forward, the wind against my face as I drove myself further—all of it.

I craved those moments of physical exhaustion because they overpowered any emotions.

The steady rhythm of my feet hitting the pavement surrounded me, a dull, repetitive sound that somehow managed to steady my mind.

As I ran through Fayetteville, everything looked the same, frozen in time. It felt strange—almost jarring—when my own life had shifted so drastically it seemed like centuries since I'd last been here.

I'd shut everyone out back then.

Calls to my mom had become nothing more than an obligation, each one brief and distant. I'd built walls so high that no one could scale them.

No one, except Noah.

Somehow, he'd managed to slip through the cracks.

As I ran, the memories came rushing back, unbidden, and I could pinpoint the exact moment when our friendship shifted. When everything between us began to change from best friends to more like brothers.

It was one of the first times we'd crossed paths after we'd graduated from our grueling two years of technical school. By then, I was already falling apart, drowning in the chaos of everything I'd been through.

It wasn't long after tech school that tragedy struck. My dad had taken his own life and the weight of that loss left me reeling. I barely had time to come to terms with it before Blakely miscarried, losing the little life we had both wanted so badly.

It felt like everything in my life was unraveling all at once, and instead of leaning on the people who cared about me, I shut them out—Noah included.

I convinced myself that breaking up with Blake was the

right thing to do. I'd become obsessed with the idea that she deserved more than I could give. If I took her away from home, she'd be alone, with no one to support her, and I couldn't shake the thought that I wouldn't be enough to make her happy. It was easier to walk away than to admit I was falling apart.

Breaking things off with her had been the hardest thing I'd ever done, and it'd sent me spiraling. That was when I started drinking more than I should, numbing myself to the pain.

Noah was the only one who wouldn't take my bullshit. He'd found me wallowing in self-pity and refused to leave me alone, no matter how hard I pushed him away.

I'd never forget the feeling of knowing he wouldn't give up on me.

I never told him how much that meant—how it felt like I'd won the lottery in the friendship department. Our conversations were a lifeline, pulling me out of the darkness and reminding me of the man I wanted to be.

I wish I'd told him how much his friendship had meant to me. How he'd kept me from falling apart when I thought I'd already lost everything.

But Noah was gone now, and I'd never get the chance to tell him.

Distracted by my thoughts, I found myself on his street, a street I'd known as well as my own as a kid.

I stopped in front of the Richeys' family home, still dark in the early morning light.

Looking up at Noah's old room, a sharp pain cut through me at the thought of that window never lighting up again.

I didn't expect to see a pair of familiar brown eyes staring back at me.

My body went rigid, every muscle freezing. My knees threatened to buckle, and I wasn't sure I could keep myself upright.

Noah?

The figure shifted, and as sunlight hit their face, my pulse steadied.

It was Mr. Richey standing in the window. I offered a sheepish smile and a small wave before forcing my feet to move again.

At least I didn't have to add "sees ghosts" to my skill set.

Running, my solace, had led me astray.

Back home, I showered and dressed for the day ahead.

Another day filled with nothing and no one.

The monotonous days had never bothered me before, but now they felt hollow.

I sat on the couch with a freshly brewed cup of coffee and rubbed the cushion next to me for Ruger to jump up. I patted his head, thankful for the comfort his presence brought me.

It had been impulsive for me to get a dog, especially with how often I was gone. But Ruger was resilient and didn't seem too bothered by my absences.

When I could, I made it a point to video call with him when I was gone. I only let Ruger stay with people I trusted, usually with my leadership or a co-worker. I hadn't made too many friends in the Air Force, not that my co-workers hadn't tried. I just never let anyone close enough to get to know me, or for me to know them.

In Fayetteville, though, my mom had stepped up and designated herself his official second owner.

An idea popped into my head.

I looked at Ruger and asked, "Wanna go for a ride?"

His ears perked at the word *ride*. He tilted his head to the side in that adorable way that only animals could pull off.

I jumped off the couch, leaving the steamy cup of unexciting coffee to cool on my table, while Ruger followed close on my heels. I'd trained him when he was a pup, and he was the best dog a man could ask for. He sat right by the front door, waiting for me.

I pulled the leash off the table I never used but didn't bother clipping it to his collar. Grabbing my wallet, keys, and phone off the same table, we walked out into the sunshine.

"Who's excited to go for a ride?"

Ruger followed me to my car, and I cringed at the sight of the purple eyesore that was my mode of transportation.

Honest to God, I never noticed how truly painful it was to look at until it had been pointed out... repeatedly.

I opened the driver's side door, and Ruger immediately jumped in, settling into the passenger seat like it was his throne.

I laughed out loud. No doubt about it—my next car needed leather seats. Dog hair was a nightmare to clean.

My thoughts drifted to the truck I'd test-driven with Blake —everything I wanted in a vehicle.

I had to admit, having Blake in the seat next to me while we drove around aimlessly had been an added bonus.

If I bought that truck, I'd never be able to remove her scent from it or not think of her when I drove it.

But would that stop me from doing it?

No, absolutely not.

I was a glutton for punishment.

If anything, I craved that connection with her. I had thought about the purchase more times than any other car I'd test-driven in the past.

Being Sunday, the dealership was closed. But maybe I'd stop by during the week.

I pulled into my mom's driveway, suddenly self-conscious. I hadn't called to tell her I was swinging by, and I didn't even know if she was home.

I knocked on the door, Ruger standing wingman at my side.

"Jamie?" My mom gave me a confused look when she opened the door. "Ruger!"

Ruger's tail wagged as he made circles around my mom, happy to see her and his second home again. The ease Ruger showed around my mom brought me a sense of relief, lifting a small weight off my chest.

I knew he'd always be well cared for, regardless of what happened to me.

"Hey, Mom, sorry to drop in unannounced. Are you up for visitors?"

My mom pulled me into a hug as she said, "You know you are always welcome."

She smiled as she opened the door and ushered us both inside. Ruger went in and made himself right at home in his dog bed that still sat in the corner of her living room.

I followed her into the kitchen and sat down at the counter.

"Coffee?" she asked.

"Sure."

"Do you still drink it like you used to?"

"Whatever is the easiest for you is fine."

Mom gave me a look.

I cracked a smile. "Once you spend time in the deserts of the Middle East and don't have the luxury of cream and sugar for your coffee, you are so desperate for the caffeine you don't care if your coffee tastes like tar. So really, Mom, any way is fine."

Her eyes widened, and she froze. I hadn't meant to shock her—or myself, for that matter. I never talked about my time overseas, not to anyone, but the words had slipped out so naturally.

I didn't miss the way she added a little extra cream and sugar to my cup, as if that small gesture could somehow make up for all the years I'd endured bitter, shitty coffee overseas.

I hid my smile behind my mug as I brought it to my lips. "Thanks, Mom."

"Of course, honey."

She brought her coffee over and sat beside me at the counter, sliding her chair close without crowding me.

Her presence was calming in a way only my mom could manage. She didn't have to do anything extraordinary—just being there, showing how much she cared, was enough to soothe my battered soul. But it also came with a sharp pang of guilt.

Who had comforted her after her husband took his own life?

Who had helped her when her entire world fell apart?

Yes, I had called her. But every time, I found an excuse to avoid talking about anything real. I'd never stopped to ask how she was really doing.

Fayetteville would always hold a special place in my heart —it was home. But I couldn't shake the negative feelings I'd tied to this place. Maybe that was why I'd avoided coming back for so long.

Still, I couldn't help but wonder if staying away had only made those feelings worse.

Would I have been a different person if I'd faced those emotions instead of running from them?

I guess I'd never know.

I looked over at my mom and realized I knew nothing about her now. What was her life like without Dad in it?

That needed to change.

"So..." I said. "What are you up to these days? Are you still working at the school teaching those little hellions?"

She beamed. "You mean first graders, and yes, I am. They are still innocent at that age. Haven't had time to learn the art of mischief yet."

My mom nudged me, implying I was the master of mischief, and to her credit, my friends and I had been.

"How about after work? Are you seeing anyone," I coughed. "Romantically?"

The question came out as awkward as it felt, considering I was asking if my mom had found someone that wasn't my dad.

She smiled to herself, a slight blush creeping across her cheeks. "Actually, I am. Do you remember Mr. Kelly?"

"Mr. Kelly, my kindergarten teacher?"

She nodded. "After your father died, I had a really rough time with everything. I lingered around school, not wanting to come home to an empty house, not wanting to be alone. Nolan —Mr. Kelly—stayed late with me, claiming he had lessons to plan and needed to do stuff in his classroom."

The guilt on my face must have been impossible to hide— something I'd never struggled with before.

My mom reached over and took my hand.

"Jamie, I am not blaming you when I say those things. It is not, and never has been, your responsibility to take care of me. It is the opposite. In fact, I'm supposed to take care of you."

"Mom..."

"No, let me finish." She took a deep breath, steadying herself. "We were all hurting, and I couldn't do anything to help you when you needed me. I couldn't take away your pain, and I feel like I failed you. First, you lost the baby, then your father." Her finger traced the rim of her coffee cup absently. "I was so lost in my own grief that I couldn't think of anyone but myself."

I reached over and pulled her into a hug, holding her close as I buried myself in her embrace.

"I'm the one who ran away," I murmured. "I'm the one who wasn't there for you. I let you and everyone else down. I've beaten myself up for years for not being here when you needed me. I'm sorry I left you alone. I'm sorry for everything."

Mom pulled back just enough to meet my eyes, searching them as if she could speak all the words I needed to hear without saying them aloud.

"I was never really alone, Jamie. I had Ella, my friends, and Nolan. I missed you—God, I missed you—but I was never truly lonely."

Her words hit me like a lifeline, squeezing my chest and unlocking some of the chains that had bound my heart for so long.

She had said exactly what I needed to hear, giving me the chance to understand that maybe I hadn't hurt her as deeply as I'd feared.

Her eyes shimmered with unshed tears, a mirror of my own emotions. The weight of our conversation settled between us— words left unspoken for years, feelings buried too deep, and the shared pain of true loss.

She sniffled. "Plus, I've always had the girls. Bingo night is still every Friday. We've been getting together for close to twenty years now." Mom pulled her arms from around me and grabbed her cup, taking a sip. "But enough about me. Tell me about you. How have you been?"

"I'm fine, Mom."

"You come home to attend a funeral for your best friend. You see your ex-fiancée—who you are clearly not over, by the way—in a relationship with your best friend's brother. You're not fine."

"Wow."

"Not exactly an easy homecoming."

I couldn't stop the grin that spread across my lips. "No. Not really."

"Which is exactly why I'm having a barbecue tomorrow. I thought it would be fun to let loose a little after everything that has happened."

"What?"

"So, do you have plans tomorrow, Jamie? Can you come by?" Mom's smile grew.

"Mom..."

"All your friends said they would come. Including Blake."

"But..."

She leaned over and kissed me on the cheek, knowing she had won this battle with me.

If she was throwing a party, I wouldn't let her down by missing it.

I let out a groan, torn between the thrill of excitement and the weight of despair.

Chapter Twenty-Three

BLAKELY

11 YEARS OLD

My first day at my new school in Fayetteville had finally arrived.

I wasn't nervous, not really.

After everything I'd been through, starting a new school was the least of my worries.

Plus, I'd already made friends. I knew the guys I met at the park went to this school, and I had every intention of seeking them out. No one wanted to be *the new girl* and sit alone at lunch. Even I didn't want that label.

My grandma was the one who dropped me off at the office for my first day of sixth grade. My dad had worked all night and was *too tired* to bring me. Just another way he showed me how unimportant I was to him.

The office attendant took me to my locker and gave me my class schedule. I looked around for the guys, for Jamie, but I didn't see them.

My first class, Geography, went smoothly. No one tried to talk to me, and I did the same in return.

It wasn't until my second class, Algebra, that I sensed his eyes on me.

"Hey! Blake!" Jamie shouted as he leaped off the desk he had been sitting on and made his way toward me.

I grinned. "Hey, Jamie."

"How's your first day going?"

"This is only my second class."

Jamie put his hand on his neck, "Yeah, I guess you're right."

"It's been alright, though. No one has said much to me."

"Well, come hang out with us. There's plenty of chit-chat to go around." Jamie threw his arm around my shoulders like we were old pals and pulled me over to where he'd been sitting with Wes and Noah.

"Nice to see you guys again," I said.

"'Sup," Wes nodded.

"Same. Welcome to *Westover Middle School*," Noah said with a smile.

Seeing their familiar faces, I already felt better about my new school. "Where are the other guys?"

"Well," Jamie said, "Liam and Erik are in seventh grade. So, we run into each other in the halls, but that's about it."

"Oh, I didn't realize they were a year older than us."

Jamie nodded as the bell rang, and the teacher entered the classroom.

"Students, please find your seats."

I looked around, unsure where to go. The classroom was filled with rows of desks, one behind the other. Luckily, the teacher saw me before everyone was settled.

"You must be Ms. Mason. Have a seat at the empty desk to your right. And since you seem to know Mr. MacIntyre already, go ahead and pull your desk to his so you can share his book until I can get you one."

As I pulled my desk to Jamie's, a chill ran down my spine. I looked over my shoulder to see a pretty brunette glaring daggers at me.

When class ended, Jamie helped push my desk back. "Let me see your schedule."

I handed it to him and watched as his gray eyes scanned the paper.

"Nice! We have the next two classes together." He smiled, and my legs went a little unsteady. His smile was filled with sunshine, rainbows, and happiness; all the things I no longer had in my life.

Once again, Jamie wrapped his arm around my shoulders and pulled me along, and I stuck to him like glue.

Our third period was Biology, and Jamie asked our teacher if he could sit with me in the back. As my new lab partner, he offered to share his book again, but this time I opted for my own.

Fourth period was Art, and surprise, surprise, Jamie insisted I sit with him at his table. Art, however, was a more free-structured class, with big tables set around the room. Jamie sat in the corner with four other students, including the brunette from Algebra.

As soon as we sat down, she threw herself at Jamie, doing everything she could to get his attention.

Her goal was far from subtle, and I wasn't sure if Jamie and this girl had a history. She was determined to get his attention and let me know I wasn't good enough to sit with them.

After Art class, Jamie told me to meet him in front of the office, and he would walk with me down to the lunchroom.

After watching how the brunette acted in Art, whose name

I learned was Charlotte, I wasn't sure I understood exactly where Jamie stood in the sixth-grade hierarchy.

Was he considered one of the *popular* guys? It was obvious from her actions that Charlotte thought he belonged to her.

And if I was honest with myself, her rejection hurt more than I thought it could. I didn't know her, but I only wanted to make friends and be liked by everyone.

Charlotte had already found a reason to hate me.

As I opened my locker to put my notebooks away, the door slammed shut. Startled, I turned, ready to receive the onslaught of apologies from whoever almost shut my hand in the locker.

Instead, I met Charlotte's dark brown eyes as she gave me a slow, deliberate once-over, disgust written all over her face.

She sneered at my hand-me-down clothes like I was an insect she wanted to chase out with a fly swatter.

To her, I was just an imposter, a nuisance, and I would wear out my welcome soon enough.

"Hey, you almost shut my hand in the locker," I said.

"Ask me if I care."

"You should!"

"Who do you think you are? Coming into my school like you own the place."

"But I didn't!"

Charlotte smacked my books out of my hands, sending my notebooks and pens skidding across the cement floor.

"Why don't you keep your nose to the ground and away from those who can't stand to be near trash like you? You look like you carry diseases. Ew." Charlotte laughed out loud, her voice drawing in a small crowd.

My eyes burned as I bent down to pick up my things, willing myself not to cry in front of her.

"Yo, Charlotte, better book that nose job now—you're gonna need it!" a voice I didn't recognize called out.

I turned to see a girl with dark brown hair and golden eyes run toward us. I couldn't move as I watched this girl shove Charlotte, face-first, into the wall of lockers and grab my hand. She pulled me along as she shouted, "Better luck next time, skank-a-saurus!"

Charlotte's shrill scream rang out as she yelled, "You better watch your back, New Girl!"

We finally stopped running once we made it out of the hallway and into the front lobby. The people in the halls were getting scarce as they anticipated the bell ringing.

I bent over, hands on my knees, and breathed in deeply. "Thanks for that."

"Anytime," she said.

"My name is Blake."

The girl stood up, and I recognized her from Art class. She had sat at the table next to me. "I'm Cadence. Nice to meet you."

"I guess I made an enemy on my first day. Not that I know what I did to make her hate me so much."

"Charlotte is just mad that Jamie MacIntyre and his friends are showing you around. She's worried she could be dethroned."

"That would never happen."

"Tell her that."

"She wouldn't listen to me even if I tried."

Cadence shot a quick glance over her shoulder. "Think it's safe to go to lunch? I'm starving."

"Do you want to eat lunch with me? Well, me and the guys."

"So, you do know them? Jamie wasn't just being nice and showing the new girl around."

"We met at the park in our neighborhood. That's all. But yeah, I do."

"It seemed weird that he had taken you under his wing, but I'm glad you had someone. Starting a new school can be tough." Cadence and I walked toward the main office.

"Oh, and Blake?"

"Yeah?"

"You may have made an enemy today, but you made a new friend too."

We were grinning fools by the time we found Jamie, our new camaraderie the beginning of a solid friendship.

"Jamie, meet my new friend, Cadence. She's joining us for lunch."

"Likewise. It's always nice to put a name to the face of a classmate." He paused. "Are you ready? We can introduce Cadence to the guys."

And from that day on, the three of us walked to lunch together—always.

I rubbed my tired eyes as I stared at my empty computer screen. The cursor blinked at me, taunting me, pointing out that I hadn't written a single word in the last 45 minutes I'd been sitting at my desk. It was 6:45 AM after another restless night. Sleep had become a stranger to me.

Dean had stayed the night, but no matter how many times I shifted, I couldn't sink into real sleep. Eventually, I'd given up and tried to get some work done.

All the good that did me.

My coffee was cold next to me, and I couldn't get the words to flow onto my keyboard. I exhaled heavily, pressing my forehead to the desk, willing the words to come.

I usually had no problem writing. I loved to write. It was so unlike me to struggle this much with a piece. Was it the weight of this piece—the responsibility of honoring Noah, not just for myself, but for Dean's family and the entire community? Or was it because writing this article solidified the fact that Noah was really gone?

By 7:30, the silence was broken by the shuffle of blankets as Dean stirred in the bedroom. I sighed and shut my laptop—still blank.

"Morning, sweetheart."

Even though I'd heard him, his voice still made me jump. He leaned down, pressing a kiss to the top of my head, his touch warm and gentle. I couldn't help but smile as I took in his bare chest, pajama pants, and tousled bedhead. Even half-asleep, his movements carried an easy confidence, his tousled hair and sleepy smirk making him look effortlessly charming.

"What?" he asked.

"Nothing, just admiring."

"Well, it's only fair to let me admire in return." Grabbing my hand, he pulled me into him and kissed me, his hands running from my shoulders to the back of my neck.

"Now *that* is a good morning kiss." He pecked me on the nose before walking into the kitchen to grab a mug. "So, what are you doing up so early?"

I shrugged. "I couldn't sleep. I keep thinking about the article on Noah. I want it to be perfect—I want to do him justice and show the world what a kind person he was. And, on top of that, my promotion depends on this piece too."

Dean returned from the kitchen, steaming cup of coffee in hand. He set the mug down on my desk before resting his hands on my shoulders, his touch releasing some of the tension I carried. He looked into my eyes, and I didn't see a single trace of the anger or jealousy from the other night.

"You're putting too much stress on yourself, Blake. You

won't be able to embrace your creative juices if you're too worried about the outcome. Just take a deep breath and let the words flow. Whatever you write, I know it will bring my brother honor."

His words spread warmth through my chest, and I squeezed him. "Thank you, Dean."

"Anytime, sweetheart. Have you had a chance to talk to my parents yet?"

"No, and I haven't been able to interrogate you, either."

"Don't tempt me with a good time."

"Do you think we could swing by their house today?"

Dean grabbed his mug and moved to the couch. "They have plans this afternoon. They said something about a gathering."

I dropped my head. "Oh crap. That's right. Mrs. MacIntyre is having a barbecue today. She asked if I'd come, and I'd said yes without really thinking about it."

Dean looked at me, his eyebrows furrowed. "You agreed to go?"

"Well, yeah... we have the day off, and when Mrs. MacIntyre asked, I couldn't say no. She has always been there for me, even before Jamie and I were together."

Jamie's name barely left my lips before Dean tensed, the easy warmth between us shifting ever so slightly.

Sitting down next to him, I wrapped my arms around his shoulders and snuggled into him.

"Come with me, Dean."

"I hate to be a downer, sweetie, but that wasn't in my plans for the day."

"Aw, please?"

Dean hesitated, exhaling slowly, like he was weighing his options.

"Pretty pretty pretty please?" I flashed the most adorable

puppy dog face I could muster and watched him fight the urge to smile as the corners of his mouth turned upward.

"Do you really think you can keep getting your way when you bat those beautiful eyes of yours?"

"Not sure, but I'm going to keep trying."

Dean pushed out a sigh. "Fine. But I don't want to be there long."

"Yay!" I gave him a quick kiss before jumping up. "Now, for breakfast. Does scrambled eggs or French toast sound better?"

"Scrambled eggs, always. You know they're my favorite."

Of course they were. Just like French toast was mine.

Walking up to the MacIntyre's home, I was a bundle of nerves. Emotions swirled through me like I had tossed them in the dryer for an extra cycle to get the wrinkles out.

I was excited to speak with the Richeys about my article.

Thrilled—but also nervous—to see Mrs. MacIntyre again.

And worried about what feelings being here might stir up.

But the thought of seeing Jamie again? That left me anxious. After how things had ended the last time we saw each other, I couldn't help but worry about the emotions he might drag back to the surface. And right now, I was trying my hardest to keep things good with Dean.

But walking through the front door, the nostalgia hit me.

I had spent so much time here growing up. Everything about this house was comforting and familiar. The warmth, the smells, and the grounding sense of safety it always seemed to provide.

Following the sounds of voices and laughter, we made our way through the house and to the backyard.

"Blake!"

My head followed the sound of my name as Jamie's younger sister Ella ran toward me. She threw her arms around me. "It's so good to see you! I'm sorry I didn't get the chance to catch up with you after Noah's funeral. I've been meaning to check in and see how you've been."

"It's okay. That was a weird day for everyone. Let's get together for lunch soon."

Ella grinned, her smile so much like her brother's. "That sounds amazing. Text me. And make sure you stop and say hi to Mom. You know she misses seeing you around."

"I will. Thank you."

Ella's words filled me with happiness. Jane MacIntyre was like the mom I never had, and I missed her companionship.

Dean handed me a red Solo cup filled with a delicious sparkling punch, and I unconsciously drained it while giving Dean's family half of my attention.

Not before long, I excused myself with the intention of getting a glass of water. When in reality, I couldn't stand still anymore.

Movement seemed to be the only thing that would ease the knots in my stomach.

I followed the string of pictures hung on the walls and found myself at the top of the stairs, in front of the last MacIntyre family photo ever taken.

And I remembered the day well.

It was the day Jamie and I had graduated from high school. We had no idea the tragedies we would face in the upcoming years.

My hand moved to my stomach, holding the place where mine and Jamie's baby had been.

That little life had been so unexpected, but everything I'd ever wanted.

And I'd been so happy.

A thud from down the hall made me jump. My breath caught as my eyes landed on the slightly ajar door to Jamie's old room.

Curiosity got the better of me.

I knocked quietly and stepped inside.

Jamie sat on his bed, head in his hands. His body was rigid, his muscles twitching like he was stuck inside the prison of his mind.

"Jamie?" I whispered.

I reached out, my fingers brushing his shoulder.

He jumped to his feet, fists raised, wide-eyed and panicked.

"Jamie? It's me."

His rapid blinking slowed as the tension drained from his body.

"Blake? What..." His voice cracked.

"Jamie, I think you had a panic attack."

Chapter Twenty-Four

J AMIE

As I took in Blake's worried expression, I wondered if I was dreaming.

Just seeing her settled something inside me, slowing my racing heart. But just as the world around me started to sharpen, her words cut through the fragile comfort her presence had created.

"I think you had a panic attack."

I glanced around.

I was still in my room, but when had Blake come in? What had she seen? What had I done?

A slow burn crept up my neck as I grasped for a memory that wasn't there.

I'd come up here to breathe, but the picture on my nightstand of Blake and me caught my attention, steering my thoughts straight to her.

She lived in my head, rent-free.

I had locked those memories in a box and drowned them in the deepest part of the ocean.

So, I retraced every step, pacing as if I could physically walk myself through the past.

I had joined the Air Force, graduated basic training, and proposed to Blake at my graduation. There was no ring, just a promise—to love her forever. I was ready to take her anywhere and everywhere with me.

After that, I entered Combat Control school, and that's when everything started to go downhill.

During training, Blake and I struggled with the distance and the lack of communication we had grown used to. Basic training had been a taste of what we would experience over the next two years, but nothing could prepare us for the challenges ahead. Each phase of my special training was held in a different city across the U.S., making it difficult for her to visit. Add in my grueling training schedule, which left me drained and unable to support her as she needed, and the strain between us only grew.

During the eight-week Combat Control Apprentice Course at Pope, I was finally able to see her every weekend. We rekindled our relationship, working to strengthen it as my graduation date approached. Later, during my Special Tactics Training at Hurlburt Field in Florida, she visited me for her birthday weekend.

Three weeks later, Blake called with news that left me ecstatic: I was going to be a father. I couldn't wait to start a family with her and finally begin our lives together.

Two months before graduation, they shipped me across the country to Joint Base Lewis-McChord in Washington. I couldn't take her with me until we were married, and between my training schedule and her work toward her journalism degree, getting home to apply for a marriage license and plan our small wedding proved a challenge. We didn't feel the need to rush it. We knew we'd get married—it was just a matter of when.

Looking back now, I realize that had been a mistake. Not having Blake—my anchor, my safe place—had sent me spiraling.

Three weeks after graduation, our baby was gone.

My family came to see me graduate and officially become a Combat Controller. I didn't realize at the time that it would be the last time I'd see Blake pregnant.

As I paced my room, reliving those memories, my pulse quickened. The events that followed came rushing back, and my chest tightened as I braced myself for what I knew was next.

Three weeks after my graduation, we lost the baby. I flew home for five days for Blake's procedure—it was all the time I could give her. I was heartbroken, but I didn't have the bond she had. I tried to console her as best I could, but in truth, I looked forward to returning to Washington just to escape the grief. Watching her grieve the life we'd lost was unbearable.

I hugged my mom and dad before heading back, unaware that I'd be returning a month later for my dad's funeral. I never could have predicted he would take his own life.

Everywhere I turned, I saw my dad—his laughter, his presence—memories that felt like lies now that I knew he'd never been at peace.

The funeral was a blur. In the days that followed, I pulled away from everyone. Seeing Blake without her little baby bump hurt more than I could have imagined.

I cut my time in Fayetteville short and returned to Washington faster than I should have. I was indifferent to everything around me, blind to the suffering of those I loved.

The next six months blurred into nothing.

The things I saw over there followed me home. Carnage I wanted to forget but couldn't.

Everywhere I turned, I lost someone I loved. And then... Noah.

Noah's lifeless body was the last thing I saw before Blake's touch yanked me back from the edge.

I hadn't heard her knock. Hadn't sensed anyone else in the room—until her small hand found me, grounding me to the present.

Instinct took over. My body moved before my mind caught up, ready to strike down whatever enemy stood before me.

But it wasn't an enemy—just a pair of familiar, worried green eyes staring back at me.

I must have looked like a damn fool.

"Jamie?" she said again.

I forced my hands down, willing my body to relax. Bewilderment shone in Blake's eyes. She had never seen me like this before. I felt stripped bare, like I was standing under a spotlight with nowhere to hide.

Muted laughter and clinking glasses drifted in from the backyard, a stark contrast to the silence suffocating us.

If Blake noticed my embarrassment, she didn't comment on it. Instead, she watched me, sympathy softening her features. She wanted to help—I could see it in her eyes. I only had to let her.

But I didn't. I couldn't.

As much as I wanted to let people in again—to rebuild the bridges I'd burned—I just... couldn't.

Letting people in only gave them the power to hurt you.

Caring about someone—loving them—only ever ended in devastation.

"Sorry," I muttered, my voice rougher than I intended.

Her cheeks flushed that soft, familiar pink. On her, it was

beautiful. On me, embarrassment painted me in blotchy red, like I'd been sunburned.

"No, it's... fine."

Blake tucked a strand of hair behind her ear, her green eyes searching mine—hopeful, waiting for me to let her in again.

I needed to deflect. I cleared my throat and put on the best fake smile I could muster.

"Naw, don't worry about it. Everything is fine. Why don't we head back down to the party?"

Blake hesitated before nodding, her gaze piecing me together like a puzzle with missing edges. I knew her well enough to know she didn't buy into my nonchalant attempt to brush off what she saw, but she respected me enough to leave it alone. At least for now.

We made our way downstairs and ran into my mom in the kitchen. She gave us a curious look before turning to head back outside.

"Hungry?" I gestured toward the food.

My mom had prepared a spread of typical party food. Platters and large serving bowls sat on the kitchen counter, heaped with chicken wings, hot dogs, hamburgers, potato salad, macaroni salad, mixed greens, corn, coleslaw, rolls, mashed potatoes, and an assortment of desserts.

"Yeah. Sure."

I handed Blake a plate and gestured for her to start. I followed, blindly grabbing food, my thoughts too tangled to care what landed on my plate.

As I moved closer, her scent wrapped around me—lavender and coconut, just like always.

Blake said nothing, just blinked at me, confusion creasing her brow.

"Cat got your tongue?"

"I'm fine." Her pitch was off just a little, and if she had

been talking to anyone else, they might not have noticed. But I did.

Annoyance curled in my gut.

This was why I kept most of my nightmares to myself. I wanted to prevent people from looking at me like I was broken. We took two steps from the counter before she stopped and turned toward me.

"I'm sorry, Jamie."

"For what?"

"I always painted you as the bad guy in my head. You turned into the villain of my story. But I never once thought about you. What you went through before you left. And then overseas. The pain you endured."

I didn't answer immediately, unsure of what to say.

I was the problem. Always the one causing pain to those closest to me. Forever atoning for the sins I'd committed.

"I am the bad guy."

"Jamie, don't do that."

"No, Blake. Just... don't." My tone came out cold, final— killing the conversation before it could start. And I meant it. I didn't want to talk about it. This conversation was over. I had no intention of discussing those pieces of me with her or anyone. Ever.

Her eyes narrowed, searching mine, as if trying to expose me for the fraud I was. Then, with a quiet resolve, she lifted her chin, squared her shoulders, and stood a little taller. She reminded me of a flower blooming before my eyes—strong, resilient, beautiful.

"I understand," she said.

And then she was gone, leaving only the faint trace of her perfume in her wake.

I watched her walk straight back to Dean—her place, her choice. She settled beside him, pressing a kiss to his cheek, lacing her fingers through his like it was the easiest thing in the world.

That familiar burn flared in my chest, a feeling I was getting far too used to.

I had no right to feel angry. No right to feel jealous. But it still ate me alive, watching him touch her the way I used to.

But that didn't stop the fire from burning anyway.

Chapter Twenty-Five

JAMIE

"Don't look so glum." A hand clamped down on my shoulder, jolting me out of my thoughts. I turned to see Wes, with Liam and Erik right behind him, smirking like they'd just walked in on something entertaining.

A slow smile tugged at my lips.

"Just be your naturally charming self, and she'll come back to you," Wes added with a knowing look.

"What charming self? I don't remember Jamie ever being the smooth one," Liam said, fist-bumping me.

"Liam's right. The charming one has always been me," Erik piped in, throwing back a swig of his beer.

I laughed. "When did you guys get here?"

"Oh, we've been here. You were just too preoccupied to notice," Wes said, not-so-subtly glancing toward Blake.

"Let's get the guest of honor a beer and sit down," Liam said, guiding me toward a table set up in the grass. Wes popped open a bottle and handed it to me.

The four of us settled in easily, conversation flowing like no time had passed since I'd joined the Air Force and left home. I wasn't the only one who'd moved away either—Liam had chased his fashion dreams to California. Only Wes and Erik had stayed behind.

"You leave in two days, Liam?" I asked between bites of food.

"Yeah. Morning flight. I have to be back in Cali for a big meeting that afternoon."

"So, we going out tomorrow night for a last hurrah?" Wes lifted his beer.

"As if your lady would let you out," Erik scoffed, nudging Wes's arm.

"I don't need Liv's permission," Wes shot back.

"Yeah, right. We'd be two drinks in, and she'd call, '*Wesley Parker, you get your ass home right this instant.*'" Erik did his best impression, voice high and exaggerated.

Liam joined in. "*Wesley. I need you right now.*"

"*Wesley? Wesley, are you even listening to me?*" Erik added, hands on his hips, laying it on thick.

"Whatever." Wes scowled, taking a swig of his beer. "She does *not* sound like that."

We erupted into laughter, drawing attention from nearby partygoers. But as the jokes faded, a familiar ache settled in my chest.

I didn't know much about Wes and Liv's relationship, but Erik and Liam clearly did. Even Liam, who lived across the damn country, was more in the loop than I was.

I'd been gone too long.

I wanted to change that.

"Uh-oh," Erik muttered into his beer can.

I followed Erik's line of sight and spotted Addison Kennedy walking in with her family.

"What?" Wes asked, brow furrowing—right before his gaze landed on her.

His whole face changed, shifting from annoyance to something dangerously close to longing. It was almost comical. He looked like a kid who'd just realized his favorite toy was stuck behind a glass case—just out of reach, but still taunting him.

I leaned back, arms crossing over my chest. "Wonder what would happen if she gave you the time of day."

Liam tipped his beer in Wes's direction. "Yeah. It's like watching a dog salivate over a bone."

Erik let out a slow exhale. "Two dogs, actually. Jamie's just as bad."

Wes scoffed. "Oh, screw off. I'm just surprised to see her here, that's all."

Liam flicked his gaze toward me. "And Jamie's just *casually* staring at Blake like she's the last drink in a dry county."

"You all talk too much," I said.

"Nah, we just call it like we see it," Liam said, stretching his legs out under the table. "This is basically *The Bachelor: Small-Town Edition.*"

"Right," Erik said, tapping his fingers against his beer can. "Except in this version, one of the contestants already has a girlfriend—" he nodded at Wes "—and the other one *had* the girl, then screwed it all up." His eyes cut to me, his expression full of mock pity.

Wes lifted his beer. "Hey, leave me out of this. I'm perfectly happy with my girl."

I sighed, reaching for my drink. "Appreciate the support, assholes."

Liam set his beer down with a dull thud. "Just keeping things fair, man. Gotta keep the commentary balanced."

Wes nudged the bottle closer to me. "Drink up, Romeo. You're gonna need it."

The conversation carried on, but I wasn't listening anymore.

Across the yard, Blake's gaze flicked toward our table—again.

Not that I had room to judge.

Because I couldn't stop staring at her either.

Blake laughed at something, then stood, excusing herself. I watched as she walked toward the house, every muscle in my body screaming to follow.

"Be right back," I said, pushing up from the table.

Wes let out a low whistle. "Go get her, lover boy."

Their laughter followed me, but I didn't care.

I caught up with her just as she grabbed a cup of punch and turned to head back outside. Stepping in front of her, I held the door open.

"Are you having a good time?" I asked, my voice lower than I intended.

She startled slightly, inhaling sharply before recovering with an eye roll. "What's it to you?"

"Well, it's *basically* my party. It's my job to make sure it's fun."

She rolled her eyes again, but this time, I caught the hint of a smile. "Having a blasty blast."

"Well, then my job here is done."

She shook her head but didn't walk away. Instead, her expression turned more serious. "Hey, speaking of jobs, can we set aside some time to actually talk about the article on Noah? No messing around, no distractions."

I pressed my lips into a thin line. I wasn't ready to let her in enough to give her what she wanted. Not yet. "This article is really important to you."

"It is. Not only do I get to let the world see what an

amazing person Noah was, but it'll also prove to the board that I'm ready for my promotion."

"Promotion?"

"There's an editor position opening at the paper. Mr. Taylor already pushed my resume forward for consideration. He said the job is mine as long as this article is solid."

I swallowed hard. "Wow, Blake, that's... that's incredible."

"Thanks. I just hope I get it."

Fuck me. That changed things.

If opening up about Noah meant furthering Blake's career, then I'd do it. I owed her that much. Maybe if I helped her, it would chip away at the mountain of guilt weighing me down.

I cleared my throat. "I'm sure you will. You're a talented writer. Any paper would be lucky to have you as their editor."

"Oh yeah?" Her eyes narrowed playfully. "What do you know about my talents?"

My pulse jumped. Shit. I paid for a subscription to the Fayetteville newspaper *just* to read her articles, but there was no way in hell I was admitting that.

Rubbing the back of my neck, I muttered, "My mom tells me about your writing."

"Uh-huh."

Before I could defend myself, the gate beside us squeaked open.

"Oh. My. Gawd. It really *is* you, Jamie."

Before I could react, a brunette with too much perfume and even more cleavage yanked me into a suffocating hug.

I barely recognized her until she pulled back, smiling like a cat with cream.

"Charlotte?"

"The one and only," she said, winking.

I heard Blake exhale sharply. "Hi, Charlotte."

"Oh! Sorry, Blake, I didn't see you there," Charlotte said with syrupy sweetness. "How have you been? How's that *hunk* of a man Dean doing?"

Blake's expression was unreadable. "We're fine. Thanks for asking."

"I'm so happy for you two. You guys look *so* in love whenever I see you around town. Makes a girl like me wish she could find someone like that."

She turned to me then, raking her gaze over my body, not even bothering to hide it.

But her words stuck in my mind like a needle to the ribs.

Blake and Dean—*so in love.*

Did they sit at home and talk about forever? Did he know her the way I did—her favorite songs, the way she twirled her hair when she was nervous? Did he get to hear her laugh when she woke up in the morning, tangled in his sheets?

The thought was a slow, twisting knife.

I shoved it down and forced myself back to the conversation.

Blake tilted her head, her expression one of fake sympathy. "Sorry you haven't found the one yet, Charlotte. I'm surprised, considering how many guys you've *tried* to date."

Charlotte laughed. "Oh, honey, I have *standards.*" Her gaze flicked to me again. "I don't plan to settle for just *anyone.*"

Blake's fists clenched at her sides.

Charlotte slid closer, pressing against me. "I've been waiting patiently for a *real* man."

I stiffened.

Blake's lip twitched. She was one smart remark away from throwing hands. And I wasn't sure who would be the receiver of them—Charlotte or me.

Before things could escalate, Blake turned on her heel.

"You know what? I'll figure something else out for the article, Jamie. Don't waste your time."

And just like that, she walked straight into Dean's waiting arms.

Chapter Twenty-Six

JAMIE

I didn't get the chance to talk to Blake for the rest of the party.

By nightfall, everyone had left, the October chill creeping in earlier than usual thanks to the fall solstice.

I lingered at my mom's house, helping her and Mr. Kelly clean up while Ella sat sprawled on the couch, her feet propped on the coffee table.

"Mind giving us a hand, El?" I asked, walking past with another bag of trash.

She didn't even look up. "Nah, I'm beat. Plus, it was *your* party. You should be the one cleaning up."

I shouldn't have been surprised. She was always looking for a way out of manual labor.

It took some time, but Mr. Kelly and I got all the tables and chairs taken down, stacked, and the garbage taken out while Mom put away the rest of the food. Soon, the four of us settled into the living room, drinks in hand.

I watched Mom and Mr. Kelly—Nolan— interact, something warm settling in my chest. They were *good* together. The way she looked at him, the way her laugh was lighter, more sincere... she looked happy.

And knowing that took one more weight off my shoulders.

One less burden to carry.

I took a slow sip of my beer, leaning back against the couch, content for the first time in a long time.

Ella plopped down beside me, setting her phone on the armrest.

"Hey, Jamie."

Something in her tone pulled me out of my thoughts. "What's up, El?"

"I need to ask you something." She hesitated, her fingers twisting in the hem of her hoodie. "Something pretty serious."

I sat up, brows pulling together. "Go on."

She hesitated, chewing her bottom lip.

A strange sensation settled in my gut. What the hell could she be nervous to ask me?

"I heard something earlier at the party and wasn't sure if there was any truth to it."

The unease sharpened. "Just ask, Ella."

She shifted beside me. "I overheard the Richeys talking about Noah. Blake was asking them about his time in the military, and your name came up. Dean mentioned letters Noah sent him. Then... he said Noah wrote him one the night before he died. Told him you were on that mission with him."

Her voice lowered. "Dean sounded angry, Jamie. Like he was blaming you for what happened."

The room tilted—just slightly, but enough to make my stomach churn.

I clenched my fists, forcing a slow, controlled breath through my nose.

Keep it together. Don't let it pull you under.

Ella wasn't done. "I know you don't like to talk about it, and I've tried to respect that, but I don't want anyone spreading lies about you. You're my brother, and—" Her voice caught before she straightened her shoulders. "I might not always show it, but I'm *so* proud of you. And I sure as hell won't let a woman-stealing scumbag talk crap about you."

A short, humorless snort escaped me. Scumbag was right.

Mom's hand found my back, rubbing slow circles. "It's okay, dear. You don't have to talk about it if you don't want to."

My throat tightened.

"It's okay," I managed, though my voice was hoarse. "Just... give me a second."

I sensed everyone holding their breath, waiting while I got myself together. My hand found the back of my neck, fingers pressing into the tense muscle, while my other hand drummed against my thigh.

But... this was my family.

And for the first time in years, talking to them didn't feel terrifying.

So I took a breath.

And I told them about Noah.

I told them how he died saving my life, how the mission should have been a success, how he should have come home with me.

Even through the gasps, the quiet sniffles, the sharp inhales of breath—I kept going.

When I finally finished, the room fell silent. The kind of silence that pressed in on all sides, thick and heavy.

Mom and Ella sat frozen, tears streaking their faces, and even Nolan's eyes looked glassy.

But I couldn't shed a single tear.

The first one to move was Mom. She pulled me into a tight embrace, arms wrapping around me like she was trying to piece me back together.

For the first time in a long time, I let her.

My body sagged against hers, relief hitting so hard it left me lightheaded. I didn't know letting it out would feel like this.

Maybe it wouldn't be so bad to let them in once in a while.

Ella sniffled, wiping her face. "So... why would Dean say all that?"

Mom pulled away, dabbing her eyes with a tissue. "I can think of one reason."

I stiffened. "Mom." The last thing I wanted was to talk about Blake and Dean's relationship. "It doesn't matter."

But the thought burned anyway.

The idea that Noah's parents might believe I played a role in their son's death—that Dean might be feeding them those lies—left an acidic knot in my stomach.

"It *does* matter," Ella snapped. "You did nothing wrong. It was the wrong place, the wrong time. How could anyone have known? It could just as easily have been *you* who—" Her voice cracked.

Nolan cleared his throat. "I've known you a long time, Jamie. And I don't believe for a second that anyone could think you'd ever deliberately hurt someone."

Something in my chest loosened—just a little.

"Thanks. That means a lot."

"And I appreciate you trusting me with something so personal," Nolan added. "I know it isn't easy, seeing me here with your mother. But I'm honored to be part of this."

I exhaled, shaking my head. "Mr. Kelly—" I hesitated, then corrected myself. "Nolan. I'm just happy to see Mom happy. So welcome to the family."

His grin was warm. "If we're family now, how about just calling me Nolan?"

"I'll try. But that still seems weirder than seeing you with my mom."

Laughter filled the space around us, the tension easing.

Except for Ella.

She stayed quiet, eyes far too knowing as she studied me.

Eventually, we all said our goodbyes. I walked outside with Ella, the cool air biting through the warmth of the house. As we reached the driveway, she suddenly stopped in front of me.

"God, you *still* haven't gotten rid of that car?"

I scoffed. "She's a classic. Probably worth a fortune."

"To *who?* Someone who's blind and nostalgic for the smell of mothballs?"

"Hey, hey. Be nice to Betty."

I started to step around her, but she grabbed my sleeve.

Her eyes shone too bright in the dim light.

"El, don't. Don't look at me like that."

"That wasn't the first time you watched someone die, was it?"

A lump formed in my throat.

Her grip tightened. "Jamie... it *wasn't*, was it?"

I stared at her, but no words came.

She exhaled sharply, blinking fast. "It all makes sense now. Why you've changed so much. Why you carry yourself like..." She gestured vaguely. "Like the weight of the world is strapped to your damn back."

I took a slow, measured breath. "It's my job, El. *Someone* has to do it."

A strangled noise left her lips. Then she was in my arms, sobbing into my chest.

I held her while she cried.

Cried the tears I couldn't.

The darkness stretched around us, swallowing the sound of her heartbreak. And even though she cried, my chest swelled with something I hadn't felt in a long time.

Love.

Chapter Twenty-Seven

Blakely

20 years old

My stomach lodged in my throat as I watched Jamie assemble his gear.

With every piece he strapped on, every buckle secured, a piece of me died inside.

I didn't want him to go.

I didn't want him to leave me.

I had just gotten him back, and I wasn't sure I could survive losing him again.

But the words wouldn't come.

I stood frozen, my throat locked in a vice, unable to tell him how much I needed him. How much I loved him. These were our last moments together—for who knew how long—and I couldn't even form the words to make sure he knew.

Tears burned my cheeks as he secured his helmet. The deep rumble of the helicopter echoed in the background, a cruel reminder that time was slipping away.

He could be back tonight. Or in six months.

We had no idea. And that terrified me.

Jamie slung his gun over his shoulder, then turned toward me.

His eyes mirrored mine—pain, regret, fear... love.

He reached for my hand, pressing his lips to my knuckles before pulling me in. I expected a quick embrace, something rushed and desperate. But then...

His other hand found my waist.

He moved.

And I followed.

Just as we always had.

We danced in the dim light of the hangar, and my heart felt like it might burst apart in my chest. But in his arms, I knew he would put it back together again.

I pressed my cheek against his shoulder, willing the God of Time to slow down. Just a little longer. Just a few more seconds.

A sharp knock on the metal door shattered the moment.

It was time.

A strangled sob ripped from my throat as I threw my arms around his neck, clutching him tighter, desperate to push past the layers of his gear and get as close as I could.

He crushed me against him, his breath hot against my skin, his hold strong. But not strong enough to keep him here.

A tear slipped down his cheek, catching the dim light before he captured my mouth in a kiss—desperate, carnal, reckless.

He poured every ounce of his love into that kiss, our tears mixing in a salty, bittersweet goodbye.

Another knock at the door. Louder. More insistent.

Jamie pulled back, his forehead resting against mine. His gaze burned into me—no words needed.

Everything he felt, everything I felt, was right there. Undeniable.

Then he took a step back.

And another.

With every step, he took more of me with him.

His fingers slipped from mine.

And I shattered.

I woke up with his ghost in my head.

The dream had been so real, so vivid, that I reached up before I even realized it—touching my cheek, startled to find it wet.

The weight of the past still clung to me, wrapping around my chest like a vice. I could still hear the echo of the helicopter, feel the press of Jamie's lips against mine.

Seeing him yesterday—weak, vulnerable—had knocked me off balance. Jamie was the strong one. He always had been. He picked me up when I fell, held me together when I crumbled.

Even at his dad's funeral, he had been oddly composed.

Maybe that had all been an act.

A sobering thought struck me.

There was a side of Jamie he didn't let anyone see.

The old Jamie had been open with his feelings. This one didn't seem to know what to do with them.

I had meant it when I told him I always thought he was the bad guy in our story. That I had convinced myself he was heartless, that he had abandoned me without a second thought.

But what if I had it all wrong?

What if he hadn't left because he didn't care?

What if he had needed me to pick him up off the floor for a change?

That thought hit me like a truck.

Looking back, Jamie never talked about his grief. He consoled *everyone else*—including me—but who had consoled him?

How had I not seen it?

I scrubbed a hand down my face. It didn't matter now. The past was done.

Still, it didn't stop the ugly knot of jealousy that twisted in my stomach when Charlotte threw herself at Jamie.

Hypocrite.

I had moved on. I had fallen in love again. But the idea of Jamie with someone else? Unacceptable.

And then there was Dean.

His insistence on dragging Noah's letters into every damn conversation had pushed me to my limit last night.

It felt like he was hell-bent on taking Jamie down.

By the time he pulled up to my house, I had barely let him put the car in park before muttering something about a migraine and bailing.

Dean had left with a scowl.

I hadn't cared.

I was done talking about it. And I meant it.

Shoving the thoughts aside, I got up, determined to start fresh. A stop at Starbucks was necessary—half out of caffeine addiction, half out of some stupid, masochistic hope that I'd run into a certain someone.

No such luck.

I dropped Kate's coffee off at her desk before settling at my own.

"Lunch today?" she asked.

"Sam's Deli?"

"Definitely."

"It's a date."

The simple routine grounded me.

I just needed to keep reminding myself I was a badass bitch.

I had worked my way up to this position. I didn't need to waste time worrying about Jamie or Dean.

This promotion was as good as mine.

I pulled up my writing software, fingers poised over the keyboard.

Nothing.

The cursor blinked. Taunting. Mocking.

Jamie's words echoed in my head.

"Cat got your tongue?"

I groaned, pressing my forehead to the desk.

"Things are going well, I see."

John's voice startled me.

Lifting my head, I forced a sheepish smile.

"It's okay," he said, sliding a manila folder onto my desk. "I have another project for you."

I did not like the way he grinned.

"What is it?"

I opened the folder. Inside, a single sheet of lined paper bore a name, an address, and the words 'The Phoenix Foundation.'

I looked up. "What's the story?"

"A new foundation to help military members coming back from overseas cope with PTSD and integrate back into their lives. One of the guys here at Pope started it."

Something inside me tightened. Jamie's haunted expression flashed in my mind.

I nodded. "I'll go now."

John waved me off. "Call if you need anything. And take an extended lunch if needed."

Grabbing my purse, I stopped by Kate's desk.

"I overheard," she said. "Text me when you're done, and I'll meet you at Sam's."

Pope Army Airfield felt different now.

The excitement I had felt as a kid—clinging to Jamie's hand, wide-eyed at the military world—was gone.

I followed my GPS to the address, parked, and stepped inside the brick building.

A deep voice startled me. "You must be Ms. Mason."

I turned to find Chief Master Sergeant Campbell.

We exchanged pleasantries, and he led me to his office.

I took in the awards, the framed pictures of his family... and the rack of military coins.

Jamie had told me about those.

I was settling in, flipping open my notebook when Campbell asked, "Where should we start?"

"Why don't you tell me about the origins of the foundation. When was it implemented? How many military members has it helped so far? What was the inspiration to start it?"

"Actually," he said, scratching his chin, "I'm not the best person to talk to about this. Let me call down the guy who started it."

A few minutes later, there was a knock.

I turned.

And my heart stopped.

You've got to be frickin' kidding me.

Chapter Twenty-Eight

BLAKELY

"It's good to see you too, Blake." Jamie's voice held a grin as he shut the door behind him and took the seat beside me.

Across the desk, CMSgt Campbell's eyebrows lifted. "I take it you two know each other?"

Jamie rubbed the back of his neck. "You could say that."

"You're the one who created this foundation?" My voice was even, giving nothing away.

"Well, yeah." He shifted, settling his arms on the armrests. "But I had help getting it off the ground. If you don't want to talk to me about it, Chief can answer all your questions."

Another crossroads. Involving myself with Jamie, or letting him walk away.

I squared my shoulders. "It's fine, Jamie. Let's just focus so we can finish this interview. I need to get out of here by noon. I have plans."

Jamie's expression flickered at that, but he gave a short nod.

Chief Campbell leaned back, arms crossed, watching us with a smug, knowing look. "So, how do you two know each other?"

"Jamie and I were high school sweethearts." I met his gaze coolly. "He joined the military and left me behind."

Jamie's jaw tensed.

Turning back to my notes, I forced my focus onto the interview. "Now, moving on to the foundation. What information do you want to share? What is it you want the public to know?"

Jamie cleared his throat. "We hope to spread awareness to military members who need support, letting them know they aren't alone. Eventually, I'd like to expand this to other bases. Right now, it's exclusive to Pope, but my goal is to have a chapter available at every military installation."

I jotted notes as he spoke, keeping my expression neutral.

"What does the foundation actually do for service members?"

Jamie leaned forward. "Right now, we offer one-on-one time for anyone who feels like they need to talk. Just having someone listen—someone who's been through the same thing—can help. We focus on curbing feelings of isolation, teaching coping mechanisms, and helping guys determine whether they need professional support. The biggest goal is making sure they don't feel alone."

Chief Campbell added, "Tech Sergeant MacIntyre is working on funding for a 24-hour hotline."

I paused mid-sentence, glancing at Jamie. "Oh really? Tell me about that."

Jamie exhaled, rubbing the back of his neck again. "Well, my thinking is that if we're available *anytime*, we can help when it's most needed. During the day, when you're surrounded by people, it's easier to keep it together. But at night—" his fingers curled into a loose fist against the armrest,

"—when you're alone, that's when the demons come out to play."

The words sent a chill through me.

My pen hovered over the paper.

I lifted my gaze, studying him. "Sounds like you're speaking from experience."

Jamie's expression gave nothing away. "We all have skeletons in our closets."

I hummed, scribbling down his words but filing away the weight behind them.

The silence stretched, broken only by the scratch of my pen.

I cleared my throat. "Next question. Why did you start this foundation?"

Jamie hesitated.

Long enough for me to connect the dots myself.

If I were a betting woman, I'd say he started it for men like him.

Guys who had seen things they couldn't unsee. Guys who felt alone, trapped in their own heads, not knowing where to go. Guys who suffered in silence.

He suffered. Or maybe, he still was suffering.

Something warm pressed against the cold edges of my frustration.

Pride.

This was the Jamie I had fallen in love with. The one who wanted to help others, even when he couldn't help himself.

He exhaled, rubbing his fingers along his jaw. "I've seen too many guys struggle and not know where to turn. I wanted to help as many of them as I could."

"You saw a need and filled it," I said.

His lips twitched. "Exactly."

My grip tightened around my pen.

I needed to hold Jamie at arm's length. I wanted to. But every time I saw him—every time I gained another layer of understanding—it became harder to cling to my anger.

It was easier to be mad at someone for hurting you. Easier to paint them as the villain.

But once you started to see why they did what they did— once you saw their pain—everything got messy.

Blurred.

I closed my notebook and forced my voice into neutral territory. "I think I have everything I need. Do I have permission to use both of your names?"

Jamie and Campbell exchanged a look before nodding.

I stood, tucking my notebook into my bag. "Thank you. I'll reach out if I have follow-up questions. It was nice to meet you, Chief Campbell." My eyes flicked to Jamie. "Tech Sergeant MacIntyre."

Jamie smirked. "I'll walk you out."

"That's not necessary."

"It is, actually." His lips pressed together in amusement. "Technically, you need an escort."

I exhaled. "Fine."

We walked in silence, the tension stretching between us like a frayed wire.

At the door, we naturally turned toward each other, hovering on the edge of something neither of us was ready to name.

Jamie spoke first. "Blake, I just wanted to say thanks. For yesterday."

"I didn't do anything."

He shook his head. "You pulled me out of my memories."

My chest tightened. I didn't know what to say to that, so I didn't say anything.

Instead, I stepped toward the door. "I'll see you around, Jamie."

"Blake."

His voice stopped me.

I turned over my shoulder, brows lifting. "Yes?"

His throat bobbed as he swallowed. "Let me know when you have time for the interview about Noah. I'll be there."

Something shifted inside me.

I nodded once, then turned and walked to my car, pulling out my phone.

> Leaving now, meet you at Sam's in 15. See you then

I hit send and gripped the wheel, heart pounding for reasons I didn't want to name.

Chapter Twenty-Nine

BLAKELY

I pulled into Sam's Deli exactly fifteen minutes later, barely registering the drive.

Jamie's words still echoed in my head, unraveling everything I thought I knew about him.

The more I learned about his past—the things he had endured, suffered, survived—the harder it became to hold on to my anger.

I was letting him in.

Letting him slip past the walls I had painstakingly built from the wreckage he left behind.

I frowned, drumming my fingers against the steering wheel.

When was the last time Dean had consumed my thoughts like this?

The realization unsettled me.

Stepping out of my car, I closed my eyes for a moment, letting the October sun warm my skin. A distraction. That's what I needed. A normal girls' lunch with Kate, where my thoughts weren't tangled in Jamie MacIntyre.

She pulled in behind me, barely out of her car before groaning, "Ugh, I am *so* glad to be out of that stuffy office."

The wind whipped through her brunette hair, making it float around her like a damn supermodel's wind machine was hidden nearby.

"Mr. Taylor got you drowning in projects again?" I asked.

"Of course." She rolled her eyes, shouldering her bag. "Not that I mind being busy, but I swear even I get cross-eyed after a while."

"We all do."

Inside, we placed our usual orders and grabbed a table outside.

Kate's lunch was an entire feast. A meatball sub, a side of fries, and a brownie for dessert. Meanwhile, I stuck with my usual—a turkey sub with all the fixings.

She could eat whatever she wanted and never gain a single pound. Life wasn't fair.

"So..." Kate took a bite of her sandwich, eyes twinkling. "You never told me the story behind *Mr. Dreamboat.*"

I blinked. "Who?"

"The guy who stopped by the office last week."

Oh. Jamie.

I exhaled, picking at the crust of my bread. "I don't even know where to start."

Kate reached across the table, squeezing my hand. "How about at the beginning? It looked like he really rattled you."

My throat tightened. He had. More than I wanted to admit.

"He broke my heart," I said, voice quieter than I intended. "Completely shattered it."

Kate nodded, chewing slowly. "I sense a *but* coming."

I hesitated. "It's been five years since he left. Since he broke off our engagement. But... now that he's back, we've talked a little. And I'm starting to see why he did what he did."

She sipped her drink, waiting.

I swallowed hard. "What pushed him away."

"Things are never black and white."

"I know," I admitted. "But it was easier—simpler—to hate him. To let him be the bad guy." My gaze drifted to the passing traffic. "Because if he isn't the bad guy..."

Kate didn't miss a beat. "You're afraid of falling in love with him again."

My head snapped up. "No. I love Dean."

"Exactly."

I blinked. "What?"

"You *love* Dean," she said, voice slow, deliberate. "But you're not *in* love with him. You love him like a brother."

A sharp heat crawled up my neck. "I definitely wouldn't do the things I do with Dean with my brother."

Kate threw her head back with a laugh. "Geez, I *hope* not."

I rolled my eyes, stuffing a bite of my sandwich in my mouth to avoid responding.

She leaned forward, tone serious. "Look, physical attraction isn't the same thing as *love*. People have sex all the time without being *in* love. What matters is whether you and Dean have something *deeper* than what it is now."

A lump formed in my throat.

"Because if you don't..." she continued, "you two have no future. Hunky Dreamboat aside."

I groaned, rubbing my temple. "Why can't things just be easy?"

Kate shrugged. "If there was no bad in the world, you wouldn't appreciate the good."

I glanced down at my barely touched sandwich.

Kate nudged my foot under the table. "Hey."

I looked up.

"You know you can talk to me, right?"

A genuine smile tugged at my lips. "Yeah. Thanks, Kate. I mean it."

And I did.

She was one of the few genuine friends I had left after Cadence moved away—even if her words cut through me like a lance.

Chapter Thirty

JAMIE

The rest of my workday passed quietly.

No fires to put out, no unexpected disasters.

But calm didn't always mean good.

It just meant the next disaster was around the corner.

For now, I'd take the reprieve.

After leaving the office, I took Ruger for a run, letting the steady rhythm of my feet against the pavement clear my head. Even called the dealership about the truck I'd test-driven last week. If everything went smoothly, tomorrow might be the day I finally traded Betty in.

I stepped out of the shower just as my phone buzzed on the nightstand.

ERIK

Dinner and drinks for Liam's last night?

I grabbed the towel, rubbing it over my hair as I texted back.

I'm there. Just tell me when and where.

WES

Gotta double check with Liv, but shouldn't be a problem.

LIAM

Can't have goodbye drinks without the guest of honor. I'll be there. Just let me know the details.

ERIK

How about Stadium Club?

I'm down for that. I've been itching to beat Wes at a game of pool again

WES

In your dreams, MacIntyre.

ERIK

Should we invite Blake? She's one of us.

LIAM

Jamie's call, he's the one who had to go and fall in love with her and ruin the whole group dynamic.

Thanks, Liam.

LIAM

Anytime, bro.

I have no problem seeing her. Go ahead and invite her.

As soon as I hit send, my stomach tightened.
The idea of seeing Blake again gave me an instant high.
She was a drug.
And I was desperate for my next fix.

ERIK

> I'll text her then. Let's meet at 5:30. That gives us 30 minutes to order happy hour apps.

I checked my watch.

Just after 4:30.

Plenty of time to get ready.

I walked to my dresser and grabbed a black Under Armour shirt before pausing.

Should I try to look nicer if Blake shows up?

Scoffing at myself, I put the shirt back and pulled out a navy-blue polo and gray flat-front shorts. October or not, I ran hot.

After getting dressed, I ran some gel through my hair and brushed my teeth for good measure. Not that I was planning on kissing anyone, but no one wanted to be the guy with bad breath.

Ruger sat by the door, ears perked.

I scratched behind them. "Be a good boy while I'm gone."

He let out a quiet huff, clearly unimpressed with my plans that didn't include him.

The familiar rumble of Betty's engine filled the driveway.

If things went well tomorrow, this would be one of my last rides with her.

A pang of nostalgia hit as I ran a hand over the steering wheel.

"You've been a good car," I muttered, giving it a light pat.

One of the only constants in my life.

By the time I pulled into the lot, the guys were already there.

We exchanged handshakes and shoulder claps, the kind of unspoken greetings that meant more than words.

I scanned the bar, my chest tightening slightly when I didn't see her.

There was still a chance she'd show.

We grabbed a table, and I pretended to look at the menu. But every time the front door opened, my eyes flicked up.

Erik sighed, giving me a look. "She's not coming."

I tensed. "I'm not looking for her."

"I think we all know better than that," Liam said.

"She texted me before I pulled in," Erik added, voice softer this time.

I didn't respond.

I Didn't need to.

The disappointment settled low in my stomach, curling like smoke.

I forced my gaze back to the menu.

A waitress came by, taking our drink orders—beers all around. I scanned the food options, but nothing sounded appealing.

Still, I knew I should eat.

If history told me anything, tonight would get rowdy.

Our conversation was light at first, the alcohol not yet working its magic on loosening our lips just yet.

But that's what nights like these were for.

For laying it all down, no judgment, no pretense.

I hadn't realized how much I missed this.

Missed *them*.

I'd cut them out of my life without thinking. Convinced myself it was easier that way. That I was protecting myself.

But had I?

Had I actually protected anything?

If anything, I had just missed out.

Wes leaned back in his chair, studying me. "Don't go getting all dark and broody just yet, MacIntyre. The night's still young."

I grinned. "What could I possibly have to be dark and broody about?"

Erik scoffed. "Oh, wait. I know this one. You come home to see the love of your life in love with someone else?"

Liam let out a low whistle. "Ouch."

I shrugged. "He isn't wrong."

"Yeah, but leave it to the resident asshole of the group to point it out," Wes said.

Erik raised his beer in a mock toast. "Somebody's gotta do it."

"And you're weirdly good at it," Liam added.

Erik smirked. "Oh, don't get too comfortable, Liam. You're next. I'm just warming up."

Liam groaned, already reaching for his beer. "Not until I have another drink."

The waitress came back, dropping off our food, and conversation took a backseat to eating.

It was easy to tell a lot about someone by what they ordered.

Liam—grilled chicken salad, same as me. Health-conscious. Image to maintain.

Erik—a loaded burger. Well-rounded. A pain in the ass, but it was part of his charm.

Wes—appetizer sampler and a burger. Stress eating.

It was clear he was trying to eat some of his feelings. I didn't want to push him on it.

Not yet.

But when he was ready to talk—I'd be here.

We all would.

After finishing up our food and another round of beers, Erik decided shots were a good idea.

Which meant, whether it was a good idea or not—it was happening.

We raised our glasses, clinking them together.

"Work tomorrow be damned," Wes muttered before we all threw them back.

The tequila burned, but I barely felt it.

Because for the first time in a long time, I felt like I belonged again.

And for now, that was enough.

Chapter Thirty-One

JAMIE

"To getting us all back together again!" Erik shouted.

We raised our shot glasses, slamming them back in unison. The tequila burned on the way down, leaving behind a familiar warmth that settled deep in my chest.

The buzz started just beneath my skin, like a slow hum in my veins.

Liam grabbed his glass. "Who's up for a game of pool?"

"I'm in," I said, pushing away from the table.

We walked to one of the open pool tables, the silence comfortable, expectant. We'd all been drinking long enough to know that this was how it started. The shots, the banter, the games.

The deeper conversations would come later.

They always did.

I grabbed a cue stick, rolling it between my palms. "You want to break?"

Liam lined up his shot, eyes narrowing in concentration. "Sure."

The crack of the balls rang through the bar, sharp and sudden, like distant thunder in a summer storm.

I moved around the table, lining up my shot. "So... had enough alcohol to talk about your troubles yet?"

Liam arched a brow. "Have you?"

I sank the six ball into the corner pocket. "Solids." I twirled my cue stick. "And I think I'm getting there."

Liam let out a short laugh before sinking two striped balls. "My wife left me." He exhaled, voice calm. Too calm. "About a year ago."

I stilled.

Shit.

I glanced up. "I'm sorry, man."

Liam shrugged. "I couldn't stop her. Thought we were happy. She never told me otherwise."

"She never gave you a chance?"

"No."

I took my next shot, sinking the three and five balls back-to-back. The weight of his words pressed down on me.

"Damn," I muttered. "I'm sorry."

Liam bent over the table, lining up his next shot. "You haven't heard the worst part."

I pushed off the table. "I think we need more beer for this."

Grabbing our empty cups, I made my way to the bar, ordering another round.

Beer. Tequila shots. *Because why the hell not?*

By the time I returned, Liam had sunk another ball. We knocked back the shots, chasing them with sips of beer.

The burn was slower this time.

My limbs felt heavier, my movements sluggish.

But my mind? Lighter.

I leaned over the table, eyes scanning the balls, trying to focus through the buzz.

Liam exhaled. "Belle left while I was at work. Everything in the house was normal—nothing out of place. The only thing missing was some of her belongings." He paused, shifting his beer between his hands. "Coming home to an empty house like that... scared the shit out of me."

I looked up.

"I thought something had happened to her," he admitted. "Called her over and over. No answer. Eventually, her mailbox filled up. I couldn't leave any more messages."

I took my shot. The crack of the balls filled the silence.

Liam set his drink down. "I had nothing to go on. My only comfort was that she took things that mattered to her. It meant she left *willingly,* not forcefully." He let out a bitter laugh. "I searched everywhere. Scoured the internet. Hired a PI. For a year, it was like she'd vanished off the face of the planet."

A long pause.

Then—

"Until last week."

The next crack of the pool balls startled me.

I hadn't realized how invested I was in his words.

"What happened last week?" I asked.

"The PI finally got a hit on her credit. She applied for a mortgage." Liam dragged a hand through his hair. "In Arizona."

My grip tightened around the cue stick. "Okay... so, at least now you know she's okay."

Liam nodded slowly. "Yeah. But here's the kicker—she applied as a co-borrower."

I froze.

Which meant—

"She's not alone," Liam muttered, finishing the thought for me.

Shit.

My stomach sank. I could already see where this was going.

"The other name on the mortgage?" Liam swallowed. "Asher Jennings."

His voice was low, edged with something raw.

"Asher," I repeated, testing the name. It felt wrong in my mouth.

"Asher was a *friend* of mine," Liam said, knocking back half his beer. "We met in school in NYC. Hit it off fast. When Belle and I started dating, *he* was the one who helped push us together." He scoffed. "A year before she left, Asher moved to California. Struggled to find a job at a fashion house. I owned my own company by then, so I hired him."

I could already feel the train wreck coming.

"I thought I was helping him out. Didn't realize a year later, he'd run away with my wife."

A long, tense beat passed.

"You didn't suspect?" I asked. "When they *both* disappeared?"

Liam shook his head. "Asher told me he found a job in New York. Left two months earlier. Belle was my entire focus after she was gone." His jaw flexed. "He wasn't even on my radar."

I exhaled, setting my cue stick aside. The game was long forgotten.

"Were there any signs?"

Liam's laugh was hollow. "Looking back? Yeah. Plenty." He swirled his beer, gaze distant. "They got close. But I thought he was just looking out for her." He inhaled sharply. "I worked all the time. Constantly traveled, trying to get my brand off the ground. I can see now how naïve I was."

"Success came at a price."

Liam nodded. "Liam Knight Creations is a multi-billion-dollar company. It's growing every day." His throat bobbed. "But I lost the one person who pushed me to chase my dreams. The person who fine-tuned my designs. The one who ate *ramen noodles with me* every night when I couldn't afford anything else."

The pain in his voice hit like a blade to the gut.

I knew that feeling.

The hollow ache of losing someone who once felt like home.

Liam shook his head, as if that would chase away reality.

"I just can't believe she ran away with *him*." He looked at me, frustration flickering beneath the hurt. "One decision—to help a friend—changed everything." His voice dropped. "Why didn't she just *talk* to me? Why didn't she tell me she was unhappy? Maybe I could have saved us."

"You really loved her," I said quietly.

Liam's gaze locked on mine. "I would've given up every penny I had to keep her."

A heavy silence settled between us.

I let the words hang there for a moment before asking, "And now?"

Liam's jaw clenched. "She can rot in hell for all I care. They both can."

But I knew better.

It wasn't anger talking.

It was heartbreak.

If she walked through that door right now, it wouldn't change the fact that he still loved her.

Liam exhaled sharply. "Anyway. Enough about me. Let's talk about *your* problems."

I arched a brow. "I don't have problems."

Liam smirked, tapping his fingers against his beer. "Says

the guy who got jumpy over the possibility of Blake showing up tonight."

I rolled my shoulders, taking a slow sip of beer.

Liam's hand landed on my shoulder.

"You still love her," he said simply.

It wasn't a question.

It was a statement.

One I was trying like hell to forget.

Chapter Thirty-Two

Jamie

I leaned against the pool table, absently tracing the Carolina Panthers logo a local artist had painted on the wall.

The smell of fried food clung to every surface in this place, thick with the scent of beer and nostalgia.

Don't Stop Believin' played softly from the jukebox, a song I'd heard a million times but never really listened to.

My thoughts were too tangled up in Liam's words.

It was embarrassing—and maybe a little painful—to realize that everyone around me knew exactly how I felt, even when I wasn't sure myself.

Like I was standing on the wrong side of a one-way mirror.

Everyone I cared about could see into my heart.

But when I looked, all I saw was myself.

Liam leaned his arms on the table, studying me. "Have you and Blake talked about what happened?"

"No." I gripped my glass in my hand. "And I don't plan to bring it up."

"Why not?"

"She's with Dean. Happy, it seems." I took a sip of beer, forcing the words down like they didn't sting. "I don't want to reopen old wounds."

"Or heal them," Liam countered.

My jaw tightened. "I don't think so."

"Because it makes you uncomfortable."

I exhaled sharply. "Are you trying to make me feel better or calling me out for every flaw I have?"

Liam smirked. "If I did that, we'd need all night."

"Ha ha."

His expression softened. "I'm only saying this because I finally have closure. Two weeks ago, I would've said something completely different. But now that I have all the information about Belle leaving, I can finally move on."

I didn't miss the weight in his voice.

He leaned back, rolling the hem of his shirt between his fingers. "For the last year, I've been in limbo—waiting for her to pop up around some corner or hear tragic news about her on some prime time TV show. Now, I know where she is. I know the truth. And that means I can let go."

His eyes locked onto mine. "You and Blake never got that. Maybe it's time."

A muscle in my jaw ticked.

"All I'm saying is—give her the truth. Let her make the best decision for herself."

I let out a bitter chuckle. "And what if I bare my soul to her, show her every inch of my tormented, messed-up self—and she still chooses Dean?"

Liam lifted his beer. "Then at least you'll know. And you can finally stop pining over someone you'll never have."

I stared at the amber liquid in my glass before draining it.

How the hell did I end up in the hot seat? I came here to help him.

But damn it, his words made too much sense.

I rubbed the back of my neck. "I need another beer."

Liam grinned and knocked back the rest of his.

As we walked toward the bar, I spotted Wes and Erik locked in a heated debate, arms waving wildly.

Liam chuckled. "What do you think it is this time?"

"Something completely stupid."

Sure enough, when we got closer, Erik turned toward us. "Hey guys. How was the game?"

Wes's head snapped up. "Hey! Don't turn around like you *won* this argument."

Liam grinned. "You two always argue, and neither of you ever win because the other refuses to acknowledge it."

Their laughter died down, and a comfortable silence settled between us.

But something gnawed at me.

It was too quiet in my head.

Because for the first time in years, in the presence of the only people I trusted...

The darkness didn't come.

And that scared me.

Liam broke the silence first.

"You know," he said, voice softer. "It's weird, isn't it? Noah wasn't always here when I visited, but knowing we'll never get to see him trip over himself again? Never hear his dumb jokes? That's a surreal feeling."

I swallowed hard.

Apparently, I wasn't the only one missing him.

Erik nodded. "Yeah, I keep thinking I'll get a phone call from him. Like it was all a mistake."

A lump formed in my throat. *I wished it was.*

"I'd give anything to make it a joke," I muttered before I could stop myself.

All eyes snapped to me.

Liam's hand landed on my shoulder. "Shit, Jamie. I forgot you were the one who brought him home. I can't imagine the weight you carry."

"I..."

Was I really considering telling them?

That I hadn't just escorted Noah's body home? That I'd been there when he took his last breath?

That he had died saving me?

My throat closed up.

But the relief I'd felt after telling my family last night, the way they still accepted me...

I wanted that with my friends.

I didn't want to be alone anymore.

And that what was what Noah had wanted in the first place. His dying wish.

I cleared my throat and glanced over my shoulder, making sure no one was within earshot.

"I didn't just escort his body home." My voice came out low, uneven. "I was there. When he died."

The weight of my words sank between us.

No one moved.

No one breathed.

I swallowed hard. "He—Noah—he saved my life." The words felt too big, too heavy. "Took a bullet meant for me and..." My throat threatened to clamp shut.

"He died," I forced out. "Because of me."

The silence stretched so long I thought I'd drown in it.

Wes exhaled first. "Jamie. Fuck."

Erik's usual smirk was gone, replaced by genuine compassion. "Why didn't you tell us sooner?"

I shrugged. "How could I? I took away someone we all loved. It feels like I killed him myself. How am I supposed to face that?"

They all looked down at their drinks.

The quiet felt deafening.

I braced myself for their anger. Their hatred.

But when Liam spoke, his voice was calm. Knowing.

"It makes sense now."

I frowned. "What?"

Wes nodded. "No, he's right."

I let out a hollow laugh. "What the hell are you two talking about?"

Liam and Wes shared a look.

"The way you carry yourself," Wes said. "Like the weight of the world is on your shoulders. You've changed, Jamie."

Erik studied me like he was seeing me for the first time.

"Gone is fun Jamie," Liam added. "The guy who always had some reckless, brilliant idea that got us into trouble."

I crossed my arms. "I grew up."

"No." Wes shook his head. "You used to give everything to the people you cared about. Now? You don't talk about yourself. You just... exist."

Erik scoffed. "And old Jamie would never let Blake walk away without a fight."

"New Jamie doesn't stand a chance," Liam added.

Erik snapped his fingers. "Oh! I get it now. All these bad things happened to Jamie, and now he doesn't know how to enjoy life anymore."

Wes clapped his hands together in mock applause. "Bravo. Took you long enough."

"Shut it," Erik muttered. "I'm adding valuable insight here."

Liam and I exchanged a look.

They bickered like brothers. Always had.

It felt... normal. Real.

Erik lifted his glass to his lips. "Jamie, none of us blame you. And you shouldn't either."

Liam slung an arm over my shoulder. "Noah wouldn't want you to live like this. His death is proof that nothing's guaranteed. So live, man."

Determination shone in his eyes.

"Are you ready to take your own advice?" I asked.

Liam clinked his glass against mine. "I am."

Wes and Erik followed suit.

We drank.

And for the first time in a long time, I didn't feel alone.

Chapter Thirty-Three

BLAKELY

My mind ran a marathon all day, nonstop.

Kate's words kept circling in my head, pushing me to figure out what I wanted. Jamie. Dean. My past. My future.

I didn't have an answer, and the thoughts swirled, dragging me down like water spiraling in a drain.

Despite my mental chaos, I'd managed to work on the article about Jamie's foundation all afternoon. The words had come effortlessly, my focus locked in for the first time in weeks. But after struggling with writer's block recently, I wasn't taking any chances. I packed up my work to bring home, determined to finish.

A knock at the door pulled me from my thoughts.

"Come in," I called, already knowing who it was.

Dean walked in, his usual confidence radiating off him, but something in his eyes sparkled differently tonight.

"Hey, sweetheart. Still working?"

I nodded, tapping my laptop screen. "Yeah, inspiration hit, and I wanted to take full advantage."

"Did you eat dinner at least?"

I glanced at the clock. 8:07 PM. "Yeah, I had some soup."

His brow furrowed. "You should've eaten a real meal."

He kissed the top of my head, and I forced a small smile. "I know, I know."

Dean pulled out a chair at the dining table, sitting beside me. "So, what's this article about? It's not the one about my brother, is it?"

"No," I said carefully. "This one is about a program helping soldiers returning from combat."

His expression darkened instantly. "Ah. I see."

I felt the shift, the way his whole body tensed.

"It's a great program," I added quickly. "It's designed to help those who feel lost or uncertain about what they experienced while deployed." The words rushed out, as if I could smooth over the sudden edge in his voice.

"And how did you hear about this program?"

I blinked. "Mr. Taylor assigned it to me. Why?"

Dean leaned back in his chair, crossing his arms. "Just curious. You know you can't believe anything MacIntyre says, right? I wanted to make sure he wasn't feeding you lies about his so-called achievements."

His meaning was clear as day.

Dean wasn't upset about the article. He was upset that Jamie was connected to it.

Kate's voice echoed in my head, urging me to look deeper into my relationship with Dean. To figure out if what we had was real or just convenient.

Looking at him now, I wasn't sure I liked what I saw.

"Dean," I said carefully, "you're being unfair."

"I'm serious," he shot back. "That guy is a liar. You can't trust anything he says. He always paints himself as the victim."

Irritation prickled up my spine. "There's a chance you don't know the whole story."

Dean's jaw clenched. "Are you saying my brother was lying in his letters? That he made things up?"

"No, Dean, I'm not saying that. I'm saying none of us know what really happened. Noah is the only one who knew the full truth."

Dean's eyes burned with conviction. "I don't need to piece together clues. I already know who's responsible for Noah's death. Jamie MacIntyre."

The weight of his words hit me hard.

He didn't just believe Jamie was responsible—he was convinced of it.

And that realization pissed me off.

I felt a deep, instinctual need to defend Jamie.

But at the same time, I saw the pain beneath Dean's anger, the raw grief that made him desperate for someone to blame.

The journalist in me knew that every story had three sides. One side, the other, and the truth.

So why, when I barely knew anything about what happened, was I so quick to jump to Jamie's defense?

Dean's voice snapped me back. "Why aren't you on my side with this?"

"I'm not picking sides, Dean."

"And that's the problem."

His words stung, mostly because I didn't have a response.

I should have been able to reassure him. To say something that would ease his pain. That's what a good girlfriend would do, right?

But Dean wasn't thinking clearly.

And I couldn't bring myself to lie just to make him feel better.

Before I could answer, my phone rang.

Cadence.

Dean's eyes flashed with frustration.

"Are you kidding me? You're gonna answer that? Right now?"

"It's Cadence," I said, grabbing my phone. "She never calls me. Something could be wrong."

Dean scoffed. "Something is wrong—with me. I should be your priority right now."

His words were like a bucket of ice water dumped over my head.

Dean didn't talk to me like this.

I searched his face, looking for the man I fell in love with.

But all I saw was someone I didn't recognize.

"I'm not pushing you aside," I said slowly, keeping my voice even. "But she never calls. She could be in trouble."

Dean's stare hardened. "So she matters more than me?"

"That's not what I'm saying."

"No, but that's what it sounds like."

I opened my mouth, but he pushed back his chair. "I'm tired. I'm going home."

I didn't fight him. I didn't have it in me.

He wasn't listening.

And honestly? I was too drained to keep trying.

"I'll text you later," he muttered, grabbing his keys. The door clicked shut—just shy of a slam.

I let out a slow breath, dropping my head onto my desk.

What the hell just happened?

My phone buzzed again.

I sat up, expecting Dean. Maybe he'd changed his mind.

Maybe he'd realized how weird that whole conversation had been.

But it wasn't Dean.

It wasn't even Cadence.

It was Jamie.

> We should get together and talk.

A rush of emotions tangled in my chest.

I wasn't sure if I was annoyed that he was texting me while out with his friends...

Or relieved that it was him instead of Dean.

I stared at the message for a long moment before typing back.

> Oh yeah? About what?

> Everything.

My breath hitched and my curiosity heightened. Jamie had never been forthcoming with his emotions, and the fact that he was offering an olive branch meant a great deal.

> Everything?

> Everything.

My fingers hovered over the keyboard, hesitation curling around me like a shadow.

I knew where he was. I'd been invited. The choice was mine.

But it wasn't just curiosity pulling me toward him—it was

something deeper, something greedy. I wanted answers. Needed them. I'd spent too long piecing together fragments of a story I barely understood, and now Jamie was offering me the full truth.

Before I could talk myself out of it, I got up and changed. Not for Jamie. Not to impress anyone. Just because I wanted to feel good about myself.

At least, that's what I told myself.

But the restless energy coiling in my chest told a different story. My hands were unsteady, my stomach hollow, like I'd had too much caffeine.

As I drove to Stadium Club, I pulled out my phone and called Cadence. She picked up on the second ring.

"Hey!"

"Hey yourself," I said, gripping the steering wheel. "Sorry I missed your call. Everything okay?"

Cadence let out a breath that was more frustration than relief. "That's a loaded question."

I frowned. "Tell me anyway."

She was quiet for a beat. "Elijah and I got into a fight."

I tensed. "A bad one?"

"Not yelling or screaming or anything. But it felt... off. Like, we weren't speaking the same language anymore, you know?"

I nodded, even though she couldn't see me. "Yeah, I get that."

A humorless laugh slipped from her. "I just—I don't know what's happening. We've been together for so long, and now it's like we don't even know each other. Or maybe we do, and that's the problem."

"Cadence," I said carefully, "you guys have been solid for years. Maybe it's just a rough patch."

She hesitated. "I want to believe that. But we've both been so focused on work, on making something of ourselves, that we forgot to actually live. And in the process, we've changed. Or at least, I have."

I knew that feeling all too well.

"You don't think he's changed?" I asked.

"I think he's holding on too tightly to what we were," she admitted. "And maybe I am too. But Blake, I don't even know if I want the same things anymore. The person I was when I met him? She doesn't exist."

Her voice cracked on the last word, and it hit me harder than I expected. Because I knew exactly what she meant.

"Sounds like you need a break," I said. "Why don't you come home for a bit? Stay with me if you want."

Cadence sighed. "I wish I could."

I swallowed the lump forming in my throat. "I get it. Just... you know I'm here, right? Always."

"I know," she murmured. "I miss you."

"Miss you too."

Silence stretched between us, but it wasn't uncomfortable. Just full of everything neither of us had said.

"Things have been crazy here," I admitted, staring at the glowing sign of the restaurant as I pulled into the parking lot.

"With Jamie?"

I hesitated. "Yeah. And Dean."

She hummed. "Sounds complicated."

"You could say that."

"Do you want it to be complicated?"

Her question settled deep in my chest. I wasn't sure I had an answer for her.

Before I could even try to explain, her voice dropped. "Crap, Elijah's home. I don't want him thinking I called you just to talk about our fight."

I smirked, trying to lighten the mood. "Even though that's exactly what you did?"

She laughed softly. "Exactly. I'll call you later, okay?"

"Don't stress about it. We'll talk soon. Love you, Cay."

"Love you, too."

The line went dead, but her words lingered.

She didn't know if she and Elijah wanted the same things anymore.

And suddenly, I wasn't sure if Dean and I did either.

The closer I got to the entrance of Stadium Club, the more my emotions tangled into something I couldn't unravel. My breath felt too shallow, my heart beat too fast, and I wasn't sure if it was anticipation or nerves.

Maybe it was the possibility of finally getting closure with Jamie.

Or maybe it was the realization that I wasn't ready for it.

I reached for the door handle, bracing myself for whatever came next—

Only to feel like a proverbial door had slammed in my face.

Chapter Thirty-Four

BLAKELY

Burning, fiery rage coursed through my veins.

Jamie sat at the bar, Charlotte pressed against him, her arms wrapped around his neck, her body flush against his, lips locked with his in a lover's kiss.

My stomach twisted, heat rising to my face as my hands curled into fists at my sides. How dare he?

He had texted me—me—while carrying on with her? He knew how I felt about Charlotte, knew what she had done to me, knew what she was capable of. And yet, there he was, letting her kiss him like she had a right to.

Shame and humiliation crept up my spine, slamming into me with the force of a memory I had long tried to bury.

Charlotte's sharp laughter.

The whispers behind my back.

The smug, knowing smirk she wore every time she tore me down.

down.

And now? She had her hands on Jamie like she belonged there.

Jamie pulled away first, his head turning, his gaze locking onto mine.

His eyes widened, the haze of alcohol flickering with clarity as he registered me standing there, watching. Catching him.

For a split second, I saw it—the regret, the guilt.

But I wouldn't let him see how much it affected me. I wouldn't give him that satisfaction.

Lifting my chin, I tore my gaze from him and searched the room for Liam. My pulse pounded in my ears, my emotions a mess of anger, hurt, and something far worse—betrayal.

I hadn't come here for Jamie.

At least now, I could tell myself that.

Liam was sitting at a table in the corner with Erik and Wes. I made my way toward them, needing to be anywhere but here.

When I tapped Liam's shoulder, he turned, his eyes widening at the sight of me before a slow grin spread across his face.

"Blake," he said, pulling out the empty chair beside him. "Didn't think you were coming."

I slid into the seat, forcing a small smile. "Changed my mind."

Liam's gaze flicked past me, then back again, his expression unreadable.

Wes leaned back in his chair, a smirk playing on his lips. "Hey, Blake. You here to drink us under the table?"

I let out a short laugh, but it was hollow. "Tempting."

Erik pushed his chair back. "I need another drink. You?"

I nodded. "Beer."

As Erik walked off, Liam studied me. "So, what made you change your mind?"

"It didn't feel right letting you leave without a proper goodbye."

I tried to hold his gaze, but my eyes betrayed me—flicking, unbidden, back toward the bar.

Jamie was still sitting there.

Charlotte was gone, but Erik had stopped beside him now, talking in low tones.

Liam's hand landed on my arm, drawing my attention back. "Give him a little understanding, Blake. He's been through a lot."

I stiffened. "I—"

"Here you go," Erik said, dropping a beer in front of me before taking his seat across the table.

"Thanks." I took a sip, letting the cool liquid soothe the fire burning in my chest.

"Hey, guys."

The sound of his voice sent an involuntary shiver up my spine.

Jamie slid into the open seat beside me, the scent of cedarwood, alcohol, and something unmistakably him invading my space.

Liam and Erik mumbled a greeting. I said nothing.

Jamie shifted closer, his knee brushing mine. He leaned in, his breath warm as he whispered, or tried to whisper—his voice was rough and hoarse from the alcohol.

"Blake."

I kept my eyes on my beer. "What?"

"Can we talk?"

I took another sip. "I have nothing to say."

"Then why are you here?"

"To say goodbye to Liam and see my friends."

Liam let out an exaggerated sigh. "As much as I love being the center of attention, I'd rather not be caught in whatever the

225

hell this is." He stood, motioning to Erik. "Darts while we wait for Wes to get his balls back from Liv?"

Erik let out a booming laugh. "Only if you're ready to get your ass kicked."

I took a deep breath, eyes closing for a moment before reaching for my beer again.

Jamie fidgeted beside me, shifting in his seat, restless. I knew he was watching me, waiting for me to give in and look at him.

I wouldn't.

I would not.

Erik walked past the table, dropping two fresh beers in front of us with a wink. "Looks like you two need these."

"Thanks," Jamie muttered.

I grabbed the beer, took a long drink, then turned to him, ready to shut this down.

"Blake, about what you saw... with Charlotte... it wasn't what it looked like."

I exhaled through my nose. "Jamie, it doesn't matter."

"It does to me."

I shook my head. "I have no right to decide what you do and who you do it with."

"You're right."

I blinked, caught off guard. "What?"

"You have no right to judge me," he said evenly, his voice void of any drunken slur now. "Or feel any way about it. You're in a serious relationship. You have been for a while, from what I'm told. You don't get to criticize my actions."

His words hit me like a slap, sharp and cutting.

He was right. I had no claim over him. No reason to feel jealous. No reason to let it bother me at all.

Except... it did.

It *really* did.

And Jamie saw it.

"But Charlotte?" I pressed, needing something to justify why it had gutted me so much.

"That's the part I want to explain." Jamie sighed, scrubbing a hand down his face. "I didn't even know she was here. I was talking to Kyle behind the bar when she came up beside me. When I turned around, she was just... there. She grabbed my arm, said something, and before I knew it, she kissed me."

I swallowed. "And you kissed her back."

Jamie's brows pulled together, his lips parting slightly. "I think I did."

The admission sliced through me.

I pushed back my chair, ready to walk away—to get as far away from him as possible.

"Wait." His hand shot out, grabbing my wrist. "Blake, I'd never hurt you on purpose."

"That's what you keep saying," I snapped. "But you keep hurting me, Jamie. And I'm stupid enough to keep letting you."

His grip loosened slightly, but he didn't let go. His eyes, so glassy, so raw, held mine. "I'm sorry I kissed Charlotte when the person I wanted to kiss was you."

I stilled.

"What?"

"Blake, I haven't dated anyone seriously since you. I haven't had anything real. And when Charlotte kissed me, for a second, it felt nice to be wanted. To kiss someone. But the whole time, I wished it was you."

His confession was everything I'd once wanted to hear.

And yet... it destroyed me.

Before I could stop myself, my fingers brushed his cheek.

He leaned into my touch, his eyes fluttering shut. "Please, stay."

I swallowed hard. I couldn't do this.

Not now. Not when my emotions were this raw.

I had to leave. Drunk Jamie was vulnerable, too honest, saying things I wasn't ready to hear.

"I've gotta go."

"Wait," His voice cracked. "Blake... please."

"I want to have this conversation, but not when you're like this," I whispered. "We'll talk tomorrow, Jamie."

His lips curved into a lazy smile, "Okay."

"Will you let me know when you get home safe?"

A ghost of a smile touched my lips. "Don't forget. Or I'll worry."

"Oh, Blake," he murmured, his voice thick with something unreadable. "You're always on my mind, babe. I won't forget."

Heat rushed to my cheeks, my stomach twisting.

I nodded, turned, and walked away.

My phone vibrated in my purse as I climbed into my car, surprised to see a message from Jamie.

Miss you already, babe.

I needed to get out of here. Before I did something really, really stupid.

Chapter Thirty-Five

BLAKELY

17 YEARS OLD

PE was the worst part of my day. I hated everything about it—sweating in the middle of school, pretending I had any athletic ability, and worst of all, enduring Charlotte and her pack of wannabes.

She had tormented me for as long as I could remember. Most of it was petty—name-calling, minor pranks—but lately, her cruelty had escalated. Graduation couldn't come soon enough. I just had to survive a few more months, and then I'd never have to deal with her again.

I hadn't told Jamie about it. He had to have heard the rumors Charlotte spread, the lies she whispered into the right ears, but he always defended me. I didn't want him to see me as weak, as someone who needed protecting. I wanted to be stronger than that.

I stepped out of the locker room, adjusting my gym shorts,

and walked into the gymnasium where the rest of the class gathered for our basketball lesson.

Lucky me, another opportunity for someone to throw a ball at my head.

A cluster of students stood in the corner, whispering and snickering. A few others leaned into each other, their eyes flicking toward me before quickly looking away.

Unease crawled down my spine.

I glanced down at myself—no toilet paper stuck to my shoe, no forgotten clothing item. I looked... normal.

I kept walking, trying to shake off the growing tension curling in my stomach. Then I heard it—the loud, shrill laugh that had become the soundtrack of my torment.

Charlotte.

Of course.

"Of course, it's true," she said, her voice exaggerated, smug. "I don't know... let's go find out. Blake!"

My stomach plummeted.

I ignored her, walking faster toward Cadence, who stood near the bleachers, waiting for me with an easy smile. Almost there—

"Blake, wait up!"

A hand clamped down on my shoulder. I turned, already bracing myself.

Charlotte's grin was razor-sharp. "Just wanted to ask—how much do you make every night?"

My heart slammed against my ribs. "What?"

"Don't play dumb, Blake." Her laughter was a calculated dagger, slicing through the air. "Everyone knows your dad is a worthless drunk who can barely support you. You rely on handouts just to survive."

Heat crawled up my neck.

Everyone was staring now. The conversations in the gym

had quieted, attention shifting toward us like wolves drawn to fresh prey.

"Charlotte, I'm not playing your game today."

Her smile widened. That sinking feeling in my gut grew.

"Oh, come on. Were you too busy playing someone else's game?" Her voice dripped with mock sympathy. "Is that why you're cranky today? Didn't get enough sleep?"

My nails bit into my palms. "I don't know what you're talking about."

Charlotte let out a fake gasp. "Are you sure?"

I turned away, but her next words froze me in place.

"How does Jamie feel about your... extracurricular activities?"

Slowly, I turned back. "What?"

Charlotte cocked her head. "Does he know?"

"For the love of God, Charlotte. Know what?"

Her grin was pure malice.

"Your prostitution, of course."

The world tilted.

The breath in my lungs turned to stone, the gym growing unbearably hot.

A sickening wave of silence passed over the room before the whispers started, spreading like wildfire.

"My... what?" My voice barely escaped my lips.

"Well, that's what I heard, anyway." She flipped her chestnut hair over her shoulder, her eyes gleaming with sick satisfaction. "Everyone's talking about how you have to pick up the slack for your pathetic dad by sleeping around. Lizzy told me you have some high-class clients, and they just love the whole forbidden aspect." She leaned in as if confiding a secret. "Bet they tip nice."

A few kids snickered.

I clenched my teeth so hard my jaw ached. "You're disgusting."

She ignored me, her expression turning dreamy as she sighed. "I just don't understand what Jamie sees in you."

And suddenly, it all made sense.

She was still in love with him, and trying to get his attention. That's why she continued to do this.

I thought she'd given up on him.

Charlotte's gaze darkened with resentment. "I mean, he's gorgeous, sweet, a total catch. You? Not so much."

Fury burned through me, but before I could open my mouth, someone stepped beside me.

"Leave her alone, Charlotte," Cadence said, her voice sharp and unwavering. "You know damn well none of your lies are true. Go find someone else to waste your time on."

Relief flooded my chest.

Charlotte's jaw tensed.

I puffed out my chest. "The only one sleeping around is you. Trying to get attention because the guy you actually want is taken—by me."

Charlotte's eyes flashed with fury.

A whistle blew from the doorway, signaling class was starting.

Charlotte leaned in one last time, her voice low with promise. "You'll regret that."

I swallowed hard as she turned away.

I barely made it through class. A basketball to my shoulder. One to my back. A particularly vicious one to my thigh.

I was relieved when gym ended. For once, I actually wanted to shower, letting the hot water soothe my aching muscles. Cadence hurried, saying she had to meet her boyfriend, and by the time I finished, the locker room was empty.

At least, I thought I was alone—until I saw it.

My combination lock lay discarded on the ground, the metal twisted where it had been forced open. Dread coiled in my stomach as I reached for my locker, already knowing what I'd find.

Empty.

No clothes. No backup gym uniform. Nothing.

A lump lodged in my throat, thick and suffocating.

And then I heard it—Charlotte's laugh. Sharp. Triumphant. The sound of victory.

I swallowed hard, my fingers tightening around the edge of the locker. Every instinct screamed at me to break down, to let the tears fall, but I refused to give her that satisfaction.

I had two choices—hide in the locker room and hope someone eventually noticed I was missing, or step out there and face her head-on.

With a deep breath, I wiped the unshed tears from my eyes, squared my shoulders, and pulled my towel tighter around me.

Then, with as much dignity as I could muster, I pushed open the locker room door and stepped into the foyer.

Laughter erupted the second they saw me.

Heat flared up my neck, my cheeks burning as the weight of a dozen stares crashed into me. My grip on the thin towel tightened, my fingers digging into the worn fabric as I fought the rising sting of tears.

Charlotte smirked. "Oh, Blake. Seducing the entire school now? Look at you, wandering the halls like this."

"Give me back my clothes, Charlotte." My voice came out weak. I hated myself for it.

"I have no idea what you mean."

I clenched my fists. "Enough. Give them back."

She tapped her chin. "Hmm. Something's missing."

Before I could react, she grabbed my towel and yanked.

Air whooshed from my lungs as the fabric disappeared.

Laughter exploded.

I dropped to my knees, hands scrambling to cover my body as sobs wracked my chest.

"Not until you learn your place," Charlotte sneered.

"Hey!"

Jamie's voice thundered through the hallway.

The laughter died instantly.

Warm fabric enveloped me as Jamie crouched beside me, wrapping his jacket around my shoulders. His arms came around me, shielding me from the stares, the humiliation.

His chest vibrated as he shouted—at Charlotte, at everyone who had laughed—but I didn't hear any of it.

I was drowning.

And Jamie was the only thing keeping me afloat.

Chapter Thirty-Six

JAMIE

I woke up feeling like my head had taken a tumble in the dryer—thumping, turning, twisting in ways it wasn't meant to. The drum-line in my skull kept playing as I fought the pull of sleep, craving the dreamless oblivion I'd just left behind.

But my alarm, shrill and relentless, reminded me that getting up was non-negotiable.

Baby steps.

I forced myself into a sitting position, wincing as the room tilted. I didn't even remember coming home last night, so at least I was relieved to find myself in my own bed.

My feet hit the floor, and regret hit me just as hard.

Okay, that was dramatic.

But still, I regretted every decision I made last night—at least the ones involving tequila. Though, to be fair, Erik was the one who'd started throwing shots at us all.

Grabbing my phone, I planned to send him a message

expressing just how much I appreciated his friendship this morning, but Blake's name on my screen stopped me cold. The last thing I did before passing out was talk to her.

My pulse thudded in my ears as I scrolled up to read our conversation.

> Miss you already, babe

> Stop messing around. I just left. Text me when you get home.

> I'm being 100 percent totally honest. I could spend every minute of every day with you and still not get enough.

I cringed.

> Jamie, please don't.

> I'm sorry, Blake. For everything.

And when she didn't text me back, I kept going.

> I'll do all I can to make it up to you.

> I really miss you.

> Everything about you.

> We are all getting Ubers home, should be home soon.

> I'm home. Safe and sound.

> It was good to see you tonight. You looked so beautiful.

And there it was—proof that I was a complete and utter disaster.

Even worse, my last unsent message sat in the text box, a gem that, by some miracle, I'd fallen asleep before sending.

I love you.

I groaned, running a hand over my face. This was bad. I sounded like a clingy ex who couldn't move on. Like a piece of dog hair clinging to a sweater no matter how many times you brushed it off.

No wonder she stopped responding.

I was about to throw my phone across the room when it rang in my hand.

Blake.

Shock slammed into me for the second time that morning.

Taking a deep breath, I answered. "Hey." I tried to sound like I hadn't made a complete ass of myself last night.

"Hi."

An awkward silence settled between us. Neither of us knew where to start.

"I just wanted to check on you," she finally said. "You seemed pretty messed up when I left. And then all the messages..."

"Yeah..." I exhaled, scrubbing a hand down my face. "I was just reading through my lovely Shakespearean verses. I'm sorry about that." Heat crept up the back of my neck, humiliation settling in.

"It's fine," she said, then hesitated. "I'm sorry I fell asleep before you made it home."

"So my thoughtful confessions put you to sleep, then?" I tried for humor, anything to lessen the sting of embarrassment.

"What if they had?"

"Then I'd feel even more like an idiot."

She laughed, and damn, it was the best sound I'd heard all morning. "Well, I can save your pride a little. I was just tired. I

237

fell asleep on my couch, which isn't something that happens too often."

"That makes me feel better. Though, only a little. And I am sorry. I never meant to throw any unwanted feelings at you. I know you're with Dean, and I don't want to make you uncomfortable, but I'd like to be friends. Or at least not avoid each other at any public gathers."

"No, it's okay. Really." She paused. "Actually, it was nice to get an idea of what you were feeling. You're always so guarded with your emotions."

Her words hit deeper than I wanted to admit. I cleared my throat. "I try to be, anyway."

"Why?"

How the hell was I supposed to answer that?

Tell her I kept people at arm's length to protect them? That anyone I cared about always seemed to end up hurt?

I was trying. Trying to let people in, to tell those closest to me what I'd been through. But instinct was hard to fight. My first reaction had always been to shut down, to keep myself locked away.

"Isn't that the question of the year?"

She let out a small laugh. "You said you wanted to talk last night."

"I did."

"What did you want to talk about?"

I hesitated. "That's an in-person conversation. And maybe one that needs a little alcohol to loosen the lips."

"Like last night." It wasn't a question.

"I was a bit extra chatty last night," I admitted. "But maybe we don't need *that* much alcohol for a friendly talk. Last night was excessive."

She laughed, and the sound settled something inside me.

A comfortable silence stretched between us before she inhaled softly. "Well, I just wanted to check on you."

"Thank you," I murmured. "I feel slightly less mortified now, so I appreciate it."

"Anytime," she said. "I'll talk to you soon."

"Bye."

I stared at my phone long after the call ended, unsure how to process the mix of emotions twisting inside me. Embarrassment, sure. But also... something else.

Something dangerous.

Something I couldn't afford to feel.

Enough of this.

I pushed to my feet, shaking it off. Today was the day I was finally getting that truck.

All day, I'd gone back and forth with John, the dealership's salesman, finalizing the details. As much as it pained me to part with Betty, it was time to move on.

A mantra I was trying to apply to all aspects of my life.

By the time I pulled into the dealership after work, my excitement had grown. John and I shook hands, sealing the deal with a classic *nice doing business with you* gesture.

There was only one person I wanted to show this to.

I pulled out my phone and sent Blake a quick text.

> Hey. I know it's getting late, but can I swing by your house? I want to show you something.

> Sure. Everything okay?

Yeah, sorry. I didn't mean to alarm you.

It's okay. Do you need my address?

That might be helpful...

Lol

"Here you go." John handed me the keys, nodding toward the truck. "She's all yours, man. Enjoy."

I grinned, shaking his hand. "It's been a pleasure. You'll be seeing me around."

Sliding into the driver's seat, I inhaled deeply. That new car smell mixed with something I swore—probably imagined—smelled like Blake's perfume.

I plugged her address into Google Maps, gripping the steering wheel. The roar of the engine rumbled through me, an echo of something deeper.

Pulling out of the lot, I gave Betty one last glance.

This was good. This was right.

One step forward.

One step closer to healing.

By the time I pulled into Blake's driveway, I didn't even take a second to admire her house. I was already out of the truck, knocking on her door.

She answered almost immediately, her blonde hair down, wearing black leggings and an oversized teal sweatshirt.

Comfortable. Familiar.

"Hey!" She smiled. "Come in for a second."

She popped the door open and walked away before I could tell her I wanted her to see what was outside.

I stepped inside and froze.

Everything about her house felt like... *us.*

The same blankets on the couch. The same coffee cups we

used to have. Little details that pulled me into a different life. The familiarity of it caught me off guard, and when she set her phone down on her desk and walked back toward me, for a millisecond, I was living a different life again.

A life that wasn't mine anymore.

A life I had no right to still want.

She turned back, tucking her phone away. "So, what's up?"

I cleared my throat, shifting my weight. "I wanted you to be the first to see my newest upgrade."

Her brows furrowed as she scanned me, looking for something different. The way her gaze moved over me sent a rush of warmth through my chest, even though I knew she wasn't checking me out—not in the way I wanted her to, anyway.

"It's not on me," I clarified, a slow grin tugging at my lips. "It's outside. In your driveway."

Her eyes widened, excitement flashing in them. "Jamie. You didn't."

I grinned. "I did."

"I knew it! I knew that truck was perfect for you!"

She ran outside, and I followed. The sky had deepened into rich hues of orange and violet, the last traces of sunlight stretching over the pavement. Even in the fading light, the truck gleamed, every detail reflecting just how damn perfect it was.

Blake didn't hesitate. She popped open the driver's side door and climbed in like she belonged there.

And maybe she did.

A shiver of belonging ran through me as I watched her, fingers skimming over the buttons, exploring every feature with a giddy kind of excitement. It reminded me of the first time she'd ever ridden in my old truck, the way she'd stretched her legs across the seat and made it hers.

It was hard to look at her like this and not want us to be

what we had been before. Harder yet to not wish she felt the same way.

But she wasn't just dating anyone. She was with Dean—Noah's older brother. And I refused to cause their family any more pain.

So, as I watched Blake run her hands over the steering wheel, her lips parting in a soft smile, I did my best to sew up the parts of me that wanted to fix what I had broken. I shoved them deep, burying them somewhere they wouldn't resurface every time I saw her.

I wanted to be there for her, to support her, no matter what it meant for me.

And that included telling her the truth about what happened to me.

Chapter Thirty-Seven

Blakely

Jamie's smile was contagious. He bounced on the balls of his feet as I climbed into his truck. The new car smell hit me, mixed with hints of cedarwood and lavender— Jamie's scent. A part of me swelled with pride for him. He'd always worked so hard, never one to spoil himself, and I had a feeling that hadn't changed.

I jumped out and stood in front of him, my lips curving into a smile. "Congratulations, Jamie. It's a beautiful truck."

"I don't think I would've even looked at it if it wasn't for you. So, thank you." He smiled, and my chest ached.

I hesitated before speaking. "Listen, Jamie. I'm really happy for you, but... why me? Why did you want to show me your truck first and not Wes or Erik?"

His expression softened. "I know, I know—I'm not an idiot. I don't want you to think I'm here trying to pull you away from Dean. I meant what I said earlier. If it's possible, I'd like us to be friends. We were close before we were... well, us. We were

243

best friends. And I'd like to have you in my life again. I'll take whatever I can get."

I swallowed, torn between his words and the unshakable weight in my chest. "I don't know, Jamie. I don't know if I can be friends with you."

A flicker of disappointment crossed his face, but he nodded, his jaw tightening. "I understand. Will you at least think about it?"

I sighed. "I can do that."

He smiled, but it didn't reach his eyes. Instead, they carried the storm raging inside him. "Well, I know it's getting late, and I just... I had to show someone my new ride. Thanks for letting me swing by."

I watched as he walked back to his truck, feeling the weight of unspoken words between us.

"Anytime," I murmured.

Jamie paused with his hand on the door and glanced over his shoulder. "Oh, and Blake?"

"Yeah?"

His lips lifted into a small smile. "I love your house. It fits you perfectly."

Then, with a nod, he climbed into his truck, started the engine, and backed out of the driveway. The low rumble of the motor faded as he disappeared down the road, leaving an odd emptiness in his wake.

I hadn't expected Dean to pull in right after Jamie left.

My stomach twisted. "Oh shit."

I wasn't hiding anything from Dean, but I knew exactly how he felt about Jamie. This wouldn't go over well.

Maybe he won't realize.

Dean parked and got out quickly, his gaze snapping to me.

"Was that Jamie MacIntyre?" His voice was sharp.

Scratch that.

"Yeah, it was."

His expression darkened. "Why was he here? I thought your relationship with him was only work-based?"

"Yeah, it is. He only stopped by for a second."

Dean's jaw ticked. "Why?"

I glanced around at my neighbors' houses, feeling suddenly exposed. "Come inside, Dean. I'll answer all your questions."

"Damn right you will," he snapped.

I froze. He had never spoken to me like that before. A warning bell rang in the back of my mind, but I pushed it aside. I could understand why he was upset—Jamie hadn't been here for work—but that didn't give him the right to be disrespectful.

As soon as we stepped inside, I closed the door, shutting out the outside world.

"Dean—"

"Answer me, Blake," he cut me off.

My spine stiffened. "Don't talk over me, and don't talk to me like that."

"Well, stop doing stupid stuff, Blake." His voice was mocking now, sneering.

I narrowed my eyes. "Stupid?"

"Not only are you in a relationship, but you keep seeing the one person I absolutely cannot stand. The person responsible for the death of your friend—my brother. You know what that is, Blake? That's called betrayal."

He turned his back to me, walking toward the couch.

I sucked in a breath, frustration clawing at my throat. "But Jamie didn't kill him."

Dean spun around, stalking toward me. "And not only do you refuse to cut him out of your life, but you defend him at every turn."

"I do not!"

"Then why was he here?" he barked. "Tell me. Now."

He jabbed a finger in my face, and I fought the urge to grab it and bend it back. My patience was running thin.

"I mean it, Dean. Don't talk to me like that. It will get you nowhere, fast."

His expression twisted with something I couldn't place. Hurt? Rage? "I don't even know who you are anymore," he bit out. "Your lack of loyalty hurts more than I can put into words. I can't trust you. You don't have my back when I've always had yours."

My stomach twisted. "That's not fair! You're not even letting me talk without making assumptions."

"Because I can't trust what you say."

"No," I shot back. "Because you refuse to acknowledge the truth."

His eyes flashed. "You know what? I don't need this. Do whatever the hell you want, Blake. I'll see you later."

Dean stormed past me and slammed the door on his way out.

I stood there, stunned, my pulse pounding in my ears.

Closing my eyes, I exhaled slowly, trying to make sense of everything. Jamie saying he missed me. Dean accusing me of betrayal.

One man from my past, stirring up old feelings I'd spent years trying to bury. Another, the man I was supposed to be building a future with, looking at me like I'd personally driven a knife into his back.

I felt like I was being ripped in two.

Jamie was my history—messy, complicated, but real. Every look, every word, every unspoken thought between us still had the power to pull me under, no matter how much I tried to fight it.

And Dean... Dean was supposed to be safe. Steady. The right choice.

So why did his anger feel like another chain wrapped around me, tightening with every accusation?

It all swirled together—regret, confusion, frustration—until I couldn't tell what hurt worse: the weight of Jamie's words or the sharp edge of Dean's.

A headache pounded at my temples as I pressed my fingers to them.

I needed space. I needed clarity.

I needed to talk to someone before I drowned in this mess completely.

Swallowing hard, I walked into the kitchen, put the kettle on, and reached for my phone. The comforting scent of peppermint tea filled the air, but it did nothing to settle the storm inside me.

And most importantly, I needed to figure out what the hell I was going to do next.

Chapter Thirty-Eight

BLAKELY

I didn't want to bother Cadence. She already had enough on her plate, navigating her own relationship, and I didn't need to drag her down with mine too.

I grabbed my phone to call Kate, but my thumb hovered over the screen when I saw Jamie's name still sitting at the top of my call log.

This morning, I'd woken up in a cold sweat. Seeing Jamie and Charlotte together had triggered a string of terrible memories, and they'd followed me into my waking moments like ghosts refusing to be laid to rest.

Reliving those memories filled me with anxiety, like I was seventeen again—standing there, humiliated, naked, while people laughed.

But Jamie had saved me that day.

And I'd craved that same comfort this morning.

Impulsively, I'd called him, needing to hear his voice, needing that grounding presence that had once pulled me out of the worst moment of my life. He'd been mortified over the texts he sent last night, but I barely even read them. My only goal had been to hear the strong notes of his voice, to let his laughter settle my nerves the way it had back then.

None of that helped me now.

Shaking off the lingering haze of the morning, I tapped FaceTime on Kate's contact and waited impatiently as it rang. The second she answered, relief washed over me. Her hair was wrapped in a towel, and she wore pajamas, looking cozy and unconcerned, like she didn't have a care in the world.

"What's up, chickadee? Boy trouble?"

"How did you guess?"

She snorted. "Your face. It's all wrinkly."

I laughed, already feeling lighter. She had a way of breaking up tension with humor, and God, did I need that right now.

"Yeah, well, I'm having some serious trouble, and since you weren't at work today, I didn't get to fill you in on all the juicy details."

"Ugh, can't help it when I gotta take Gran to the doctor. But I'm invested in this drama, so spill."

I told her everything.

Dean's behavior last night. Seeing the guys at the bar. The way Jamie had looked at me. And tonight—Dean acting normal all day, then snapping out of nowhere.

When I was finished, Kate sat there for a second, absorbing it all.

"I mean, I get why he's upset," I admitted. "He doesn't like Jamie, and I keep talking to him."

"But almost every time you've talked to him, it's been because of work," she pointed out. "If Dean hadn't left you last night, you would've stayed home with him instead of going out.

And tonight was a total fluke. What are the odds of that happening again?"

"Exactly! But none of that gives Dean a right to talk to me like he did. That's what's really bothering me."

"As it should. Has he ever acted like this before? Because, not gonna lie, Blake—it's coming off a little controlling."

I hesitated. "No, not really."

Kate arched a brow. "Not really?"

I chewed my bottom lip. "I mean... he's always liked having things his way. He doesn't like when I change plans or do something different."

"Hmm."

"What?"

"Sounds a little controlling to me."

"But it's never been like this."

"Or maybe you just didn't notice. Or care. When did you start seeing it?"

I scoffed. "Our relationship has been up and down since Noah died and Jamie came back."

Kate let out a low whistle. "So he's jealous. He's threatened by Jamie and is afraid of losing you. But little does he know, his behavior is what's gonna push you away."

"I wouldn't go that far."

"So you like this version of Dean?"

"Well... no. But that doesn't mean he'll always be like this."

Kate gave me a knowing look. "Blake, this side of him will always be in there. It's coming from somewhere. And even if Jamie isn't in the picture anymore, what happens if you start working with some super-hot guy? What's Dean gonna do then? That kind of jealousy doesn't just go away, chickadee. It stays. Doesn't matter if the super-hot guy is actually into me. Dean will only see the green monster. Envy."

I laughed at her joke, but her words landed harder than I wanted to admit. "I see what you're saying."

Kate just nodded.

I groaned, pressing my forehead against my palm. "Why did Jamie have to come back and ruin my life again? Everything was fine before."

Kate's expression turned serious—something I didn't see from her often. "Was it, Blake? Or is this some blessing in disguise?"

My stomach twisted. "What do you mean?"

"I can only tell you what I see. And what I see is that Jamie brings out a side of you that you locked away. You're livelier. More animated. It's like you're finally seeing the world in color again. With Dean, you were always on autopilot—like you had the 'perfect relationship' because there were no fights, no tension, no friction. But you weren't *you* anymore."

I swallowed. "You're only saying that because you're living vicariously through my life right now."

"You're not wrong." Kate grinned. "My love life is so dry right now. Maybe I should find myself a military lover. You've got a bunch of guy friends, right? Hook me up!"

"No way am I unleashing you on my guy friends. You'd break all their hearts."

She shrugged. "You've got a point."

"Besides, the only two who are single are Erik—who you *hate*—and Liam. But Liam is in California."

"I can do long-distance. Is he hot?"

I laughed. "Yeah, but I don't think of him that way. He's like a brother to me. But you might've heard of him. You wear some of his clothes."

Kate gave me a confused look. "What do you mean?"

"Liam Knight. The fashion designer."

Her jaw dropped. "OF LIAM KNIGHT CREATIONS?"

"The one. And he's recently single."

"You *know* Liam Knight? Why am I just now learning this?"

I laughed. "Liam grew up here. We went to school together."

"So every time you've talked about your guy friends and mentioned Liam, you meant *Liam Knight*?"

"Yes, Kate, can we move on?"

"No. I need another minute to process. I can't believe you never told me."

I put my hand over my mouth. "It never came up."

Kate took a deep breath. "Okay, I'm ready."

"For ...?"

"To move on."

"Great... back to... "

"Wait!" she shouted, startling me. I was going to kill her.

"What, Kate!?"

"Does he wear boxers or briefs?"

"Oh my god, Kate! Stop it!"

But we both erupted in a fit of laughter. Once we calmed down a bit, I felt better. But I was still unsure.

"So, what should I do, Kate?"

Kate hmm'ed as she thought for a moment. "Honestly? It sounds like you need some time to yourself to figure out what makes you happy. When was the last time you've done something for yourself?"

"I'm trying to get promoted. That's for me."

"But is it? Or is it because of some deep need to feel fulfilled by being successful?"

"Wow. That's deep."

"Right?" Kate raised her eyebrows.

"Okay, too much on my plate to tackle that one, but I can try to fit in a little extra me time. But I love Dean. I can't just break things off with him. Besides, Jamie said he just wanted to be friends."

"Bull."

"What?"

"Bull shit."

I put my chin in my hand. "And, pray tell, why do you say that?"

"That man loves you more than anything. It is so obvious from the way he looks at you. He is only saying that to make you happy. It's a self-sacrifice thing."

I sighed. "What am I supposed to do with that?"

"I don't know. I just wanted you to know that it was bull-shit." Kate shrugged.

"And that is so helpful. Thanks." Sarcasm dripped off my words like a leaky faucet.

"No problem, chickadee. Now, I'm going to get off this phone before my hair dries like this. It will scare all the hot guys away if I let that happen."

I chuckled. "Okay. And thanks for talking to me. I feel a little better now. No closer to solving my problem, but feeling better."

She blew me a kiss and ended the call.

I leaned back, her words echoing in my head.

Maybe it was time to focus on *me*.

Chapter Thirty-Nine

BLAKELY

17 YEARS OLD

Two days after my encounter with Charlotte, the whispers hadn't stopped. The hallways were still alive with cruel murmurs, the weight of them pressing into my skin like sharp, invisible nails.

Every day, it hurt a little more.

Every day, it chipped away at the walls of steel I had built around myself, breaking me down in a way I swore I'd never let happen.

And now, it seemed Charlotte had finally done what she set out to do—tear down my reputation completely.

It was only a matter of time before Jamie realized he couldn't be in a relationship with someone who was labeled a prostitute. Even though the rumors weren't true, they clung to me like oil in water, impossible to shake.

Hell, I was still a damn virgin.

Jamie knew that. At least, I thought he did. It should've

been obvious—I'd never had a serious boyfriend before. But boys didn't always think things through, and he had an entire football team around him, feeding him who knew what.

It didn't change the fact that Jamie was the captain of the team, well-liked, respected. And now, because of me, people would see him differently.

I didn't want that.

I didn't want to be the reason people looked at him and saw anything other than the incredible guy he was.

My thoughts spiraled so fast that I didn't notice him approaching from behind until his arms wrapped around my shoulders.

"Hey, babe," he murmured against my ear.

I stiffened, still locked inside my own head.

Jamie frowned, his arms tightening around me. "I feel like I'm hugging a board. What's wrong?"

I swallowed hard, trying to find my voice. "Jamie, I..."

But the words tangled in my throat. How was I supposed to tell him? How was I supposed to say the one thing I feared most?

That I wasn't sure I deserved to be with him anymore.

My eyes welled with tears, and Jamie's expression shifted instantly. The worry in his storm-gray eyes reached straight into my chest, unraveling me.

"No," he said, tugging my hand into his. "Not here. Let's go."

He led me to his car without another word, driving us to the place that had always been ours—the old park where we'd met as kids. Where we'd spent countless afternoons together, long before we ever fell in love.

He parked under the towering Red Maple trees and climbed out, coming around to open my door. Jamie didn't need words to reassure me—his presence was enough.

I took his hand, the warmth of his palm grounding me as he pulled me toward the faded mulch surrounding the playground equipment.

When we reached the monkey bars, he grinned.

"No way," I said immediately.

"Don't be a chicken, Blake."

I shot him a glare. "I'm not a chicken. I just know I'm not as nimble as I used to be."

Jamie's gaze swept over me, slow and appreciative, the heat in his eyes unmistakable. "Oh, I doubt that, babe."

A flush spread across my cheeks. He would never know how much his teasing words meant to me. How even after everything, he still looked at me like I was the only girl in the world.

With the ease that came from years of football training, he reached up, grabbed the bars, and swung himself up in one effortless motion, perching on top like we used to when we were kids.

He smirked down at me. "Come on, babe. Get that cute little ass up here."

I rolled my eyes, but my heart was hammering.

I jumped to grab hold of the bars, pulling my feet up and wrapping them around the poles before hoisting myself up. Jamie watched with an amused grin, offering no help as I struggled—but the second I made it, his arm wrapped around my waist, pulling me against him.

A rush of warmth spread through me as we sat side by side, looking out over the park. Everything seemed so much bigger when we were younger. The slides, the swings, even the monkey bars had shrunk, or maybe it was just me.

Maybe I'd just lost the ability to see the world the way I used to.

"It's okay, Blake. I want you to stop worrying about it."

I glanced at him, startled.

Jamie exhaled beside me. "I know you're worried about the rumors and how they're affecting me."

"What?"

He looked straight ahead, fingers laced loosely between his knees. "But I'm here to tell you, they don't. Not in the slightest. They aren't true, and frankly, I'll beat the ass of anyone who has the balls to say otherwise."

I let out a shaky laugh, but fear still clawed at my chest. "How do you know they aren't true?"

Jamie turned to me, brows pulling together. "Because I know you, Blake. Better than anyone."

I dropped my gaze to my lap, my fingers picking at a loose thread in my jeans.

His hand found my chin, tilting my face up so I had no choice but to meet his eyes. "I mean it," he murmured. "It doesn't matter what they say because I know the real you. And nothing else matters."

His grip tightened around my hand.

"They can't stop me from loving you."

My breath stalled in my throat.

My heart stilled.

Everything stilled.

"You..." My voice barely came out. "You love me?"

He nodded slowly, his thumb tracing soft circles over my knuckles. "With every fiber of my being. I'm in love with you, Blakely Mason."

I couldn't breathe.

I couldn't think.

My heart flip-flopped inside my chest, skipping beats like it had no idea how to function anymore.

"Jamie, I..." I shook my head, fumbling for words.

His fingers moved from under my chin to brush against my lips. "You don't have to say anything."

I let out a small laugh, shaking my head again. "You misunderstand."

His expression flickered with uncertainty. "Oh."

I inhaled deeply, forcing myself to speak. "I'm not just saying this because you did. I'm not saying it because I feel obligated. You *have* to know—I've been in love with you for years."

Jamie's eyes darkened, his breath hitching.

And then he moved.

One hand threaded into my hair, the other gripping my waist as he pulled me to him. His lips brushed against mine— soft, questioning, like he needed to make sure I meant it.

I did.

I parted my lips, and the second I did, Jamie deepened the kiss, his tongue sweeping against mine in a way that set every nerve in my body on fire. We had kissed countless times before, spent hours wrapped up in each other, but nothing compared to this.

This was desperation.

This was devotion.

This was love.

I had worried that Jamie would think less of me because of the rumors, that he would see me differently.

But he didn't.

He believed in me.

He *loved* me.

And no matter what anyone said, I knew one thing with absolute certainty.

I would always believe in him.

I would always love him.

With every fiber of *my* being.

Chapter Forty

JAMIE

For the first time in a long time, I didn't feel like a storm cloud was hanging over my head. The thoughts that usually haunted me seemed distant, like they had finally loosened their grip.

My mom was happy in her new relationship. Blake had found someone who made her happy. And so far, every person I'd confided in about Noah told me the same thing—there was nothing I could have done to change what happened.

Maybe I wasn't cursed after all.

Yeah, I had endured more tragedy than most people saw in a lifetime. But maybe—just maybe—it wasn't my fault. Maybe it was time to stop punishing myself, to let my walls down. To let someone in again.

Of course, if I had a choice, that person would be Blake.

But I didn't have a choice. Not anymore.

The only thing I could do was be there for her.

I stirred, feeling the familiar weight of Ruger pressed

against my side. His deep brown eyes blinked up at me before he rested his head on my chest.

"Good morning, boy," I said, scratching behind his ears.

His tail thumped lazily against the bed, content. I didn't mind that he slept with me—it made me feel safer, like he stood guard while I rested, keeping my nightmares at bay.

I ruffled his fur. "Who's a good boy?"

He let out a soft huff, his warm breath fanning over me.

Since it was still early, we headed out for a run. I felt lighter than usual, my body moving faster, pushing harder. Ruger matched my pace effortlessly, his tongue lolling as we ran through the quiet streets.

By the time we got back, I threw together a quick breakfast —scrambled eggs for me, grilled chicken for Ruger.

"Bon appétit," I said, even though he had already inhaled his food.

Yeah, I was that guy. The one who believed his dog deserved better than dry kibble every day.

I picked up our dishes and set them on the counter, and that's when I saw it.

A small orange tiger plushie.

Blake had won it for me at the county fair when we were seventeen. She'd been determined to break the stereotype—to be the girl who won a prize for her guy.

I had forgotten I'd unpacked it last night.

For years, it had been buried deep in my deployment bags, or displayed on my dresser. I had taken it with me everywhere— through every base, every mission, every sleepless night. It was my way of holding onto her. Of holding onto who I used to be.

I ran my fingers over the worn fabric, a faint smile tugging at my lips.

Some things never lost their value.

I gave Ruger another pat before heading out. "Be good, buddy," I said, grabbing my keys.

Meetings consumed my morning, one after another, until I barely had time to breathe. By the time I finally sat down at my desk for lunch, my phone rang.

I glanced at the screen and smirked.

"Liam, I'm surprised you're calling this early."

His dry chuckle came through the line. "8AM, you ass. I've been at work for two hours."

"Wow. You have no life, workaholic."

"Takes one to know one."

"Touché."

"I didn't call to bust your balls," he said, though I could hear the amusement in his voice.

"Oh yeah? Then why are you calling? You rarely call me at all."

"My turn to say *touché*."

"Point taken."

"I just wanted to check in," he admitted. "See how you're handling the whole *supporting Blake dating Dean* situation. Made any progress?"

"It's been like, one day, Liam. No."

"Figured. When did you get to be such a sissy?"

I snorted. "You're being extra grumpy this morning. Miss Fayetteville already?"

"Maybe."

"You could always move home."

"Tempting, but no. I'm busy trying to build an empire."

I leaned back in my chair. "Well, now that your focus is in the right place, you shouldn't have trouble with that, right?"

"That's the thing. I can't focus."

Something in his tone caught my attention. It wasn't like Liam to admit something like that. "You okay?"

He sighed, the sound heavy. "I don't know. Maybe it's just jet lag, but... I feel like I lost something."

"You *just* found out your ex-wife is alive and well, and on top of that, she's in a serious relationship with another man. You have every right to be a little off."

"I had my lawyer draw up divorce papers. He just brought them to me."

"Ah. There it is."

"Yeah."

I exhaled slowly. "Sounds like a good day to go drinking."

"It's *eight in the morning*."

"So, early bedtime too. Makes you well-rested for tomorrow."

Liam huffed a quiet laugh. "Nothing's more pathetic than drinking alone."

I knew the feeling all too well. "You really don't have anyone out there to grab a drink with?"

Silence stretched for a few seconds before he let out another sigh. "Sad, isn't it? I've pushed everyone away."

"No," I said quietly. "Sounds like self-preservation at its finest. Something I know well."

Liam was the one person I'd always looked up to—the one who had his life together, the one I never imagined would need advice from *me*.

And yet, here we were.

"So," he asked, "what would *you* do if you were me?"

I thought for a moment before answering. "I'd throw myself into work today. And every time I felt my focus slipping, I'd slap myself and get back to it. Then, when the workday is over, I'd go home, hit the hard stuff, and pass out before my brain has time to play the regret montage."

"Do that one often?"

"Yep. How do you think I've managed to start a foundation, stay in peak physical condition, and still be the overall badass that I am?"

"Humble, aren't you?"

I grinned. "But it worked. Wash, rinse, repeat until you're ready to move on."

"Sounds a little like alcoholism to me."

"Well, you'll be back in two weeks, and I'll set you on the straight and narrow when you get here."

"Oh, I am?"

"Yeah. You agreed to do a charity fashion show to raise money for *The Phoenix Foundation.*"

"... I did?"

"You don't remember?"

"Two weeks is a really short time to throw something together."

"But you're *Liam Knight.* You can do anything. Plus, what a noble reason to throw yourself into work."

He was quiet for a moment before sighing. "You know, you could just ask. You don't have to manipulate me into doing things."

"But where's the fun in that?"

Liam let out a soft chuckle—the first real one since we started talking.

"Fine. Two weeks," he said. "I'm not bringing any new pieces, but I'll raffle off the clothes, and all proceeds will go to your foundation."

A grin spread across my face. "Have I told you how much I love you, man?"

"Don't start with me," he warned. "I've got a busy day ahead of me and a night of drinking to prepare for."

The lightness in his voice told me he'd be okay.

And if he wasn't?

He knew where to find me.

And I knew where to find him.

"You know I'm here for you, right?" I said seriously.

His response was typical Liam—gruff, blunt, but sincere.

"Yeah. Whatever, asshole."

Chapter Forty-One

JAMIE

The rest of my day went smoothly. I resisted the urge to text Blake, reminding myself to give her space.

So, when I got home from work, I took Ruger for a long walk and decided to take some of my own advice—I needed to unwind.

Instead of sitting in my cold, empty apartment, I climbed into my truck and headed into town for a drink. After being in Blake's house last night, surrounded by warmth, memories, and life, my place felt lifeless in comparison. Ruger was my only real source of comfort at home, but tonight, the thought of being alone just didn't sit well with me.

I texted Wes.

Me: *Feel like grabbing a beer?*

A few minutes later, my phone vibrated.

Wes: *Hell yeah, I'm in.*

I smirked, shaking my head. Wes had always been good at sneaking away when he needed a break.

Archway's was exactly what I needed—low-key, familiar, and known for having the best burgers in town. I slid onto a barstool, ordered a beer, and within five minutes, a firm hand landed on my shoulder.

"What's good, brother?"

I turned to see Wes grinning down at me.

"Glad you could make it."

"Yeah, well, Liv isn't happy that I'm ditching her again, but I couldn't pass up a chance to have a beer with my best bro."

I raised a brow. "Is Liv *ever* happy?"

"Whoa, whoa, whoa," he said, holding up a hand. "No girl talk tonight."

"Fine."

Wes paused. "So, how's Blake?"

I shot him a look. "You just said no girl talk."

"I meant *you* couldn't talk about girls. *I* can."

I exhaled through my nose. "I don't think I agreed to that. It's either all or nothing."

"Fine." Wes sighed dramatically, then leaned forward. "Liv seems extra moody these days. I don't know what's gotten into her. I can't seem to make her happy."

Another one of my friends with relationship problems. And *I* was the one they wanted to talk to? What a funny turn of events.

"You're in luck," I said, grinning. "Dr. Jamie is in the house and seeing patients."

Wes punched my arm. "Shut up. I was just asking about Blake. I don't need your help."

"But maybe I *want* to help."

"Like I'd take relationship advice from *you*."

I shrugged. "Take it or leave it, man. Just because I messed things up with Blake doesn't mean I can't see what's going on in your relationship."

Wes scoffed just as the bartender walked up.

"What can I get you guys?"

"I'll have a Bud Light, draft, and the burger," I said.

Wes took a second before nodding. "Yeah, same."

As the bartender walked away, I turned back to Wes. "So, what is it about you that Liv finds so annoying?"

"I don't know. *Maybe everything?*"

"Well, that *really* narrows it down."

"Like I said, I'm not looking for advice."

"Touchy." I changed the subject. "Good news—I convinced Liam to come back in two weeks to put on a fundraiser fashion show for me."

Wes' brows lifted. "Really?"

"Yeah. He didn't even fight me that much."

"What do you need a fundraiser for? Doesn't the military have, like, endless amounts of money?"

"Not exactly," I said. "And the military doesn't run *The Phoenix Foundation,* so they don't fund it. We're volunteer-run and donation-funded, which means we have to hustle for money."

"You should ask Blake to cover the fashion show for the paper," Wes suggested. "Would give you an excuse to spend more time with her."

I scowled. "That's actually a great idea. Thanks."

Wes grinned. "I'm full of them, thank you."

The bartender returned with our drinks, and I held up my glass.

"Cheers, man."

"Cheers."

We clinked our glasses and took a drink. The bar was lively but not overwhelming, with a football game playing on the TV above the counter. The Panthers were up against the Cardinals, and we both fell into comfortable silence as we watched.

I hadn't had time to keep up with football since joining the military, but I'd always loved it. Seeing the players on the field sparked something inside me, a reminder of how much I'd enjoyed the game back in high school.

Maybe I'd look into coaching.

The thought caught me off guard, but... it didn't sound bad. In fact, it sounded like something I might actually enjoy.

Who the hell was I turning into?

The bartender slid our plates in front of us, and we dug in, eating between easy conversation.

"You think Carolina will go far this season?" I asked, gesturing at the screen.

Wes shrugged. "As long as they keep their heads on straight, they've got a shot at the playoffs."

We finished our food, talking stats and team changes until I overheard the guy next to me grumbling about the weather.

"What's this about a storm?" I asked Wes.

He waved a hand dismissively. "You know how it is. The weatherman always makes it sound like the end of the world, and then we get a drizzle. I'm not worried."

I nodded and finished my beer.

Wes stretched, then exhaled heavily. "You think you're ready for a family?"

I blinked at him. "A family?"

"Yeah. A wife. Kids."

I ran a hand through my hair. "I want one, of course. But will I ever be *ready*? Probably not. No one is. I think you just take it as it comes." I huffed out a quiet laugh. "But being single makes that a little difficult."

Wes didn't laugh. He just stared into his beer. "Liv told me she doesn't want kids."

I winced. "Didn't you... already know that?"

He shook his head. "We never talked about it. But Addy and I... we did. We both wanted three or four kids."

"Kids weren't something people *usually* changed their minds about, especially women. Some women just didn't want to go through pregnancy, and that was fair."

"That's what Liv said," Wes muttered. "That she didn't want to ruin her body for a baby."

I stayed quiet, letting his words sink in.

"I just wondered if it was something you thought about," he continued. "Maybe I was crazy for wanting the whole *dream*— white picket fence, a dozen kids running around."

"I don't think you're crazy at all."

In fact, as I pictured it—coming home to someone, being a husband, a *dad*—a longing twisted inside me so fierce, so sharp.

It wasn't something I'd allowed myself to think about in years.

And yet... suddenly, it felt like *everything*.

I swallowed hard and forced my thoughts elsewhere.

Wes flagged the bartender. "Can I grab the check? Sorry to eat and run, but I need to get home."

The bartender set our bills down. "Have a great night."

I threw some cash on the counter and stood. "I should head out, too. Ruger gets worried if I'm out too late."

Wes barked out a laugh. "At least *you* have someone to go home to."

I joined in his laughter, pushing open the door—

And bumped into someone coming in.

"Shit—sorry about that," I said, stepping aside.

Then I heard it.

A voice dripping with hostility.

"Why, if it isn't the man of the hour—Jamie MacIntyre."

A chill shot down my spine.

Dean.

Nicolette Terry

Spitting my name like a curse.

Chapter Forty-Two

Jamie

I couldn't move. My feet were cemented to the pavement as Wes stepped onto the sidewalk beside me. He stopped abruptly when he saw Dean in front of me.

Dean swayed slightly, his eyes bloodshot and filled with rage. He was obviously drunk—but that didn't make sense. Dean was a master of control. He never let himself be vulnerable, especially not in public.

Something had pushed him over the edge.

The sidewalks of downtown Fayetteville were packed with people during the dinner rush. The energy around us buzzed, but as soon as Dean's voice rang out, everything shifted.

"Why did you kill him, Jamie?"

My body stilled. My blood ran cold.

The people passing by slowed their steps, heads turning. A public spectacle was unfolding, and Fayetteville thrived on small-town drama. A crowd began to gather, waiting for the inevitable explosion.

"Dean..." My voice barely left my throat.

"I asked you a question." His face was red, his eyes wild. "Why did you kill my brother?"

A vice tightened around my lungs.

Wes stepped forward, gripping my arm. "Hey. That's not fair. Jamie didn't kill Noah."

Dean didn't hear him. Or maybe he just didn't care. His hateful glare stayed locked on me as he grabbed the collar of my shirt.

"How could you do that to him? You're a disease. A poison that infects everyone you touch."

My breathing picked up, trying—and failing—to match the frantic pace of my heart. My vision darkened, a tunnel closing in around me.

I glanced at the crowd forming around us, familiar faces staring back. People I'd known my whole life. People I'd grown up with. Their expressions hovered somewhere between pity and fear.

They didn't know what to believe.

Their uncertainty burned through me like fire.

The crowd suddenly shifted as someone pushed through. A cop.

Dean let go of my shirt, but didn't move away from me.

"Everything okay, gentlemen?" Officer Lucas Carter asked, looking between us.

"It won't be until this man is behind bars for murdering my brother," Dean spat.

Lucas narrowed his eyes. He recognized Dean's intoxication immediately. He wasn't stupid—he knew our history. Knew that after a few drinks, something like this was bound to happen.

"You two go on home," he said, voice firm. "No one is getting arrested tonight." He turned to Dean with a pointed look. "At least not yet. Make sure you don't drive home."

"But that man is a murderer!" Dean roared. "He killed my brother!"

Lucas sighed, placing a hand on Dean's shoulder. "Come on. Let's get you a ride home."

Dean's voice grew more distant as Lucas guided him toward his squad car. "You can't just let him go free. He could kill someone else!"

The words hung in the air long after he disappeared down the street.

I was frozen. Trapped in the middle of the sidewalk as the world crashed around me.

He's right.

How had I let myself forget?

People *forgiving* me didn't erase the truth. The weight of my sins hadn't disappeared. I was responsible for Noah's death.

Whispers rippled through the onlookers like an unstoppable tide.

Do you think he really did it?

He isn't that sweet kid anymore.

Maybe that's why he and Blake broke up.

I heard he made her get an abortion.

I heard he told her the baby wasn't his.

That whole family hasn't been the same since Scott MacIntyre killed himself. Maybe Jamie really is capable of murder.

A wave of nausea hit me so violently I thought I might throw up right there on the street.

Wes grabbed my arm. "Jamie. Don't do it, man. Don't go back there. You know it wasn't your fault."

But his voice was drowned out by the whispers. By the suffocating weight pressing against my ribs.

I was unraveling.

Wes yanked me away from the crowd and shoved my keys into my hand. "Get in your truck. Go home. Get away from this."

I was on autopilot, numbly nodding as I turned and walked away.

When I opened my apartment door, Ruger greeted me with a friendly yelp, his tail wagging.

But it wasn't just Ruger.

Blake was kneeling in the kitchen, scratching behind his ears.

She looked up at me, standing quickly. A soft blush colored her cheeks. "Sorry. I didn't mean to just let myself in." She fidgeted. "One of the maintenance guys was unlocking your door when I got here. He let me in—probably thought I lived here too. He said he needed to inspect your fire alarms. But once I got inside, I couldn't leave this pretty puppy all alone."

She smiled at Ruger, giving him one last scratch.

Normally, the sight would have warmed my chest. Ruger was fiercely protective of our space. If he'd let Blake in, it meant something. Animals didn't trust just anyone.

But tonight, I felt nothing.

I just stared at her, waiting for her to explain why she was here.

She cleared her throat and rubbed her arm. I knew I was making her uncomfortable, but I couldn't bring myself to care.

"I came to show you something," she said hesitantly. "But then I saw this on your counter." She gestured toward the plushie. "I can't believe you still have it."

The tiger.

The one I'd taken with me *everywhere.*

I didn't want to talk about the past. Didn't want to sit here and pretend things between us weren't completely fucked.

"Jamie?" Blake's voice softened. "Are you okay?"

"Fine." The word was clipped, hollow. "What did you need?"

She recoiled slightly, like I'd struck her.

"I... I'm sorry to bother you." She wrung her hands, biting her lip.

I clenched my jaw. "Can you just tell me what you came for so you can leave?"

The color drained from her face. I knew—*knew*—I was being cruel. Knew I'd hate myself for it later. But the darkness inside me didn't care.

"Blake. What do you need?"

She straightened her shoulders. "I'm sorry for bothering you."

"Then leave."

Her breath hitched. Tears welled in her eyes.

She turned on her heel and walked out. The door slammed behind her.

Still, I felt nothing.

Sensing my unease, Ruger pressed his head against my leg, his silent way of offering comfort.

I moved into the kitchen, eyes landing on the plush tiger. That's when I saw it.

A small stack of papers, freshly printed.

I picked them up, skimming the title:

Doing Better for Our Service Members: The Phoenix Foundation

By Blakely Mason

Her article.

She'd come here to show me her finished piece. She hadn't

even turned it in yet. She'd probably wanted to make sure the details were right. That was the kind of journalist she was.

My hand trembled as I read.

Blake had taken the most important thing I'd ever done with my life and written about it with the kind of understanding only she could give.

My throat tightened, bile rising as I forced down the emotions clawing their way up.

I turned my back to the counter and slid to the floor. Ruger was at my side in an instant, his worried eyes locked on me.

Pulling my knees to my chest, I rested my arms on them, clutching Blake's article in my shaking hands.

And then, for the first time in years, I laid my head down and let myself break.

I let myself cry.

Chapter Forty-Three

Blakely

That night, my sleep was dreamless. Maybe it was from sheer exhaustion after spending hours curled up on the couch, drowning in self-pity. Or maybe it was because I was just... drained.

I'd been excited to show Jamie the article on his project, eager to share how it had come together. But instead of getting that moment, he had pushed me out before I even had the chance.

I'd fought back my tears on the drive home, but the second I stepped through my front door, the dam broke. I collapsed onto the couch, sobbing into my hands as the weight of it all pressed in on me.

Something had happened to Jamie last night—something bad. That much was obvious. He wasn't the same man who had shown up at my house Wednesday night, full of warmth and teasing smiles. But knowing that didn't make his rejection hurt any less. I had expected it in the beginning, braced myself for his usual push-and-pull, but slowly, he had worn me down. Letting myself trust him again, even just as a friend, had been a mistake.

I finally dragged myself to bed, completely spent, and slept straight through my alarm.

Despite running late for work, I still stopped at Starbucks.

As I drove, the radio warned of the incoming storm. The forecast called for high winds, heavy rain, and even the possibility of tornadoes. Everyone was advised to use caution, but I had little faith in the weatherman's accuracy.

I eyed the sky skeptically as I walked into the café, already doubting the warning. The morning was too bright, too beautiful to believe a storm was coming.

But the second I stepped inside, something felt... off.

People glanced at me, then quickly looked away, as if they'd been caught talking behind my back. It should have been my first clue, but I was too focused on getting my coffee to pay attention.

That was, until I heard the whispers.

Jamie's name.

I turned, scanning the café until I found the source—Mrs. Jenkins and Mrs. Brown, huddled near the pastry case, their heads bent together. The second they noticed me watching, their eyes widened.

I had no patience for gossip. Not after everything I had been through. Not after knowing firsthand how cruel rumors could be.

"And what exactly were you saying about Mr. MacIntyre?" I asked, my voice sharp and direct.

Mrs. Jenkins glanced at Mrs. Brown before answering. "We were only talking about what happened last night."

My stomach tightened. "What happened last night?"

Mrs. Brown leaned in slightly, her expression smug, like she was relishing the chance to share.

"You know, the fight," she said.

Ice spread through my veins.

I had no idea what they were talking about. I had spent the morning forcing Jamie from my mind, but now, I was being dragged back in.

"Mrs. Jenkins, what do you mean?"

She pursed her lips. "I'm surprised Dean didn't tell you, since he was involved."

"What?" My voice barely came out.

Mrs. Jenkins' eyes gleamed, delighted to be the one delivering the story. "Last night, Dean and Jamie got into it downtown. People saw them arguing in the street. Dean was yelling about Noah, saying Jamie was a murderer. Things got heated, and the police had to step in before it turned violent. No one knows exactly what started it, but my friend who was there said she heard your name come up."

My breath caught.

Mrs. Jenkins took my silence as an invitation to keep going. "I can't believe Jamie wasn't arrested. Dean is a saint for letting him walk free, but I don't know how I feel about having someone so violent in our town."

Mrs. Brown tsked beside her. "I never knew Jamie was capable of such terrible things. I can't believe he killed his best friend. When I saw him at Noah's funeral, he looked so upset. Now we all know it was just an act."

"Makes you wonder if his father's death was really a suicide or something else," Mrs. Jenkins mused.

That was it.

My fists clenched. "You can't be serious." My voice came out louder than I intended, sharp with anger. "Are you actually suggesting Jamie killed his father? Or that he killed Noah? Do you have any idea what Jamie has been through? What he's sacrificed for this country—for you?" My pulse thundered. "How dare you? You don't deserve his sacrifice."

Neither of them spoke. They just stared, wide-eyed, as I turned on my heel and walked out.

I forgot all about my coffee.

My hands trembled as I gripped the steering wheel, but the adrenaline carried me straight to Dean's office.

I flung open the door to Dean's office, startling Stephanie, the receptionist.

"Ms. Mason, how are you?" she asked, wide-eyed, clearly trying to mask her shock.

"I hope Dean is available right now, because I'm going in whether he is or not."

I didn't wait for a response, striding past her desk and down the hall.

Dean was a successful lawyer, known for taking care of his clients and winning cases. I had always admired his tenacity, convinced that his determination came from a genuine desire to help people. But now? Now I wasn't so sure.

Maybe it was never about justice—maybe he just hated to lose.

I shoved open the door to his office without knocking. Dean's head snapped up, irritation flashing across his face.

"I'll call you back," he said into the phone, his gaze locked onto mine. "No, I'm fine. Blake just walked in."

He set his phone down and studied me, his scowl deepening.

Looking at him, a wave of emotions crashed over me—anger, pity, sadness, resentment, and bittersweetness.

I loved him. I did. I had only ever wanted the best for him.

So how had he become a stranger?

How had we drifted so far apart without even realizing it?

Noah's death had changed everything, forcing us to see ourselves—and each other—differently. And in doing so, it had exposed the cracks we'd been too blind, or maybe too afraid, to acknowledge.

"What's up?" he asked, his tone edged with annoyance.

"We need to talk."

"I gathered that much. It's not like you to barge in here like this." He gestured toward the chair across from his desk, the one he reserved for the clients he needed to intimidate or impress.

Since I was neither, I refused. "I'll stand. This won't take long."

For the first time since I'd stormed in, something flickered across his expression—something unsettled. Proof that the Dean I had once loved was still in there somewhere.

"Okay," he said warily.

I wasn't sure where to start, so I just plunged right in. "Dean, what happened last night?"

He snorted, crossing his arms over his chest. And just like that, cocky Dean was back.

"What do you mean?"

"Don't play games with me. What happened last night?"

"Well, you obviously already heard about it, so the town gossips must be doing their job." He narrowed his eyes. "Unless Jamie told you."

"Jamie is not the point of this conversation."

Dean smirked. "But I have a feeling he will be."

I sneered right back. "I don't know what you mean by that."

He laughed, leaning back in his chair. "Last night, I ran into Jamie. I'd been drinking. Nothing wrong with drowning my sorrows every now and then." He shrugged. "Anyway, I told him exactly what I thought of him—every word I could muster in my drunken state. It's not my fault we drew a crowd. Or that Officer Carter happened to walk by and decided to step in."

"Officer Carter?" I asked, my stomach twisting. "Why was he involved?"

"He was on patrol, Blake. He wasn't there to arrest anyone —just to break up a scene. He's the one who drove me home."

I stared at him. "Why didn't you call me? You knew I was home all night." My voice came out quiet, a whisper of realization.

Dean just shrugged.

"You're starting rumors and trying to hurt someone on purpose," I said, my anger rising. "You can't possibly think that's okay."

Another shrug. "I don't see why you even care about Jamie. He hurt you. Badly."

How could I explain my past to him? The trauma I had carried since high school? The pain I had endured because someone wanted to hurt me—for entertainment, for revenge, just because they could.

Dean's gaze sharpened. "Why, Blake? Spit it out."

I lifted my chin. "I guess you don't remember that I was the victim of cruel rumors and bullying in high school."

His eyes widened slightly. I had finally stunned him.

"So, it doesn't matter if you're spreading lies about Jamie or someone else. I would be just as upset if it were anyone."

Dean scoffed, crossing his arms. "I doubt that." He tilted his head, studying me. "Now that you say it, I do remember you being bullied. But why haven't you ever talked about it? Not once in all these years?"

"Why would I?" I shot back. "You think I should've sat you down and relived every horrible memory just to satisfy your curiosity?"

"You're asking me to open up about my feelings, but you won't do the same?"

I exhaled sharply, my frustration mounting. "That's not the same, and you know it."

Silence stretched between us.

I swallowed hard, gathering my courage. "Dean... we're not the same people we were when we first got together. We don't want the same things anymore. We never used to argue like this. We were happy." I gestured between us, my voice breaking. "What the hell happened to us?"

Dean's jaw tightened. "You really don't know?"

I crossed my arms. "Why don't you enlighten me?"

He leaned forward, his eyes burning into mine. "Things changed when Jamie came home."

I groaned, exasperated. "Jamie again? Why do you keep bringing him into this? You're mad about me bringing him up, but you're the one who won't stop talking about him!"

"Because I trusted you," he snapped. "I trusted you to be faithful. I trusted you to have my back and to support me."

He slammed his fist on the desk and stood abruptly, his anger pulsing through the room.

"I trusted you," he repeated. "And you broke that the moment you let him back into your life."

"It was for work, Dean. Stop being dramatic."

He laughed bitterly. "Oh, cut the shit, Blake. It wasn't just for work, and we both know it. The phone calls, the little meetings, the truck test drives? You still love him. Hell, you probably love him more than you ever loved me."

I couldn't answer.

Because maybe, deep down, he was right.

His eyes darkened. "And that's what makes this worse. Jamie killed my brother, and you ran straight to him. You should have been by my side, but instead, you were by his."

He turned away, staring out the window. His voice dropped, quiet but razor-sharp.

"Sometimes I feel like I can't even look at you."

His words sliced through me, and I sucked in a sharp breath. Tears burned the backs of my eyes. "I never meant to hurt you."

Dean let out a low, bitter chuckle. "And yet, somehow, you were too busy worrying about Jamie to notice how deeply you were hurting me." He exhaled hard, scrubbing a hand over his face. "You know what? It doesn't even matter anymore."

I shook my head, barely able to comprehend the finality in his tone.

Dean met my gaze, his expression eerily calm. "As much as I love you, and as much as I wanted a future with you, it's obvious we're no longer on that path." He picked up his phone. "I'll get your things together and have them sent to you."

The emotion was gone from his face, his voice, his entire being.

And just like that, it was over.

Dean didn't even look up as he pressed his phone to his ear.

"If you don't mind," he said flatly, "I have a call to make."

I swallowed past the lump in my throat and turned for the door.

I shut it softly behind me, feeling emptier than ever.

Chapter Forty-Four

JAMIE

Hell.

Fire, brimstone, and self-loathing. That was where I sat as I tried to look busy at my desk, even though my mind refused to focus on anything other than the look in Dean's eyes as he called me a murderer.

I was stuck in my own personal version of hell.

The word *murderer* had followed me into my dreams and clung to me through the morning. Standing in line for coffee had been an exercise in restraint as people openly stared, whispering behind their hands. No one stood too close. It was as if they thought getting near me might make them *catch* the murderer disease. Or worse—maybe they feared that if I got emotional, I'd turn on them next.

I sighed, dropping my head into my hands.

Dean's words had gutted me, but the worst part?

I had told myself those same things a thousand times before.

Only now, hearing them from someone else, they had weight. They weren't just intrusive thoughts whispering in the back of my mind—they were *real*.

I had been *starting* to let people in again. Finally at the place Noah had wanted me to be. But in all those years of keeping my distance, I had never been hurt by another person.

And right now? That solitude sounded better and better.

"MacIntyre."

I looked up as CMSgt Campbell walked into my office.

I stood. "Hey, Chief. What's up?"

"The base is releasing everyone early—bad weather rolling in. Pack up and head home. Take your laptop in case anything pops off."

"You think it's really going to get that bad?" I glanced at the window. A few clouds had started to gather, but it didn't look ominous yet.

Chief shrugged. "Who knows. They're calling for severe thunderstorms, possible hail. But you know how reliable weather guys are. Either way, enjoy the rest of the day off. Go, relax or something. I'll call you if I need anything."

It wasn't unusual for the base to close early for bad weather, especially in the South. Snow, hurricane rains, ice—if there was even a *chance* of dangerous road conditions, they erred on the side of caution.

"Yes, sir. Have a good weekend, Chief."

"You too, MacIntyre."

I watched him leave, but something about this didn't sit right.

The hairs on the back of my neck lifted as I glanced at the dark clouds rolling in.

Shaking off the unease, I packed my laptop and headed out.

The wind had picked up slightly, carrying the thick scent of coming rain. The air felt damp and heavy, clinging to my skin as I crossed the lot. By the time I reached my truck, the first raindrops started to fall.

Great.

I had things to do—prep for the fashion show fundraiser, finalize a few details—and now half the town would be shutting down because of the storm. Not to mention, I still had to pick up Ruger from the groomer, and I *knew* he was going to be pissed. Nothing like a freshly groomed dog getting dumped into the middle of a downpour.

And I was right.

Ruger made his displeasure known the second I lifted him into the truck, shaking himself off *everywhere*.

"It's okay, boy," I ran a hand over his head as I pulled onto the road. "The rain'll be gone by tomorrow."

But even as I said it, I wasn't so sure.

The further I drove, the worse the storm got. By the time we pulled into the apartment complex, the sky had *opened up*, sheets of rain hammering the pavement. The wind howled, and the first crack of thunder rumbled overhead like Zeus himself had decided to pick a fight.

"I guess it's gonna storm after all," I muttered as I parked, cutting the engine.

Ruger whined as I helped him down, both of us rushing toward the stairs.

Then, just as I reached my door—

I froze.

My breath caught as I realized something was *off*.

The lock.

It had been pried open.

Someone had broken into my apartment.

My pulse slammed into high gear, my breathing shallow. Ruger's ears perked, his body stiffening beside me. He wasn't wagging his tail or leaning into me for comfort—he was at full attention.

Unlike yesterday, when he had greeted Blake like an old friend, *this* time was different.

This time, he was ready to attack.

I gripped the handle of my Gerber knife, flipping out the blade with one smooth motion.

Breathe.

Count backward from ten.

It was a trick I had learned overseas—going into a situation worked up never ended well.

Ten...

Nine...

I forced air through my nose, steadying myself.

Eight...

One last deep breath.

I reached for the doorknob and eased the door open.

A gust of wind slammed into my back as the storm raged behind me.

Lightning streaked across the sky, flooding my apartment in *blinding* white light.

And sitting on my couch—

A shadowed figure.

Waiting.

Someone was inside.

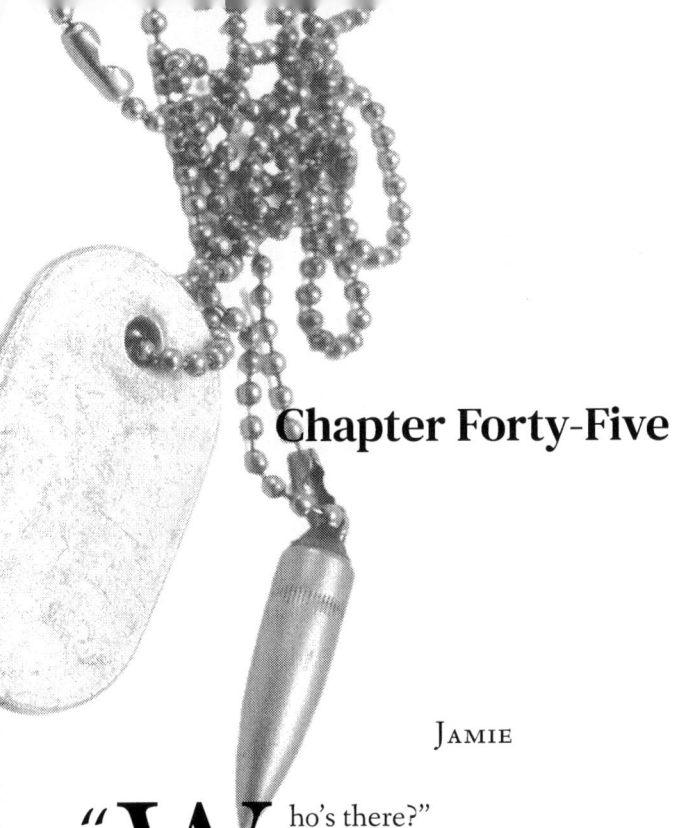

Chapter Forty-Five

JAMIE

"Who's there?"

The figure shifted, and I braced myself for an attack. Ruger growled low in his throat, his stance rigid, muscles coiled. But all the figure did was raise his hand.

"Who are you? What do you want?"

"Jesus, calm down," the voice scoffed. "No one's here to rob you of your measly belongings."

I knew that voice.

"Dean?"

"Don't sound so surprised."

I pushed the door open fully and stepped inside. Lightning flashed, illuminating the room in stark white light. Dean sat in one of my living room chairs, still dressed from work, but his hair was disheveled, the top buttons of his collared shirt undone. He looked... off.

"Hope you don't mind," he said, holding up a glass. Ice

cubes clinked against the sides as he swirled the liquid. "I helped myself to a drink while I waited. This shit is terrible, by the way. Can't you afford something better?"

"I don't drink anymore."

Dean let out a derisive snort before tossing back the rest of his drink.

I didn't move from my spot by the door. Something felt wrong. My instincts, sharpened from years of knowing when a situation could go sideways, told me not to ignore it. I signaled Ruger to sit, and he obeyed, but his body remained tense, his lips curled just enough to show his teeth.

I kept my knife hidden in my hand, but I knew, deep down, if Dean had come for revenge, I wouldn't stop him. If I could take his pain—his family's pain—and make it my own, I would. Just as Noah had done for me.

Dean stood, setting the empty glass on the counter. He looked completely at home, like he belonged here. Like he had a right to be in my space.

"What do you want, Dean?"

The rain lashed against the windows, the wind howling with a vengeance.

"I came for justice." His voice was steady. "Justice for Noah. For my family."

A strange sense of relief settled over me.

If this was it—if this was the moment I finally paid for everything—I wouldn't fight it.

I stepped toward him, closed my knife, and shoved it into my pocket. "Do your worst."

In the distance, a siren blared. A warning. But neither of us paid it any mind.

We were too deep in our own personal storm.

Dean's jaw clenched, his fists curling at his sides. "I want to know. How could you do that to someone who trusted you?

Someone you claimed to care about? It's your fault he's dead!"

"Yes," I said, the word barely above a whisper. "It is."

Dean pulled a knife from his pocket, the blade catching the dim light. He held it steady—too steady. His grip was sure, his body eerily still.

Ruger jumped to his feet, ready to launch, but I grabbed his collar. Not yet.

"Noah knew you were messed up," Dean spat. "He told me himself. He knew you were dangerous to be around."

"Noah always seemed to know me better than I knew myself."

Dean's lip curled in disgust. "And you let him stay anyway? When you knew it would hurt him? What kind of piece of shit are you?"

He stepped closer. I held his gaze, letting the shame settle in my bones.

Outside, the storm raged. The wind screamed. The rain slammed against the glass like a fist. Lightning split the sky, illuminating Dean's face just enough for me to see the fury in his eyes.

"He trusted you." His voice rose with each word, raw and guttural. "He believed in you. He thought you were a good person. You let him down when you should have protected him."

I squeezed my eyes shut, but it didn't stop the memories from flashing behind my lids.

Noah pushing me aside. The sound of the gunshot.

The way his body jerked before collapsing into my arms.

The blood. So much blood.

"He looked up to you, and you killed him!"

"I did everything I could!" The words burst from my chest like a battle cry. "I did everything I could to save him! I have replayed those minutes over and over, trying to find a way to change it. To stop it. To save him. But every time, all I see is Noah taking the bullet meant for me. Noah dying in my arms. Me, helpless to stop it."

The air between us went still.

Dean's chest heaved, his face so much like Noah's it physically hurt to look at him.

Tears tracked silently down his cheeks.

I did everything I could.

I dropped my gaze to Ruger, his wet nose pressing against my palm, grounding me. I ran a hand over his head, the motion automatic, familiar. Steadying.

"So do what you will," I said, my voice barely audible over the storm. "I won't stop you."

Dean's breath shuddered. "It wasn't just Noah you took from me."

His next words sliced into me.

"You took Blake, too."

I flinched. "Blake?"

"She's been slipping away since you came back. Moving toward you, away from me." His voice was bitter, the pain thick beneath the anger.

He reached into his coat pocket and pulled out a familiar book.

Jane Eyre.

Blake's copy.

Dean turned it over in his hands, his lips curling as he studied the worn pages.

"She reads this all the time. I never thought much of it." His grip tightened. "Until I dropped it, and the book flipped open to the dedication." He flipped it toward me. "From 'your Jamie.'"

My stomach twisted.

Dean pulled a piece of folded paper from the back cover. The moment I saw the slanted handwriting, I knew. A love letter. One I had written to Blake years ago.

My throat went dry.

"She kept this," Dean read the words like they physically pained him. "All these years."

He crushed the note in his fist before tossing it to the floor, his face twisting in disgust. "I have loved her since we were kids. You stole her from me then. And once I finally had her, you stole her from me again."

His voice turned venomous. "Although now, looking back... maybe I never really had her at all."

Something inside me cracked at the truth of it.

Dean's eyes snapped back to mine, burning with fury. "I am no one's stand-in." He pulled the knife higher, pointing it at my chest. "I deserve more than that."

"You're right," I said quietly. "You do."

Dean's grip tightened. His knuckles turned white.

He exhaled sharply, eyes wild. "Everything leads back to you, MacIntyre." His voice was ice. "You stole my brother. You stole Blake. You have taken everything from me."

The knife inched closer.

Ruger let out a sharp, warning yelp—

And then everything shifted.

The air grew heavy, suffocating. The pressure in the room dropped so fast my ears popped.

Ruger snapped to attention, nose pointing toward the window.

I followed his gaze—

And felt my blood turn to ice.

A massive, churning funnel cloud barreled toward us.

Dark. Ominous. Alive.

For the first time in my life, I felt true, unshakable fear.

"Run!" I lunged for Dean, shoving him toward the hallway.

He stumbled, tripping over his own feet as I dragged him toward the bathroom and pushed him and Ruger into the tub.

The storm was here.

And it wasn't going to leave anything behind.

The wind screamed through the cracks of my apartment, the roar drowning out even my own thoughts. I tightened my hold over the tub, my body a shield between the storm and the two lives beneath me. Debris slammed against the walls, glass shattered, and the very foundation of my world groaned under the pressure.

Ruger whined beneath me, his body pressed against Dean's, and I could barely hear Dean's sharp, panicked breaths over the chaos.

Hold on. That was the only thought repeating in my head. Hold on.

The walls trembled, and then, with a deafening crack, the roof tore away.

The suction was instant. A force stronger than anything I had ever fought against ripped at my body, trying to tear me away, trying to pull me into the churning vortex above.

I clung to the edges of the tub, my fingers digging into the slick porcelain. My muscles screamed from the strain. Dean's hands latched onto my shirt, gripping me like a lifeline.

"Jamie!" His voice was raw, barely audible over the howling wind. "Don't let go!"

"I won't," I gritted out, though I wasn't sure if I was reassuring him or myself.

Another explosion of sound—something massive slammed into my apartment, the impact sending shockwaves through my bones.

The Story That Ties Us

The world around me was unrecognizable. Darkness. Debris. The relentless pull of the storm.

And then—silence.

Chapter Forty-Six

BLAKELY

After seeing Dean that morning, I went to work determined to finish my article on Noah. I told myself I could set aside my personal drama—just long enough to get it done. The deadline was looming, and yet, every time I tried to put words on the page, they got harder and harder to write.

I couldn't talk about Noah without thinking of Dean and his family. And every time my mind went there, it inevitably jumped to Jamie—because he was there when Noah died.

It was a never-ending cycle.

John thought I was the best person to write this article because I had been so close to Noah. But maybe that was exactly why I shouldn't be writing it.

After two wasted hours, I finally caved and asked John if I could take the rest of the day off. He barely looked up from his desk before waving me away. He had already planned to send everyone home early because of the storm, unwilling to take any risks with his staff's safety.

Stepping outside, I pulled my jacket tighter around me as I walked to my car. The storm had rolled in fast—too fast. Thunder cracked overhead, and the air buzzed with static, leaving the fine hairs on my arms standing on end.

I started my car, shivering as an odd chill settled deep in my bones.

The sky was eerie—that unsettling in-between of dark and light, when everything feels just a little... wrong.

The wind howled, rocking my car slightly. I gripped the steering wheel, unnerved.

No wonder John had shut down the office early.

But as I sat there, staring out at the storm through the windshield, I felt the weight of something heavier than the weather pressing down on me.

I didn't want to go home.

The thought of sitting alone in that empty house while a storm raged outside left me feeling... hollow. My mind was already in shambles after the last two weeks. If I sat in that silence too long, I might drown in it.

I backed out of the parking lot, with no real destination in mind.

Dean? No. We had been too angry this morning. We needed space.

Kate? She was still at work, no doubt wrapping things up with a tight-lipped determination. I didn't want to get in her way.

My fingers tightened on the wheel.

I had no one.

For the first time in a long time, I ached for Cadence.

Without thinking, I kept driving. The city blurred past in

streaks of gray and muted headlights. It wasn't until I stopped at a red light that I realized where I had been going all along.

Jamie's apartment.

I dropped my head to the steering wheel, exhaling shakily.

I guess that answered that question.

The light turned green. A strong gust of wind slammed into the side of my car, making it sway.

Cars weren't supposed to move like that.

My stomach twisted as I squinted through the rain-streaked glass. The storm was worsening—fast. And I was still a few minutes from Jamie's place.

I should turn back.

I should go home.

Instead, I gritted my teeth and pressed forward.

The sirens started wailing.

My radio cut out, then came back, repeating the same automated tornado warning over and over. My fingers went numb around the wheel.

I could see Jamie's apartment complex in the distance—just barely—but a massive wall of black clouds was racing toward me, swallowing the horizon.

The rain became a solid sheet, blinding me.

I couldn't see.

My breath hitched as panic flooded my system. For the first time, I felt truly afraid.

I didn't have time to think.

Instinct took over.

I yanked the wheel, veering off the road just as the wind roared, ripping across the pavement. My tires skidded before I slammed the car into park.

I threw the door open and ran.

Down into the ditch. Into the wet grass.

I barely had time to cover my head before the sound hit me like a train.

A tornado doesn't sound like a freight train. That's a lie.

It screams.

A guttural, rage-filled howl that tears through everything in its path. A noise that would follow me into my nightmares. It cried out as if it were in pain as it ransacked the earth in its version of justice.

I curled in on myself, arms over my head, body shaking as the wind roared around me. My jacket did nothing to stop the rain. The ground beneath me was pure mud.

But I didn't move. I couldn't move.

Time stretched. Warped.

Maybe it was minutes. Maybe it was hours.

Debris pelted my body—small things, wood, paper, bits of who-knows-what. I barely registered it.

Then, just as suddenly as it had come—the wind was gone.

I peeled my face from the soaked ground, forcing my arms to move. My legs trembled as I pushed myself up, gasping for air.

And then I saw it.

Jamie's apartment complex was—pure carnage.

My legs buckled. I collapsed back onto the ground.

No. No. No.

The destruction looked like something from a war zone. The roofs were peeled back. Walls had been ripped clean off. Debris was everywhere—trees, broken glass, chunks of drywall. Personal belongings were scattered like dandelion fuzz, ripped from homes and tossed into the streets.

A strangled, broken sound ripped from my throat.

I was on my feet before I even realized I was moving.

I didn't think.

I didn't stop.

I just ran.

The closer I got, the heavier my limbs felt, like cement had filled my veins.

People were emerging from what was left of their homes. They stumbled out of doorways, dazed, their faces slack with shock.

I ignored them.

I only had one goal.

Jamie.

He was here. He had to be here. He wouldn't have left.

I spotted his truck, still parked in front of the complex.

Hope shattered.

A sharp, burning pain stabbed through my chest.

No.

Please, no.

I just got him back.

I had spent years mourning Jamie—grieving him as though he had died. I had finally let myself forgive him. We had just found our way back to each other.

He couldn't be gone now.

Not like this.

My breathing hitched. The panic built—too fast.

The world tilted.

Darkness rushed up to meet me.

I was unconscious before I even hit the ground.

I woke sometime later, disoriented and convinced I'd just had the worst nightmare. But as my mind surfaced from the haze, the steady beeping of machines pulled me back to reality.

My head throbbed, my mouth felt like sandpaper, and the

scratchy hospital gown irritated my skin. I ached to be in my own bed, in my own pajamas—somewhere familiar.

I reached for the call button, pressing it with sluggish fingers. I needed to get out of here.

A nurse appeared seconds later, offering a warm but professional smile. "Glad to see you're awake, Ms. Mason." She moved to my bedside, checking my vitals with practiced efficiency.

"I want to go home." My voice was hoarse, unfamiliar—even to me.

She shook her head gently. "I'm sorry, but we need to keep you overnight for observation. You took a pretty bad hit to the head. It took ten stitches to close the wound."

I blinked, trying to process her words. "What?"

Instinctively, I reached up, my fingers grazing my scalp—then winced. A dull, radiating pain bloomed beneath my touch.

The nurse continued her work, speaking as she moved. "I'm guessing you didn't even realize you were hurt. The ambulance brought you in from an apartment complex, along with a few others. I can't imagine what you went through."

Her words snapped my foggy brain into focus.

Others?

My heart slammed against my ribs as I struggled to sit up. "You said they brought in other people—" I swallowed, my throat constricting. "Was Jamie... was Jamie MacIntyre one of them?"

The fear clawed up my chest.

What if I had lost him?

What if I never saw those gray eyes again? Never heard him say my name?

The nurse's expression softened. "I'm sorry, but I can't disclose patient information without consent. I can only tell you that five people were brought in from the same complex."

She hesitated, then added, "The paramedics mentioned a guy who refused treatment, even though he was visibly injured. He was more worried about helping everyone else."

A breathless, choked laugh escaped me before I could stop it. The motion sent a sharp jolt of pain through my skull, making me wince. "That sounds exactly like him."

The nurse smiled. "There have been no reported fatalities from the tornado so far. That should set your mind at ease."

Relief washed over me, leaving me exhausted in its wake.

I managed a weak smile. "Thank you."

The moment my head hit the pillow, the tension drained from my body. My heavy eyelids fluttered shut, and I surrendered to sleep—grateful, relieved, and just a little bit hopeful.

I woke up late the next day, stiff and uncomfortable. My head still throbbed from the stitches, and I was more than ready to go home. I sat anxiously in bed, waiting for the neurologist to complete the exam that would determine whether I could be discharged.

As I picked at my mediocre hospital breakfast, a timid knock sounded at the door.

"Come in," I called, not bothering to look up. Nurses had been in and out all night, and I figured this was just another routine check.

The door clicked shut.

"Hey."

I turned at the sound of the familiar voice.

Dean stood near the door, dressed casually in jeans and a sweater. His hands were tucked into his pockets, his body language radiating discomfort.

I set my fork down, pushing the tray aside. Turning toward him, I waited for him to speak.

"I wasn't sure if I should come or not," he admitted.

"No, I'm glad you did." And I was. After everything, it was nice to see a familiar face.

Dean shifted slightly. "They're limiting visitors in the hospital right now. I had to use my connections to get in here."

"Did your mom get you in?"

"Yeah. She did."

I wasn't surprised. Dean's mom worked as a nurse in the cardiac wing—of course, she had enough pull to get him past the restrictions.

But why were they limiting visitors? Before I could ask, Dean answered the question.

"They're only allowing family because of the influx of patients," he explained. "A lot of people got hurt in the tornado, and this was the best way to make sure everyone gets the care they need."

That made sense. Fewer bodies in the hospital meant less chaos, less confusion. And it eased some of the quiet worry I hadn't allowed myself to acknowledge.

"At least it helps keep things under control," I murmured.

Dean nodded. Silence settled between us, thick and uncertain. Then he took a few steps closer, stopping at the edge of my bed.

I gestured for him to sit, and after a slight hesitation, he did.

"Dean, I'm sorry about yesterday," I said softly.

But he shook his head. "No, please, let me." He cleared his throat, looking down at his hands. "I'm sorry for the way I acted. I've been so overwhelmed with losing Noah, I couldn't see past my own pain. I didn't stop to think about anyone else."

My chest ached at the raw honesty in his voice.

"It's okay, Dean," I told him. "You weren't wrong to feel

those things. You lost your brother. And I did reach out to Jamie—I did see him. Your emotions were valid."

"But my actions weren't." His jaw tightened, his fingers tapping restlessly against his thigh. "But don't worry. I've had my come-to-Jesus moment, and I can see a little clearer now." He exhaled, shifting forward. "I need to take time to deal with my grief and pain. But until I overcome it..." He hesitated, then met my gaze. "I think it's best if we still part ways."

I nodded, swallowing past the tightness in my throat. I hadn't had much time to process our breakup, to really sit with what it meant. But maybe that was a blessing.

Dean reached into his jacket and pulled out a book, setting it gently on the bed beside me.

I sucked in a sharp breath.

Jane Eyre.

The cover was scratched and torn in places it hadn't been before. The pages were warped, wavy from water damage.

I looked at him, confused. "What happened to it?"

Dean shrugged. "Long story. Maybe we save it for another day."

Something about the way he said it made me pause. His voice was even, but there was a weight behind his words—like he was telling me something without actually saying it.

I studied him. He looked exhausted, the bags under his eyes darker than I had ever seen them.

"Dean... is everything okay? Did something happen? Was someone hurt?"

He shook his head. "No. Everyone is fine. Everything is okay." His lips pressed into a thin line before he added, "I just wanted to bring this back to you. I know how much it means to you."

I swallowed hard, running my fingers over the frayed edges of the book.

Dean watched me for a moment, then stood, straightening his shoulders. "I need to work on myself," he said. "To become a better person. A person worthy of someone like you."

I offered him a small smile, even as my throat tightened. "I'll be waiting."

Dean smiled back—but it didn't reach his eyes. Instead, his gaze softened, filled with something distant and unreadable. He studied me for a long second, like he was trying to memorize everything about me in that fleeting moment.

Like he would never see me again.

"I doubt that."

My stomach twisted. "What?"

"Nothing." Dean shook his head. "Get some rest, Blake."

He turned toward the door.

"I'll talk to you soon," he added over his shoulder.

I watched him go, an odd sense of finality settling in my chest.

"Bye, Dean," I murmured. "And... thanks for bringing this by. It means a lot."

With a curt nod, he disappeared through the doorway.

The moment I was alone again, I let out a deep sigh, sinking back into the pillows.

I knew I would have to process everything eventually. But right now, I was so damn tired.

Thinking—feeling—took more energy than I had to give.

It felt too good to let my eyelids close, so I didn't open them when a nurse came in to take my vitals.

Chapter Forty-Seven

BLAKELY

Being in a hospital was a unique form of torture. The food was terrible, the machines were noisy, and the beds were so uncomfortable that, despite being a place meant for people to get better, you could hardly rest.

To my surprise, Mrs. Richey was the one who came in to discharge me. And to my even bigger surprise, she handed me my cell phone, my favorite leggings and sweater, my Ugg boots, and—best of all—my car keys.

"Dean," she said simply, as if that explained everything.

She reviewed my discharge orders, running through the usual warnings: come back if you feel dizzy, confused, or lethargic; get plenty of rest; drink lots of water.

But she didn't mention a single thing about Dean and me breaking up.

Had he not told her yet? It had only happened yesterday, and with the tornado, it probably wasn't high on his priority list. Still, it felt like a small blessing. I didn't have the energy to deal with any awkward "mom of your ex-boyfriend" conversations.

Before leaving, Mrs. Richey reached out and gave my hand a squeeze. "Now, Blake, if you need anything—anything at all—you just call me, okay?"

"Thank you, Mrs. Richey," I said automatically. "I will."

I wouldn't. But I appreciated the sentiment.

She gave me a knowing look. "You know we'll always be here for you. No matter what happens."

She pulled me into a warm embrace, pressing a kiss to the top of my head before walking out the door. I blinked back the sudden sting of tears.

After changing into my clean clothes, I finally felt like myself again. Then I picked up my phone... and my heart stopped.

Jamie.

> I can't stop thinking about you. I'm sick with worry. Please call me when you can. I need to hear your voice.

His words hit me like a punch to the chest. The anguish and desperation were clear, and my first instinct was to call him back, to reassure him that I was okay.

But... I wasn't ready.

Sitting in that tiny hospital room, my mind had been spinning, looping over and over again around the same questions.

What did I want?

Who was I?

Was I happy with my life?

Could I be happier?

I had too many thoughts and no clear answers.

Before I could dwell on it, another message caught my eye —this one from Dean.

> I had one of the nurses grab your keys for me. I parked your car in the hospital parking lot. Feel better soon.

I typed out a quick response.

> Thank you so much! You have no idea how much this means to me.

My heart swelled when I saw Cadence's name.

> OMG, Blake! Are you okay? I heard about the tornado and you being hospitalized. GIRL, WHAT ARE YOU DOING WITH YOUR LIFE? Call me. XOXO.

I laughed, already anticipating the chaos of our conversation. I'd call her as soon as I got in the car.

Then I saw it.

A missed call.

From my dad.

My throat tightened. He had called yesterday, around the time I'd left work. I hadn't heard my phone ring, not that I would have answered it. But this time... he'd left a voicemail.

With shaky fingers, I lifted my phone to my ear.

His deep, gravelly voice poured through the speaker, sending a rush of emotions through me.

"Hey, Kiddo. I wanted to check in and see how life was treating you. I saw that your friend had passed, and I wanted to make sure you were doing okay." He paused. "I also wanted to tell you that I'm working on getting my life back together. I hit rock bottom about two months ago and... I haven't had a drop of alcohol since."

I gasped, my free hand flying to my mouth.

"I'm trying to make amends in my life," he continued. "Trying to fix the things I've broken. And... well, I wanted to tell you in person, but you're not taking my calls right now, and I understand why. But I want you to know, I'm sorry. I'm sorry for all the times I wasn't there for you. I'm sorry I let you grow up without both a mother and father. If I could do it over, I would in a heartbeat."

A sob built in my throat.

"I hope we can get together soon," he added, voice quieter now. "Maybe for a cup of coffee or something. My treat. Love you, Kiddo."

Tears flowed freely down my cheeks.

It was all I had ever wanted. All I had ever dreamed of as a kid—for my dad to stop drinking, to start living again.

For years, I had needed him. But he wasn't there.

But now? Now he was finally giving sobriety a chance.

And maybe... maybe that meant we had a chance, too.

I wasn't ready to let him back in just yet. But maybe, soon, I would be. Maybe we could get that coffee—as father and daughter.

I wiped my tears on my sleeve and stepped into the hallway, ready to leave this place behind.

Dean had parked my car right in the visitor's lot out front. Relief flooded me. I didn't have to call an Uber, didn't have to figure out how to pick it up later.

And, miraculously, my car was fine.

There were a few minor scratches, but otherwise? She was okay.

Just like me.

The parking lot and surrounding area bore the scars of the storm—leaves, branches, and debris littering the pavement. Trees bent at odd angles, but they were still rooted. The buildings across the street had minor damage, but nothing catastrophic.

We had made it through.

I climbed into my car and backed out of the space before dialing Cadence.

She answered on the first ring. "Thank God. I've been waiting for your call. Holy hell."

I laughed. "Yeah, it was… an experience, for sure."

"What happened?! Jamie wasn't sure how you ended up at his apartment, so he couldn't tell me how you got hurt. Ten stitches, though? Ouch. Did they shave your hair?"

I stiffened. "Jamie? You talked to Jamie?"

"Yeah! Funny how that's the only thing you heard." She huffed. "He was the one who called me and told me. He was so worried, Blake. You could hear it in his voice."

I swallowed hard. "It's been an eventful few weeks."

"Uh-huh. We'll get to that. But first, seriously—how are you feeling? I feel bad chewing out an invalid."

I laughed again. "I'm fine. Just a headache and some bruising, but otherwise okay."

"I'm glad to hear it. I was worried about you." She took a breath. "Okay, next order of business: Jamie freaking MacIntyre. Spill."

I sighed. "There's nothing to spill."

"Okay, and I'm not addicted to Reese's Cups or in a relationship that sucks the life out of me."

I blinked. "Wait, what? Things are still rocky with you and Elijah?"

"Yes, but that's not the point. Blake, how could you not talk to me about this? About Jamie? You've been dealing with all of this alone, and I had to hear about it from him instead of you? That's not okay."

And with those words, the weight of everything finally hit me.

I exhaled, my throat tightening. "I'm sorry. I knew you were going through your own drama, and you didn't need mine, too."

"Blake, that's for me to decide. I'm pissed at you for not coming to me. I will always be there for you. No matter what."

The lump in my throat thickened.

"I don't even know where to start, Cadence."

"How about the beginning?"

I sighed. "When I first saw him, I was so determined to show him how fine I was without him. I pushed him away, which was good and smart for my self-preservation. It took me a long time to get to where I am today. But then, Mr. Taylor assigned me to do an article on Noah."

Cadence made a knowing sound.

"For the article, I was supposed to interview Jamie. So we spent some time together. And I found it harder and harder to hold on to my anger. I wanted to be near him again. To laugh with him. To be his friend."

"And Dean?"

"Oh my God," I groaned. "Totally psycho over Jamie and me spending time together."

"Understandably."

I frowned. "You think so?"

She scoffed. "Blake. You and Jamie had that ride-or-die, once-in-a-lifetime love. Dean knew that. Hell, everyone knew that. So with Jamie coming back, it was only a matter of time before you two found each other again."

"That means nothing. That was before he ripped my heart out and trampled on it."

"Blake. Come on." She huffed. "I don't even need to be there to see you two giving each other those longing looks across the room to know you'd find a way back to each other."

I squeezed my eyes shut. "But there's so much pain there. I don't know if I can."

"You don't know if you can what?"

I hesitated. "I don't know if I can trust him with my heart again."

Cadence sighed, her voice gentler now. "It's not easy. But you know what? Hearts grow with people. Not only have you grown, but so has he. He's changed, Blake. And it's up to you to determine if the new Jamie is worth your forgiveness."

"My forgiveness?" I echoed.

"Uh-huh." I could practically hear her nodding. "Once you forgive him—for leaving you, for hurting you—everything else will fall into place."

I swallowed hard. "I didn't even tell you that Dean and I broke up."

"You didn't have to, hun. I'm your best friend."

I grunted. "You make it all sound so simple."

"It is simple," she insisted. "When you truly love someone, everything is simple."

"I feel like you're speaking about more than just me."

"Another talk for another day." She brushed it off. "Today is just about you."

"Fine." I blew out a breath. "So... what should I do?"

"Well, that's up to you."

I groaned. "Cadence."

"Nope. I'm not making this decision for you. What do you want to do?"

"I don't know."

Cadence barked out a laugh. "I think you do. You just don't know how to admit it to yourself."

I gripped the steering wheel tighter. "What do you want me to say? That seeing Jamie these past two weeks has made me feel more alive than I have since he left? That I've been sleepwalking through my life, and now I feel awake for the first time?"

My voice broke, but I didn't stop.

"That the idea of losing him again made every muscle in my body tighten until I couldn't breathe?" Tears blurred my vision, spilling freely. "That the thought of him with another woman crushes my chest like I'm having a heart attack?"

Cadence stayed quiet, letting me get it all out.

I sniffled. "That during the few times I've seen Jamie, I've felt more passion and desire than I ever have for Dean?"

Cadence exhaled. "Well. I'd say it's a start."

I pulled into my driveway just as the sobs took over. It felt so good to let it all out. To stop ignoring the truth, to stop burying the feelings I'd tried so hard to suppress.

Through my tears, I whispered, "I love him."

"I know."

"I still love him."

"I know."

I wiped at my eyes, voice raw. "What do I do?"

"Tell him."

"But I..."

"Blake," she interrupted. "Tell him."

A shaky breath left my lips.

"Okay."

Chapter Forty-Eight

Blakely

After talking with Cadence, I felt more like myself than I had in months. The things I wanted... the things I needed... I knew what they were again.

As I stood in the shower, I let the hot water cascade down my back, loosening the tension in my muscles. The steam curled around me, clearing my head and washing away some of the weight I'd been carrying.

I dressed in jeans, a sweater, and my favorite pair of Converse—nothing special, but not my usual leggings. I even swiped on some mascara and blush, just enough to add a little color to my face. I wouldn't admit it out loud, but I wanted to look good when I saw Jamie.

When I finally told him I was ready to forgive him.

I grabbed my phone and keys from the counter, but the second I saw Jamie's name on my screen, my heart stopped.

Meet me at our park... please.

The timestamp said he'd sent it an hour ago.

I ran out the door, not even bothering to lock up, and prayed he was still there.

The drive was a blur. I broke more traffic laws than I cared to admit, my fingers gripping the wheel like it could somehow make me get there faster. The sun had set about thirty minutes ago, leaving only the dim glow of streetlights to guide me. The days were getting shorter. Colder.

And as soon as I pulled into the parking lot, nostalgia hit me like a punch to the chest.

This was where we met. Where we became best friends. Where he first told me he loved me.

I killed the engine and immediately noticed something was off. The park had no lights, aside from the dim ones near the lot, but there was a glow around the playground equipment. My pulse kicked up.

Was something wrong? Had something happened?

"Jamie?" I called, stepping onto the pavement.

As I moved closer, the blur of lights came into focus, and my steps slowed. String lights hung from the trees, the swing set, the slide—soft, warm, and flickering in the night. But it was the ones over the monkey bars that stopped me in my tracks.

Jamie stood beneath them, hands behind his back, like a man waiting at the altar for his bride.

Except Jamie wasn't some polished, well-dressed groom.

Light-wash fitted jeans, a blue button-up, and a pair of white sneakers. His hair was a little messy, and the lights cast long shadows over his face, making it impossible to read his expression. But when he heard my footsteps, he lifted his chin and smiled—a slow, breathtaking smile worth more than every cent I had to my name.

"You came." He reached for my hands.

I let him take them. "I'm sorry I'm late."

"I'm just happy you're here."

I looked around, taking in the effort he'd put into all of this. "Jamie... what is this?"

His fingers tightened around mine. "It's my big grand gesture."

I let out a soft laugh. "Your what?"

"The part of our love story where I do everything I can to prove I can't live without you. I'll grovel, I'll beg—I'll give you the shirt off my back if that's what it takes to get you to listen."

My heart swelled so fast it hurt.

"You can start the begging now, then."

Without hesitation, Jamie dropped to one knee.

I gasped and yanked at his arm. "Oh my God, I was kidding!"

He grinned but didn't move. "But I'd do it."

"But you don't have to."

A shiver worked down my spine, and before I could hide it, Jamie was already rubbing my arms.

"I'm sorry. It's too cold. This wasn't a good plan."

I shook my head. "Are you kidding? This is perfect. This is our spot, Jamie. The fact that you picked here to talk means everything."

His chest rose and fell with a deep breath, and a look of sheer determination crossed his face.

"I love you, Blake."

Jamie's voice was low, steady, unshakable. A declaration, a vow, a truth carved into his soul.

"More than words can express, more than I know how to comprehend. Without you, I've been walking in a shadow, just a quarter of the person I was before. You make me better in every way, and I am so damn sorry for the pain I caused you." His hands trembled as he reached for me, his fingers ghosting over my skin before he cupped my face. "I would never want to hurt you, and I think about what I did every day. It was unfair for you to go through that alone because I couldn't handle myself. We could have lifted each other up. We could have been there for each other. But I tore us apart, and I made that pain so much worse. And for that, I am sorry. I'm sorry for every moment I stole from us. For every second you felt alone."

Tears blurred my vision before I even felt them fall.

Jamie's thumbs caught them before they could escape, his touch gentle, reverent—like he was trying to wipe away years of hurt in a single stroke.

"But despite how sorry I am, I'm also incredibly selfish." His voice thickened with emotion, his thumb grazing my cheek in slow, agonizing circles. "I can't leave you alone. I can't walk away from you. When I climbed out of the rubble of my apartment and found you on the ground with paramedics surrounding you, I lost it. I couldn't think straight. I'm almost certain I acted like a complete idiot."

A choked laugh slipped from my lips. "According to the nurses at the hospital? You did. A complete idiot."

Jamie groaned, already shaking his head.

I grinned, drawing out the moment. "Apparently, you yelled at the paramedics for not letting you ride in the back of the ambulance with me. Then, when they offered to let you ride up front, you used some... colorful language to let them know how you felt about that atrocity. And when they refused to let you in at all, you—"

His eyes squeezed shut. "I don't want to hear this."

I bit my lip. "Jamie... you chased the ambulance to the edge of the parking lot."

His cheeks burned red.

"I was afraid I lost you." His voice dropped to barely above a whisper, like saying it too loud would unravel him completely. "And I couldn't handle losing you twice."

"That's the thing, Jamie." I threaded my fingers through his, grounding us both in the moment. "You never actually lost me. I've been here the whole time."

Jamie's chest rose and fell with a heavy breath, his eyes scanning my face like he was memorizing every detail.

"I lost my way," he admitted, his forehead pressing against mine. "In my sorrow and grief, I lost my way." He exhaled sharply. "I am hoping you can find it in you to forgive me, Blakely."

I smiled so wide it hurt. "I've already forgiven you, Jamie. I did a long time ago without realizing it. I hated you for leaving me when I needed you the most. Losing the baby was the hardest thing I've ever gone through, and you—" My throat tightened, thick with emotion. "You weren't there. You failed me."

Jamie flinched, like I had physically struck him, but he didn't look away.

I cupped his face, forcing him to see me, to really see me. "But I know now that you never meant to hurt me. Whatever you were going through... it had to be so dark, so unbearable, that you couldn't think straight. And after a while, I stopped waiting for an apology. I stopped needing an explanation. Because deep down, I knew you weren't the villain I tried to make you out to be."

His hands covered mine, his touch desperate and unsteady, like he was terrified I would disappear if he let go.

"I'm sorry it took me so long," he whispered, his breath brushing my lips.

I shivered, and his hands immediately dropped, his brows knitting in concern.

"Let's go somewhere warm," he started, but I wasn't ready to let him go.

"But first."

I grabbed the front of his shirt, yanking him to me, crashing my lips against his.

Jamie's reaction was instant and primal.

A groan rumbled in his chest, and suddenly, I wasn't just kissing him—I was consumed by him. His arms banded around me, pulling me flush against his body, his hands sliding down my back, gripping, exploring, claiming.

Heat exploded through me, chasing away the cold October air. My fingers knotted in his hair, and he tilted his head, deepening the kiss, his tongue sweeping against mine, teasing, tasting.

I moaned into his mouth, and that sound—that tiny, uncontrollable noise—was all it took.

Jamie growled, his grip tightening, his hands skimming down my sides before one slid under my sweater, his fingers branding my skin with fire.

God, I'd forgotten what this felt like. The electric pull, the ache, the desperate, unrelenting need.

He kissed me like he was starving—like he'd been dying of thirst, and I was the first drop of water to touch his tongue.

When we finally pulled apart, we were both panting.

Jamie rested his forehead against mine, his breath ragged, his voice hoarse with unspoken promises.

"God, I love you." His hands tightened on my waist. "So damn much, it hurts."

My heart ached from the sheer force of it.

I ran my fingertips along his jaw, memorizing the scruff, the warmth, the familiarity of home. "I love you too. Always."

Jamie kissed me again, this time slower, softer—savoring every second like he was afraid to wake up from a dream.

When we finally broke apart, he cradled my cheek.

"I swear on everything, Blake, I'll never walk away again. Never."

I smiled through my tears. "Just don't make me come hunt you down."

Jamie let out a rough laugh, then kissed me one last time—a vow sealed in warmth and devotion. "I promise."

Lacing his fingers through mine, he led me toward his truck, pulling me tightly to his side.

"Come on. I'll drive."

The butterflies in my stomach felt like a rollercoaster drop—that weightless, stomach-in-throat, giddy-with-a-side-of-nausea kind of feeling.

I watched him as he climbed into the driver's seat, his movements easy, comfortable, like a man who had finally found solid ground again.

"I'd take you to my place, but... "

I barked out a laugh. "Funny."

"I try."

I smirked, settling into my seat. "Where are you staying until you find a new place?"

"My mom has graciously taken me in."

I arched a brow. "And how's that going?"

Jamie groaned, resting his head back against the seat dramatically. "Terrible. Absolutely terrible. She doesn't let me sulk or wallow in self-pity in peace."

I giggled, and something inside me unclenched at the sound. It had been so long since I had laughed with Jamie like this.

"So, Jane told you to make peace with me?"

He cut me a sideways glance. "Kind of. She told me to find my happiness. Gave me the closest thing to an ass-chewing I've ever heard come out of her mouth. Made me do some soul-searching of my own."

Jamie reached across the console, his hand landing on my thigh, his touch grounding me. "Blake, you are my happiness. I could never be truly happy without you."

I swallowed past the sudden tightness in my throat.

"But my mother's kick in the ass helped me see it clearly. That... and almost losing my mind while you were in the hospital. I couldn't even see if you were okay. I was so afraid, Blake. So damn scared."

I placed my hand over his and gave it a gentle squeeze. "I'm here. I'm fine."

Jamie looked over at me, his smile soft and full of something I couldn't name. His fingers flexed, gripping my thigh a little tighter before he turned back to the road.

He kept his hand on my leg the whole drive.

The warmth of it anchored me, kept me from waking up from this dream—the too-good-to-be-true moment where Jamie and I had finally found our way back to each other.

But this wasn't a dream.

This was real.

And I was ready.

I could be a journalist anywhere. Jamie wouldn't be in the military forever. One day, we'd settle down. One day, I'd focus on my career. But right now? Right now, I just wanted to be with him.

I had made this choice years ago, and I was ready to make it again.

Supporting Jamie through missions, deployments, injuries, hell... even PT tests—I'd do it all.

Because that was what being a military spouse was.

It wasn't for the faint of heart.

It took courage—so much courage—to love someone whose

job would always come first. To know that I would never be his top priority.

To know that sometimes, his duty to his country would be more important than me.

I looked over at him from the corner of my eye, drinking in every familiar detail. The bridge of his nose. The shape of his lips.

Jamie was worth it.

He was worth every sacrifice.

And I hoped—more than anything—that he finally realized it, too.

Chapter Forty-Nine

BLAKELY

Walking into my house, we acted like teenagers after confessing our feelings—shy glances, hesitant smiles, the kind of giddy nervousness that made my stomach flutter. I felt like my old seventeen-year-old self despite being twenty-six.

"Can I get you anything? Drink? Snack? Anything before we talk?"

Jamie rubbed the back of his neck and laughed. "Got anything strong? I'm not exactly looking forward to this conversation."

"I've got some whiskey?"

"Perfect. Thanks."

I frowned as I grabbed the bottle of Jack Daniels and two glasses. "Why are you nervous?"

I poured our drinks, waiting for him to answer, but Jamie stayed silent, his gaze locked onto my hands like he was trying to work through something in his head. I slid a glass to him, and he swallowed hard before knocking it back in one shot. He set the glass down a little too forcefully.

"Sorry," he muttered with a weak smile.

"It's okay." I refilled his glass. "Let's go sit on the couch."

His sigh was heavy as he followed behind me, his steps too quiet for a man his size. I curled into my usual spot and grabbed my blanket, the one that had seen better days but would always be my favorite. Jamie sat beside me, pulling me close, like it was instinct, like it was where I had always belonged.

"You still have this?" Jamie traced the fabric, his fingers brushing over the frayed edges.

I nodded, emotion catching in my throat. "Of course, Jane made it for me for my eighteenth birthday."

Silence stretched between us, thick with everything we hadn't said yet. Jamie held me, my head resting on his shoulder, his fingers skimming slow, soothing strokes along my arm. I could have fallen asleep like this—if it weren't for the anticipation tightening my chest. I wasn't afraid of what he had to say. I knew Jamie better than he knew himself. Nothing could change how I felt.

"Well," he exhaled. "I guess I better rip the band-aid off."

I lifted my head and met his gaze. Those storm-cloud eyes —haunted, conflicted, raw.

Jamie took a deep breath. And then he began.

"I've seen a lot of death. Caused a lot of death." His voice was steady, but something dark coiled beneath it. "Every time I went back overseas, I left pieces of myself behind. Every time I took a life, I felt some of my own slip away. At first, I didn't even notice. I think you saw it before I did." He paused. "I never dealt with it. I shoved it down, told myself I'd handle it later. But it changed me. I pushed you away when I should have pulled you closer. Hell, I pushed everyone away." His fingers flexed against his knee. "But you? You're the one I regret hurting the most."

My throat tightened, but I didn't dare interrupt.

"It really started when we lost the baby." His voice dipped lower, heavier. "I remember being so damn confused—why I was so wrecked over someone I'd never even met. But I was. Knowing I'd never get to hold our little boy tore me apart. Your pregnancy was a surprise, but I was so fucking happy. I was ready. I couldn't wait to start our life together as a family."

Jamie took a shaky breath. His hands trembled, so I took one, lacing our fingers together. He gripped me like a lifeline.

"Then everything happened with my dad, and I didn't know how to deal with it. I was so angry—so fucking angry that I couldn't think straight. How could he do that to us? Just leave us like that?" He looked away, jaw clenched. "That's when I started suppressing everything. And when I lost myself completely."

Tears silently slid down my cheeks, but I didn't wipe them away. I wouldn't stop him, no matter how much it hurt to hear how much pain he had been in.

"Six months after I graduated from training, Remember that deployment?" His voice had turned flat—emotionless, almost mechanical. "That was my first taste of real combat. It should have wrecked me, but I was already numb. I broke off our engagement and isolated myself completely. I thought..." He swallowed. "I thought I was toxic. Death followed me wherever I went. My job. My family. My entire life. I couldn't escape it."

Jamie let out a bitter chuckle. "And I thought putting distance between us would keep you safe."

I squeezed his hand, but he barely seemed to feel it.

"I was a zombie. Just existing. Then, one day, I ran into

Noah overseas. And you know what he did?" A ghost of a smirk flickered across Jamie's lips. "He beat the shit out of me."

Shock rippled through me. "Noah?"

Jamie chuckled, shaking his head. "Yeah. He saw what a hollow, lifeless piece of shit I'd become, and he thought if he hit me, I'd fight back." He shrugged. "Spoiler alert—I didn't."

"But why would he do that?"

Jamie hesitated. His fingers tapped a slow, uneven rhythm against his leg. His chest rose and fell like he was gearing up for something big.

"Because I lied to you." He exhaled sharply. "When I told you why I joined the Air Force, I didn't tell you the whole truth. I said it was my way out, that I'd always wanted to serve. But that wasn't my dream, Blake. It was Noah's."

I froze. Everything inside me stilled.

"That day he was supposed to sign his enlistment papers? He panicked. I could see it all over him—the sweat, the shaking hands. He was about to back out." Jamie stared at the floor. "And I couldn't let him walk away from something he'd wanted his entire life. So I stepped up. I signed first. I pushed him into it." His voice dropped. "Looking back, I used to wonder if I should've let him walk away. But a few weeks ago, I finally realized—Noah would have never forgiven himself if he had. He loved it, Blake. The job. The mission. The purpose."

Jamie inhaled deeply, bracing himself.

"And for the first time in weeks... I don't blame myself for his death."

My breath caught. God. His voice—the sheer weight of those words.

"Jamie." His name was barely a whisper.

"But how could I have known? How could I have predicted what would happen?"

His voice cracked, just slightly. But I heard it.

Jamie clenched his jaw, his body coiled so tightly, I could feel the tension radiating off him. I reached for him, but before I could say anything, he kept going.

"Noah and I joined under the buddy system. We trained together, which of course, you know. But then... we got stationed apart." His fingers dug into his thigh. "I let myself believe he was better off without me. I stopped keeping in touch. And then..."

He swallowed hard. Too hard.

"That first time I saw him again? He hit me. Hard. I'll never forget that look in his eyes, and he said, 'You helped me when I had no one else. I'll get you out of this if it's the last thing I do.' Of course, I thought he was full of it, but he kept tabs on me after that. He called and emailed me all the time. And unknowingly, I let him in.'"

Jamie's voice broke completely. His breathing turned ragged. He squeezed his eyes shut like he was trying to block out a memory too painful to relive.

I couldn't take it anymore.

I pressed my palm to his chest—felt his heart racing wildly beneath my fingertips.

"Jamie." I covered his shaking hand with mine.

He exhaled slowly, pressing his palm over mine.

"I'll be okay." His voice was barely above a whisper. "I just need to get through this."

I nodded, fighting past the lump in my throat.

"Then I'm right here."

And I was. For as long as he needed me.

Chapter Fifty

BLAKELY

I watched Jamie struggle to speak, his body coiled tight, like a man on the edge of a battlefield, not sure if he'd make it out alive. The weight of his past pressed down on him, thick and suffocating. I wanted to reach for him, to tell him it was okay, that he could let me in. But there were no words that could ease what he carried.

So I waited, letting the silence stretch between us, letting him find his way through the storm of memories dragging him under.

"On my last deployment, we were given a mission to clear out a village. We were looking for a high-value target, someone crucial to the enemy's infrastructure. Because of how important he was, they assigned two teams—my unit and Noah's. The night before the mission, Noah and I stayed up talking. It was the first time in years I let myself believe that maybe—just maybe—I could have my old life back. That I could come home and make things right with you."

His Adam's apple bobbed as he swallowed, his fingers clenching into fists on his thighs.

"Noah encouraged me to reach out, to fix what I broke. He told me to stop running, to stop pretending I didn't still love you. But he never mentioned you were dating his brother... I imagine he left that part out on purpose."

Jamie let out a humorless laugh, shaking his head before dragging a hand over his face.

"I went to bed that night thinking about you. Imagining what I'd say, how I'd try to make you understand why I left, why I stayed away. I told myself if I survived that mission, I'd find you. I'd make things right."

His breath hitched, his voice turning hoarse.

"But we weren't ready for what happened. We took the target's compound fast. Too fast. Our confidence made us sloppy. We were ambushed before we even realized what was happening. The enemy surrounded us, trapped us inside the compound walls. We couldn't call in an airstrike because the bastards were too close. It was chaos. Gunfire, screaming, the smell of smoke and blood in the air."

He exhaled sharply, eyes distant, lost in a battlefield that no longer existed except in his mind.

"I remember the moment I knew I was dead. An enemy soldier ran through the breach in the wall, his rifle aimed right at me. I heard the shots. Felt the impact."

I gasped, my hands covering my mouth.

Jamie's voice dropped to a whisper. "But it wasn't my body that hit the ground." His eyes met mine, tortured and full of ghosts. "It was Noah's."

The air rushed from my lungs.

"That son of a bitch." His voice cracked. "He jumped in front of me."

Jamie scrubbed a hand down his face, but I saw the tears

trailing down his cheeks before he could wipe them away. "There were two bullets. One hit me in the arm, the other hit Noah right where our armor was weak. I tried to stop the bleeding. I tried to save him. But it was too late. He couldn't breathe. He—he took his last breath in my arms."

Jamie shuddered, sucking in a ragged breath before letting it out slowly, like he was trying to stay afloat in a sea of grief. "He gave up his life for me, Blake." His voice was barely a whisper now, raw with pain. "And it's my fault. I took Noah from his family, from his friends. From you. I'm the one who should've been buried in the ground, not him."

I reached up, wiping the tear that slipped down his face. Jamie stilled at my touch, like I'd broken some kind of trance, like he hadn't even realized he was crying. My heart didn't just break for him—it shattered completely.

"Noah would never have blamed you."

Jamie nodded, his grip on my hand like a lifeline. "I know. And I've finally started to believe it." He swallowed. "Noah wanted me to live. He wanted me to come back to you. He fought like hell to keep me alive, and I can't keep dishonoring his memory by wasting the life he saved. I'm ready to stop running from my past. To stop being afraid of what I feel for you."

His eyes locked onto mine, vulnerable and unwavering. "I love you, Blake. I've always loved you. And if you'll still have me, I swear to God, I'll spend the rest of my life making up for the time I stole from us."

I didn't hesitate.

I climbed into his lap, straddling him, pressing every inch of my body against him, grounding him in the present, in me. My hands traced his face, his jaw, his lips—like I was memorizing him all over again. Jamie's breath hitched, his lashes fluttering closed as he leaned into my touch.

Then, I kissed him.

Jamie groaned, deep and needy, like he'd been starving for this, for me. His hands gripped my hips, pulling me closer, harder, like he was afraid I'd disappear if he didn't hold on tight enough.

He kissed me like I was his air, his salvation, his entire goddamn universe. Like he needed to erase the years of pain and regret, to put back every broken piece.

My hands threaded into his hair, tugging just enough to make him groan against my mouth. His grip on my waist tightened, fingers digging into my skin as he angled my head, deepening the kiss.

It was desperate. Hungry. Completely unhinged.

His tongue traced along my lips, seeking entrance, and I let him in without hesitation. Everything else fell away.

The past. The pain. The war he'd been fighting inside himself.

There was only this.

Only him.

Jamie pulled at me like he could never get enough, like I was his light after years of darkness. Like he was drowning, and I was the only thing keeping him afloat.

I let my hands roam, feeling the firm planes of his chest, the familiar strength beneath my fingertips. Finding the buttons of his shirt, I pushed it off his body. I wanted to see it. Needed to see the mark.

The fresh scar.

The wound left behind by the bullet that could have killed him. The skin was still healing, slightly red, slightly raised. A brutal reminder of how close he'd come to never making it home to me.

Jamie flinched when my fingers brushed over it.

"Does it still hurt?" I whispered.

"Not as much as it used to."

"Jamie..." I traced my fingers over the scar again, gentler this time. He closed his eyes, his breathing uneven.

"I can still hear it," he murmured, his voice barely audible. "The gunfire. The shouting. The sound of the bullet tearing through the air. The smell of blood and gunpowder and sweat. I can still feel Noah's weight on me, still hear his last words, still see his face in my dreams. It's like I never left that battlefield."

Tears burned in my eyes.

"But all dreams end," I whispered, cupping his face. "And even the darkest nights are followed by morning light."

Jamie exhaled shakily, his forehead pressing against mine.

"And I finally have my light."

He pulled me back into him, kissing me harder this time, with a raw desperation that set my entire body on fire. This wasn't just a kiss. This was a claiming. A promise. A vow.

And I never wanted it to end.

Need pulsed between us, thick and inescapable. The air was charged, humming with electricity, an invisible force pulling us closer, drawing us into the inevitable. It had always been this way—chemical, undeniable, all-consuming.

He pulled at my clothes, the fabric whispering against my skin before landing somewhere on the floor, forgotten. Jamie looked at me like I was something sacred.

Like he could hardly believe I was real, that I was here, choosing him.

There were no doubts. No hesitation.

I wanted this.

Needed it.

Craved it in a way that refused to be ignored.

I wrapped my arms around his neck, pressing my lips to his, letting him taste my need, my hunger, the ache that had been dormant for too long. But just as my body melted into his, just as I surrendered to the fire consuming us, Jamie pulled away.

His hands framed my face, his breath ragged, his forehead pressing against mine.

"Blake, wait."

Confusion flickered in my chest. His touch still lingered, his fingers trembling against my skin.

"Jamie, it's okay."

His eyes—God, those eyes. Haunted and stormy and filled with a pain I wanted to erase.

"I don't want to hurt you again." His voice was hoarse, barely above a whisper. "I don't want to move too fast and ruin this."

My heart clenched. It wasn't just about what he wanted—it was about what he thought he deserved.

I cupped his face, tilting his chin so he had no choice but to look at me, to see me, to understand.

"Jamie, listen to me." My voice was steady, unwavering. "You're not hurting me. You're healing me."

His breath caught, his grip tightening on my waist.

"We've spent so much time running," I whispered, brushing my lips against his. "I don't want to run anymore."

Jamie exhaled sharply, like my words had shattered something inside him, breaking down the last of his resistance.

And then, he kissed me.

Not gently. Not carefully. Not like I was fragile.

He kissed me like he was starving. Like I was the only thing keeping him alive.

And I was ready to give myself to him completely.

Chapter Fifty-One

JAMIE

I didn't deserve this.

The thought came unbidden, sharp and insistent, but Blake's hand in mine silenced the voice before it could take hold.

She was here. With me. After everything I'd put her through, after every mistake I'd made, she was still here.

I didn't know what I expected when I told her everything, but it sure as hell wasn't this—wasn't her, standing in front of me, looking at me like I wasn't broken. Like I wasn't ruined.

Like I was worth loving.

My chest tightened as she reached for me, and I fought the instinct to pull away—not because I didn't want her. God, I wanted her. But this wasn't just about want.

It was more.

She was more.

I didn't want to take from her—I wanted to give. Give her

every part of me, the way I should have all those years ago. Give her everything I'd been too much of a coward to offer before.

She slid off my lap, her fingers lacing through mine as she stood, her emerald eyes locked on me like I was the only thing in the world she saw. And maybe, for the first time in my life, I was.

Then she held out her hand. Waiting. Letting me choose.

She'd always been beautiful, but right now, with her shirt discarded on the floor, she was breathtaking. And she was choosing me.

Despite my past.

Despite my scars.

Despite everything.

I was done running. I was ready to be the man she needed.

So, I took her hand.

She led me down the small hall to her bedroom, the anticipation stretching between us, thick and heavy. When she turned to face me, a coy smile tugged at her lips as she unbuttoned her jeans and pushed them down her legs.

Blake stood before me, bare except for the soft lace that barely covered her, and whatever control I had left snapped.

I had tried—tried to hold back, to savor the moment, to go slow. But seeing her like this, bathed in the dim light, every inch of her so damn perfect, made restraint impossible. I could feel the moment my rational self drowned beneath the hunger clawing through me.

A low curse slipped from my lips as I reached for her, my hands finding the heat of her skin, my pulse hammering in time with the need rising inside me.

And there wasn't a force in this world that could stop me from showing her just how much I needed her.

"You're still wearing too many clothes, Blake."

Her lips parted, a breathy, knowing smile curling at the edges.

"Fix it, then."

A growl rumbled deep in my chest as I stepped into her, my fingers sliding up her back, my lips capturing hers again, deeper this time, more desperate.

My fingers traced the delicate strap of lace clinging to her shoulder before I unclasped the back, letting it fall down her arms, baring her to me.

She was everything. Every dream, every regret, every whispered prayer I didn't think I deserved to have answered.

And she was mine.

She gasped as I stepped forward, forcing her back. The back of her knees hit the mattress, and I pushed her down onto the bed.

I towered over her, watching the way her breath came in short, needy little pants, how her body arched toward me, silently begging for my touch.

"You knew exactly what you were doing," I murmured, my voice low, dangerous, laced with possession. "You knew I'd lose my mind the second I saw you like this."

Her breath hitched, her pulse fluttering beneath my fingertips.

"Say it," I ordered, tilting her chin up so she had no choice but to meet my gaze.

Her tongue flicked out to wet her lips, and I nearly lost my damn mind.

"Say what?"

"That you're mine," I growled, my fingers sliding into her hair, fisting the soft strands as I tilted her head back. "Say it, Blake."

A small, desperate sound escaped her throat as her hands

pressed against my chest, nails digging in just enough to make me feel it.

She was shaking. But not with fear.

With need.

With anticipation.

"I'm yours," she whispered, her voice breathless, wrecked.

"That's right," I said, dragging my lips down her neck, my teeth grazing just enough to make her tremble. "And no one will ever touch you again."

My grip tightened in her hair, my voice dropping lower, rougher.

"Do you understand me?"

She nodded, her breath coming in short, needy gasps.

"Words, Blake," I warned, my lips ghosting over her collarbone before pressing hot, open-mouthed kisses along the delicate skin.

"Yes," she gasped. "I understand."

A dark satisfaction settled deep in my chest.

Because this?

This was exactly where she belonged.

I tilted her head back further, dragging my teeth along the delicate curve of her throat, savoring the way her pulse thrummed wildly against my lips.

She trembled, her body taut beneath my hands, every soft, needy breath fueling the hunger tearing through me.

But it wasn't enough.

Not nearly enough.

I straightened, looking down at her, bare except for the lace still clinging to her hips. My fingers traced along the delicate waistband, a slow, teasing glide that had her arching into me, silently begging for more.

Not yet.

I was going to savor this.

I hooked my fingers into the thin fabric, giving it a light tug —not enough to remove it, just enough to remind her that I could. That I would.

Her breath caught, her hands sliding down my chest, tracing the ridges of my abs before finding the buckle of my belt.

"You're still wearing too many clothes," she murmured, throwing my own words back at me.

A deep, rumbling laugh vibrated through me, but it was cut short when her fingers deftly unfastened my belt and popped the button of my jeans.

Blake's eyes met mine, a quiet challenge burning in them as she slowly dragged the zipper down.

Fuck.

She was playing with fire.

My jaw tightened. I had no control left to hold me back.

Then she dipped her hand beneath the waistband of my boxers, just barely brushing against me.

With a growl, I grabbed her wrist, squeezing it as I kicked off my jeans and boxers.

Her eyes widened, breathless anticipation lighting up her features.

I could see it—the way she wanted me to lose control. The way she wanted me to take her apart piece by piece.

I climbed onto the bed, caging her beneath me, the warmth of her skin searing against mine.

"You have no idea," I murmured, my lips brushing against hers, "how many nights I lay awake, wanting you like this."

Her breath hitched.

"How many times I dreamed about having you beneath me again. About making you mine again."

I moved lower, my lips trailing down her neck, lingering over the spot where her pulse raced.

"How many times I swore I'd never touch you again—because I didn't deserve you. But in those quiet moments alone, I let those thoughts of my need for you consume me. Let them break me."

Blake's hands slid up my back, her nails digging in, a sharp, sweet pain that sent a shudder down my spine.

"Jamie..."

My name on her lips was my undoing.

I yanked the lace underwear from her hips, my grip rough, possessive, worshipful. She gasped, a soft, breathy sound that sent a surge of heat straight through me.

I pressed against her, skin to skin, nothing left between us. My body molded to hers, and I felt everything—the way she arched into me, the way her body responded to my touch like she was made for me.

Blake's green eyes searched mine, shining with something that nearly broke me—love, trust, everything I thought I'd lost.

"You forgive me?" My voice barely more than a breath. I needed to hear it.

"I forgave you a long time ago. I was just waiting for you to come back to me."

Fuck.

I let out a shaky exhale, pressing my forehead to hers. "I love you," the words ripped from somewhere deep within me. "I love you so damn much that I can't breathe unless you're with me."

Her fingers traced over my jaw, soft, reverent. "Then show me."

Our eyes locked, a silent understanding passing between us.

And then I sank into her, into every piece of me that I'd left behind the day I walked away.

Blake's lips parted on a sharp inhale, her nails biting into my skin. But I didn't notice. There was nothing else but the feel of her.

I let out a guttural curse as I moved, every slow, deliberate thrust an unspoken vow.

"You feel that?" I growled.

"Everywhere," she whispered.

I gripped her hips tighter, anchoring her beneath me. "Good. Because no one will ever touch you like this. No one will ever love you like this. Like I do."

A soft moan slipped from her lips, her head falling back as her body clenched around me.

She reached up, threading her fingers through my hair, tugging me down, fusing our mouths together. A kiss so desperate, so full of love, so perfect.

"God, Jamie..." she cried, and goosebumps spread across my skin.

"Say it again."

"Jamie... Yes!"

I lost myself in her, my rhythm deepening, pushing harder—faster. I couldn't stop now if I wanted to. I could feel her tighten around me, her body tensing as pleasure overcame her, as it blinded her to everything else but me.

Her back arched as she broke apart beneath me, calling my name, her release shattering through her.

A sound I would play on repeat for the rest of my life.

I knew I wouldn't last, not with the way she was gripping me, pulling me in, giving me everything.

So I moved faster, taking what I needed, chasing the high only she could give me.

"I. Love. You. Blakely."

With a final curse, I let go.

The world faded into nothing as I collapsed beside her, my body still humming, my pulse thrumming in sync with hers.

The Story That Ties Us

Blake wasted no time in snaking an arm around me, curling against my chest.

"I love you, too, Jamie. Forever and always."

I let out a slow, contented breath, running my fingers through her hair as she pressed her lips to my collarbone.

After all these years—the pain, the distance, the heartbreak — we were finally whole once again.

We'd found our way back to each other.

Right where we belonged.

Epilogue

TWO WEEKS LATER

JAMIE

Liam had thrown together one hell of a show. Standing backstage, I was still in awe of how everything had come together in record time. Leave it to someone with connections like him to secure the Cape Fear Botanical Gardens for a last-minute fashion show. But everything had turned out perfectly, and I was in shock.

My life had completely changed in two weeks—for the better.

That tornado had torn apart pieces of the town, but also my life and Blake's. But the proverbial windstorm we went through had helped set us back on the road to each other, and we were better for it.

We had spent the last two weeks getting to know each other again, both with and without our clothes on. I was so happy that I didn't recognize myself in the mirror. That shit-eating grin didn't fit my face, but I couldn't shake it. Blake made every-

342

thing in my life better. She accepted me for who I was, flaws and all, while accepting my past. She let me back in, even though I hurt her. Her love and forgiveness were things I'd never take for granted again.

There were moments when the fear I'd lose her again consumed me, and self-doubt tried to take control, but I could pull myself out of it. Something I'd struggled with before.

Progress was progress, as they said.

I felt a hand on my shoulder. "It's almost the finale. Ready?" Liam gave me a knowing look.

I took a deep breath. "Too cheesy to say I was born ready?"

Wes laughed. "I expect nothing less from you."

"At least I have someone now. Erik still doesn't seem to even like girls."

"Yeah, and you're one hundred percent whipped by that girl too. At least I have my freedom."

"Oh, more than one hundred percent." I agreed, as we all laughed.

Warmth rushed through my chest once again. I had everyone I cared about around me: Liam, Erik, Wes, my family, and Blake. We were only missing a special few—Noah, my father, and our baby.

Admiration and appreciation welled up inside me. "Liam, thanks for doing all this. You have no idea what you are doing for the foundation and for me."

Liam simply smiled. "Anytime."

All of us stood there, best of friends, as we waited for the MC to conclude the show.

"Thanks so much to everyone who came out today, and don't forget, all proceeds go to an excellent cause—the Phoenix Foundation. Please give a warm welcome to Jamie MacIntyre, founder of the Phoenix Foundation."

I straightened my red beret and smoothed down the front of

my blues jacket. Chief insisted I wear them today, and they were the most uncomfortable thing you could ask anyone to wear. The lights from the show glinted off the metal surrounding my ribbons displayed on my chest. My career achievements were on display for all to see. They didn't bring me as much sorrow as they had before. I was proud of all I had done to protect those I loved.

I stepped onto the stage, temporarily blinded by the lights.

"Hi, everyone," I said into the microphone. "Thank you for coming out today to support something so near and dear to my heart. For those who don't know who I am, I'm Tech Sergeant Jamie MacIntyre, and I grew up here in Fayetteville. I know many of you in the crowd came out to see a Liam Knight Creations fashion show, but I thank you for coming anyway.

I'm here to raise awareness for the service members who experience combat overseas and come home feeling lost. The ones that have trouble sleeping, have difficulty moving on, or," I paused, swallowing the lump in my throat, "who are alive after watching their best friend die.

The Phoenix Foundation was named after one of my best friends who was there for me during my rock bottom—Noah Richey, an Air Force Combat Controller whose call sign was Phoenix. He picked me up and set me on the path to find peace and to heal.

This foundation is here to help those service members in need, to be there for them through the transition back into everyday life. To help them find a way to heal—anything from a simple phone call in the middle of the night to helping them find peace through different forms of therapy. Whatever it is, we are here to help those who need it.

So, thank you for all your donations tonight, and a big thank you to Liam. I couldn't have done this without you, buddy."

I turned toward the edge of the stage where the guys stood.

"How about a big round of applause for one of my best friends, Liam Knight, and LKC?"

I could see Liam's eye roll from where I stood in the middle of the stage, but it didn't stop my grin. Liam reluctantly made his way towards me, first shaking my hand and then pulling me into a bro hug.

"You're such an ass," he said in my ear with a smile on his face.

"I know."

Once the applause died down, Liam and I made our way off stage. I heard the MC wrap up the end-of-the-show announcements, telling the guests about refreshments and the after-party.

I was nothing but jitters now. My nerves shot through me like an electrical current. I didn't know why I was anxious, but I was.

"You got this. I'm going to find Liv and introduce her to Liam. She's a big fan and is mad I haven't introduced them yet. But I can't wait to hear the big news."

"I'll be at the bar. Drinking," Erik said. "Good luck!"

"And me," Liam said. "I'll be around, trying to blend in and avoid basically everyone."

"Still can't shake it?"

Liam shook his head. "She hasn't signed the papers yet. I haven't even heard from her. It's like a nightmare that never ends. I just want to move on."

I understood—I did—but I was finally on the other side of the mountain, and I knew there was hope. "You know, Blake told me once all dreams end eventually, and every night turns to morning light. Or something like that. But you get the idea. It will get better. I'm living proof."

Liam looked at me like I had just sprouted two heads.

"God, you two make me want to throw up. New love and all that."

I laughed. "I wouldn't call this new love."

"You're right. How about the love that was too stupid to realize you'd never be able to be with someone else as long as the other was still alive?"

"That works, but I feel like there is an insult in there somewhere."

"And you'd be right." Liam placed his hand on my shoulder again. "Jokes aside, I'm happy for you two."

"Thank you."

"Now go get her, tiger."

I shook my head, a grin spreading on my lips, as Liam disappeared.

I looked at my watch. It was 7:50 PM. I had told Blake to meet me under the wisteria tree behind the stage at 8:00 PM. I reached down and grabbed the small paper bag I had hidden backstage.

The moon was full and bright, lighting my way like a beacon to my destiny. The tree was far enough away from the party that we could have a few quiet moments to ourselves.

"Hi."

I heard her familiar voice and turned toward her. My heart skipped a beat when I saw her.

She was stunning by the moonlight.

Her blonde hair, almost platinum in the darkness, was pulled away from her face into a simple updo. The skin-tight black rhinestone dress Liam had gifted her showed off her curves, while the generous slit up the side gave an eyeful of her long legs.

She was every man's fantasy, and she was all mine.

"Hi," I said.

"I missed you today."

"I know. Me too. It's been a long day."

"I bet you're ready to get home and go to bed."

"Not exactly."

"Oh?"

Clearing my throat, I pulled the tiger plushie out from behind my back along with a single white peony. Blake eyed them suspiciously.

"Do you remember when we got this?"

"Of course."

"You were so proud of yourself for winning it. I almost didn't have the heart to take it from you."

"But I won it for you!"

"I know, but it brought you so much happiness, and I wanted you to keep that happiness."

"It made me happy to give it to you."

"Maybe so. But that was the day I realized I would marry you."

Blake chuckled, and my pulse fluttered. I took another deep breath.

"I've done many things wrong in my life, but finding you was the best thing I ever did." I swallowed hard, my heart pounding in my chest. "After breaking off our engagement, I carried this tiger everywhere. I couldn't bring myself to let go, even though I knew I was broken. I still needed you then, and I need you now. I will always need you in my life."

I revealed the diamond ring I had slid onto the plushie's little paw and sank onto one knee, watching Blake's eyes widen in surprise.

"Jamie?" Her voice was barely a whisper in the night.

"Blakely Mason," I said, steadying myself. "I have hurt you in the worst possible way. I left you when you needed me and only thought of myself."

"I really hope there's a 'but' somewhere in this proposal."

I let out a breathy laugh. "But... I want to spend the rest of my life making it up to you. To show you I am worthy of your love and affection. I can't imagine my life without you in it, and I'm sorry it took me this long to get back to you."

Her eyes shimmered with unshed tears, and I reached for her free hand, squeezing it gently between my fingers.

"I realize we just began our relationship again after all these years, but we already know each other, and I don't want to waste any more time. You are my past, my present, and my future. I love you, Blake. I love you more than I can ever put into words. Please say you'll be my wife... again."

Silence stretched between us.

My heart pounded so hard it was painful.

For the first time since dropping to my knee, I felt the crushing weight of what if? What if she wasn't ready? What if she wanted more time?

I had been ready to run down the aisle with her the second she let me back into her life, but that didn't mean she felt the same.

Then, her lips parted, and she whispered the one word that made my entire body exhale in relief.

"Yes."

I blinked. "What?"

"I said yes!"

She threw herself at me, sinking to her knees in front of me and wrapping her arms around my neck.

"Yes, yes, yes. A thousand times, yes."

I inhaled her familiar scent, a smell that reminded me of home, as I pulled her closer to me.

"Thank God. I was getting worried there."

She laughed against my shoulder before pulling back, her fingers curling into my jacket. "Just don't bail on me this time, okay?"

"I'll go to Vegas with you tomorrow if that's what you want."

"Don't tempt me."

"Mmm," I hummed, pressing my lips to hers.

It was a kiss that sealed everything.

A kiss that tethered me to this moment, to her, to forever.

She was mine.

And this time, I wasn't going anywhere.

"I love you too, Jamie. Always."

BLAKELY

Jamie and I arrived at the after-party hand in hand. I rubbed my thumb against the ring on my finger for the umpteenth time since he'd slipped it on.

I was giddy.

No other word could describe the sheer joy coursing through me.

I was going to marry Jamie MacIntyre.

For most of my life, it was all I had ever wanted.

I glanced at him out of the corner of my eye. Men in uniform were a cliché for a reason, and Jamie? He was their poster child. The epitome of rugged confidence, with that strong jawline, those stormy gray eyes, and that devil-may-care smirk that followed me into my dreams at night.

We made our rounds, greeting guests, making small talk. These people had known us our whole lives—had watched us grow up—and none of them seemed surprised to see us back together. It was as if we had been written in the stars all along.

Dean's accusations against Jamie had been put to rest.

After everything, he'd come forward and admitted he'd let his emotions cloud his judgment. He had no proof—only grief and misplaced anger. He had apologized, and though the town gossips had had their fun spreading the drama, it was officially a thing of the past.

Now, I was with the man I was always meant to be with, on my way to being a part of his family again.

Jamie tensed beside me, and I followed his gaze to see Mr. and Mrs. Richey walking toward us.

"It'll be okay," I whispered.

They surprised us both by pulling us into warm embraces.

"We are so happy to see you two back together," Mrs. Richey said, her voice thick with emotion.

"But I..." I faltered, caught off guard.

"Oh, honey," she said, squeezing my arms, "just because you and Dean didn't work out doesn't mean we don't love you the same. As much as I wanted you to be part of our family, I always knew you two were destined to be together."

Emotion clogged my throat. "Thank you, Mrs. Richey. That means so much to me."

"And you, Jamie." She turned to him. "Dean told us everything. I'm sorry I didn't come to see you sooner." She reached for her husband's hand, her voice trembling. "Noah was a kind soul. He loved his friends like family. He wanted you to live, Jamie. And I can't fault him for that." She sniffled, wiping at a stray tear. "We don't hold you responsible for his death. There wasn't anything you could have done. Once Noah made up his mind... well, that was the end of that."

Mr. Richey stepped forward and placed a firm hand on Jamie's arm.

"I know you carry the weight of what happened, but son, we don't blame you. And we still love you."

Jamie's face contorted with emotion, his chest rising and falling with deep, measured breaths. Then, without a word, he let go of my hand and pulled Mr. Richey into a hug.

A man without a son.

A boy without a father.

I had to blink back my own tears as I watched them find a moment of peace together.

Then, just as the moment settled, Mrs. Richey gasped.

"Blakely Mason. Is that a ring I see on your finger? When did this happen?"

A warm flush crept up my cheeks as Jamie's hand found mine again.

"Yes, just this evening."

Her face split into a delighted grin. "Well, congratulations, you two! We are so thrilled for you both. And Blake, if you need any help with wedding planning, you just holler and let me know."

"Thank you, Mrs. Richey. You have no idea how much your love and support mean to me."

"Of course, honey. Now, if you'll excuse me, I need to find myself one of those cute little desserts I keep seeing. All this crying has worked up an appetite."

I squeezed Jamie's hand as Mr. Richey dipped his head before following his wife toward the dessert table.

"I'm glad we had the chance to talk to them," I said. "It feels like closure. We can move forward now, no lingering doubts."

Jamie nodded. "You're right. But you do realize she's about to tell every person who will listen that we're engaged."

"Yep. Look. Mrs. Tilly is already her first victim."

Jamie sighed. "I guess I should tell my mom before she does."

"We better."

Just as we started searching for Jane, I heard my name called.

John.

I turned to Jamie. "You go ahead. I'll come find you in a few."

"Okay, babe." He leaned down, pressing a quick but molten-hot kiss to my lips. "I miss you already."

"Get out of here."

His laughter followed him as he walked away, that familiar sparkle in his eyes making my heart flutter.

As John approached, I composed myself.

"I hear congratulations are in order, Blake!"

"Let me guess—Mrs. Richey?"

"Of course." He smirked. "She told me about your engagement, but I meant congratulations on your promotion."

"My... what?"

John's grin widened.

"I just heard from the board—they absolutely loved your piece on Noah. The way you captured his character and wrapped it into the hometown hero story was perfect. A true tribute to a man who deserved nothing less. That's why they were so impressed with your eye for detail and your ability to craft impactful narratives." His eyes twinkled. "Blake... they want you as editor."

I blinked, trying to process what he was saying.

I got the promotion?

When the paper printed the article a week ago, a promotion had been the furthest thing from my mind. My life had been so chaotic, I'd been focused on damage control, not career moves.

"I... I got the promotion?"

John chuckled. "Yes! And it's well deserved."

"But Mr. Taylor..." My mind raced. "I just agreed to marry Jamie."

"I know. So many good things happening at once."

"But... Jamie's bound to leave Fayetteville at some point."

Being a military spouse meant constant relocations. How could I keep a consistent career?

John placed a reassuring hand on my arm.

"And we'll cross that bridge when we get there. You worked hard for this, Blake. It's time to enjoy the fruits of your labor."

Emotion swelled in my chest.

"I... Thank you. Thank you so much, Mr. Taylor." I didn't know what else to do except throw my arms around him. He had been my mentor, always pushing me to do my best.

He chuckled, patting my back. "Now go back to your man. Lord knows you two can't keep your hands off each other."

My cheeks burned as he winked.

Twice in one night, I was utterly speechless.

A proposal from Jamie.

A promotion at work.

Although... things tended to happen in threes.

What else could possibly happen?

I turned, scanning the crowd for Jamie—

And there was my third surprise.

"Oh my God! Cadence!"

I threw my arms around her.

"What the hell are you doing here?"

She hugged me back just as tight. "I had to come home and support my friends." She pulled back, beaming. "Congratulations, by the way. Apparently for both an engagement and a promotion."

I giggled. "Thank you."

But as I looked at her, I noticed something... off.

Her usual spunk was missing. She was anxious, shifting her gaze around the party like she expected someone to appear out of nowhere.

"Where's Elijah? Is he here?"

Her smile faltered.

"No. We had a fight."

A fight? Cadence never seemed unsettled.

I studied her closer.

"Did something happen?"

She let out a shaky sigh.

"I met someone."

Thank you SO much for going on this journey with me and reading my first published full length novel.

Not ready to say goodbye? Keep reading for a special excerpt of *The Music That Ties Us* that stars none other than Cadence Copeland and Damien Walker.

WANT EVEN MORE??

Download The Night That Ties Us for a **FREE** special prequel Novella to Cain and Isabella's twisted one night stand turned forced proximity full length novel.
https://BookHip.com/ZRMSSCP

One night was supposed to be the end... until it became the beginning.

The Music That Ties Us: Chapter 1

Cadence

<u>Summer</u>

Excitement for tonight coursed through me. It had been too long since I'd gone out and spent time with my sister, just the two of us, and there was nothing better than seeing a live band play.

Jade had been pumping me up for this concert for weeks, claiming this band was her newest obsession. I didn't listen to rock music often. Not because I didn't like it, it just wasn't my usual go-to.

But music resonated with me in all forms, so my anticipation for the night grew as the hour got closer.

Touching up my make-up, I grabbed my outfit off my bed and got dressed. Summer was in full swing, so I decided on jean shorts and a floral tank.

Since I didn't need to impress anyone, I left my dark brown hair in a messy bun.

The front door opened and I heard Elijah call, "Hey, babe."

"In here," I yelled.

Elijah walked into our bedroom, loosening his tie as I zipped my clutch. That beginning honeymoon phase of our relationship ended a long time ago, and it'd been a long time since we greeted each other with a welcome home kiss.

He threw his suit jacket on our bed before studying me. "Are we going somewhere? Do we have plans?"

"I'm meeting with Jade, remember?"

"No. I don't."

"She's taking me to The Music Factory to see a band."

He stilled. "Where?"

"The Music Factory."

"That place is a shit hole. You can't go there."

I crossed my arms and shifted my weight onto one leg. "Elijah, stop. You're being ridiculous."

He ran a hand through his hair. "Cadence, imagine if someone saw you there. People would begin to think *I* go to places like that." He pretended to shiver. "Call Jade and tell her you're not going. I won't allow you to tarnish my reputation by being seen somewhere so beneath us."

Speechless, my mouth fell open. All my eagerness for the night drained from my body. Tension filled my limbs as a fire burned inside me. I took a deep breath, trying to calm myself. He rarely talked to me that way.

"Listen," I said, crossing my arms over my chest. "I don't know what kind of day you had, but you don't control what I do. You don't get to tell me I can't go somewhere with my sister. If you have a problem, we can sit here and discuss it like adults."

He let out a sigh and stepped closer to me. "I'm sorry. I didn't mean for it to come out like that. You know that my parents take the Powell name extremely serious."

And I did.

Elijah was the son of a prestigious family. Charleston had its own royal hierarchy, and the Powells were high on that list as one of the founding families and well-known throughout the area.

When he'd first brought me to visit his family in South Carolina, I was shocked to see the upbringing he'd come from.

In the halls of Villanova, Elijah had simply been a normal college kid who stayed up too late having fun, studying only when absolutely necessary, and playing music on his guitar.

But in his family home, he'd become a completely different person. He'd been stiff, unfeeling, and missing that love for life he normally exhibited. When we returned to school, he reverted to the man I knew once more. I thought it had been a fluke, just a bad weekend, but after we moved to Charleston together, I realized that the Elijah I met at college was the fluke.

He no longer played the guitar—said he didn't have time for 'silly' things anymore. But that had been one of the things about him I'd fallen in love with. Back then, we had shared our passion for music—the melodies, the lyrics, the rhymes—but now there wasn't much we shared anymore.

"It's fine," I said responding to his apology. I grabbed my clutch. There was no truth to my words, but what else could I say? Escalating this fight was the last thing I wanted to do right now. "Listen, Jade is going to be here in a few minutes. Let's talk when I get home, okay?"

His eyes narrowed, a clear sign of his unhappiness about my decision to go, despite him wanting me to stay, but he kept any further comments unspoken. *Smart man.*

"You could always come with us. We used to go see live bands all the time." Maybe we'd reconnect again and reignite that spark we seemed to have lost. Back to when we couldn't keep our hands off each other and the world spun around the two of us. It'd been so long since I felt connected with him.

Elijah scoffed, unbuttoning his dress shirt. "Hell no. I'm good."

He'd answered quickly, proving his priorities. Sadly, I was never one of them. Deflated and defeated, I gave him a quick kiss on the cheek as Jade honked her horn from the driveway.

"I'll be back soon. Love you."

I turned away from him without waiting for a response.

It wasn't until I walked downstairs that he finally replied, "Love you, too."

"Hey, girl! Are you excited?" Jade squeaked as I climbed into her car.

Jade was never anything other than who she was. There were items scattered around the inside of her car and it was a little messy, but it smelled just like her. The mingled scents of raspberry and vanilla. The familiarity alone helped me relax.

I couldn't help but smile. Her vibrant energy was infectious, and I tried to soak up some of her positivity to counter the unsettling way I'd left things with Elijah.

Jade Hardy and I were stepsisters. My dad and her mom married after my parents split. Unfortunately, their marriage only lasted a few years. Despite the break-up, our sisterly bond continued to grow over the years. It didn't matter that we weren't related by blood. We were sisters in all the ways that mattered.

Funny enough, my dad had met Jade's mom in Charleston on one of his business trips. Who'd have guessed I'd eventually move here years later?

"I got you a pick-me-up," Jade said.

Staring at the unnaturally red beverage in her cupholder, I almost got a contact caffeine high from its nearness alone.

"As good as Code Red is, I gave it up after last time." Mountain Dew might be delicious, and Code Red was my favorite flavor, but it was about three days' worth of my sugar intake and it gave me the shakes.

Jade shook her head. "That's mine. Yours is right here."

She thrust a styrofoam cup into my hand, and I took it with narrowed eyes. "My mom always told me not to accept an open container from a stranger."

"Good thing I'm not a stranger. Just drink it, you dork."

I pulled the plastic straw into my mouth and drank, sipping desperately, like an alcoholic taking their first swig of liquor. Dr. Pepper from the soda fountain. "Oh my god, you're a saint."

Jade giggled. "I know."

As she pulled out of the driveway, I cast a longing glance at my house as we drove away. There was a part of me that secretly wished Elijah would appear at the window, waving or at least watching us leave. Any hint that our brief fight had bothered him as much as it did me.

But he didn't.

With both cars tucked away in the closed garage and all the curtains drawn, our house felt vacant. An empty shell instead of a welcoming home.

I let out a heavy breath and took another sip of my drink.

Jade glanced my way. "Okay. What's wrong?"

I didn't want to tell her. I couldn't handle her judgment of my relationship or have her blame Elijah. Even when he was wrong, I always felt a deep-seated need to defend him. "Just a little mix-up with Elijah. He didn't realize I was going out tonight."

"Aw, he misses you."

I snorted. "Yeah, that's it."

Jade peeked at me from the corner of her eye, but kept her focus on the road. "Is it something else then?"

"No, it's really nothing. A simple misunderstanding." An exchange I honestly didn't want to talk about and would love to forget. Talking about it kept the emotions he'd triggered at the forefront of my mind. I just wanted to let them go and enjoy tonight.

It was easy to be myself with her, and I needed that. "Now. Keep your eyes on the road and tell me about this band."

She perked up immediately, and her chest puffed up in delight.

I had executed a perfect change of topic.

"Oh my gosh, Cay." She gushed, and changed lanes without using her turn signal, causing the driver of the car behind us to blare their horn. "They are so amazing. The band's name is Rebel Rebellion. All of the band members are so nice and down to earth. I can't wait to introduce you to them. Their music just gets to me, you know?"

And I did. It was how I felt when I listened to songs that resonated with me. Like the artist wrote the melody for me and only me.

"It doesn't hurt that the guys are easy on the eyes, either." She grinned wickedly.

"So, do you follow them because you like their songs or because you think they're hot?"

Jade laughed. "I mean... both. Can I say both?"

We erupted into a contagious fit of giggles, each burst of laughter peeling away layers of stiffness and I felt more and more like myself.

"Well, there's no better way to get ready for a concert than to jam out to the songs ahead of time. Put them on!"

Jade grinned. "I thought you'd never ask."

Despite the venue being located just across town, the trip from my house on John's Island took us a full hour. The connectors between islands were busy on a good day, but they were a complete mess during rush hour. We didn't mind the traffic, since it gave us plenty of time to relax and listen to music.

When we finally reached The Music Factory, we were giddy from the caffeine and in the middle of a sugar rush—a sugar rush we planned to continue with a few sugary cocktails.

We bounced on the balls of our feet as we paid our cover then went inside. The bar, lined with red cushioned bar stools, was the first thing we saw when we walked through the door. One of the male bartenders lifted his head to greet us, before shaking a drink.

This was the first time I'd stepped inside this place, and I couldn't believe how intimate and cozy it was. I'd expected a grand hall with high ceilings and bright lights, but The Music Factory was the opposite.

I blinked rapidly, allowing my eyes to adjust. The lights were dim, except behind the bar and on stage, and there were only eight tables for guests to sit. The stage was up against the far wall, and there was plenty of room in front of it for everyone to get up and dance to the music.

I was warm, despite the air conditioning working hard to keep the heat at bay. Thankfully, I'd kept my hair up instead of styling it down and having it stick to my neck.

As we walked toward the bar, Jade grabbed my arm, her long nails digging into my skin. "There they are!"

My gaze followed hers to where four guys stood around a

foldable table filled with Rebel Rebellion merch against the far wall. The other bands had tables set up too, but it was clear Jade had only one destination in mind.

"Come on. Let's go say hi."

She pulled me along, and her enthusiasm overflowed as we got closer.

"Hey! You made it out again," one member said, his lips curling into a smile.

"But this time, I brought my sister. This is Cadence."

The stranger offered his hand in a welcoming gesture. His curly, blonde hair tumbled just past his chin, framing a face set with chocolate brown eyes and a smile that radiated warmth and sincerity. He dressed simply in a graphic tee and black jeans. "I'm Hudson. Nice to meet you."

"Hudson is the drummer," Jade added.

"It's nice to meet you. I'm looking forward to the show."

"And I'm Shane, guitarist." A man slid smoothly into place beside Hudson, gently edging him aside. He dressed entirely in black, his ensemble complementing the light brown-colored hair that cascaded to his chin. With his hair parted on the side, I could only see one of his dazzling hazel eyes until he swept the locks back. When I put my hand in his, he leaned into me and smiled. "It's always nice to meet our fans."

"I wouldn't say I'm a fan since I haven't heard you play yet."

Shane smirked. "It's only a matter of time."

"Causing trouble already, Shane?" A tall figure emerged behind him. He sported a white baseball cap worn backward, allowing wisps of brown hair to escape and hang over his deep brown eyes. His lip piercing, the hint of stubble on his face, and the mischievous curve of his smile pulled me in.

"I never cause trouble." Shane crossed his arms.

"I bet your mom would say differently," Hudson said.

Shane grunted in response.

"Colton, this is my sister, Cadence," Jade interjected. "Cadence, Colton."

Colton squeezed my hand tighter than a customary handshake, and I tilted my head. "And what part do you play in this band?"

"Bass guitar."

"I see."

"And that over there..." Colton directed my attention to a form along the wall. "Is our other guitarist, Jeremiah." He was dressed in all black, stationed near the venue's door with a phone held to his ear. The only visible details from this distance were his dark polished nails and the sleek black color of his hair, all combining to add an air of mystery and charm to his presence.

I turned to Jade. "Didn't you say there were five of them?"

"Our lead vocalist is still on the bus, probably fixing his hair." Colton chuckled.

"Why am I not surprised?" Jade wrapped her arm around mine. "We're going to get ourselves a drink. We'll come back to chat later."

"I'm glad you made it to another show, Jade. And it was nice to meet you, Cadence," Colton said.

"Same to you," I said over my shoulder as Jade pulled me away.

"So, what do you think so far?" Jade asked as soon as we were out of earshot.

"Honestly, I'm surprised we could meet them like that. I just assumed there would be a swarm of screaming fans. I'm not sure why, but I didn't think they'd be so..."

"Normal?"

"Yeah. Exactly."

"What can I get you ladies?" the bartender asked as we walked up to the bar.

"I'll have a Sex on the Beach." Jade grinned at me.

Of course she would. It was her signature cocktail.

"Malibu and pineapple for me, please." I loved how they brought my mind to a beach somewhere in the Caribbean. "So, exactly how many times have you seen them play? They seem to know you pretty well."

Jade shrugged. "Maybe four or five? But I've talked to them at every show. I'm just surprised they remember my name. They meet countless people."

"Well, you are quite unforgettable."

Jade tended to overlook the fact that she was gorgeous. Even though Jade and I weren't biological sisters, we still looked the part. Her hair was long like mine and the same shade of dark brown. We were both petite and considered short. The only significant difference between us was the color of our eyes. Hers were a deep brown, whereas mine were the color of amber.

The bartender placed two glasses in front of us. "You ladies are all set. Thank the gentleman down at the end."

Jade and I grabbed our drinks and turned to smile at a middle-aged man dressed in a button up and dress slacks. Jade waved to him, but the person walking in behind him immediately drew my attention.

Captivated, I watched as he walked into the bar like he owned the place. There was an undeniable confidence in his bearing, a magnetism that made it impossible for me to look away.

Adorned in a simple white henley tee paired with gray jeans and black combat boots, his attire hugged his body, accentuating his well sculpted physique. There was a hint of color marking his skin above the collar of his shirt and up the side of his neck, and I suspected that wasn't the only tattoo on him. With each step he took, light glinted off the chain draped from the front pocket of his jeans to the back. His deep red hair was tousled effortlessly atop his head, perfectly outlining the striking features of his scruffy, but handsome face.

Transfixed, I remained motionless as he made his way to the table of guys Jade and I had just left. As he circled behind it and greeted the members of Rebel Rebellion, a wave of realization washed over me.

Then, he lifted his head, and his gaze met mine. His eyes were a piercing shade of icy blue, and they ensnared me in an unbreakable hold.

I inhaled sharply, my cheeks warming. He totally just busted me for ogling him from across the room, and now there was no escaping the intensity of his gaze. A gaze that seemed to see right through me.

"Perfect timing!" Jade said, snapping me out of the spell. "I just saw Damien. Come on."

I allowed Jade to lead me once more, fully aware of our destination and the person she intended to introduce me to.

But little did she know, we'd already had our own introduction.

The Music That Ties Us: Chapter 2

Cadence

I couldn't explain the simmering heat that grazed my body from Damien's stare as we approached. He took me in from head to toe, an intense look as he assessed me. Walking around the table to greet us, he smirked.

"Hey, Jade. It's good to see you again." He pulled her into a quick hug before turning back to me. "And you are?"

I lifted my chin, pulling my shoulders back and standing tall. "Cadence." I stuck out my hand. "Jade's sister. Nice to meet you..." I purposely left my sentence hanging, trying to pretend Jade hadn't already told me his name and everything else she knew about him.

"Damien Walker."

The moment his fingers clasped mine, I sensed it.

A jolt.

A bond.

An electric attraction.

His warm hand in mine sent a wave of goosebumps through

my body. I was acutely aware of him, and in that instance, it was as if everyone around us disappeared. Leaving only him and I, his soft skin pressed to mine.

I pulled away, frowning.

Damien recovered quickly, stepping closer and acting as if he'd felt nothing. "This is your first show, isn't it? I'd remember if I'd met you before."

He smiled at me, but something shone more profound behind those cool blue eyes. Something fierce. I could tell he was intrigued by our little exchange as he analyzed every tiny detail.

"Ha. Yeah. Cadence's boyfriend doesn't let her out much."

My head snapped toward Jade. "Gee, thanks."

"Boyfriend, huh?" Damien paused. "He sounds like a real winner."

I looked at Damien, but the heat in his eyes had disappeared, replaced with a note of indifference as he moved away from us.

"Are you excited about tonight's show?" Jade asked, not picking up on the change in his attitude as he turned to face her again.

"Of course. I love what I do. Meeting new people and being on stage. I have the best job in the world." He crossed his arms, and without his piercing gaze on me, I noticed all the pieces of jewelry that decorated his body: small gauges set in his ears, a stud in his bottom lip, and another in his nose. His accessories matched, with beaded and leather bands wrapped around his wrists, and a string of beads around his neck. I could see colorful ink on his wrist, peeking out from under his sleeve.

"I can only imagine." Jade smiled wistfully.

As children, Jade and I thought we'd become famous singers when we made it to adulthood. In those days, we'd been positive we would find our big break and sing the songs we wrote with our choreographed dances. We even came up with stage names and picked which cities to tour as the amazing duet of Kodi and Rhyan. But as we grew up, we stopped planning for our big gigs and stopped writing those songs. Eventually, those dreams became nothing more than part of a child's vivid imagination.

"Speaking of which," Damien said, his face expressionless. "I should get back to the bus. I need to get ready. Warms ups and all that." He turned toward his bandmates. "You know where to find me."

And without a moment of hesitation, he vanished and took all the warmth in my body with him.

Colton threw his arm around my shoulder as a gust of cold air made me shiver. "Don't let our lead singer's hot and cold attitude get under your skin. He's always like that."

"Why would it bother me? I just met him."

And I meant every word. Damien's actions, or lack thereof, didn't affect me at all.

Whatever tension or weird energy had passed between us, it meant nothing.

I would go home tonight to Elijah and never think about Damien Walker again.

"We're gonna head to the bus and get ready for the show, too." Hudson turned his head to Colton. "You comin'?"

Colton nodded and looked at Jade and me with a grin. "See you from the stage."

"Let's find a table until the show starts," Jade said as we watched the guys walk out of the vendor's entrance.

I followed her like a lost puppy to a table near the bar.

I hated to admit it, but being here felt entirely out of my element. The hem of my shirt had risen up my back, so I pulled it down before I wrapped my arms around myself to stave off the chill from the AC.

Now that the climactic event of 'meeting the band' was over, I looked around, wondering if I could sneak out and call an Uber.

Oh my God. I let my shoulders sag, and my eyes flutter closed. *Idiot.* Was I seriously trying to leave? After Jade had practically begged me to come and share this with her. This is exactly why I needed to get out more. I needed to live a little.

Jade was right. I rarely went out as it was, and even less without Elijah. Clearly, I needed to change that. Surviving a night on my own would be easy peasy lemon squeezy. Besides, I was here with my best friend. I didn't need anyone else.

I finished my drink, hoping the small amount of alcohol would help me relax. Unfortunately, Malibu Rum wasn't exactly potent, so I felt nothing.

The first band of the night made their appearance on stage and music soon filled the small space. I winced as a thunderous sound enveloped us. Beside me, Jade moved to the music, loosening up with each beat.

The noise overwhelmed me. The pounding of the drum and the cry of the electric guitar agitated my nerves. I took a deep breath and tried to enjoy it as much as Jade did. The rock band was called Twisted Elements, and their intense sound was so different from what I usually listened to. Something about the tune didn't sit well with me. It was harsh in my ears, lacking the melodies I craved to hear.

"I'm going to get another drink. Want anything?" I yelled over the music.

"Yeah, I'll have one more."

I grabbed her empty glass and walked to the bar.

"Can I get a vodka cranberry and a Sex on the Beach, please?"

"No problem. Anything else?" the bartender asked.

"Yeah, a shot of tequila."

"Sure thing, sweetie." A twinkle sparkled in his eye as he looked me up and down.

Rolling my eyes, I turned sideways and leaned against the light chestnut wood, watching the band on stage giving everything they had. I only wished I enjoyed their performance more.

I held onto the hope that Rebel Rebellion would give a better show. Jade wouldn't be here if they sucked. There was no way I could suffer through this much longer.

The bartender placed the shot and our drinks in front of me. I grabbed the shot glass and tipped my head back. The warmth ran down my throat and into my belly, quickly soothing my restless nerves. I smiled as I set the glass back down, and the bartender pushed another shot across the bar.

"This one is on the house."

My gaze dropped from the bartender to the glass, and back up again. He was kind of cute, kind of not. He looked like he prioritized arm day at the gym over leg day and he was shorter than I preferred. With spiked-up dark brown hair and matching eyes, he wasn't anyone I'd write home about.

"Thanks," I said with a grin, playing my part. I downed the shot with a wink before placing a few bills on the bar, grabbed my drinks, and walked away.

The alcohol made its way through my veins, the signs unmistakable. My limbs grew heavy, but I welcomed the lightness in my mind that came with it—a perfect contradiction. The aggressive rumbling music no longer bothered me, and I let myself relax.

It seemed I was more distracted than I'd realized. I returned to the table as Twisted Elements finished and the members of Rebel Rebellion were climbing on stage to set up their equipment.

"Great timing. Let's head toward the stage."

I handed Jade her drink and raised an eyebrow. "We aren't going to sit here?"

"Now, where's the fun in that?"

Once again, eagerness radiated off her in waves. Her attitude was so infectious that I couldn't stop my mouth from curving into a grin to mirror hers.

I gestured. "Lead the way."

I followed her as we walked through the crowd, allowing my own spark to tingle within. I had a new pep in my step. Was it from the alcohol or actual excitement? I wasn't sure. But it didn't matter. I was finally having fun.

My gaze bounced between the band members I'd just met, watching Colton set up the amps, and Hudson perfect the position of his drums.

And then *he* appeared.

He strolled onto the stage as if it were just another ordinary night, unaware he would bare his soul to the entire establishment.

Damien.

Immediately, his gaze locked onto mine, causing my breath to catch in my throat. Once again, he fascinated me with the passion behind his gorgeous eyes.

He had transformed his attire, now cloaked entirely in black and leather, his hair sculpted and standing on his head in a faux hawk. It should be a crime how, with every stride he took, he exuded a blend of unshakable confidence and smoldering sex appeal, mesmerizing everyone in the room. With his shirt sleeves rolled up I could see the intricate tattoos that lined his arm, and I loved the way the color contrasted against his dark clothes.

"I'm so excited!" Jade squealed beside me, and I let my gaze fall to her.

When I turned back to the stage, Damien was bent over plugging in his microphone.

The spell was broken.

I lifted the corner of my mouth. "Me too."

I took a large gulp of my drink, trying even harder to chase away the unsettled feeling that burrowed in the pit of my stomach whenever I saw Damien. A feeling that grew stronger each minute.

It felt like a premonition, like this one night would irrevocably change my life forever.

While they ran through sound check, the crowd gathered around the stage.

A palpable sense of anticipation and exhilaration buzzed through the air.

Damien looked out into the audience, enjoying every second he was in that spotlight, before his gaze settled on me with a mischievous grin.

And then they played.

Indescribable sensations washed over me as the chords on the guitars rang out. The hair on my arms stood at attention, waiting for what would come next. As Hudson hit the drums, it reverberated throughout my entire body. Each beat felt responsible for pumping the blood through me instead of my heart.

When Damien stepped up to the middle of the stage and stood before his microphone, he already had me in a trance.

His gaze met mine briefly before popping back out to the crowd. "Who's ready for some rock' n' roll?" Damien laughed into the mic as the audience roared. "I can't hear you!"

When the first note left his lips, his voice caressed my body like an old lover.

Primal and sensual.

Velvety smooth.

And undeniably sexy.

His words enthralled me, and I surrendered, a more than willing prisoner.

Broody and intense, Damien was tantalizing. Like a damn walking aphrodisiac. Performing on stage, he was breathtakingly beautiful. The way his eyes lit up and his face scrunched up with joy as he vocalized all the emotions of the song. He moved with ease, at home in the lights and in front of the crowd. But it was the grin that spread across his lips, showing off his perfect white teeth, that revealed the true ecstasy he felt.

Around me, the world was alive, but Damien alone ensnared my attention. My body swayed, entirely under his spell as the melody coursed through me. I let it consume me, move me, a symphony of sensations that was as intoxicating as it was exhilarating.

A wave of tranquility washed over me. At this moment, I didn't have to be perfect Cadence on display for others to watch, or walk around with the label of Elijah Powell's girlfriend. I could just be myself. Be who I truly was.

Music was an escape for me, it always had been. A place that always welcomed me with open arms. It never let me down. I'd lose myself in the beat and belt out the lyrics as if they could make my problems disappear.

Damien's rich, powerful voice tempted me, resonating deep within my soul and demanded my undivided attention.

"With every step, I'm drawn to your flame.
Consumed by a desire, I can't contain."

The Music That Ties Us: Chapter 2

Damien cried into the microphone.

I moved my body purposefully, jumping and dancing, losing myself in the sea of strangers around me. The air was stuffy, heavy with the electric energy coming off the stage.

Damien put everything within him into this performance.

He was born to be on stage.

The crowd grew thicker around us, pushing Jade and me closer together, all equally bewitched by Rebel Rebellion's music. So, it had to be a coincidence when I found Damien's eyes on me once again. *Right?*

> *"Can't break free from this hold on me,*
> *I'm lost in your chaos, can't you see?"*

It was like he was singing directly to me, which was crazy. He wouldn't be able to pick me from a lineup. But while he held my gaze, he kept me hypnotized.

My body warmed from his attention, heat settling deep in my lower belly. His words... they turned me on.

He turned me on.

When the last note faded at the end of their set, Damien finally looked back out over the crowd. "Thank you all for coming out tonight. We appreciate each and every one of you. Be safe out there and don't do anything we wouldn't do, which leaves a lot open for your interpretation." The crowd laughed with him. "But remember: We are Rebel Rebellion!"

Then the lights came on, blinding us all, and snapping me from the trance I'd fallen into.

The guys stepped offstage, out of sight, but I didn't want the music to end. I wanted more.

Jade turned toward me with the biggest grin on her face. "Amazing, right?"

I wouldn't be able to explain my emotions if someone held

me at gunpoint. I struggled to regain my composure and anchor myself back to reality. So I settled on a simple, "Yeah."

"Come on, let's go to the bar and grab a drink while we wait for them to return to their merch table."

As we ordered another round, I used my hand to fan my warm cheeks, the temperature inside now an inferno.

Jade collapsed against the bar. "Ugh, I could watch them perform every single day."

I honestly couldn't argue with her. "Where is their next show?"

"Unfortunately, they travel north tonight. Somewhere in Ohio, I think."

"Hmm."

Jade's disappointment about Rebel Rebellion's show being over was understandable. She loved the band and was sad to see them leave. But for me, the night ending meant that I was returning to my everyday life, exactly how it had always been. My golden carriage would be turned back into a pumpkin at midnight.

The tiny snippet of freedom I'd experienced tonight would disappear.

That realization scared me.

"Oh! The guys are back. Let's say hi, and then we need to start thinking of heading home." Jade sighed dramatically. "Work tomorrow and all that."

I laughed. "Adulting is the absolute worst."

She wrapped her arm around mine as we left the bar. "Remember the days we built forts in the basement as kids?"

"Yeah."

"And all we had to worry about was beating the next boss on whatever RPG we were playing."

"Uh-huh."

"Those were simpler times."

"And we had a curfew, no money, and were huge nerds."

Jade laughed. "We're still nerds. Just being a nerd nowadays is considered cool."

I joined in her laughter. "Yeah, you got me there. We're the OG nerds."

A crowd had surrounded Rebel Rebellion's merchandise table, and we hung back waiting for it to die down. The band kept up the best they could as the fans gushed and raved about their performance. Women asked for their signatures, and not all requests were for appropriate places

I couldn't hide my grin when Damien's cheeks reddened as he swiped his black Sharpie along the top of a woman's breast who was old enough to be my grandmother.

But he was all smiles and welcomed everyone to the table.

Once the crowd had dissipated and Jade and I were among last few left, his smile slipped when he noticed me.

Was I imagining things?

Shane approached us. "So, Cadence. How did you like your first show?"

"You guys were fantastic up there. I really mean it."

Colton threw his arm around me. "So, we converted you into a fan then?"

"Absolutely." I smiled up at Colton. "And Damien." I turned my head toward him. "You were incredible."

Damien narrowed his eyes. "Thanks."

I was about to ask him what his problem was, but Jade grabbed his bicep, and his previous smile slid into place. "I swear you guys get better every time I watch you play."

"Aw, thank you, Jade. That means a lot." Damien pulled her into a quick embrace.

This couldn't be my imagination. Damien was totally giving me the cold shoulder. He showed Jade his fun, flirty side, while all I got was his side-eye and one-word answers.

I didn't like it when people were upset with me. As a people pleaser at heart, I wanted everyone to like me, and when they didn't, it gnawed at me, consuming my thoughts. It compelled me to try even harder to get him to like me.

I moved out of Colton's reach to stand beside Jade and tried to engage with him again. "Hopefully, I'll be able to make the next show."

"It's okay if you can't." Damien didn't even look at me.

What. The. Hell.

Well, screw you too, buddy. Even I had a limit to how much I would try. It was rare, but I guess there were people in the world who just didn't like me. But it didn't make sense. I'd done nothing to him.

I turned toward Hudson, Shane, Colton, and Jeremiah. "You guys are seriously great. I hope you'll be back in South Carolina soon."

Met with a round of 'thank you's, I perked up and turned back to Jade. "Are you ready?"

"Yep! See you guys next time!"

We walked out of the stuffy bar and into the warm, damp air. The breeze coming off the ocean was a welcome respite on a summer night in Charleston. I shivered as a new sense of foreboding washed over me.

"That was so much fun," Jade said as we climbed into her car.

"It really was. Thank you for bringing me along."

"Of course! I can't *not* drag my sister to meet some of the coolest people I know."

She giggled as she maneuvered out of the parking lot, barely missing two parked cars and a streetlight, and began our drive home.

We were quiet, lost in our own thoughts, and as we got closer to my house, I felt my grip on my newfound independence slip away. Vanishing before me like an early morning fog as the sun rose.

When she pulled into my driveway, she handed me a CD.

"What's this?" I asked.

"I knew you wouldn't get one yourself, so I bought you Rebel Rebellion's CD. I had Colton get everyone to sign it, too."

I opened the cover, and sure enough, each one of their scribbled signatures decorated the inside. They were unreadable, but I could make out the capital D. I ran my finger over his name, still bothered by the fact that he so clearly disliked me.

Maybe that was the reason for my fascination with him. I was drawn to him simply because I couldn't stand knowing he didn't want to be around me.

"Thank you for this."

Jade pulled me into an awkward hug over her center console. "Anytime. And thanks for coming with me tonight."

"I'm glad I came." And I was. I learned something about myself tonight. Being attached to Elijah ensured I acted a certain way out in public. I just never realized that somewhere along the way, I'd made his rules my rules too.

Don't draw attention to yourself.

Don't be obnoxious.

Don't be too loud.

Be calm, cool, and collected at all times.

When I walked in, the house was completely dark. Elijah usually went to bed early, so it was no surprise.

I made my way through my home effortlessly. Sticky and sweaty from the bar, I walked to our ensuite bathroom for a shower.

The steam enveloped me, and I rolled my head from side to side, trying to release the tension. My body felt wound up and jittery. Like I needed to run a marathon or scream at the top of my lungs into the night sky.

I squeezed the back of my neck, seeking any form of relief. My other hand trailed down my shoulder to my chest, where my heartbeat quickened.

I knew what I needed, what I wanted.

Moving my hand over my breast, I inhaled sharply as my fingers moved over my taut nipple. Continuing down over the planes of my stomach, I slowed just below my belly button.

I didn't make it a habit of touching myself. Orgasms were usually better when shared with a partner. But right now, I didn't want to share this with anyone.

I closed my eyes as I pushed my hand lower.

Biting my lip as my fingers found my clit, swollen and needy. I knew I'd find my slit wet and slick. It had been that way since Damien had ensnared me within his grasp.

Moaning as I found my rhythm, I spread my thighs wider to give myself more room. Leaning my back against the wall of the shower, I pulled my foot up on the edge of the tub and nearly finished as soon as I pushed two fingers into my core.

The stream from the water hit my sensitive skin like needles as I bucked against my hand.

Pleasure surged through my body as my breathing grew ragged and I tightened around my fingers.

The last thing I saw before I came apart, was a pair of icy blue eyes and a devilish smirk.

The Music That Ties Us:
Chapter 3

Damien

I woke slowly to the sound of another grown man snoring.

Groaning loudly, I pulled my pillow over my ears, trying to drown out Hudson's blatant bragging about his being asleep while I tossed and turned.

My bunk vibrated as the bus rumbled down the road. Normally the motion soothed me. Today it irritated me.

It had only been about two weeks since we'd played in Charleston. This leg of the tour focused on the eastern side of the country and we were on our way to Columbia, South Carolina. An overnight drive from Pittsburg, PA.

Lucky for us, our tour bus had everything we needed. A shower, a place to sit and eat, and an area in the back where we would pull out the instruments and have an impromptu jam session when we needed a moment to breathe.

My bunk was the only area on the bus that was truly my own, and even though I couldn't stretch out completely without my head hitting the wall, it felt like my home away from home. That's how it was when you were six foot three.

But the curtains were far from soundproof, and I swear Hudson wanted to test my patience as his snores grew louder.

The six bunks were in the middle of the bus, with three on either side stacked on top of each other. Even though Hudson's bunk was on the opposite side of mine, it was still within arm's reach.

Slamming my eyes shut, I tried to fall back into dreamland. To no avail.

I growled, frustrated with myself. I wanted the sleep, *needed* the sleep. But lately, I got less and less.

I grabbed my phone from under my pillow, squinting as my irises adjusted to the sudden onslaught of light.

A dozen or so notifications popped up on my screen. Most were from our social media accounts relaying comments from fans. I always made it a point to respond to anyone who reached out. It was important they knew how much we appreciated their support. How much *I* appreciated their support.

We wouldn't be here without them.

I clicked on the text notification, surprised to see a message from Jodie.

Jodie was the nurse hired to take care of my sister. My stomach jumped into my throat.

JODIE

> I'm taking Violet to the ER. She's having some trouble breathing.

It took all of my restraint to keep from bolting out of my bunk. Steadying my shaking hand, I skipped texting back and immediately called her.

Jodie picked up on the second ring. "Hey, Damien. I'm sorry to bother you so early."

"It's fine. Don't ever feel like you can't call me. How's Violet doing?"

"I'll be honest. It's not looking good. The doctors think the cancer is back."

Words caught in my throat. My vision blurred as I thought about losing another person I loved.

"We're waiting on some test results to come back."

I let out a long breath. "Is she awake? Can I talk to her?"

"Yeah, hang on."

I heard a door opening and closing and some shuffling before Violet said, "Hey."

She sounded weak and tired, and it broke my heart not to be there for her. "Hey Vi. How are you feeling?"

"Stop. I can hear the worry in your voice. I'm not ready to kick the bucket yet. Still got a few more fires to raise, if you know what I mean."

I chuckled. "I'm sure it will take more than your cancer returning to knock you out. We aren't that lucky."

"Damn right, you're not. I can't leave my brother to fend for himself. Fuck cancer. It can't keep me down." Her voice grew gravely despite her words, and she erupted into a fit of coughs. I didn't want to force her talk, I only needed to hear her voice.

"Vi. I need you to stay focused on getting better and out of the hospital."

"You can count on it."

"Will you hand the phone back to Jodie?"

"Yeah. And remember, I love you, Rascal."

"I love you, too." Her old nickname for me stirred some- thing in my chest as more rustling came through the speaker before Jodie came back on.

"Anything she needs, anything at all. No questions, send me the bill. I'll take care of it."

"Violet is lucky to have you."

"I'm the lucky one. She took care of me when I had no one else."

I was instantly brought back to when I was twelve years old and finding out our father had fallen off an electrical pole and died. He was a lineman, and I couldn't understand why he would free climb a forty-foot pole, only to have his gaff not grip enough and fall to his death. The helmet he wore stood no chance of protecting his head, not from a fall like that. Our dad had been our sole caretaker after our mom had run off with my dad's best friend. Without him, Violet and I had no one left.

But the person who took the brunt of the tragedy was Violet. At sixteen, she took it upon herself to become the household provider. I couldn't begin to imagine what she had done to keep warm meals on our table and a roof over our head.

Violet was the only woman in my life who'd never hurt or betrayed me. And I could never repay her for all she gave up to make sure I never went without.

And now, she was a happy mother of two.

"Where are Grant and Maylee?" I asked.

"Legally, they are old enough to stay home alone, but I didn't want to risk it while they slept. Marianne came by to watch them while we're gone."

"How much longer will the doctors keep her?"

"Honestly? I don't know. They won't release her until they figure out why she can't breathe."

I squeezed the bridge of my nose and tried to push back the emerging migraine. Grant and Maylee didn't deserve this. They'd already been through so much in their short lives.

"Anything the kids need—a sitter, entertainment, whatever —I'll take care of it. Violet doesn't need to worry about anything but getting better."

"Okay. I'll keep you updated."

"Thank you, Jodie." I let my head fall back against my pillow.

"You take care of yourself, too. The last thing we need is for something to happen to you. I'll be in touch."

We hung up, and seconds later, Shane pushed my curtain aside and leaned down into my bunk looking like a bat in a cave.

"She okay?"

"Not great. But hangin' in there."

"I'm sorry, man."

I ran my hands down my face. "Nothing anyone can do. But thanks."

"We'll be back home soon. Only a few more shows on this tour."

"Not soon enough. The kids need me."

Shane didn't answer right away. He scrunched his brow as he said, "I know you love those kids, Damien. But isn't there someone else who can help take care of them? Somewhere they could stay while Violet gets better and you tour?"

I had to fight the red-hot anger as it bubbled inside me at his words.

My jaw tightened. "I'm all they have. I won't abandon them." I never wanted them to feel like I did as a kid. Like I wasn't good enough. That no one cared about me. That no one loved me.

Shane sighed. "I know you won't. Just remember, I'm here if you need anything." Shane straightened and the curtain fell back into place. "All you have to do is ask."

But that was the problem, wasn't it?

I wasn't one to ask for help.

I could do it myself.

Most people didn't realize the behind-the-scenes work that went into playing a gig. Besides the actual performance, we had to set up and tear down, perform equipment checks, book with the venue, and arrange for travel. Even though we'd signed with a label, most of those duties fell squarely on our shoulders.

Colton put an amp down beside me. "That's the last of it. Now we need to set up the merch table."

I huffed, moving my hands from my hips to wipe the sweat from my forehead. "Always something to be done."

Colton smirked. "Don't worry, Princess. We won't have you do too much."

I turned to face him. "What?"

"I said don't worry. Before the show tonight, you'll have plenty of time to press your outfit and style your hair."

Glaring, I raised my chin. He was barely taller than me, but I could scrap with the best of them and I wasn't afraid to get my hands dirty when needed. One of the consequences of going through the teenage years without parents. "I've had a really shitty morning. I don't have time for your immaturity right now."

"Hey, guys. Let's cool it down, okay?" Hudson said, stepping between us.

I scoffed as I turned and started walking away, yelling over my shoulder. "It's your lucky day, Colton."

I walked out into the afternoon sun, my fists clenched tight, ready to hit something, anything. Anger, frustration, and helplessness pulsed through me, and I couldn't quiet the storm. There were times when Colton and I didn't see eye to eye. The phrase 'too many cooks in the kitchen' applied, but I couldn't see how this little tussle was related. As far as I knew, we had been on the same page with band stuff for a while.

As we completed the preparations for the show, the weight of my emotions pressed down on me. I felt like a metal wire, each moment winding me tighter and tighter. Worry for my sister and the urgent need to be with my niece and nephew gnawed at me. It was only a matter of time before the tension became too much to bear and I snapped.

Colton and I stayed out of each other's way for the rest of the afternoon. As patrons arrived at the venue, I put on my most friendly façade. The last thing I needed was my resting bitch face to be misinterpreted by someone who came to enjoy our music.

Standing behind the merch table, I took in a deep breath and rolled my shoulders, forcing the stiffness away and allowing the muscles in my body to relax.

It wasn't only passion that drove me, music was part of who I was. I found myself in every note, every harmony, every song.

It was the essence of my existence and coursed through my veins. Without music, I felt nothing but emptiness.

I needed it. I craved it.

It was all of me, and just knowing I'd be performing soon improved my mood. None of my worries could touch me on stage.

But then I sensed her gaze on me.

I knew it was her without seeing her. There was something about her aura that resonated with mine. Her unexpected appearance caught me off guard, and I was already fighting to keep my head above water.

Fuck.

My mood instantly plummeted. Something about this girl lit me up like Fourth of July fireworks. I plastered on a charming expression to hide the unease that swirled inside me.

"Damien! Hi! We made it." Jade was all smiles as I walked out from behind the table and pulled her into a hug.

"I didn't realize you'd be here." I let her go, and she automatically stepped back—next to *her.*

"Honestly, we weren't sure we would make it in time. Traffic was a mess. But you know we wouldn't miss it for the world."

I finally turned to acknowledge her.

Cadence.

Of course, I remembered her name. Even though I tried hard not to.

She was beautiful, but in a way that made you wonder if she knew just how beautiful she was. Petite, but feisty. Clearly, she had no problem holding her own. Despite a slim waist, her shorts hugged her curves, and there was definitely enough of her to hold to. But her most striking feature was her honey-colored eyes. They had pulled me in from the very first time I'd held her gaze across the bar back in Charleston.

There was electricity behind them, passion. And I'd sought that light the rest of the night.

Idiot.

She couldn't know she'd left an impression on me. That of all the women who had propositioned me since that night didn't hold a candle to the fire that burned within me for her. Something like that would only make me vulnerable, and the last thing I needed was another groupie to get the idea that I wanted more from them. I wasn't that kind of guy anymore.

Always so full of yourself. She already has a boyfriend, fuck-face. She doesn't want you, anyway.

Whatever.

As soon as I'd found out she had a boyfriend, it was like the proverbial ice bucket had been dumped over my head. I didn't usually fuck around with other guy's girls. And if I needed to keep telling myself that to keep my thoughts on the straight and narrow—to stop from imagining myself peeling off every piece of fabric covering her skin—that's what I'd do.

"I didn't think I'd be seeing you again..." I paused. "Cassie?"

God, I was an ass.

She crossed her arms over her chest, giving me a better view of her cleavage, an adorable pout forming on her mouth. "It's good to see you too, Derek. I mean, Damien."

I bit the inside of my cheek, fighting excruciatingly hard to keep the smirk from my lips.

Tou-fucking-ché

Jade giggled. "Damien. You remember my sister, Cadence."

"Ah. Right. Cadence. My bad."

I looked away from them, deliberately steering clear of Cadence's penetrating gaze. Even though I was deep in my own denial, I couldn't shake the remnants of what echoed inside me the last time I'd been caught there.

Undeniable desire.

Profound hunger.

Insatiable need.

I needed to get out of here. To escape that magnetic pull of her presence. "Enjoy the show. I'm heading to the bus."

Moving away without sparing them another glance, my lungs burned, my muscles ached. I knew I was being a dick to Cadence, but I didn't know how to be anything else.

Besides, you know what they say. When a guy was mean to a girl, it meant he had a crush on her.

The guys knew better than to interrupt me during my warm-ups. It was something I didn't mess around with, ensuring my voice was at its peak for each performance, since it allowed me to be up on that stage. I had to make sure I took care of it.

I soon forgot about Cadence and the unwanted fascination between us as I became entirely absorbed in my music.

Back in the venue, I stood just off the stage and waited for Hudson to hit the drums and start our set. That familiar sensation of adrenaline and excitement came over me. I was sporting an ear-to-ear grin as the guitars picked up their part and the melodies merged.

The roar of the crowd pulsed through my ears. Their passion and anticipation were so thick in the air I could stick my tongue out and taste it.

I didn't get nervous about our shows. Sure, I felt normal jitters, but it wasn't anything close to fear. I loved it up there. And honestly, the stage lights were so damn bright I usually couldn't see into the crowd. The only people I was aware of were my bandmates.

So tell me why, as soon as I ran onto the stage, gripped the microphone in my hand, and sang those first few notes, I found those mesmerizing golden eyes once again.

I felt her gaze all over my body. And I fucking loved it.

Giving every piece of my soul into my performance, I locked eyes with her. I knew she was watching me so, naturally, I wanted to impress her.

Her and the rest of the crowd, of course.

But the mesmerizing way she moved her body to my music enthralled me. If eye-fucking was a legit thing, I'd have fucked her all the way across the county and back. At least twice.

I hated that I saw her, *desired her.* I wanted nothing to do with her, but I was a glutton for punishment. And... there was just something about her eyes.

Hypnotic.

Alluring.

Irresistible.

I finished the set, praying no one could see the semi in my pants. The last thing I needed was a hard-on while on stage.

As I made my way back to our merch table, my love for music pulled me out of the haze once again. I became lost in the sea of people who came to meet us after the show. In those moments, I felt truly blessed to be doing what I do. I met new fans, greeted old ones, took photos, and signed merchandise. It was all I ever wanted to do. Make connections with people and inspire them.

I was weightless and walking on clouds. The high I felt coming off stage was potent enough that nothing could bring me down.

All the anger and stress that had swirled around me earlier —the worry about my sister, niece, and nephew—vanished. I was my best self when I was performing.

Standing for yet another photo, I contorted my face in any silly way possible, because you couldn't take life too seriously. At least that was what I told myself when I felt the weight of the world on my shoulders.

As I turned, ready to talk to another patron at the table, I caught Colton off to the side talking to Jade and Cadence.

"Omigod, I love your music," a girl said, stopping me in my tracks. "You are seriously the coolest person I've ever met. I can't believe this! Can you please sign my CD?" The girl looked like she'd just graduated high school, complete with the emo-kid starter pack of dark eyeliner, fishnets, and all-black attire.

"I'm glad you liked the show." I tried to give her my full, undivided attention, but the sound of delighted laughter distracted me. From the corner of my eye, I saw Cadence throw her head back as Colton touched her arm. The sound, angelic and pure, grated on my nerves.

"This is seriously the best day of my life. Can we please get a picture? I think I'm in love with you."

I forced out a laugh. "Of course, sweetie."

I posed for the photo, doing my best to look like I wasn't annoyed as fuck.

When Cadence smiled, those intoxicating eyes twinkled and her full lips curved. It was an entirely different side to her beauty. Her straight, white teeth stood in stark contrast to her dark hair.

She'd never smiled like that at me. But then, I'd never given her a reason to.

After the girl left the table, I called over to Colton. "Can I get a hand over here?"

Colton's smile dropped for a second as he made his way over. "What's up?"

"How about spending time with our fans instead of standing on the sidelines batting eyes at girls?"

Colton narrowed his gaze, his posture straightening as he grew angry. But he knew as well as I did, that he wouldn't cause a scene. At least not here. "Yeah. Alright."

There was no stopping the victory dance I did in my head. Just because I couldn't have her didn't mean I wanted anyone else to.

As the crowds thinned out, the day's stress came back and hit me with full force. I took a sip of the beer someone had brought me, trying to get rid of the numbness settling in my limbs. Not that it helped. I knew alcohol would only make it worse.

"Think we should start packing up?" Shane asked.

"I don't see no harm in it." Hudson shrugged.

Colton leaned up against the wall with his arms crossed, glowering. "Might as well. We need to head out soon."

Jeremiah nodded in agreement.

The patrons that remained in the bar were more focused on getting their alcohol fix than visiting our merch table. So, we began the excruciatingly mundane task of packing and taking loads to the trailer.

The humid air clung to me uncomfortably as Colton and I placed the last totes inside, when someone touched my shoulder.

"We are heading out. It's getting late." Jade reached for me as Cadence walked into Colton's arms. I watched as he rubbed her back and ran his hands over her shoulders. He smiled down at her with that crinkle in his eye.

The next thing I knew, Cadence stood before me while Jade hugged Colton. She looked as uncomfortable as I felt.

"Um..." She pulled her bottom lip into her mouth and stared at her feet. "Bye."

It was weird going from the constant eye contact she'd given me on stage to her not even wanting to look at me.

It made me angry.

I grabbed her arm and tugged her against me in a quick hug. She was warm and soft, and I was instantly aware of how seamlessly her curves fit against me. Like two pieces of the same puzzle. Despite our embrace being brief and completely innocent, it held the promise of something more, something profound, between us.

I let her go, eager to cut that magnetic connection. But what could I say? She was a beautiful brunette, with golden eyes and an ass worth worshiping.

If someone were to put in a dictionary somewhere, 'Damien Walker's type of girl' there would be a picture of Cadence next to it.

"Yeah. See ya," I said, moving away. As if pretending she wasn't there would actually help.

When they finally left, Colton turned toward me.

"The fuck is your deal, Damien?"

I closed my eyes before facing him and standing to my full height. "I'm not sure what you mean, Colton."

"Yeah, you do. You've been extra pissy lately. And can we talk about what is happening with you and Cadence? You treat her like shit but then stare at her like a fucking creep. Everyone can see it. If you want her, then grow a pair. If you don't, stop being a bitch when someone else wants to give her a chance."

"You know I don't sleep with fans." The words burned like acid in my mouth.

Colton scoffed. "At least not anymore."

I grabbed Colton's shirt and threw him up against the side of the trailer in a blind rage. "You better watch what you're saying. You don't know what tree you're barking up."

And he didn't. I'd never shared intimate details about my relationship with Vanessa and how it ended. How she stole not only the love I had to give, but made it so I no longer had the ability to receive it ever again. "Besides," I said. "Cadence has a boyfriend. She's off limits."

Colton pushed me away before walking toward the door. "So? When has that ever stopped any of us before?"

I clenched my fists and grit my teeth as Colton disappeared. Was he saying that just to piss me off or did the bastard want her all to himself?

Fuck.

Grab your copy of The Music That Ties Us and finish their captivating story.
https://a.co/d/oZaaKDx

Want to stay connected?
Join my exclusive Facebook group for all the fun and insider information:
Nicolette Terry's Rebels and Romantics Reading Group

The Music That Ties Us
Read Cadence's story. Out now!

"I don't want you."

"I don't want you, either."

Cadence Copeland's life is unraveling. Betrayed by the man she thought she'd love forever and watching her career go up in flames, she's left to pick up the pieces. A night out at a rock concert throws her into the orbit of Damien Walker—a brooding, magnetic rockstar with piercing blue eyes and a past he keeps locked away.

Damien lives by one rule—no relationships, no messy emotions. Especially not with fiery women who see straight through his defenses. His family depends on him, and distractions aren't an option. But Cadence? She's the worst kind—irresistible and utterly off-limits.

But some desires can't be ignored. As forbidden attraction turns to something deeper, secrets and scars threaten to tear them apart. Now, they must decide: is love worth the risk, or will the weight of their pasts destroy them both?

This book isn't your average rockstar romance. It has a band that's still fighting for their shot, some not-so-private intimate moments, and two people who couldn't be more right for each other.

Get yours on Amazon here!

https://a.co/d/oZaaKDx

Signed books, special edition books, and extra goodies available directly from me at www.authornterry.com.

Happy Shopping :)

Can't get enough of the gang?

Grab a FREE Novella just for signing up for my newsletter!

Cain Maddox wasn't looking for company—just a quiet moment with his book to escape his family's endless expectations. But when Isabella storms into the bar, frustrated and determined to salvage her night, their connection is instant and their chemistry undeniable.

A shared laugh over a romance novel leads to a single unforgettable night—no names, no strings, just a fleeting moment of escape.

But fate has other plans. Their lives are more intertwined than they realize, and the truth will change everything.

One night was supposed to be the end... until it became the beginning.

Grab your copy here!

https://BookHip.com/ZRMSSCP

In the mood for a Christmas Miracle?

Katerina Moretti's world is unraveling. Her beloved grandmother is in a fight for her life, and the looming weight of loss threatens to crush her. The last thing she expects is for Roman Kingsley—the childhood friend who broke her heart and vanished—to reappear as her grandmother's doctor.

For Roman, returning home was supposed to be temporary—a way to honor a promise—but seeing Kate again pulls him back into a past he's never truly let go of. As her family faces an uncertain future, Roman steps in to be the steady presence they need, even when it means risking himself.

With Christmas approaching, time is running out for Kate to save the person she loves most, while grappling with whether she can risk trusting Roman with her heart again. As old wounds resurface and new challenges arise, can they overcome the pain of the past and fight for a second chance? Can love truly be The Miracle That Ties Us?

The Miracle That Ties Us is a deeply moving holiday tale of sacrifice, family, and the transformative power of love.

Grab your copy on Amazon here.

https://a.co/d/8uc472B

Signed books, special edition books, and extra goodies available directly from me at www.authornterry.com.

Happy Shopping :)

Want more of Noah?

Noah Richey's life changed after a troublesome night out with his friends. He'd found the path he wanted his life to go. But saying you want to join the Air Force and actually signing that line were two different things. Noah would never be able to repay Jamie MacIntyre for the sacrifice he made that day when they were seventeen.

But as adults, Noah knew Jamie was lost in his darkness and needed him, now more than ever. And Noah planned to be there for him. Even if it was the last thing Jamie wanted.

Follow the story of Noah through this emotional and heartfelt novella.

Download now from Book Funnel:

https://dl.bookfunnel.com/gsyjp4wm75

Acknowledgments

There are so many people who have helped me through this journey to publish my first book. I'd love to have enough pages to thank each and every one of you, but you know who are and how much your support means to me.

My family in particular, for putting up with my late nights and leaving the house a mess. Thank you to my husband for your constant support and picking up the slack for me so I could follow my dream.

I hope one day, my boys read this and are proud of what I was able to accomplish with all the trials placed in my way.

Don't Forget The Review!

REVIEWS ARE ESSENTIAL TO HELPING INDIE AUTHORS.
SO THANK YOU!

About the Author

Nicolette has always been passionate about writing and has been creating stories since she was a little girl. Becoming a published author was something unobtainable then, but now she is living proof that dreams can come true.

Nicolette is a military spouse and happily married to her biggest supporter for over 13 years. They have two sons together and two bengal cats, Howl and Sophie. When Nicolette isn't writing, you can find her snuggled underneath a cozy blanket with a book.

Want to stay connected?
Join my exclusive Facebook group for all the fun and insider information:
Nicolette Terry's Rebels and Romantics Reading Group

Made in the USA
Middletown, DE
18 January 2026

27263470R00250